Boundless Solitude

Selim İleri

Translated by Mark David Wyers

Milet Publishing
Smallfields Cottage, Cox Green
Rudgwick, Horsham, West Sussex
RH12 3DE England
info@milet.com
www.milet.com
www.milet.co.uk

First English edition published by Milet Publishing in 2014

ISBN 978 1 84059 856 8

First published in Turkish as *Yarın Yapayalnız* in 2004

Funded by the Turkish Ministry of Culture and Tourism TEDA Project

Printed and bound in Turkey by Ertem Matbaası

Selim İleri was born in 1949 in Istanbul. He published his first short story when he was in secondary school and went on to study law at Istanbul University. His true passion, however, was writing, so he left university to dedicate his life to literature. When he was nineteen, his first book of short stories, *Cumartesi Yalnızlığı*, was published to critical acclaim. In 1998, the Turkish Ministry of Culture and Tourism awarded him the title of National Artist. He has written scripts for film and television, as well as literary columns for major Turkish newspapers. He has published twenty-two novels and seven short story collections, including *Dostlukların Son Günü*, which won the Sait Faik literary award. *Boundless Solitude* is his first novel published in English translation.

Mark David Wyers was born in Los Angeles, California and received his BA in literature from the University of Tampa. He lived in Turkey, in Kayseri, Ankara and Istanbul, and in 2008, he completed an MA in Turkish studies at the University of Arizona. His book *"Wicked" Istanbul: The Regulation of Prostitution in the Early Turkish Republic*, a historical study of gender and the politics of urban space in Turkey, was published in 2012, and his translations of Turkish short stories have been published in journals and anthologies, including *Istanbul in Women's Short Stories*, *Europe in Women's Short Stories from Turkey* and *Aeolian Visions/Versions: Modern Classics and New Writing from Turkey*, all published by Milet.

Editorial Notes

Throughout this novel, we have retained the Turkish for several types of terms, including honorifics, place names and foods. For the Turkish terms, we have used italics in their first instance and then normal text for subsequent instances. We have not italicized the Turkish honorifics that form part of a name, such as Bey and Hanım, to avoid splitting the name visually with a style change.

Turkish Honorifics

Abla: Older sister, also used as an honorific for women.
Bey: A respectful term of address used after a man's first name.
Hanım: A respectful term of address used after a woman's first name.
Hanımefendi: A respectful way of addressing a woman without using her first name.

Guide to Turkish Pronunciation

Turkish letters that appear in the book and which may be unfamiliar are shown below, with a guide to their pronunciation.

c	as *j* in *just*
ç	as *ch* in *child*
ğ	silent letter that lengthens the preceding vowel
ı	as *a* in *along*
ö	as German *ö* in *Köln*, or French *œ* in *œuf*
ş	as *sh* in *ship*
ü	as German *ü* in *fünf*, or French *u* in *tu*
ˆ	accent over vowel that lengthens the vowel

To Handan Sarp,
through whom I lived the heartache of this novel.

Everything ends with falling in love.
—Sait Faik

Last fall, after the release of my novel *The First Summer of Separation*, Handan Sarp called me.

No, not last fall. It was two falls ago. The fall of 2001. Just fall.

It was through Handan Sarp that I acquired this habit of confusing times and events. Perhaps "confuse" isn't quite the right word; it's more like becoming suspicious of them, doubting our perceptions of the past. We take everything up anew, sifting through the dregs of that which we couldn't forget.

When the violence of our experiences subsides, all that remains are scatterings of memories we may think are useless. But cause and effect arise from them, belong to them.

It's like not believing in the painting you see on a canvas, hoping to see through to the colors, figures, background, perhaps even multiple backgrounds, that the painting conceals. In a sense, scratching the surface of everything.

These are the painful scenes and stories that time perpetuates and erases, rending them apart and bringing them back together, or at least making it seem they are whole again. Agonizing portraits that, when scratched, rise to the surface and then vanish. Perhaps we sought to erase them, those portraits that speak of all that has been choked back and silenced. And at times they may cry out.

Memory has always been cruel, unable to do away with scratching and erasing.

In the beginning, I was exhausted by Handan Sarp's habit of plunging into doubt and trying again and again to resolve the same memory. But after time I began to find her stories oddly engaging. They spoke of a journey to the pain of the heart.

The neighborhood of Sıracevizler in Şişli, Istanbul: a row of apartments built up against one another; on the roofs are television antennas, some saucer-shaped and some linear, clinging stubbornly to existence. If I lean forward ever so slightly, I can see the trees in the distance, their leaves tinged with yellow. When I lean back, there is nothing but lost green.

And the sounds: the rumble of traffic, the blaring of car horns, a woman's voice from the park that suddenly pauses as it echoes—as though I'd heard a song. But actually it is silence. Inner silence, like a secret.

It was a cool, rainy day. There was the patter of rain, a sound that always stirs something in the heart. And under the rain, a woman in the park. But have I made her up? Is she a mere premonition?

I refuse to close the window in the living room. It's a strange habit of mine; until the middle of November, no matter how cold the weather turns, I leave open the windows and the balcony door. As though I want to hold on to autumn a little longer.

Summer had ended long before, there was no denying it.

The first summer of separation had passed. Many such summers had passed.

Blowing lightly in the wind, the tulle curtains were dampened by the rain. I sat gazing at the poppy flowers on the upholstery of the armchair, some of them worn and faded, and I dozed off occasionally. I was in a slump, not wanting to do anything at all. A state of pointless expectancy. Utterly pointless: how can you make things right, and where to start? The values you hold dear are trailing away, there is nothing you can do . . .

The poppy flowers had been stitched in purple thread. In contrast to the usual red warmth of poppies, this bruised purple made my heart heavy. I'd liked the fabric when I bought it. Had I liked the purple poppies, or just not noticed them? I pondered this insignificant question. An escape from life.

At that moment Handan Sarp called. When she said her name, I was stunned.

Some may laugh at the idea, but just like people, books also have a destiny. Something metaphysical moves through their peregrinations, each of them their own adventure.

Over time, as I wrote more and more novels and stories, I began to understand this.

A novel can unexpectedly lead to another. A story can lead to the birth of more stories.

I wouldn't call this chance, because the fate of some books is shrouded in loneliness and desolation. You write the book, it is published, and then it disappears from your life, forgotten.

After having written for years, I have some experience in the matter. I knew that with much of what I wrote I was running the risk of losing my readership. But I never paid heed to prescriptions for guaranteed sales. I followed my own path, as my abilities allowed. And I bowed down before the fate of my books.

At times, writing quieted the murmuring I carried within. At other times, all that emerged were vapid rants.

But there are times when writing abandons you, betrays you.

In the beginning, I was full of enthusiasm and the vigor of youth. I thought of nothing but writing. I held to the hope that by writing, I would change the world. (Did I, however, have any idea why or how I would change it?)

From one book to the next, I tried to find a niche in life. You may think that your path in life has changed, but then you realize that, in fact, you have been on the same path all along. You say something, thinking it is entirely new, but it is a mere repetition of something you've said before. You think that events bring along with them a whole new set of words.

It's all conjecture, nothing more. And when that stops, so does the writing.

I breathed life into repetition.

Youth and the promise of the future set my head spinning. I was young; like I said, I was full of enthusiasm and dreams. But isn't that the nature of youth? Writing had enveloped my being, and in my writing I wanted to reach out to the other arts as well. For instance, even though I lacked the slightest musical talent, through my writing and drawing I was trying to be a pianist. My zeal was limitless.

Film had a profound impact on me. From film to film, my interests and dreams were transformed. One day I would devote myself to becoming a piano player, but the next I wanted be a painter or sculptor. After watching a film about Chopin's life, I decided to become a composer. Such was the deluge of my inspirations.

Before going to the cinema, I would stop by Atlantik—the first snack bar in our neighborhood—and have a hot dog and carrot juice. In those days, all that was new for us: hot dogs smothered in mustard and topped with pickles, frothy carrot juice, banana frappes, toasted cheese sandwiches, large hamburgers with spicy ketchup, french fries in paper cones, toasters, blenders . . . That's why we indulged ourselves so much. And my desire for more was insatiable.

But when I think back on those days, it seems like autumn had enveloped everything. A sense of ennui clung to life.

I see only gray, leaden tones. For example, when I stepped out of the movie theater, it would be raining. In the city lights, this rain of the past, of experience, is a rain of melancholy.

A song by Vittorio Paltrinieri echoing from a record seller's shop that seemed to be the color of ash: "Portofino," which I adored! The sound of the churning sea, the rush of water, wrenches my heart. Listen to "I Found My Love in Portofino"—the sea's whispering will drive you mad, especially in the middle of the song, that mournful whistle.

I raise the collar of my trench coat. A car on Istiklal Street sprays mud as it passes by. In the shop window of Franguli's, even a dazzling brooch nestled in folds of black velvet is ashen, muffled in darkness.

Now, as I think on it, I realize that in my youth I should have known it was novels that beget novels. Every metaphysical occurrence comes forth through the gleam of intuition.

In my adolescence, I watched a film starring Kim Novak and Laurence Harvey. The title was probably translated as *Slave of Passion*, or maybe it was *Slave of Love*. A scene in that film whispered to me of the destiny of books.

Although I often remembered that scene, it never occurred to me that my books were also bound up with their fates.

The scene lived on, alone, in a corner of my memory, cut off from everything.

Handan Sarp spoke at great length about the sea. Her descriptions were not foreign to me:

It is like the crashing of waves. Life goes on. I can recall my books in the tumult of days as if they were distant echoes. The sea suddenly falls silent and there is nothing left. Then, again: the roar of the sea, the crashing of waves as they pound the shore.

Life consists of such jolts and blows.

Your heart sinks, filled with regret. The flush of enthusiasm fades, and in place of your youth, a breeze blows. Questions rush through your mind: Why did I publish that book? Did I truly think it was a testimony of our times? What arrogance! I didn't testify to anything. Hundreds, thousands of pages—all for nothing! But still, I was writing letters. Silence falls, until the sea roars and thunders again. In silence, all is forgotten, and the pain inflicted by those books subsides.

We suffer through our books. When you write about a scene, for a moment it reminds you of something. Pain, joy, or the happiness in our lives . . A flash of a smile. You were smiling at me. Glances, laughter, farewells, separation. Compared to how they felt in their full violence, what the writer puts on paper is always but a shadow. The pain that scars the heart drives you to write; it is a desperate need. But as soon as you've written it, you're struck by two kinds of torment: not being able to make the past breathe through what you've written, even though you feel it; you're consumed by it. Your feelings are drowned out by your words, which never suffice. What you've expressed is already lost.

What I'll write now will also be like that.

I watched *Slave of Love* at the Atlas Cinema. I was enthralled by the cold beauty of Kim Novak.

Films enchanted me, perhaps to the point of obsession. My family thought that, at most, I watched two films a week. But in fact, I would sneak off to the cinema three or four times.

After school, I'd say that I had to attend a course or some other event. All I needed was two hours; it wasn't hard to come up with an excuse. In those days, I lied from morning till night.

At the time, I didn't realize that the film was based on a novel; only later did I find out that the film was an adaptation of a work by W. Somerset Maugham. In any case, I watched movies based on the actors. I wasn't interested in the directors or who wrote the stories.

W. Somerset Maugham . . .

To be honest, Maugham has never been a favorite writer of mine. In fact, I've never really liked his writing.

Nonetheless, he would have an indirect impact on my journey of becoming a writer.

A while after I'd watched *Slave of Love*, I saw a signed copy of a Turkish translation of Maugham's novel *Of Human Bondage* in the shop window of the Semih Lûtfi Bookstore. The title was printed in deep blue on a yellow background, and the book had a maroon binding. The publishing life of Semih Lûtfi had come to an end long before I was even born, but he'd been known for the discount novel series he put out.

A droopy-eyed, cantankerous woman ran the bookshop of Lûtfi's publishing house. This withered woman would proclaim from time to time, "I'm the wife of Semih Lûtfi, the publisher!" The run-down shop was dank and smelled of urine. Her assistant was a short Quasimodo who never uttered a word. He cowered in the presence of the lady of the shop, his deep blue eyes timid and full of fear.

From some unknown depot, leftover copies of books would be

trundled out, novels by writers like Güzide Sabri, Aka Gündüz, Mahmut Yesari and Server Bedi. Who knows how many copies had been printed in the first place. From the Translations of World Classics series there were works such as *The Autumn of a Woman* (translated by Suat Derviş) and *Forever Yours, Empress of Portugal* (translated by Safiye Erol).

Those tattered novels captivated my imagination. The pages were tinged the color of rust and smelled musty. Even before you read half the book, the binding would split apart.

Whenever I had the money, I'd buy a few books from the shop. I still have most of them; they are carefully stacked on my bookshelves, precious as gold. My youth somehow lives on through those novels. I remember going to the Semih Lûtfi Bookstore in the mornings during summer break.

Toward eleven o'clock, bashful-eyed Quasimodo would roll up the steel shutters of the bookstore as the lady of the shop waited nearby. Then he'd open the front door with a jangling of keys, and the entry procession began: first the lady, then Quasimodo. In the shop, the lady always sat and Quasimodo stood at attention.

Rather than being put off by the sour smell and dinginess of the dim shop, I was so enchanted that I never wanted to leave. The troves of books filling the shelves begged to be explored. However, there was a strict rule: it was forbidden to touch the books.

With his long white beard, Quasimodo would rush over whenever I reached out for a book, his eyes flashing in warning. Then, the shrill voice of the lady:

"Get back! Stay where you are. Just tell me which book you want."

"*Çapraz Delikanlı*? No, not today!" she'd say. *Çapraz Delikanlı* was a novel by Aka Gündüz. The old woman wasn't about to sell the copy in the shop window, so Quasimodo would have to bring it up from the depot. A shadow of guilt would flicker across his face.

"I'm the wife of Semih Lûtfi!" she'd exclaim. "Come back in two days."

Those two days would drag on interminably. Perhaps the old woman was afraid of losing the last customer who frequented the shop; if I didn't come back, she'd be left alone with Quasimodo. Or maybe she derived a devious pleasure from badgering lovers of old books.

"What do you want with these old things? They were all read in their time . . ."

But in those novels I can feel that enthusiasm, the fluttering of my heart.

Actually I should use the past tense here, and say "felt." After Handan Sarp, it is almost impossible even to imagine that excitement of youth, the impassioned, idealistic reading, my heart stirred by old songs—"Portofino!"—and those old books.

After Handan Sarp, something turned leaden inside me.

Even now, my thoughts were drifting to *Of Human Bondage*.

In my youth I bought the book. As soon as I started reading, however, my enthusiasm faded. I had to force my way through it. That was the first novel I read by Maugham.

As I read more, I realized that the film I'd seen was based on the book. But changes had been made, and the scene that I mentioned earlier, the one that was so memorable for me, wasn't even there.

In the film, before Laurence Harvey falls madly in love with Kim Novak—it was more like lust than love, because the first time he saw her, he was enraptured by sexual desire—he was living with a woman who was a writer of popular fiction.

It was a stagnant relationship, for all appearances monotonous. Laurence Harvey felt neither love nor desire for her. But because of his weak personality and dependence on the writer, the relationship dragged on.

The novelist was older than him. She was the one in love, and her passion for him was deep, almost inexpressible. It was like an inner storm, as though the novelist always felt that the body that she touched, kissed, embraced and stroked belonged to a stranger, a body that left her poisoned through lack of love. Even if you make love a hundred times, that body will always be a stranger to you.

One evening, the young man went to the apartment he was sharing with the novelist. He'd crossed that threshold countless times, but now it was different; he'd met Kim Novak and made love with her.

There was a large gathering: music, drinks, food, conversations, peals of laughter. An old man—perhaps a second-rate poet—said it was raining outside.

The novelist, her hair pulled into a bun, drifted among the guests. She was wearing a long, conservatively cut dress. There was nothing particularly charming about her.

That's how writers of romance are: they write about the most beautiful women and the most handsome men, but if you see a photograph of them, you find a dull countenance.

The young man told the novelist that they had to stop seeing each other, and he apologized. They were standing by a window, away from the noise of the party. His lips twitched: "I'm in love with her, please forgive me . . ."

The novelist was holding a martini, but her cheerful tipsiness quickly darkened. She stammered: "Don't worry, there won't be any tears . . ." Outside, the drizzling rain glimmered on the asphalt road.

There won't be any tears.

The woman placed her glass on an end table. Then she placed her arm in Laurence Harvey's, and guided him through the dancing crowd to the door. "You can leave now," she said. "I have at least ten more novels to write, thanks to you."

I was young and inexperienced, and didn't understand how a person could be the source of novels.

I explained this to Handan Sarp.

"Yes," she said, "whether you believe it or not, people truly are the inspiration for novels and operas. Novels pregnant with pain to come. New operas that are all the same."

Although I wasn't impressed with his writing, Maugham was popular both in my generation and the one before. He was British but had settled in Paris, which he considered his second home. *Of Human Bondage* had brought him to fame. It was said that the book was based on his own life.

The Turkish translation of the title, *Slave of Love,* caused a small scandal. At the end of the Turkish version, the translators, Fikret Ürgüp and Necdet Sander, had added a short note:

"This work has been translated from the French translation, *Servitude Humaine,* of Somerset Maugham's *Of Human Bondage.* Due to an unfortunate circumstance, during the printing of our translation the book was given the title *Slave of Love.* We discovered this after a large number of books had been printed and unfortunately could not correct the error. We offer our deepest apologies to our esteemed readers for the inaptness of this title, which does not reflect the dignity of this work."

There is something disturbing about the translators' note.

What standard of values have brought us to this point? In today's world, where everything has been commercialized, who has the right to complain about the title *Slave of Love*? We should be grateful for this "unfortunate circumstance." To push up sales, we could even call it *Stark Naked with the Slave of Love*. We wouldn't feel a pang of conscience.

In the past, books would conclude with the words "The End." That was a nice flourish; the novel thus came to a definitive conclusion. But over time it was dropped, for fear that it assumed readers lacked the intelligence to realize the book had ended. But I must admit that I miss that tradition.

I used to know Fikret Ürgüp and Necdet Sander. I saw Fikret for the first time in 1970 at Kemal Tahir's house. He said he was a writer of short stories. Even though I was an aspiring literary connoisseur, I'd never heard of his work. He drank a glass of cognac. And then another. "I divide the days by the glass," he said. He spoke for a brief while longer, and then left.

He had a lisp, and his facial expressions were rather childish. He tottered as he walked. Kemal Tahir said that he used to live an orderly, respectable life. But if you ask me, I think that Fikret preferred the life of an alcoholic in mockery of blue jackets, gray pants and neckties.

The last time I saw him, he was vomiting on a backstreet in Karaköy.

In one of his stories, he wrote of a *meyhane* that was built over the water. On the walls of the restaurant there were photographs of attractive Greek women resembling Marilyn Monroe depicted as half-mermaids. Light reflected from the sea through the narrow gaps between the floor planks and flickered across the surface of the photographs in faint greens and blues. In the photographs, there were schools of small fish; clams opened their shells and gazed upon the Greek beauties. A world devoid of Marilyn Monroes is simply not livable.

In addition to being a gifted writer, Fikret Ürgüp was a skilled painter.

He thought that short stories, as a series and as a whole, shed light on life, both for the readers and the author.

I remember a drawing he had done in pencil and oil colors. It was a sketch of a wooden house with a tree in front, and the leaves were colored in greens and yellows. The drawing spoke of a deep loneliness. Had Fikret Ürgüp been lonely?

In her book *Day of Darkness*, Leyla Erbil based a character on him, changing his name to Fikret Kapadok. Perhaps as a manifesto for us all, she wrote a plaintive obituary when he died: "Fikret Kapadok has been saved from the suffering of this world. His funeral will be held after the afternoon prayer in Çengelköy."

Necdet Sander was the son of the heavyhearted poet Şükûfe Nihal. He was the owner of one of the finest bookstores in Istanbul: Sander Books. Located in Osmanbey, the bookstore was huge, two stories tall if I remember right; you could've gotten lost in there. It had everything: books in Turkish, English, French, German—anything you could imagine.

I met Necdet's mother Şükûfe toward the end of her life. She was living in a rest home, utterly alone.

We'd gone to visit my mother's grandmother at a rest home in Bakırköy. It was a sunny autumn day. The leaves were turning yellow. In those days, rest homes were a novelty in Istanbul and had just begun opening.

In my novel *Wings of Blue*, she appears as a character enthralled by imaginary love. Passion made her suffer, but she hid her pain. When I wrote those pages about love, I slipped into a trance. Love always holds us entranced. The old, shriveled woman I saw in the rest home—a haggard, unhappy person withered away by life—was infused with youth in the story as she set out to embrace life. Once again she frequented the literary salon of Abdülhak Hamid Bey, and flitted from the Parkotel to the newly opened Hilton. But she was always haunted by ill luck . . .

I'm speaking of a mystery—of mysteries, to be more precise—because it is difficult to draw a connection between *Slave of Love* and Şükûfe Nihal, to interlink all the scenes, events, places and people. But how can we brush aside or deny the fact that they're all connected in one way or another?

They all speak of the mysteries of my life. But from which part of my life? It seems as though they want me to write something. But what?

Can it be for Handan Sarp's novel? When I bring together the experiences from different periods in my life and write them down, a unity is created, and what emerges seems to be something singular.

Even when the words *Slave of Love* and W. Somerset Maugham come together, it's as though years ago the plans had been laid for this novel, Handan Sarp's novel, like a scenario. As though I had watched that film so that I could write the beginning of this novel. Perhaps that's why I remembered that scene.

Memory compiles and accumulates. Memory seems to know what we'll need, as if it has seen our future lives and determined what should be saved and what discarded.

How could I have known when I was writing about Şükûfe Nihal in *Wings of Blue* and recalled her poem "Final Memory" that one day

I would recall that poem yet again for Handan Sarp's novel and that its final quatrain would whisper a secret:

Waves, sweep me into the depths,
I too am a grain among grains of sand!
"Inseparable, together we shall dive to the depths!"
And at that point, my friend let go of my hand, and left.

Did that gaunt woman I saw at the rest home in Bakırköy remember that poem, those last lines? As she wrote them, what trials of suffering did she endure? Did she remember the pain she'd gone through? We cannot seek salvation by succumbing to the idea that pain will always be the same. Suffering is left behind in lines, stories, and novels, because new pain will come, new stings of torment.

There is one last detail I should share:

Maugham once said that Emily Bronte's extraordinary novel *Wuthering Heights* was among the best ten books ever written (and it's strange as well that the novelist said, "I have at least ten more novels to write, thanks to you"—why is it always *ten* novels?).

Maugham scoffed at people who doubted that the young Emily Bronte could've written *Wuthering Heights* in such a barren, isolated location and argued that someone else must've written it. He suggested that Emily was quite familiar with the experiences of the two main characters of the novel and was in fact both Catherine and Heathcliff.

It's always that way. The writer is a multitude of persons. Even when the narrator is just one.

I imagined Emily Bronte as two people: one braving wild winters shaken by the roaring wind and the other taking excursions among the bluebells in the heath as the season changed. As she wrote that romance, she was two people in that stone house, confronting her stone-hearted destiny. Two people she carried within.

I must confess that I was impressed by Maugham's claim that we're not one person, but rather numerous people inhabiting a single body.

He also said that by rendering these "others" the novelist creates the story's characters. But he cautioned that if we try to create a character who is not within us, not in our soul, we'll stumble and falter.

As I said, Handan Sarp phoned me. We didn't recognize each other's voices at first.

"Can I speak with Selim Bey?"

"Who's calling?"

It was natural that she didn't recognize my voice, but it was strange that I didn't recognize hers.

"This is Handan Sarp. He may not know me."

I was stunned. Scenes from *Norma*, *Macbeth*, *La traviata* and *Tosca* flashed before my eyes; a majestic soprano rang out, echoing down through the operas.

"This is Selim speaking."

"This is Handan Sarp, a soprano from the city opera. You may not have heard of me."

"Of course I've heard of you, Handan Hanım. Who hasn't?"

"Thank you, that's very kind. From your writing, I know that you like opera. But still, I was unsure . . ."

Since my youth, her voice had set my heart aflame. But was it just her voice and inflection? For years I'd admired the way that Handan Sarp was like the tragedians of the past, and I never wearied of listening to her. Her stage presence enraptured the entire opera house; the way she entered the stage, her walk, the first scene, her hand gestures, her arms suddenly spreading, the way she would take a step and then pause, her tragic expressions—as though she wanted to surge ahead of the music—and her fiery glances that stunned the audience . . . With her, all of the artificiality of opera fell away. Or perhaps it would be more correct to say that in the presence of Handan Sarp, that grand artificiality was suddenly transformed into a howl of unrivaled sincerity. Even if you'd memorized the story line and the songs, she transformed every opera into a marvel, the flourishes of music striking unfathomable depths; you found yourself enchanted, drawn in, aching to savor it again and again.

"I'm a great admirer of yours." There's no need to conceal it—my voice was trembling.

Handan Sarp replied, "I love reading your work as well."

I was stunned to hear that Handan Sarp had read my writing. (It was a period in which no one really read my work and every effort at writing came to naught.) Despite my surprise, I was still overwhelmed by the fact that I was listening to the voice of Handan Sarp. But somehow it wasn't that ringing, crystal voice I knew. It seemed flat somehow.

"I was pleased when I read that you like opera. I know that opera has always been something distant, unfamiliar. That's why we opera performers have either always looked down on our society or withdrawn into ourselves. Not being able to make people love your art . . ."

No, her voice was no longer that of a soprano.

I'd read a few interviews with her in which she had said much the same. She was of the opinion that there were just a handful of people who "truly" loved opera and that the remainder of opera-goers went just to be seen. Nor did she refrain from saying that she despised those premiere nights filled with evening gowns and tuxedos. She'd said something like: what could those women who simply wanted to flaunt their gowns and jewels understand of Verdi's passion for liberty? As I recall, she said that while opera may be foreign to Turkish society, those tuxedos and bow ties were simply preposterous.

"Selim Bey, I was undecided about whether I should call you."

"I'm pleased that you called."

"The old generation used to say 'recluse.' I've long been living like that, as a recluse. A life of withdrawal. I've imprisoned myself within myself."

The telephone was on my writing desk. I glanced at the disorder: dusty stacks of papers I was always putting off organizing, copies of the last novel, newspaper articles, books, newspaper and magazine clippings untouched for weeks that I planned on filing away, pens, empty lighters, my typewriter dusted with cigarette ashes.

"You're probably also a little like that. Avoiding public places, not mixing with crowds."

"Yes, yes," I stammered. "I do get a little anxious."

"That's why I was unsure about calling, unable to decide whether or not to disturb you. We recluses . . ."

For a moment the clutter on my desk gave way to a glimpse of Handan Sarp as Violetta Valéry. (That was twenty years earlier, perhaps more. *La traviata* was one of Handan Sarp's major successes.) Stoically, she'd listened to Giorgio Germont's pitiful entreaties, her dark glances openly scornful of the hypocritical morals of bourgeois society, and at times she seemed to belittle our morals as well; she sang despairingly of love that is destined for separation.

Yes, that was it: if Alfredo's sister is to marry someone of her own standing, and if Alfredo is living with a woman like Violetta, then . . .

As the bourgeois world, money and the sanctity of family for which Giorgio pled are silently spurned, separation and love are kindled; the duet pulls us "half-mad" opera lovers from emotion to emotion.

That season I watched *La traviata* twice.

In the piercing blue sky, groups of clouds drift idly, seemingly unsure where to go. Half white, half gray. I'm looking up through the open window, trying to pick out the shapes of figures in the clouds. (As I said: it was autumn.) In the sky, I could make out the pain of separation: the whites and the grays, locked in embrace, then drifting apart.

"If you were to come to my place one evening . . ."

"Most certainly," I said. "I would be honored."

I went to Handan Sarp's modest apartment on Sakızlı Street in Nişantası. Her apartment was painted in dark tones and had a garden in the back, which was surrounded by the other apartment buildings. We sat in the garden until well after evening fell, and when the chill became uncomfortable we went inside. We sat in opposing chairs in front of the windows that ran the length of the wall facing the garden, which was dappled in dim light. "It's like the liqueur in your novels," Handan said, twisting her lower lip into a wry smile, as we drank cherry cognac.

The cognac was left over from the previous year. That summer (the summer of 2001) she hadn't made cherry cognac or vodka. When cherry season had come around that year, she'd passed the greengrocers with a vacant stare, her soul bundled in sorrow. The cognac we were drinking was perhaps all she had left; she may not ever make it again.

I listened to Handan Sarp. A number of times I went to her apartment, and she came to mine. We continued meeting up until she had told me all of her story, and she also entrusted me with her pieces of writing, which she referred to as "somniloquies."

After our first meeting, I always kept my small tape recorder on. She encouraged me to do so, and even suggested that we "work" with the tape.

Her voice was hoarse. "I've lost my voice," she said to me. "I no longer have a voice." Most of her writings—her "somniloquies"—were stained with tears.

The tearstains distracted me from the technical side of my work. In the face of such candor, I gave up trying to wrest perfection from the narrative. In fact, as I wove it into writing, I wasn't disturbed by the way it was cluttered, scattered and disorganized. My primary goal was authenticity. (Over time, however, I began to doubt whether or not I could complete it.)

Personally, I don't like explanations. Nevertheless, Handan Sarp began her story in the following way:

"Selim, the title of your book is *The First Summer of Separation*, but you didn't explain the separation. You talked about the gardens. I, too, like gardens. You wrote of Ayhan's suicide, and Sevim's collapse. I once compared one period of my life to Sevim's life. Then there is Old Bobi and Gülderen. You wrote of Gülderen's liqueurs, and how she listened to recordings of *La traviata*. But the separation . . . You didn't explain the parting one bit. I can even say that you wrote a lie of a novel. Let me tell you what separation truly means."

Love is always the same.

All loves resemble one another. No matter if they are between a man and a woman, or between two women or two men.

People hesitate to speak of the last two. Not so much now, but they did in the past. Now there is a little more tolerance, and a lot of brazenness and banality.

I was afraid too. Set aside showing it, talking about it or living it in the gaze of society; I couldn't even admit it to myself. I tried to repress my feelings, to destroy who I was. I acted like another person, and even dressed like them. For a long time I was someone else: a prim, demure girl.

Since I'm not going to live to be a hundred, I must've lived out more than half of my life by now but I've never talked about it. I couldn't. I kept silent. I was distant from everyone. Little by little, my close friends pulled away. I sensed a decay, a sickness. "What a frigid woman she is," they'd say. I've never let anyone ask about my private life.

Wasn't it Virginia Woolf who fainted when her nephew asked her if she was a lesbian? I understand perfectly. It's painful. Why would they ask such a question?

I've never asked anyone about their sex lives.

"Lesbian": I don't like that word. In Turkish we have a much better word, *sevici*. At least it doesn't pain the heart so much. It comes from the word *sev*, meaning love—it's as if the word wants to speak of love. "Lesbian" has an air of science, as though they want to sit you down with a few pages of medicine. Poor Sappho; day in and day out, she spoke of longing and burning passion, but rather than listen to her sorrow, they got hung up on Lesbos.

Before, it was sexual perversion, and now it's sexual preference. After having lived out more than half of my life, I can laugh now—bitterly.

Have you ever looked it up in the old dictionaries? Sevici: a woman with the perverted desire to make love with other women rather than men. Why "rather than men," why "perversion"? Now, dictionaries are more tactful; they say "female homosexuality." For years that term tormented me: I wanted to make love with other women rather than men . . .

"As long as it harms no one else, no one can interfere in another's sexual preference." Today, that's what they say to you; they're so kind as to show you the way. You can walk down that thorny path alone.

I walked alone.

I read somewhere that the Turkish word for love, *aşk*, comes from the word for two vines that become intertwined as they grow. Intertwining, perhaps one slowly strangling one another, destroying the other.

Why do they meddle with love?

Meddle with whom or what we fall in love with, and our reasons why?

Can't a person fall in love with a painting? Especially when it's sexual love?

There is a nude by the artist Çallı which depicts a woman getting dressed behind a screen. We see her from behind: she leans over to pull on her thin, black silk stockings; her black hair spills over her shoulders, and there is the pure pink of her thighs, the tautness of her breasts, half-hidden, and her blue dress, draped over the screen, has an ashen sheen . . .

After she has dressed and gone out into the street—her high-heeled shoes stop at the corner—where will she go? It's as if she were going out to make love.

How many times I gazed at that painting, intoxicated; how many times I brought myself to satisfaction gazing upon it. And then nothingness.

I should explain this to you, Çallı's painting. One night I'll tell you.

We're sitting at my place. In a while you'll get up and leave. You're afraid of taxis, but I'll pay the fare. You don't want to take it. Your family will ask where you've been at this hour. You're afraid, but can't bring yourself to leave. Ah, you!

Love is always the same and there is suffering in every love: at the beginning, middle and the end. Love consists of suffering.

Even though we've felt the same pain, "theirs" is the love between a man and a woman, while mine is a "lesbian" love. Would you believe that I've been in love so many times, but my love went unanswered? I was driven from love.

There was one time, just one time . . .

But I'm not ready to talk about that yet.

To speak of that, of you . . . You!

("Selim Bey, to use that word of which you are so enamored, it was a 'romance.'")

She loved me, I know.

The strange thing is that I, who have been driven from love to love, understood this love only later, much later. After it was gone.

It came and went. But now we are like one person. In parting, we've become one.

I, Handan Sarp, can make the two of us live on, in parting. In separation, we are together. Love carries on within me, even more violently, more passionately, more terrifyingly! It was so heartfelt, so deeply shared, with her . . .

With you . . . We don't need to speak, we fall silent in this dream of love, and we have no need for words. Without a single word we explain everything, we feel everything.

You could say, "In that case it isn't over." And I can say, "What's it to you!"—indeed, what of it! If I say that after love, in separation, that we have come together, you'll just stare at me blankly.

Maybe she too would just stare. She, whose name I'm still not ready to recall.

You . . .

When I remember your name, will the pain begin to subside?

Will I awake one morning without thinking of her? The painting is fading away. That's how it'll be. The painting will fade.

("Isn't it easier for you? I hope you don't expect me to believe in the fictional characters in your novels. The people in this novel are fictional, and any similarity between the characters in this novel and real people is coincidental . . . There should be some irony between us and the readers. You can write as much as you want and as you write, consume it all. Nothing will be left. Nothing should remain.")

I awake to the night. At night, they return. Silently, I rise from bed. The city's silhouette from ten years before begins to emerge, in Nişantaşı, on the Bosphorus, in Kocamustâpaşa. I'm afraid to turn on the light. When I do, the neighborhoods, the silhouettes, the life in the city will be resurrected. I'm content with memories. Memories bring pain, but they don't suffocate you. To relive everything is fatal. I cross a deserted street; the city is in my genes. A candle melts and the waxen tears weep, and at the holy tomb of Şem-i Dede—Who? He left behind a name, and perhaps some mercy—there is a dim light, and I can't bring myself to touch the iron bars. As I cross the street, the lights of showcases shine viciously down: brand-name watches, jewelry, cosmetics, a tiger lilly orchid. Şem-i Dede falls silent; this is unfamiliar to him. She . . . You, every morning and every evening you passed in front of them, and every morning you came from Şem-i Dede and every evening you returned to him. One morning, in Kireçburnu, I looked up at a magnolia tree growing behind a wall, billowing with blossoms, and I stood waiting for the sound of the sea.

How will I explain this? Where will I start?

I'm sitting beneath the crepe myrtle. This year, despite the season its flowers are still in bloom, fuchsia with a violet glimmer. This tree is a small thing that breaks apart: the slight trunk, the branches sprouting to the left and right, stretching forth—it's like a fan, a breath of solitude.

From now on, I shall be alone.

We often sat together here. Summer nights. On summer nights we drank and ate dinner. I explained opera to her . . . To you. Because you didn't know about it. Because for me, opera was reality itself. We listened to music, and sometimes I sang along to *La Gioconda*, and you liked the song "Suicidio!"

Suicide! Death! That became our song.

Over time you learned about opera and you came to love it. The songs and howls out of nowhere.

You asked me: "Why do they scream and shout the songs? Why do you sing like that?" You were laughing and your radiant eyes laughed as well, deep hazel and thick-lashed. "Are arias sung like that too, shouting and screaming?"

"Opera is the scream inside us. The words that we can't say. The music insists, and we give it a voice. And in the end, we can't hold the scream back."

We were looking at each other, smiling. You were young, almost a child. And I was older, but still young as well.

"Yes, we always sing that way. Screaming."

For a long while, the singing in opera, the arias and duets which were so different from the songs you loved, remained an enigma for you. My eyes would open wide as I sang, and you thought it was strange how my mouth would open so wide and my neck would strain. You laughed, embarrassed.

Over time, you began laughing less. If only you'd kept laughing.

Yes. A scream.

Just once, here in this garden beneath the crepe myrtle, we began to feverishly make love. Just one time. Apartment buildings surrounded us on all sides. Do you think I cared? Me, cowardly conformist Handan Sarp? My unhappiness was endless; knowing that I would lose you and that I despised our relationship which was already over, I sought a fantasy, no matter how trite. I kissed you. I saw the purple flowers aflame in the settling darkness of night.

My eyes filled with tears of pleasure and pain. The flowers, ablaze, swayed in the breeze. I lowered my head to your breasts. The buttons on your blouse were fake pearl. One by one, I undid the buttons. You didn't push my hand away, but you paused. "Handan," you whispered.

My dear—this is the first time I've ever addressed you that way, here in this desolate garden of night, far from you, farther and farther as time goes by—that night, I kissed you. I held your left breast in my palm. Your heart was pounding, and your nipples had stiffened. Pale with fear, you looked at me.

Dusk hadn't settled, and you wanted to cover yourself with the sprigs of pink flowers. Embarrassed. Afraid.

In the beginning of our relationship, when I was afraid . . .

My dear, I'll explain it all.

For years, I never once called her "my dear." Not even "sweetheart." It never occurred to me. For us, love must've been so forbidden that the words "my dear" were only for "other" kinds of love and so I . . . No, I don't even want to finish that sentence.

It was only after our life together fell apart that I realized we were lovers.

Was I perhaps repulsed by the idea of calling her "dear"?

Why did you do this? I don't know to whom I can release this scream inside of me. You left me.

(As the author, I should note that the lines above in italics are not taken from my meetings with Handan Sarp but are a quote from one of her somniloquies. It may not be necessary for me to say this, but I've broken up the flow of the narrative in this way to suit the flow of *Boundless Solitude*. Sİ)

The days drag on, as if I'm reliving the same day over and over. I wait for evening so that I can know that the day has actually passed. I think of nothing but memories. Like strikes of lightning: the flash of a moment, a frozen image, a searing luminosity. The moment may be short, but when it fades away, it leaves in its wake a surge of emotion that drives you to the brink of despair. In my thoughts, I go back to the image. I'm forced to relive it, as well as suffer the pain of that loss. Only then is calm restored. Until it strikes again. And when it does, a new round of suffering. That evening in the garden, I was watering the plants. Dusk was settling: radiant blues, reds, and pinks lingering in the sky, colors of deception. In the windows, lights began to flicker on. In these apartments, people live with their families. Until that thought occurred to me, I was pleased with the evening. But then the stab of the knife: you are alone! This is how I wanted it, so why should I be upset? Evening no longer soothes my heart. I feel the jab of our separation. The garden, weary of my complaints, slumbers.

The buttons on your blouse were fake pearl. Aside from the clothes I gave you as gifts, you had to sew your own dresses and buy inexpensive outfits. Perhaps it was the pearls I wanted to kiss that night. Pride and the sweat of labor.

Embracing, we went inside, gingerly undressing each other. I would be saved from those buttons, your bare skin against mine.

Bare skin! To punish, and be punished.

Even today, after our separation, I'm still aroused by the memory of our lovemaking that night.

No, I'm not aroused. I feel nothing. Even then it was foreign to me. I had stiffened, taut with nerves. It's just an illusion; it will pass.

("The drinks have gone to my head. Selim, did you notice that I've been addressing you informally. I feel a certain closeness between us. The same kinds of people as in your novel live here on this street. That first summer! Ayhan was still alive . . . He hadn't killed himself yet."

I didn't tell her that she was mistaken. Ayhan's suicide is revealed at the end of the novel, but at the beginning of *The First Summer of Separation* everything has already occurred, including the suicide. The writer just tries to give shape to the order of events. And it is the same in Handan Sarp's novel).

If we've truly lived something, our experiences will never be forgotten. ("Promise me you'll write that!") You don't forget. And since I've suffered so much, that means I haven't forgotten.

I haven't forgotten her. Her name . . . No, her name will only bring even more pain. I should erase her name from my memory. I should give up on telling this tale of romance; others will just call it perverse—but if it is, let it be so! I'm done, I won't go on.

I can't.

I must go back.

You were so close, and yet so distant. But now that distance is gone. We're closer than ever. You destroyed my life when you were closest to me.

You approached me at Nedret's boutique. But you weren't aware of what it meant. You were somber, weary. Resigned to domineering spoiled rich women. You're my sibling, my spiritual twin.

That's what I'd thought: my spiritual twin. We had so much pain to share, so much rebellion. Life would appear before our eyes. A sudden revolt. The two of us, struggling against what others have suffered through.

Nedret said: "Let's do the jacket in beige."

"No," I replied. "As our young seamstress here suggested, it'll be in green, with brown cuffs."

I trusted you.

My life . . . The life of a young man, of a young woman, of that woman whose life was in ruins. Where should I begin? ("I should tell you a little about my life, shouldn't I? For the book. But I don't know, do we need it to describe our relationship, my relationship with her? If I'll be turned into a character in a book, if the novel about our lives will truly be written . . . But still, the characters in novels also have parents.")

It seemed autumn would never end. The weather turned cold at the beginning of September and for a few days it rained. Did she also like the rain? I don't know; I never asked. There was a lot I didn't ask. And now, asking has lost all meaning.

I'd said that after the rains began, the weather would stay cold. But in the middle of September, summer returned. For a few days it was stiflingly hot. And then fall settled back in.

I like the word "fall," but could never do without "autumn."

Never could I part from the words that I love. I've never parted from words. I've never parted from anyone.

Every evening, I place a wicker chair under the crepe myrtle. Then those games of deceit known as memories begin, one by one. I swathe them in the pink of the flowers. They blossom, invigorated. In that pink, negativity fades away. I try to drive it away.

Like that old wicker chair rocking ever so slightly, I'm caught in a tide of memories.

At times, I'm brought back to my childhood, to a memory of being at my grandmother's house in Pendik on the fringes of Istanbul. ("Don't worry, I'm not going to indulge in nostalgia for the grand mansions of past days.") It was a world of women; my grandmother was widowed, my aunt Nadire had never married, and my mother and father had divorced.

One night, we were returning from the cinema ("This is where you ask me the name of the cinema . . ."). My aunt, easily thirty at the time, had wept during the sad romantic film, which was titled *Bouquet of Jasmine*; the film starred Belgin Doruk and Göksel Arsoy. I remember the name of the film because my grandmother had said, "This year, our jasmine didn't bloom." As I gazed at the sky—it was a star-filled moonless night—you could even see the distant procession of stars in the Milky Way. My eyes on the sky above, I stumbled as I walked and gripped my mother's hand.

I've thought long about the tricks that memory plays. There are spans of years that I don't remember. But then a rather ordinary detail, such as a stage in an opera, somehow remains lodged in my memory. The others are smudged, hazy, fluid, but that one emerges in all its vibrancy: my grandmother's words about the jasmine not blooming become entwined with the stars.

My aunt Nadire was still hopeful that one day a charming Göksel Arsoy would come ringing the doorbell. The heaviness of that evening, the mournful ending of *Bouquet of Jasmine*, in which Göksel and Belgin separate forever, had put a damper on her hopes. No one was going to ring the doorbell, no one was going to say, "Nadire, will you marry me?"

For me, the promises of the Milky Way are dangerous. I pitied my aunt, but at the same time I was angry with that woman who was getting older day by day.

My mother asked, "What's wrong? You didn't insist on having an ice cream." We were passing the Petek Patisserie. I always got clotted cream and cherry. Sometimes cream and sour lemon. At other times, ice cream with a slice of chocolate-biscuit cake.

But that night I didn't want any. Aunt Nadire's Göksel Arsoy . . . I was painfully discovering why she was waiting for a Göksel Arsoy but also knew why he hadn't come.

We passed the patisserie. All I said to my mother was, "I'm a young woman now." And it was true in every sense.

My mother didn't understand. She tittered, "You're right, dear, elegant young women don't eat ice cream after midnight."

We opened the gate of the garden, and in the light filtering through the branches and flowers of the silk tree I could see my aunt's silhouette: she appeared like a flat-chested, hipless ghost with her unattractive face that always seemed to be on the verge of tears and her long thin neck. I felt sorry for her. Also at that moment I felt a stirring within me, a desire for beauty, like that which men seek in a woman's face and body.

I wouldn't say that I dislike men. Quite the contrary; I also pitied the men who were blind to my aunt's need for love and compassion, as well as her instinct for motherhood. I saw the storms of passion that raged in the heart of this woman who fantasized about giving her heart to a man like it happened in films and novels. No, I was simply revolted by maleness but also by femaleness.

Stars and jasmine. Years later I was Tosca, throwing myself into the void, into death. The Italian director had put star-patterned filters over the lights and the sky glimmered. Singing "Colla mia!" I leaped into the void. Ah, Scarpia, to settle accounts in the presence of God! There were human voices calling out and the crescendo of echoing music as I gazed upon the twinkling stars. Every time, my grandmother's words, "The jasmine didn't bloom this year," enveloped Tosca's impassioned tale in mercy. A shiver running down my spine, I would emerge for the curtain call. "Where is this scent of jasmine coming from?" I would whisper. No one understood.

Aside from the silk tree and jasmine, the only other flowers were the hollyhocks. The rest were fruit trees. My grandmother would gather the flowers of the hollyhock and make cough syrup with her secret recipe.

The jasmine flowers couldn't be dried. They were never sprinkled over the laundry. I remember sachets of lavender, but not jasmine.

Gleaming white sheets scented of jasmine may have been a myth, but the legend of Çalıkuşu was true. At first utterance, the two may seem incongruent. I should point out, however, that some of those myths are baseless. For example, the one about the sheets and the jasmine. Those "snow-white" sheets always had blue stains from the detergent. It never dissolved completely and would blotch into stains on the sheets. I despise the tales of housewives. Also, there is this notion that jasmine grows in everyone's yard, as though Istanbul were awash in jasmine.

But the legend of Çalıkuşu isn't like that. As the novel *Çalıkuşu* became more and more popular, all of Istanbul was pulled into the struggle for freedom during the fight against the Greeks in Anatolia. At the center of that struggle was the happiness of Feride. My grandmother told the story again and again, tears in her eyes. If Feride were happy, if the novel ended happily, then the War of Independence would be won.

That's how the legend of Çalıkuşu took on such proportions.

And that's why, in my grandmother's heart, my nickname was Çalıkuşu.

We'd go to Pendik when the green plums were in season and I'd spend my entire summer climbing among the branches of her fruit trees. No, that's not quite true. When we got there, the green plums would already be splitting open on the ground, so every summer was something of a disappointment. Especially in those days, those green plums meant the arrival of spring.

Not exactly. I liked the plums, but only later did they come to symbolize spring for me. From the day they come into season, for two or three weeks I eat green plums. Through them I live the refreshed green of spring, the scent of grass and flowers. But these last two summers, the first days of summer . . . No, not now, let's not go back to that same pain.

Then we'd return to Istanbul, to the unripe cherries, peaches, and apples that I ate; in my childhood, I spent all my days in those fruit trees. Just like Feride. But at the time, I hadn't yet read the story of her life.

And that's why I never understood why my grandmother always called me Çalıkuşu.

"Çalıkuşu, dinner's ready!"

"Be careful, you'll fall down, Çalıkuşu!"

"Çalıkuşu, wash your hands before you sit at the table!"

I had no idea what a çalıkuşu was, and never guessed that it was a novel. It frustrated me, and I imagined brooms and green beans, all sorts of strange things.

Later I learned that it was a rather small bird that lived in shrubby landscapes, a bird with black-spotted wings, a red head, and feathers that turn greener toward the body. Despite its size, it has a loud call. Was Feride like that? Perhaps, in a way. As for me, even though I was rambunctious, I tended to be a quiet child. To keep away from prying eyes I'd sneak off to the trees and not make a peep.

My grandmother would say, "Çalıkuşu, why are you so quiet? Why don't you sing out like the other children?"

Grandmothers are always beloved.

You too loved your grandmother. I feel nothing; just disconnected from myself, broken off. I'm going toward the sea. The dark, horizonless sea of night. The night sea beckons me. And since I feel nothing, the open sea cannot frighten me.

The sea calls. I have nothing here on the shore. As I move toward the sea, as I'm reunited with the sea, I recall the most painful memory. Your grandmother's funeral and the small neighborhood mosque built by the architect Sinan all those hundreds of years ago. Your grandmother . . .

Tonight, that memory comes. Now, when I want to erase you from my thoughts.

You were crying on the phone. She had died in your arms.

I was leaving for a recital, one more time—now I know that it was the last one—because I was playing Mimi and death was with me as well, in the last act.

You said that if I called you after the recital, you wouldn't be at the boutique. "She got worse in the morning, and we didn't get her to the hospital in time. She died in the taxi."

How did you get her down two flights of stairs? On a stretcher? Did your father and Hüseyin carry her down? Was she able to take a few steps? Just a few hours earlier, she'd been fine, and had even asked for some rice soup.

You were crying. It's unbearable when you cry. When anyone cries.

You weren't at the boutique. You'd returned home with the body. The house was cold. Because of the corpse. It was so cold that the coal stove could've been lit. I glanced around the set. From where I was, I could see an unlit stove in the poor attic apartment. I compared the stove of "La bohème" with the one at your home. Which was colder? Which was more run-down?

I clutched the phone. "When will the funeral be?"

"Tomorrow, after the noontime prayer."

Prayers and opera—could the two possibly go together? Where and when? It was strange but I'd ceased thinking about death and was pondering the question: "Which mosque? Where?"

"You don't need to come. Don't you have a recital?"

Let me make a correction: it wasn't an attic apartment, it was a loft in Paris. Or was it Italy? Why are my memories so jumbled? Mimi comes to light the candle that went out. She sees Rudolf.

You said that you heard the sound of the instruments. The loud moan of the trombone. Now, forever, those instruments are playing for the sea, the night, the sky unbroken by a horizon.

"It's the recital for the last act. I'll call you when it's over."

I enter the courtyard. The waves are crashing over me. You know that I was always afraid of being with your family; I never showed it, but I was afraid. Maybe you never knew, or perhaps you forgot long ago.

It could be that you've forgotten everything. You were lost in the sea. That's why it calls out to me. Like I said: tonight the sea is calling me. The night sea. It shrouded our memories with a deep blue curtain.

Among my memories there is one of the day I entered the courtyard of the mosque designed by the master architect Sinan. But it wasn't the noon prayer, it was the midafternoon prayer. Midafternoon, and the sun was tumbling down. It was the beginning of fall.

I was preparing for my role as Mimi in "La bohème." A massive stove had been made to suit the grandeur of that scene. And yours . . . I was cold the first time I came to your place, such a small stove.

My first visit. But tonight I don't want to speak of that.

Particularly, your mother: there was doubt and concern lurking behind the kindness in her eyes. Did she sense something? You, her daughter, her daughter's future . . . Who is this woman? Why are they such close friends? Is that what she thought?

I didn't know your grandmother, I'd never seen her. I may have heard her voice once on the phone. We may have spoken once: "That mad opera woman," she probably said and then called for her granddaughter.

That was in the early days. Your mother and grandmother wouldn't *have spoken of me. But I know that women talk like that. Whispered implications. The truth is never fully spoken aloud. No, they didn't talk of me. Her death was at the beginning, in the early days of our love.*

Your mother would never have dared admit that you'd become entangled in a lesbian love affair. Nor would your grandmother. Even if she had lived a few more years. She was always uncomfortable with my social standing and uneasy about opera. It wasn't an art she understood.

I didn't trap you in my net. You came to me of your own will; on judgment day you'll confess this. There should be a day of judgment, an outpouring of our sins and good deeds, our lies and truths.

I don't know why, but I feel a warmth for your grandmother. Hadn't she wanted you to sew a velvet dress for her?

She brushed your hair when you were a child. My grandmother also brushed my hair and tied it up with a large white satin ribbon. You probably didn't have a ribbon; they'd long gone out of style when you were young.

Your grandmother had wanted velvet, a jacquard cloth that shimmered, with small flowers like roses or pansies that glimmered in the folds of the fabric.

Your young heart was set on sewing it for her. You were crestfallen that you hadn't been able to find the fabric to sew the "roba" that she desired.

That's what you said to me: "Roba!" You'd learned the word "roba" from those wealthy women at the boutique, and when you said it, your eyes would light up.

There were bolts of jade green velvet, burgundy and carmine. But what you sewed was blue, without flowers, cut from scraps of cloth at the dress shop.

We asked everywhere about flowers, pansies and cloth flowers, and in the end I found out that I could have it brought from Damascus. I had it delivered secretly, not telling anyone at the boutique.

In that phone call, your grandmother thanked me. She was grateful to the woman from the opera. But her gratitude sent a jab of pain through me; such a small, wizened grandmother. It was just a few yards of fabric.

It was gray, but it had the pansies. They hadn't been able to find one in green or maroon.

Why don't I know your grandmother's name? Weren't we so close that I should've known the names of the people in your family?

Who were you? Was your family from Istanbul? Or had they come later, from a brokenhearted town in the provinces where night creeps in early? I don't know.

Why can't I say your name, or even remember it?

I hung back in the courtyard of the mosque. For a moment. A long moment. I had to brace myself for the crowd gathered there. The women had congregated in a corner. I hesitated to approach. They were wearing headscarves; I wasn't. Nor had I put on makeup. For some reason I'd worn my outdated black sunglasses. The sun had begun its descent, but it still shed a weak autumn light. The dark lenses of my sunglasses concealed me from the people, especially from your family, your circle, your social class. That's how it seemed to me.

Death and funerals should be the work of men. I saw that the men, including your father and brother, had gathered around the stone dais upon which rested the coffin. Hüseyin, your younger brother. He likes me. Used to like me. Just like your father.

The sea washes over me and then recedes. I have doubts, however, if your father, like your mother, truly liked me. In the rare times that we met, they would ask after me, smile and chat. They'd insist on addressing me formally as "Handan Hanım." But they probably didn't say that to your friends who were your age. If I think of the age difference, they were right, as I was altogether maybe two years younger than your mother.

The director insisted on "Rodolfo"—which is what we needed to do to remain faithful to the original work. He was a red-haired man, with *freckled hands and face. He found it strange that we wanted to perform Puccini in Turkish.*

It had all slowly begun to strike me as strange. Thinking on it now, playing the role of Mimi had pushed me too far. But back then, it never occurred to me.

The artificial flowers left stains on my hands. I was infatuated by them; they brought me closer to you. "In 'La bohème,' I'm a little like you . . ." Because in the opera, Mimi made artificial flowers. But you were upset by my comparison and thought I was insulting you; clouds darkened your glowing face.

You had long, narrow fingers. I kissed them and begged you. But that was much, much later. Your nails were always unpainted. How many times had you pricked yourself on a needle, recoiling in pain?

You thought I was being snobbish when I compared you to Mimi. I fell silent, as always. As if to say: it wasn't like that, you misunderstood. To hold you close . . . But I merely pulled away.

I walk toward the stage: "Si, mi chiamano, Mimi." I was entranced. Swathed in the sorrow of young seamstresses, dressmakers, tailors' assistants. Entranced. In Paris, it is snowing. Rodolfo has abandoned me. Waiting until spring, the first days of spring, spring of death. What is it that burns my eyes?

Your mother was standing among a group of weeping women. But she wasn't crying. For the others, weeping in public was a kind of show. It's a tradition that women cry at funerals. But this tumult of weeping repulses me. Men should cry as well. But still, your mother didn't shed a tear. I have no compassion for such outbursts.

As I sing, my voice is rent by emotion. I plead for Rodolfo. Have our hands become joined like our hearts? The candle goes out. We're left in utter darkness.

No matter how much it hurt, they say you never wept when you pricked your finger on a needle.

But you . . . You're crying. I imagine: you're weeping this very evening. You're here, with me.

That day, my dear, you wept on the phone; I could have become Mimi and died.

In the evening I write you letters that you'll never read. Words and lines breathe death into one another.

I drink every night. What did you expect? I'm drunk, smoking ciga-rettes one after another—no longer will I be Mimi. I brushed away La bohème. *But I'd like to be back in the opera, back onstage. "Don't cry," I told you. My heart sunk. Tears poured from your eyes, their pupils dappled in green and olive, and I know that I'm losing control but still, your tears flow and Mimi is losing control, and at a signal from the director she tried to warm her hands in the muff that she thinks Rodolfo gave her, and now it's the final scene of parting: "Addio, dolce svegliare," let her go so she can die in silence. You killed her.*

Close your eyes which are the color of honey. I want to kiss your eyelids.

Your grandmother's funeral was held at that mosque. I know the names of operas, but nothing of mosques. The next time we were able to meet in private—a full three days later—you told me about it. There's a legend about the mosque. They say that when the foundations for the Süleymaniye Mosque had been laid, Sinan disappeared for a year. They looked for him, everyone looked for him. But he was gone. People disappear, even when the foundation collapses. Aren't both of us also lost? This small neighborhood mosque was built in the year that he disappeared. The weak sunlight is try-ing to make the leaden domes of the mosque glimmer. It's hopeless.

Your grandmother who had wanted that iridescent velvet "roba" always spoke of the mosque. Had she been born in that neighborhood? Did she arrive there as a bride? Who told her that story? Did she think that the mosque designed by Sinan honored the neighborhood?

I walked toward the door. A wooden door, framed in white marble. Both sides of the entryway were offset by black marble panels, facing one another, embossed in gold. If examined carefully, traces of an untarnished gilt dream and the anguish of beautiful days can still be seen there. Indifferent to the strange looks I received, I entered the mosque.

I avoided the crowd. I hadn't seen you. Inside, whites and blues were resurrected into a flurry of colors in the tile work. Then there was austerity, emptiness.

The men from the neighborhood were performing the afternoon prayer. I stood behind them. Hüseyin saw me and approached: "Handan Abla!" No, there was no exclamation point. He held his voice down.

I asked about you. You'd cried so much that you hid yourself away. From whom? From those women whose lives were steeped in television and gossip, those poor drab women who found entertainment in the trip to the mosque for your grandmother's funeral as they huddled about sobbing? Were you ashamed of them and of the haggard men, aged beyond their years, most of them unshaven?

No, I'm being unfair. The fault lies with the sea. It surges and swells, speaking. It says what I'm saying.

Handan Abla held Hüseyin's hand. Your brother's hand was trembling. Handan Abla was as cold as stone, just like her hands.

"We can leave now. The prayers are finishing. This is the last one." Hüseyin probably said something like that.

Handan Abla didn't object. They left.

Rodolfo wasn't to blame. He'd loved Mimi; it was the tuberculosis . . .

That night, and this agonizing night, I'm pained by the tears you shed for the death of your grandmother. Perhaps tonight even more than ever.

My grandmother and I never shared words or memories. And you know, my grandmother had always wanted me to sing.

(I said to Handan Sarp, "Later you did sing. You sang those magical songs."

It was cold, and a biting wind blew.

She shook her head: "But that's not what she wanted. My grand-mother wanted me to sing popular songs. She never listened to the kind of music I sang. She heard opera for the first time at the conservatory. But she passed away before I made my debut.")

In terms of physique, Liù might be the last character I should've ever played. But I took to the stage as Liù in *Turandot*. Thirty years have passed since then. Only now can I understand the importance Puccini had in my life.

The moon was rising. An orange and pink moon, tinged with blood. I lost myself in that full moon and my nervousness fell away. But for me, moonlight is so commonplace. It seems laughable that people gather to ogle the moon. The one on stage, however, was different. During the recitals, we were bound up together, that moon and I. Especially during the lighting rehearsal. But it was at the premiere that the moon outshone everything else. Turandot appeared on the veranda of the palace, a full moon rising behind her.

Did I say it was a bleeding moon? No, on the contrary—it was a moon that drew blood.

The critics wrote that a new star had been born. The reason was the moonlight. I was awed by the overpowering nature of Turandot and the full moon. It wasn't surprising at all that Prince Calàf suddenly fell in love with Turandot. The full moon shrouded her in secrecy. I was burdened by Liù's misery.

In fact, the moon was quite shabby. I exaggerated its allure, its pinks and oranges. It was placed there like a plate behind the veranda. As for Turandot, I won't give her name but the woman who played her was washed up and even rounder than the moon itself. But I needed something to inspire me to sing. First, it was the moon, and then it was the power of Turandot.

I had to, because when left unadorned, life is unbearable.

My chest burned with indignation, and I wept for the fate of the poor slave girl Liù. She was in love with Prince Calàf, but rather than speak of her love, she took her own life. Liù's love for Calàf meant nothing to him; he was in love with stone-hearted Turandot.

I think that Puccini knew the secret of love, of falling in love with a wicked-hearted person. Calàf asks, "Liù, why did you love me so much?" And she answers, "Because one day at the palace you smiled at me."

I have a photograph that was taken of me at just that moment. The lens captured an entirely different Handan. If I'd been in front of a mirror, I wouldn't have recognized myself, I wouldn't have seen what the lens saw: a real Liù, believing and trusting in Calàf's smile; she had gathered it up in her heart. That's why she fell in love with him and would be prepared to die for love.

Is it the innocence of youth, or the power of art?

For years I looked at that photo with indifference, not trying to interpret the image. It's difficult to purify the poison in my blood and give meaning to the past. Could I have fallen in love because of a smile?

For nights, for months I worked to reflect in my voice just how Liù could fall in love with a smile in that last aria before she dies. The music followed as if from a distance: a chorus, flute and solo violin. It was heartrending.

But was I really purified? Did the wound heal? Did I tell you that my life is a wound? Not the wound of a heart. An open, festering wound that never closed. That's why I always tried to avoid people and passion. That is, until I met her. I didn't fall in love with her, with the person whose name I can't say. In the beginning, she wasn't in love. Perhaps she was running from the pain of a previous romance. I wasn't in love at first either. I hid my life, that wound of a life that refused to heal. Maybe I smiled like Prince Calàf. I deceived her, that young woman. I smiled into a void, at goodness. I smiled at her goodness and the void I carry within, that abyss.

When I played Liù, she may not even have been born yet, or perhaps was quite young. A mere child. They didn't know that *Turandot* was being performed at the Istanbul City Opera. Neither she nor her family knew that I'd played Liù in *Turandot*.

Liù's life would be lost, unbeknownst to Calàf. And he would marry Turandot. A smile: Prince Calàf would forget that smile, it would be lost in those legendary years of Peking in an aria.

Later, when I looked at that picture and tried to recall those days, the poison welled up within me again. I was revolted by the love I saw in my eyes. I was particularly revolted by the slave girls who fell in love with princes. She looked at me, and when she smiled, I should have responded with an angry glare. That smile deceived Liù, the slave girl.

She was smiling.

It was the smile of a young woman, a working-class woman, my young seamstress. She smiled at me.

I never played Liù again.

They saw me as Turandot.

The gongs rang out. In the light of the moon, I stepped out onto the palace veranda and gave the signal to the executioner.

Then I found Liù in Elem.

Elem . . . Her name. At last I could bring myself to say it.

Elem became my Liù. I didn't understand this at the time. This is our story.

It's raining, a thin needling rain. Yet again, under the crepe myrtle, I'm unable to get up and close the windows. I'm curled into a ball on the wicker chair. Soon, autumn will be over, and I'll pass the rest of the season indoors.

This year, I'm more composed.

But last year, when fall came and went, I was like a madwoman. I could find shelter nowhere, neither in the garden nor inside.

I thought of moving out to save myself from my memories of Elem. But I didn't have the money. Just as the memories had suffused the garden, they seeped into the furniture. It was impossible for me to replace everything. And even if I had the means, I couldn't bring myself to do it; that would mean yet another separation.

I recall a line of poetry by Haşim . . .

"We are imprisoned here for eternity in exile and longing."

Exile and longing. My life.

I have no one left. They're gone, every single person. Maybe a friend or two I see occasionally, some distant relatives with whom I can't bear to even speak on the phone, and Aunt Nadire who insists on living and is filled with dreams about the future. Kadriye Hanım, who labors silently at home. For the first time, I had a longing for children. If only I'd had children . . . In the monotony of days, I feel a need for love, if I could ever love again. But then it vanishes, and just as how I feel about Aunt Nadire's dreams, I find the desire for children absurd.

The sounds of my home frighten me. They go on and on.

I picked up the book with hesitation. There were two reasons I was unsure: first, I doubted that a book that I'd read in my adolescence would invoke the same feelings. Second, there was the possibility, the danger, that in the pages of *Çalıkuşu* I would be pulled into turgid memories of Elem.

I was wrong on both accounts. I read it just as I had in the days when I devoured slices of chocolate-biscuit cake at the Petek Patisserie: one slice of cake, ten pages of breathless reading. But this time, without the cake. As for Elem, she's always with me anyway. Wherever I go, whatever I do or see, she's with me. *Çalıkuşu* and Munise didn't bring any new pain.

It was summer when I read the book. The same copy.

I don't have a large collection of books, but I always kept the works I love, taking them with me when I move. After this, I don't know. Much less the books, I can't bring myself to move again.

My first love was literature. Opera came later. I loved opera like a book among novels.

The cover is melon-pink and torn. On the first page I'd written "July 19, 1966." My signature at that time was an ostentatious "Handan" followed by a "Sarp" drifting across the page. In our garden, the garden that memory now begins to sketch.

But now I'm here on Sakızlı Street. Summer is over and I'm cold. I'm drinking the cherry vodka left over from last year. The color of the cherries has faded ever so slightly. The long, summer afternoons in Pendik were eerily silent. Now, an ambulance is passing by. The piercing sound will be drowned out in *Çalıkuşu*.

Feride is the main character. She's studying at the French high school in Istanbul, Notre Dame de Sion. In any grade, it doesn't matter. I'm scanning the lines.

Sir Alexi appears, reed-like in his black suit. Feride's head scarf is like a palace yashmak.

"Palace yashmak" perhaps no longer means anything to people today. Perhaps just to the curious . . .

Was Sir Alexi just Feride's friend, or did he have other interests?

I sketched a picture of Sir Alexi on page seven. Had I felt something at the time? Right from page seven, did I start seeing Feride in a different way from everyone else? It could've been an unconscious impulse, an instinct, a tendency. A desire to find your own sexuality, a wounded sexuality doomed from its very inception to fade in the midst of inexperience. Thinking that it was your crime, your sin, and then to suddenly find someone like yourself, even if in a novel, and take shelter there . . .

Sir Alexi's lips were vermillion. "Vermillion lips." That's how Feride described them.

Feride's lips were always tinged with purple ink stains. She constantly twirled the shaft of her pen between her teeth like a meat skewer, leaving stains on her upper lip like a mustache. At the peak of puberty, she'd felt humiliated when a close acquaintance visited her at school.

Sir Alexi: taut vermillion lips. Feride: lips stained purple, and a mustache of ink.

My heart began to speak. Perhaps not aloud. But even if it did just murmur, it was in such pain! I felt this later as well, numerous times, and spoke of the pain.

On the first page of the novel, this line had apparently caught my eye: "The sky was visible through the slats of the window shutters." I'd underlined it. Something deep inside me winced in the summer of 1966. I need the sky, even if I can only see it through the slats. And for days, the sky has been overcast, oppressive.

Later, I underlined a line about a fountain in a copse of trees.

My grandmother didn't have a fountain at her summer house. But there was a well that had always frightened me. The water had gone bitter, and it was admonished for being useless, no better than a dry well. Despite my fear, it saddened me because I thought that it could understand the rebukes. I even remember going to the well and stroking it out of pity.

Fountain or not, I always thought those old-style homes had one in the garden, which were more like small forests. That's why I'd run, like Feride, to the fountain—an imaginary one. I didn't even know about Feride's fountain. I'd merely conjured one up.

The real fountain in the novel was in a cluster of trees behind the summer house by the sea. In the center of the fountain there was an armless statue of a nude child, and Feride always thought it resembled the children of the desert. In any case, she thought it must have come from the desert. Red leaves floated on the surface of the water. Again, it was autumn. The leaves drifted across the water, revealing the red fish below. I wonder if the fish get cold; I think it's a good thing that children have fountains with red fish. In my childhood, the fountain and fish became interwoven with stories and novels.

As for Feride, one time she tried to walk into a fountain, indifferent to the fact that her grandmother had carefully dressed her up in a silk outfit and new shoes. Was it mischief, sheer naughtiness? Likely not the desire to attempt the impossible . . .

No matter how I acquired it, I had that in me as well: the desire to test the impossible. It was a passion, an obsession even.

I had recurring dreams about running in the copse of trees, peering into the fountain with its blanket of red leaves, and wanting to wade into the pool in my cotton nightgown. Just at that moment I'd awaken, never to know if I'd actually entered the water. But I'd imagine that I had and then take my flights of fancy as fact. Nobody had seen me, nobody knew, but I had waded into the fountain.

Then the pool was transformed into the sea. The charm of the small red fish gave way to a longing for the wild creatures of the sea.

I also dreamed of that: drifting out to sea. Being the sea. Existing in its purple-black water. It no longer mattered if I waded in. But still, I had a pang of regret: the red fish in the pool were alone, I'd abandoned them. Those imaginary fish pined for me.

In all truth I've never liked the character Kâmran, who had a crush on Feride. In one scene in the novel, which seems to be everyone's favorite, Kâmran brought her some chocolate bonbons. Holding the edges of her skirt, Çalıkuşu curtsied to him. Kâmran stood there smiling like a well-bred lady. Feride's hands and lips were stained with ink, as usual. That scene simply exasperates me.

What I saw in the scene were the signs of a compatible husband and wife, a perfect couple. Of course I didn't pick up on that as I was reading. Perhaps it was when I finished the novel? No, it was later, much later, after thinking on Munise and Feride and as I got to know myself better and found myself trapped.

Çalıkuşu concludes with a "happy ending" in which Feride and Kâmran are reunited: a mustachioed girl and a youth like a well-bred lady.

It was the chocolate pudding scene that typified everything. Feride and Kâmran, alone in an empty room at the nun's school. The female students were pressed against the door, trying to peer in. Both clandestine and right in the open. When it's like that, no one finds it strange: you don't drift far from moral judgments and you have a place in society's morality. No one will be interested in Feride's mustache and Kâmran's air of a lady of breeding.

That is how I came to know about happy couples.

All day long it rained. That's what autumn is: rain. For a long time now, the rain that I so loved has brought me nothing but suffering. The rain told me that I was alone and that I would always be alone.

I awoke to rain beating against the windows. I wanted to escape the sound. The roar of traffic, which the rain had driven far away, would even have been better.

I missed the idle years of my adolescence: a time when I wasn't yet exhausted, when I was bolstered by ideals that life hadn't torn to shreds. I cast *Çalıkuşu* far from my thoughts. There was only opera and singing.

I went out into the garden. The vine was turning the colors of fall, and I trimmed the yellow and red leaves. You once gave me a black porcelain vase as a gift. I placed the branches inside the vase and my hands were steady. A few yellow leaves fell to the floor. They gave their tired existence over to the vase. I wanted to protect the vine from autumn for a few days, at least a few more days, in a rainless room.

But it was in vain. The vine was exhausted; the red leaves fell until there were just dry branches in the vase, a few green leaves clinging on.

In her journal, Feride wrote of Kâmran's eyes: "Like the mossy green of the sea glowing in the sunlight." It's strange; in bright light, Elem's eyes would lose their honey color and become infused with green.

Picking up a fistful of sand, Feride threw it in Kâmran's face to sting his pensive eyes.

And I stung Elem's soul.

We were sitting at Hristo's old restaurant. He hadn't yet passed away. Like the new Hristo's, it was well-lit and had nothing like the air of a grilled meat diner. Don't ask me why I'm bringing up these memories; I'm just trying to write our history. But writing is difficult for me. If you read it one day, reading will be hard for you. In our story, I cannot skip over Hristo.

That was the first place we went together. It was fall—why is it always fall?—and a cold, drizzly night. We'd known each other for almost three weeks. You may have forgotten that we met in September. I remind you here: we met at the end of September at Nedret's boutique. Perhaps you forgot. Have you lost our memories? Do you remember the day we met? First, we went to Hristo's.

No, that wasn't the first time. We were together; we'd become close. The chains had been broken. We were at the beginning of the road, and you loved me.

The long, hall-like restaurant on the shores of the Bosphorus showed its age, and that was its charm. Monsieur Hristo sat, looking for all the world like a lobster with shriveled antennae, beside the glass display case of seafood.

Did I say lobster? I've begun speaking nonsense, my dear. In the days when we went to Hristo's, lobsters hadn't been seen for years; they'd long since been scuttled off to the fine restaurants where wealthy politicians dined. Those were the fish restaurants with foreign names that gained their fame as five-star establishments.

One time a woman approached me, and mentioned such a five-star restaurant. As she was describing it, I was introduced to a lady whose name sounded liked "Daisy" and she also started going on about five-star restaurants. She'd come backstage to give me her regards, and invited me to a lobster dinner. I let her prattle on, and thanked her.

Let Monsieur Hristo sit there, dreaming of the old days, mulling over the ghosts of lobster in the display case. The restaurant is empty. Perhaps there is no one aside from us. Only later, when my mind is clouded by drink and your fear has begun to make you squirm, only after some time has passed, will another couple arrive; they'll sit in a corner, hiding their extramarital fling, never imagining that we're a couple just like them.

No, it wouldn't occur to them. We'd be cautious. When you smiled too openly at me, I'd flash you a warning glance.

But in fact, neither at Hristo's nor at any of the Bosphorus restaurants could you smile or laugh from the heart. Even though you were born and raised in Istanbul, it was with me that you first saw the Bosphorus. I took you on walks on those languid summer evenings to the restaurants and villages that dot the shores of the strait: Tarabya, Kireçburnu, Sarıyer. In Beykoz we paused and observed the blackened fishing nets and round buoys coated in moss.

"How would I, Elem from Kocamustafapaşa, so far from the sea, know anything of the Bosphorus?" you asked me.

Something should have softened inside me. We were from the same city, but were so different. The opportunities were so abundant, but at the same time so few. But I didn't soften. I wrenched the smile from your lips when I said: "You don't even pronounce it like a real Istanbulite: it's KocamustApaşa, not KocamustaFApaşa."

There's no reason for me to write these memories or speak of them, or even recall them and try to bring them to life again. No reason at all. Our past will interest no one; not after it has failed to interest you . . . I'm just trying to pass the time, and I wish it would pass quickly. All of it.

I cannot go back to your youth, nor to your love or your attachment to me. You loved me, didn't you?

I should carry love away. That's what I should do. I should take love far away from you, from memories—our memories.

But it wasn't Kocamustâpaşa or Hristo's that I wanted to talk about. What was it that I wanted to correct by bringing that up? Your Turkish? There was nothing wrong with your Turkish. When I said "Istanbulite," whom did I really mean? It's the poor people living there today who call it Kocamustafapaşa.

Yet again I catch the scent of the sea, drifting in from the moss, fish scales, shellfish and fishing nets. But we aren't there, gazing at the heaps of nets. Still, I'm surrounded by the scent of the sea.

As for Hristo's . . . It was a work by Reşat Nuri Güntekin, the author of "Çalıkuşu." It was his other book, "The Night of Fire."

"The only novel I've read is 'The Night of Fire,'" you said. "It was a homework assignment in middle school."

We sat, you facing the sea, my back to it. I was drinking vodka openly, you secretly. "A double vodka," I'd said. "Half a bottle. A small bottle. Do you have Binboğa vodka?" Partners in crime, we mixed a little vodka into your beer so no one would see.

You had your first drink with me. And my addiction to alcohol began with you. I drank so that we could be more reckless together; it drove away my shyness that I tried to hide. What would they say about us? Always that fear! I lived in fear; it was all that was left.

We dashed into Hristo's from the taxi. A storm had broken out, churning the sea, and waves crashed against the shore. It was like the loneliness we both carried inside. But you didn't yet understand that loneliness. You thought of the two of us as one being. But we weren't. I knew that you were outside of life; I'd lived, and aged. No matter who and what you are, two people can never be "one." Sooner or later, tedium sets in, and the days are numbered. The passion may die down, perhaps be transformed into friend-ship. As night began rolling in, the dark sky was rent by purple flashes of light. In the harbor, waves tossed the boats against one another.

Elem, for the sake of all that's human, hold on to these thoughts. Don't let your new life push me and what we felt from your memory. We were two separate people, not one. Till the end, everyone must bear this separa-tion. Forever, that rift and daze; I drink myself to oblivion, finally—it's like being saved and dying. Killing and being killed.

You'd read "The Night of Fire."

I too must have read it. I did: Afife, a young woman wrapped up in dreams, finally confesses her love after years have passed. But it had faded away long ago. That night of fire had flickered out. Flickered and burned out.

After a life of so many years, you'd only read "The Night of Fire," just one novel.

"Why didn't you read anything else after that? Did you get bored of reading?" I asked. For me, novels were like opera. "I've read a lot of novels. I'm always reading," I said. I was secretly proud of this.

"Don't throw it in my face."

But I did throw it in your face; an act of petty intellectualism. If you read novels, you can be saved. Poor young seamstresses should read novels. Such absurdity!

The eyes of a young woman. Her eyes, a deep mossy green, had turned from my piercing gaze. As though looking out to sea. "The storm has gotten worse."

Look at the sea. The storm hasn't worsened. There is no storm. We weren't two people and we didn't live as individuals; we were the malignance of one. The sea is calm. The sea no longer believes in us. The sea turned us away. In this world, we have no other friends. Our old story, our love, is nothing now.

The malignance of one.

I insisted: "Tell me if you're bored of the topic. But, didn't anyone read books at home?"

"No."

The sea rejected us.

To whom can I turn? I don't know. Can I run to you? No, never.

Like a pedant, I'd wanted to blame your teachers for not teaching you to love literature. But in the end, were novels really so important? The silence was like a shard of glass. Like bleeding. Let novels rot in hell! Across from me, you fidgeted like a startled bird. I was stony. A stranger, observing, as you passed by... You're everything to me.

I'd like to sleep. If I sleep, everything will be as good as it can be—because I won't remember anything.

I was unable to cling to life, to love. You left me. I'll write that again and again: You left me.

"What did you enjoy doing then?"

A twitch pulled at your cheek: "Mostly working, to help out at home."

I fell silent. Had I no idea that people, some people, including girls, had to work?

If only I could sleep.

You lowered your voice: "My father worked for all of us. He was always working."

I looked up: "'The Night of Fire' is a good book. You might have liked Reşat Nuri Güntekin's writing."

"As soon as I finished middle school, I started working. I never read another novel." You sat there stiff and despondent. As though you'd given up on gazing at the sea, the abyss, straight ahead of you. You looked into my eyes as though to say, "I'm not like you. I don't know anything about books. Please don't go on."

I can still hear your voice.

And of course I did say something: "From now on, you should read literature."

You were saddened, because you loved me. Every word I said affected you. Hurt you. In those times, that's how it was.

I write this to the sobbing and the cries.

It's morning. Daylight. The pain of night has subsided. The daylight takes it away.

I didn't used to write my somniloquies in the morning. But today, a sudden pain shot through my heart and wouldn't leave me be. I should write more. But what?

Times of parting; your leaving, and my leaving. We committed the greatest wrong against each other, and now I shall be forever alone. Say what you will, but you too will always be alone. There's no one else with whom we are close. And there never will be. You may think there is, but one day, they'll be gone.

Our faces and bodies appear and disappear in our memories. But for you, they must be forgotten, utterly forgotten.

In that dream, I didn't cry. Last night, I didn't even dream. But sometimes in my dreams, I find myself weeping.

In the morning, I read my somniloquies. They are sheer deliria. I regret having written them; they're vessels of poison, of blood.

Elem, will you notice that as you pull away, I draw nearer? But why would you? You won't read these somniloquies. You won't even know.

In the beginning, on the first evenings we went out, the restaurants I chose filled you with fear. "Welcome," they'd say, "welcome, Handan Hanım." The headwaiter, in a three-piece suit, would rush up to shake my hand. They were probably thinking, "She's a soprano at the City Opera" but had no idea what that actually meant. "How are you?" I'd ask as I headed to a corner table. They all knew that I preferred sitting at a corner table.

When making love, Elem was close to me, but at the restaurants she was distant. On the Bosphorus, in Beykoz gazing at the buoys and fishing nets, in Ayaspaşa at the restaurant of the Madame who's now dead; everywhere and everything is but a skeleton now. Elem, our memories are but a skeleton.

Those were the middle class places where we could freely frequent as two women—one young, the other nearing middle age, a ladder propped against the brink of forty: cadaverous restaurants, bars and cafes; the strangely somber, frenzied clubs for gay men where we were graciously accepted.

You blushed. In a cold sweat, frightened and tense. You wanted to sit down at the corner table and disappear. Not knowing how to break the bread, you watched me furtively. Which was the salt, which the pepper. Your timidity gave me courage.

"Have a glass of wine. What's the harm?"

"But if my family finds out . . ."

"They won't. Drink." I called the waiter over: "Another glass, please."

You blushed a deeper shade of red. You were but a child, my dear, at the beginning of the path of your life. You entrusted yourself to my care.

"Who," I asked you, "are these people? Who are they? There's nothing to be afraid of." I lowered my voice: "What's there to fear?" But I was afraid.

I, the woman they groveled to as "Handan Hanım," a performer of an art of which they knew nothing. And by her side a silent young woman with flushed cheeks, blinking her hazel eyes at the world around her as she quickly put down her knife and picked up the fork in her right hand only to put it back down, flustered. Two people. Actually, the two of us were one. We were one, I said. We were tears.

("Selim, I was afraid of living. I cowered before life. My cowardice persisted. And yet something else drew to a close.")

Evening has fallen. The novel *Çalıkuşu* is in my lap. The thought of turning the pages fills me with dread.

But this time it isn't the fear that I won't get the same pleasure from the book. I realize that I'm fleeing from myself. Just as she fled from life, Handan Sarp is trying to escape from her own essence, unable to face reality.

I always kept a distance—from my mother, father, Aunt Nadire, Semra, Ali and Nilüfer, and not just them but also my other friends and acquaintances. In the same way, I rebuffed the advances made by Gelengül. That's such a grand name, meaning "budding rose," for a woman who prided herself on her mustache. I was a stranger at Hikmet and Mustafa's home; but then again, I also wanted them to keep a distance from me. Did I succeed? I wanted to erase Kaya from my life. And from the others—there were hundreds—I kept my distance.

Some of them don't even know the real Handan. ("If you write the novel of my life, you most certainly must change my name.") But I didn't know them either, because they also had masks. I can't count how many times I caught them gazing at their own faces in the mirror. If we're lonely when we look in a mirror, it reflects our ugly side, the one we attempt to conceal. It is repugnant, abashed and despairing, precisely because we hide it.

The wind is blowing. For a few days, the flame in the pink flowers of the crepe myrtle has started fading to yellow. The flowers will quickly shrivel to a brownish-gray. That's the end. The chill of autumn has settled in.

I saw Elem. She was looking in the mirror. The mirror was written on the page of an old yellow notebook. I miss those old notebooks with their yellow paper. The writing was faint, difficult to read. When was it written; who wrote it? That's what I was thinking in my dream.

I can feel tears welling up, but I can't cry. Elem smiles. She looks at our life, elated, thinking we can have a life together. We'll get a cat, a kitty cat.

"Why do you want a cat?"

"You don't want one? Why wouldn't you want one, Handan? It would be like our child."

It seems she forgot that I've never liked children.

I saw a garden gate, grass and a fence stretching into the distance. Elem's desire for children suddenly filled me as well. It was all written in the yellow notebook. Alone, as she looked into the mirror, she appeared so pure and delicate! It frightened me that someone could be so virginal.

I tried to close the yellow notebook. Elem said, "Everything is going to be wonderful."

Now, I'm trying to understand who Elem is.

Long before I'd gotten to know myself, through *Çalıkuşu*.

Feride had met Munise in Zeyniler, a village of which I know nothing, not even where to find it on a map.

Munise was blond-haired and blue-eyed, and had clear white skin. She was a young, orphaned girl who always wore a tattered flower-print dress, her hair disheveled.

I know her.

Feride would call her over. When all the other girls had common names like Ayşe or Zehra, this little orphan had been named Munise. She would smile with her curly-lashed eyes at Feride, whom she called "my teacher."

I saw that smile. I know that smile.

On some evenings, Munise would sing folk ballads in a nearby yard.

Those ballads were moving, heart-weary. One evening, as Feride was passing along one of Zeyniler's convoluted dirt roads, she heard a voice, and listened to the ballad as it receded into the distance, not knowing if it was Munise.

"Munise, were you singing a ballad last night?"

"Yes, my teacher."

A blondish light moves gently toward empty birds' nests that have filled with snow. The cranky, weary Çalıkuşu revives upon sensing the gaze of the small orphan Munise and perks up upon catching sight of her smiling lips and pearly teeth. Love melts her heart.

For the first time in her life, Feride felt a mother's instinct.

As for me, I was unable to ascribe meaning to my feelings. At the time, I was old enough to mother a child. Despite that, I had absolutely no desire to be a mother. As long as I can remember I've been repulsed by the way that girls play with dolls; at the same time, it has always struck me as preposterous that boys acquire a fascination for playing with toy tanks and guns. My mother's life, spent venting rage against my absent father, further pushed thoughts of motherhood from my mind.

Munise's smile, the love and compassion in her eyes (which Feride felt as though "rubbed" onto her lips), and the pure white skin that showed through the rips in her floral-print dress stirred my heart. She should be with me, at my side, and save me from the monotony and drollery of those long summer days that never seem to end. The things we would talk of, the things we would say!

Most likely that wasn't a mothering instinct.

We didn't get a cat.

Even if we'd stayed together, we wouldn't have gotten one.

I accepted my reason for being on this earth. They couldn't tell it to my face; I accepted that they couldn't tell it to my face: lesbians cannot have cats, or children. And Elem, as for you . . .

Elem: a name given to none other. Your name. I always wondered why they named you that. Whispering prayers into your ear. Perched in your father's lap. Elem. When they gave you that name, my fate was sealed.

Elem. Just like the meaning of your name, everything filled with sorrow. We'll have no children. The lives of women who love women are filled with sorrow, so long as we carry on in life, so long as we take pride in our lives. There will be no children for us.

And there was fear. Our love was fear.

And we, weren't we each other's children, each other's parents? Those empty nests that the bare branches of autumn cannot conceal. Those empty nests aren't important, my dear, as long as we have our pride.

Our cats will be death. Our children will be death. When we made love, was it not death that we spoke of? Didn't we speak of death? Have you never missed death?

I didn't want to live. I should've told you that. If I had, perhaps I wouldn't have awoken to such suffering this morning.

I awoke. It was a sunny morning. I went out into the garden in my nightgown. Autumn is returning. I looked at the apartments, at their windows and balconies. I thought about life, of what I've lost. In a window, I saw a woman reach out toward a man. I couldn't see them clearly; they spoke to one another, and their hands joined. They didn't notice me, half naked in the garden, a ruined woman.

I need to live more to find the answers. I need to know why I didn't want to live with you. I said that to myself, and plucked two yellow leaves from the vine. In other autumns, they wouldn't have saddened me. My heart sank, because every yellowing of leaves reminds me of us.

The couple joined hands. It was beautiful.

I was surprised that Feride used to dress up Munise as if she'd found a doll in the village. She'd pleat her tousled, white-blond hair into two braids, tying them off with pink ribbons. Then she'd put her into a blue dress—probably the same blue as her eyes—and pull stockings over her legs. Munise, all dolled up.

Playing with someone's personality, their identity, seemed to me to be a form of ridicule. An expression of Feride's selfishness that made me feel shame.

But did I do the same to Elem?

("When the time comes, Selim. I just can't seem to put it all together: Munise and Elem, Feride's dress-up games, my own actions . . .")

I was also surprised at the idea of a red flannel dress. I even asked my grandmother, "Can you really make a dress from flannel? What is it?" She said it is a thin, wool cloth the French call *flanel*. Feride made a "coquette outfit" from red flannel. She then later compared Munise, who was wearing a red dress at the time, to "a chocolate sweet that melts in your mouth."

At that moment, why didn't she think of those chocolates that Kâmran had brought her? Those chocolate sweets that the girls at Notre Dame de Sion made jokes about and ate. Was Munise becoming a kind of Kâmran?

The light of suns burned within Feride. She saw the sky as a huge jasmine tree that sprinkled down white flowers in the cool of evening.

In the cool of evening, the sky was always the same for me: a darkening blue, fading to black and gloom.

I constantly had to be on my guard. Aunt Nadire would ask about Elem: "She hasn't been around in quite a while. You don't mention her anymore." Again, that shirt of flame. "She's fine," I'd say. "She's working as usual." Aunt Nadire, who was fond of Elem, missed her. Elem liked her as well, referring to her as "old auntie." Elem liked people.

Aunt Nadire said, "Let's have her over one evening for tea. I'll make a cherry pie."

Elem was mad about cherries.

Like Kâmran, I used to buy her chocolates, but I'd get the ones filled with cherry liquor, and I'd watch as she ate them, her eyes closed in delight. She opened the wrapper carefully, so she could pick out any crumbs left behind.

Her mother used to make cherry jam for me. Abashed, my Munise would bring the small jar and leave it on the table. "How much is a kilo of cherries?" I'd muse, but bite my tongue, and smile. A pang of conscience ran through me.

I bought the cherry liquor chocolates from expensive patisseries like Divan. Later, I started going to La Cave to buy cherry wine, four or five bottles at a time.

Why am I so saddened by these memories?

Four letters. Four letters from Kâmran, clear as day. The mail truck, passing through Zeyniler, left four letters for Feride.

Four crumpled letters, tossed on a shelf by the stove. Munise tells Feride that she burned them, but she'd hidden them away.

Munise holds them out to her: "Take them, my teacher, someone you love sent them."

Was it Elem? Or Kâmran, Munise? An unfathomable enigma, an unfathomable ache.

Elem won't send me a letter. My somniloquies won't reach her.

I long for the mail truck that trundles through Zeyniler, the courier of novels.

In the dark room, Feride throws the letters Munise holds out to her into the stove. No, they aren't from her beloved; those are letters from an enemy. The coals of the fire had died but now burst into flame, greedily devouring the envelopes. But the last letter just won't catch flame, it curls open, revealing neat handwriting. Munise leaps and saves a piece of the last letter.

Elem saved something as well. My shattered memories, past loves. She would've listened to me; if I wept, she would have kissed away my tears.

Who was Munise fleeing from?

In Zeyniler, on the 17th of December as a storm raged outside, Feride slipped into bed "in a fever." On this page, right here: Munise, that "poor young girl" buffeted in the winds of my youth; and Feride, having lost all hope, thinking that Munise had been lost in drifts of snow in some dark corner of the night.

I closed my eyes. There was no need to read the rest. I remember: the biting wind that will blow in as the door opens, the candle blown out—like the extinguished candles of Mimi and Rodolfo—and the small body, cold as ice, that will tumble into Feride's arms.

I remember that Elem once came to me on a rainy night. Timidly, the doorbell rang. I was in the living room. Who would visit at that hour? I was hesitant to open the door. Perhaps it was Ayşe Hanım, the doorkeeper. She would tell me something, like the natural gas bill needed to be paid, or that they were going to spray for insects. It was only nine thirty.

I opened the front door. No one was there, so I pressed the button to open the street door. Then I heard the sound of steps, but because of the pattering of rain, I couldn't make out whose they were. I waited. My Munise came down the steps, sopping wet.

"Elem, what's wrong?" I asked.

She threw her arms around my neck.

"You're cold and wet. Come inside."

My young seamstress apologized for coming unannounced; she said that she'd been standing at the door, unsure of what to do. We'd never visited each other without calling first. She was too shy. I took her by the hand and led her inside.

"Take off your wet things, you'll catch cold."

I went inside and got a towel and sweat suit. When I returned, she was crying. She wept silently, in shame. Then she began to tell me what happened.

Toward evening, Nedret had caused a scene. A few meters of satin had been cut wrong for so-and-so's dress. "I'll fire all of you!" she'd bellowed, saying that she was going to deduct it from their weekly wages. When she couldn't find more of the fabric in the same color, she sent Osman to the fabric shop, where they only had it in a slightly lighter tone. Nedret—she was prone to such outbursts—lost control, and shouted at Elem: "You hussy! What the hell were you thinking?" Elem rushed out of the boutique and wandered in the rain for a few hours.

"You can quit tomorrow," I told her.

"What will I do then? How will we make ends meet?"

"Until you find a new job, you can be my assistant. I'll take care of it."

Of course, I knew that she wouldn't agree to it. But I couldn't think of anything else. I wanted to console Elem, but at the same time I wanted to get her mind off the subject.

"Have you told your family? They'll be worried about you."

She said that she'd called and told them she was going to help a bride with a dress at the Hilton.

"How could I be your assistant?" she asked. "I don't know enough about opera to be able to help you."

The tomb of the saint Şem-i Dede, washed by the rain, utterly alone. Did the saint realize that tonight, Elem didn't pass by at her usual hour?

In fact, Elem was quite helpful. She was now my seamstress. To make sure that she didn't get into any trouble, occasionally I went to Nedret as well.

Sitting in her chair, Elem would carefully examine my stage costumes and point out their faults. It may not have seemed significant that I said "sitting in her chair." But it is; not once did I invite her backstage. I couldn't. Aside from Ali and Semra, no one else from the opera knew about Elem. And they shouldn't have known. Ali and Semra would only find out later.

She was so attentive to Handan Sarp that she could pick out the slightest flaw in her costumes. Disregarding Necmi's resentment, I'd call him over to make alterations. The seamstresses would tease me, saying "Handan Hanım, you never used to know so much about sewing."

Elem had found something else with which to occupy herself: she carefully read through newspapers and magazines and if she found a line or two about me, rare as that was, she'd cut it out and file it away. I have no idea how she found so many articles.

She showed me the blue album where she kept them. The picture of my face from Turandot made her recoil: "Such hatred in your eyes," she gasped. My eyes were aflame; I studied the photograph, taking in those dark fiery eyes. I turned the pages. Elem had pasted the clippings onto the pages of the album. She'd started doing that just after our intimacy began, tracing the pages of my artistic life.

She took childish delight in the blue album. I couldn't bring myself to tell her, "No one in this country gives a damn about opera." Anger stirred within me.

That year, it seemed that summer would come early. In Zeyniler that's what they were saying. The weather had turned so warm in February that you could've thought it was May.

Feride was doing a drawing of Munise. To draw your loved one's portrait, especially in water color . . . I would've loved to have drawn Elem; her face, eyes and body that I had stroked and kissed. Nudes of her, portraits.

I have a weakness for drawings. I've always been repulsed by photographs of naked women, even those of women making love that men (and some lesbians) fawn over. But drawings and paintings are entirely different.

Paintings stir my passions, but not feelings of love. For example, I was smitten by the naked male bodies at Michelangelo's Sistine Chapel. In desire, sexual desire, perhaps there are no genders—no men, no women. Those strange youths in that church: their bodies were masculine, but their faces, hair, eyes and lips were more feminine than a woman's. Stricken, I gazed at the men's muscled legs. Powerful desire rushed through me, and the lips of my femininity became engorged. Time had left cracks across the face of Michelangelo's masterpiece, but even after hundreds of years you could still sense each and every aspect of the estrangement of the artist's soul, the incessant ache.

Just like your estrangement.

Feride and Munise separated in Zeyniler. At first Munise was happy about going, but as the day of separation drew near, she was wracked by sadness.

"My mother came to see me. She heard that I was leaving . . . Please, don't be upset with me."

Feride said to herself, "I understand the pain in your tiny heart . . ."

Enough of that *Çalıkuşu* drama. This morning, yet again those lines brought tears to my eyes. Such expressions of compassion and selflessness fill my heart with gloom. To understand more than what is hoped for . . . If only I could have done that for Elem.

For two days now it has been raining. A chill has settled in the air. This must be the end of autumn.

Munise met up with her mother and Feride joined them. She asked that the young woman remove the veil from her face. That was Munise's face. Childish, no makeup. Feride thought that Munise would also one day succumb to the same fate. She pulled Munise close, as though to protect her.

No one can protect anyone else.

Elem didn't protect me.

Feride didn't know, but I do:

Munise didn't become a prostitute. She died.

Death approached with the tenderness of moonlight. In the distance, a gramophone was playing. Midafternoon light. Death kissed Munise on the forehead, on the lips.

Feride never gave Munise a last kiss.

And I'll never kiss Elem on the lips again.

In the end, clothes are nothing more than rags and tatters. But that's not what people think. At some point in their lives, they place great importance on what they wear.

For me it was the same; I cared a lot about those rags.

One day—I'll explain what happened, if I have the courage—I hurt Elem, very bitterly, because of clothes.

And then there is this: what we wear conceals the inner "I" we cannot show to the world. It adorns that "I," shaping a new identity for others to see. You become a new person, the woman that others want.

I'll say it again: at least in certain periods of my life, I placed hope in the clothes that I wore, trying to conceal the storm brewing within.

When I fell in love, I'd forget I was something they call a "woman." But I was always careful to be well-dressed.

And that's why I went to Nedret's boutique, where the glory and high fashion of the past had given way to the coarseness and mediocrity of Turkey in the 1980s, when the economy was opened up to the world.

When you're completely naked you inhabit a closed world, withdrawn into yourself, the windows and doors of your soul sealed shut.

That's what you have to do if you want to go on existing. Both naked and shrouded in yourself, you observe the world around you. But then comes the time to dress yourself. And when you do, that's when you open up to the rest of life.

And so I'd go to Nedret's boutique.

I like Nedret. She may be peevish, among other things, but in her heart she carries a certain sensitivity and refinement for understanding people. And she's a fine judge of character. She knows innumerable women, and often their husbands, fiancés, and relatives as well. They're all more or less wealthy, at least wealthy enough to have Nedret tailor their clothes. And although she knows their fickleness, caprices and poor taste, she never speaks about them. But why? Just to avoid offending them? I doubt it.

She wants to make people happy with her designs. Silently she listens to the jealous husband who doesn't want his wife wearing a low-cut dress, knowing all the while that he wants the opposite for his mistress. She does this to spare the foolish wife's feelings, a woman who takes secret pride in the fact that her husband doesn't want her to show cleavage; she knows, as well, that the two women will end up being at the same wedding or cocktail. There are many such ruses.

("Are you bored by all the details? Today my chattiness is in fine form. Selim, have you ever been to the boutique I mentioned? I'd like to describe it to you. If only you knew Nedret...")

Nedret picked up right away on my style, which is anything but flamboyant. Or perhaps flashy, but in a furtive way. A reflection of the tides of my soul. Above all, black. Always dark tones. But there's nothing wrong with the occasional glint of color in the accents and accessories. A style that could be considered classic, quietly distant from the vagaries of seasonal fashion.

It depends on where I'm going; out of necessity, I have a few evening gowns for the galas, and others for daily attire. And the invitations of course—you have to remember that you'll be seen in that outfit in public.

But I've always wondered: why such a fuss about evening gowns? I'm shocked at the obsessions of women who go to Nedret for such dresses. Hours pass, and they still don't find a gown they like. They weep when their measurements are being taken, and then again when the gown is ready. The patience of the young seamstresses at the boutique has instilled in me a sense of shame, and also a feeling of alarm at how they're treated. Over time, an itching for rebellion has grown in me: an aria of revolt that I've never sung, never been able to sing.

So, why did I go there, when I was completely withdrawn into myself? Because I could only come to terms with the outside world when I was withdrawn. I didn't need clothing. When I mingled with the crowd, everything became crystal clear, saturated in suffering. In the crowd, I couldn't destroy my individuality. Rebellion always welled up within me when I was with the crowd. Fear, emptiness, nothingness. And then that melancholy that caught me in its arms. For my own good, I should've kept my distance from the gowns and dresses.

Nedret and I once had a strange conversation about evening gowns. She was always complaining about her weight. In those days, I'd lost quite a few pounds, and she said to me, "This time let's have a tuxedo made for you. It would suit you so well."

I felt my face turn hot in embarrassment: "Nedret, how could you think such a thing?"

"Yes, a turquoise tux. Or," she laughed, "perhaps a tux with tails."

I grew suspicious, but persisted: "I couldn't wear a tuxedo. If only I could..."

"Wear it just once. When you enter the room, all eyes will be on you."

Hoping to put an end to the conversation, I said, "I'm a soprano, not a pop singer."

She was crestfallen, but insisted on talking about the clothes of my "colleagues." No matter how their clothes ill-suit them, they strut about in the most gaudy things. But, she said, a turquoise tuxedo would give me an air altogether my own.

First, I've always despised the word "colleague."

Second, there was no way I could take pleasure in this fantasy. It was useless prattle. I responded coldly.

But at the same time, Nedret's suggestion caught my fancy, in terms of courage, of defying masculinity and femininity. But not a turquoise tuxedo: a black tuxedo, a tux with tails. Closely fitted. I wore no makeup at all, but my hair was pulled into an elegant bun. No accessories, no trinkets. I strode in, and gazed boldly at anyone who turned to look. I paused for a long moment, and then strode forward. No one could corner me; no one could make a snide remark.

Why now does that night tumble forward now from the past? Those adventures, borne forth by the slipperiness of time, leave you feeling helpless, pulled from one experience to the next.

The sparks of a hot summer night. Yes: a hot summer night, radiant with sparks. It's still radiant. Long ago the glow should've faded. Why doesn't it die down? Why does it heave forward again like this, aflame yet again, as though it promised happiness?

My Munise was excited about her new apartment but flustered that she'd be having me over.

Initially I'd been the most enthusiastic about her moving into a new place, away from the pressure of living with her parents; she deserved her freedom.

But was she just flustered? Perhaps there was worry as well. These memories, so jagged, overwhelm me. My coldness toward her persisted. My coldness toward her intimacy, her goodness. It surprised and then angered her, and she'd pull away. She may have thought that I'd belittle her house and how she hosted me.

She asked if I'd like to drink whiskey—she'd saved up to buy whiskey!—we could have a glass of whiskey, she said, and then wine with dinner. Or, she offered, there is also *rakı*. It was Saturday.

No, my dear, my coldness wasn't aimed at you. It was life . . . I just couldn't bear life. It struck me as strange to profess one's love. Love was strange to me, when I saw and felt that the world was full of pain. Love dies. "You have no right to love," I said to myself. Your kindness was a curse to me. Life was like a grape harvest. Two lonely people, at the center of the harvest: you and me. I was trying to reject this. To reject us. It was the love between a famous soprano singer and a young seamstress, but "fame" and "young" must be set off in quotes. From the outset, it was an impossible love: the love of two women; fame; a younger woman. It's unimaginable that they could be together. When you pushed all that aside and offered me your heart, it was simply out of a feeling of deep apprehension. On those evenings when you stayed with me, you'd help me clear the table, but you didn't know that you had to put the mustard in the refrigerator. After you left, I put it away. You thought mustard was disgusting. That's how I found out that you'd never had it before. At your apartment, just past the tomb of Şem-i Dede, mustard didn't exist. Like at so many other apartments. But I don't want to write about mustard, I don't want to write these lines. Won't the pain ever subside? Even in memory, won't the love between us ever heal?

It was Saturday. Even though you'd worked all day, you went to your parents' place in Kocamustâpaşa and picked up the fried zucchini patties your mother had made, and then made the long trip back to Beşiktaş. Along with dinner we had *mücver*, just because you knew I liked that dish.

Neither of us could pull off making mücver. It takes so much work: grate the zucchini and squeeze out the juice, and then mix in the flour, feta cheese and green onions, not forgetting to add an egg. When we poured it into the pan, the batter refused to shape into a patty. And we laughed till tears came to our eyes, till our sides hurt. Failed lumps of mücver floating in the simmering oil . . . But the tears I weep now no longer matter.

She'd gone shopping at the market in Beşiktaş, but wouldn't tell me what she'd bought; I had to wait until dinner was served to see her small surprise. And that's when I realized that she'd gone all the way to Yıldız and to Serencebey.

I loved going to my Munise's new apartment; I would pass by the dream-like Ertuğrul Gazi Mosque, Tomb of Şeyh Zafir, and fountain designed by D'Aronco, which belonged to neither Christians nor Muslims, and turn down Nemli Yufka Lane, gazing at the run-down wooden houses and the shoddy residence blocks until I saw that one in particular, the apartment on the top floor, Elem's place. As soon as we passed the traffic lights, I'd get out of the taxi because I just had to see those dream-like structures. But before turning onto her street I'd pause, like I were stopping for breath, and gaze down the parallel street, Çitlenbik Lane. Life on the first street was mired in poverty, and the affluence of the other, Çitlenbik Lane, was enough to make your heart sink: well-tended homes, private garages, views of the silhouette of the city and the sea, balconies looking out to the horizon.

The balcony of Elem's apartment was the size of a shoebox. There was no view of the sea. In the decrepit, unkempt garden of the sagging building, there was a mulberry tree, and sweet william and purple lilacs still managed to grow in what used to be a flower bed. When the season came, a spray of flowers, especially purple lilacs, brought to this lost garden an opulence born of sorrow; but it was an illusion, painful and absurd. Nobody collected the mulberries—they fell to the earth to be devoured by insects, and then dissolved into summer during the rain showers.

On some evenings I'd sit on the balcony and ponder the similarities between that ruined garden and my heart. Sparrows would take flight in a rustle of wings from the tree's branches, and then there would be that same sense of desolation.

We'd just eaten dinner. It was one of those Saturdays that seemed to last an eternity. I think it was the first time we had dinner at her place. A salad of sliced lettuce and tomato. Smoked tongue she'd bought at the market. Mücver. Fried potatoes and grilled meatballs. I remember that much. She was rushing back and forth from the kitchen to the dining table. Although she'd bought candles and placed them in the candelabra, she forgot to light them. The five-armed bronze candelbra was my gift to her; its lone twin is still at my apartment.

"I forgot about the candles!" she exclaimed.

"It's fine," I told her. "This is just fine." And I looked at the table. Candlelight would have hidden the flaws: cheap paper napkins, plates you'd see at a market diner, the glassware shot through with bubbles. Either from a habit acquired at her parents' house or because she was flustered, my Munise had randomly placed the service spoons. The spoons, forks, and knives were all set together. The fact that I noticed this made me despise myself. I took refuge in whiskey.

And the fact that I can still remember this . . .

Was it an obsession with order, or habituation to luxury? I don't think so. Was it a concern or fear that one day others would ridicule her? Perhaps.

I didn't tell her what was on my mind.

"Is something bothering you? What's wrong?" she asked.

Alcohol and the night bring tenderness to the heart. Before long, the rough edges were smoothed and everything had calmed. The waves retreated back to the sea.

My young seamstress was drinking wine. She'd been released from the pressures of home life, the questioning, and was drinking in gulps. She had a tendency to drink, and I was probably the cause. If we hadn't met, if we hadn't been together, would she have turned out the same way? What woman from her background, from the neighborhood where she was born and raised, could ever be on such intimate terms with alcohol?

A bolt of fear ran through me, fear of what I'd done to her. I got up, and hugged and kissed her. I kissed her eyelids. I could see that her lips were trembling with fear, but also with desire. I traced my finger across her lips.

I loved her enough to get up from the table and kiss her. Was that really love? The feeling of irritation had faded.

Now, why do I think of that night? Such memories don't beckon me. Still, I go back, heedless of the pain inside, I go back—so that I won't be lost on that immense sea.

The most vivid memory is of the fireflies. It was a hot summer night, so still that not even a leaf stirred. We were on the balcony. Fireflies flitted in the garden of the wooden house next door.

"Look, fireflies," she said. "Just like at your place!" A smile lit up her face.

Whenever the idea of smiling comes to mind, I think of her face, her smile. She was but a child, chaste and innocent—and, most of the time, lonely.

We made love to ward off that loneliness.

It was a starry night, the sky a deep blue, but the garden was shrouded in darkness, untouched by the sky's light. There was only the yellow-fuchsia, fuchsia-yellow flickering of the fireflies here and there, appearing and disappearing like ghosts. We'd fallen silent. If only she hadn't said it, if the silence hadn't been broken:

"The fireflies are praying for us . . ."

Did I tell you that Çalıkuşu met her Munise at Nedret's boutique?

(Handan Sarp described that scene in broken segments. She wasn't feeling well that day. It was much more than that; she seemed to want to disappear, wanting her life to be severed at some point.

For me it was just a scene, but for her it was an experience that plunged her into grief. She'd begin to talk, and then falter into silence. Her head was bowed, her eyes on the verge of filling with tears. Then she'd raise her head, biting her lip. She tried to smile, but in vain. It was clear that she regretted getting involved in this adventure of explaining and sharing, and was on the verge of giving up.

I acted as though I were unaware of her feelings and unease. Actually, I was undecided about whether or not I'd write Handan Sarp's story. But I was pulled in by the fervency of her narration, and I enjoyed the hours I spent with her. If she'd changed her mind, I knew I'd get the urge to write but wouldn't know what to write about.

She wanted to get off that topic and move on to something else. At one point she said, "If it were possible, if I could always be in the garden of the summer house, my grandmother calling out to me, 'Çalıkuşu!' as I mourned for the dry well and Aunt Nadire was in love with Göksel Arsoy . . . There for the first time I listened to a record that played the lovers' duet 'Parigi, o cara.' I would love to be able to go back to the wondrous voices of that woman and man as I listened, pressed against the record player, and asked, eyes agape, 'What's this? A song?' and they said, 'It's opera. An opera song.' Just as, years later, I told Elem the same thing. How much I'd like to go back to those days of summer in the garden, the fruit trees, the hollyhock flowers, my grandmother's compassion, and not having met Elem." And then she fell silent, exhausted.

Those long pauses and silences were part of our meetings, and when they happened I didn't turn off my tape recorder. She wanted to describe their meeting as if she were speaking of something insignificant, but was unable to go on.

If I'm going to write her novel, I was thinking, I'd have to try to make Handan Sarp feel as comfortable as possible and start with that record and young girl—the one with the bow in her hair—and listen to songs that she'd never heard before. She'd have to let go of herself. Whose record was that? A neighbor's? Was the neighbor a man or a woman? There's a black grand piano in that house. An empty sitting room—no, it's just a large room in a summer house. The windows are open. In the garden there are a few bristly pine trees standing among the pink, fuchsia and white roses.

Then I tried to get back to the scene of their meeting, how it unfolded.

I can more or less envision how it happened:

The neighborhood and area have changed; it's no longer Pendik and the summer house, but an apartment on Rumeli Street. It's an old apartment building with high ceilings and spacious salons, and along the length of a long corridor in the rear are workshops of varying sizes where women are sewing. The front faces the bustling traffic, looking onto the ornately decorated display cases of the shops and the idlers who parade up and down the street; there is a hint of luxury.

But the workshops in the rear face dirty, narrow dark courtyards. Aside from an occasional clump of weeds, the courtyards reek of death and are strewn with shreds of fabric and rubbish.

The salons are adorned with gilt full-length mirrors, armchairs, end tables, crystal ashtrays, mannequins swathed in the latest designs and large vases stuffed with banal fake flowers and peacock feathers.

And there are the women that Handan Sarp loathes, women benumbed to the lives of millions of other people living in poverty. They sit, drinking coffee and smoking cigarettes, flipping through design catalogs. They chat about diets, natural remedies, cosmetics and fashion, tittering over the gossip of the day. Even though most of them have had cosmetic surgery, they're still unattractive but well-dressed.

They're called into the fitting room when their turn comes. Nedret dashes from the front of the shop to the rear. Sometimes the showy thick-fringed curtain is closed to divide the room, especially when a "guest" of importance arrives. According to Handan Sarp's account, Nedret is a heavy-set woman. She never deigned to open the door for her customers, but she always walks out her important clients.

When she found out that Handan Sarp was a soprano at the Istanbul City Opera, Handan joined the ranks of those dignified customers.

It was the end of September, or the beginning of October.* A hot day, toward dusk. Istanbul has such autumn days that cling to summer. The double casement windows of the boutique were open, and the cream-colored tulle curtains fluttered in the breeze. Above the jagged cemetery-like skyline of apartment buildings, the sky was visible: a cascade of color, red fading to orange, blue and pink.

---

* Handan Sarp wrote in her "somniloquies" that she met Elem at the end of October. But summer seemed a more fitting time for them to meet. Before the end of summer . . . (Sİ)

I think that Handan Sarp would've been sitting in the salon, granting herself the pleasure of a rare cigarette to brace herself against the snobbery of the setting. A long, slender Eve cigarette. Her coal-black eyes in a daze. The previous night she'd thought about the vagaries of life till morning, and her face was pale. Lately, those sleepless nights were becoming more and more common.

As I wrote that line, a thought occurred to me:

They met in the mirror.

The young woman entered the room, timid and unsure of herself. No one noticed her presence, even though she was rather tall and tended to stand out. Her green-flecked eyes were framed with thick eyelashes. She had long, wavy hair that was light brown, almost blond. Like the other girls in the boutique, she was dressed simply, wearing a skirt and blouse. Both the skirt and the blouse were dull solid colors. She wasn't smiling. Even when the other girls giggled together, she didn't smile.

I should probably linger on that for a moment. Was it unhappiness? Why would she be unhappy? She was still young. She couldn't be despairing about the years to come. Perhaps she was just a somber person? But where did I get the idea that somber people don't laugh or smile? Because they don't fit in with their surroundings? Is it dissidence, class consciousness, rebellion?

She brought a piece of sample material to one of the women.

No, that's not when they saw each other.

Those were tedious days for Handan Sarp. I know of her ennui, because—even during one of their first conversations—she told Elem about it; and because she told Elem, she told me.

Perhaps she'd gone to the boutique that day to cast off the despondency that clung to her. She tried to act like those snide wealthy women; she put on that act because she wanted to escape from herself. But she couldn't. Cigarette in hand, she sat perfectly still, enveloped in blue and white smoke.

The young woman stood next to the customer looking at the piece of sample material. She waited, but the woman seemed oblivious to her presence. Maybe the customer would ask a question, maybe she'd swallow her pride and ask the young woman's opinion. But she didn't. The young woman was forced to silently step away, not knowing what to do.

Handan Sarp didn't, in my opinion, see her at that moment. If she had . . .

Many moments pass unnoticed. And in most of those, there is hurt.

The woman went to examine the fabric in the daylight and when she returned, she said to Nedret, "This isn't the brown I want. It should have more red." Then she took off her glasses, and placed them, along with the sample, on an end table.

Addressing the young woman, Nedret asked, "Didn't you show her the other sample?" Her voice was flat, and without waiting for an answer she went to the end table and picked up the sample: "This is dark brown."

"A little more red . . ."

Nedret said, "Of course, right away," and looked at the young woman.

She was about to step away. But then, in the mirror, she exchanged glances with Handan Sarp. It wasn't clear if Handan Sarp was observing her or her state of agitation.

But their eyes locked. Unaware of what she was doing, Handan Sarp smiled at the young woman, whose eyes widened momentarily. The soprano lowered her gaze.

She thought to herself, I should put out my cigarette, I should do something, anything. No one should see me without my mask.

Was the young woman new there? Handan had never seen her there before. It must've been the sorrow in her eyes that made Handan Sarp smile: sorrow, youth and naivete. Perhaps she was mistaken. She'd smiled and then the young woman noticed—was it pity?

She was gone. Only the wealthy, domineering women remained in the salon.

"Cutter's assistants," she thought to herself. That's what they're called: cutter's assistants. She put out her cigarette. Young women who haven't finished school, thrown into life and working as assistants to the cutters at sewing houses who cut the fabric as the fashion boutique owner requests, kneeling to the ground to take measurements during fittings. She pushed away the ashtray. Arrogant customers tuck a few lira in their pockets for a tip, either out of generosity or tradition.

Or she may be a deliverer, taking dresses to the women's homes. Perhaps that's what Nedret asks her to do. What kind of a life does she have here? But why was Handan Sarp mulling over this so intently? That young woman, caught in a whirlpool, hope ebbing away. All day she deals with women bedecked in jewels and at night returns to her small flat. One day, she may seek solace in the hope that she can break free. But no, she'll never be able to do that. Sometimes the young woman thinks that as well, that she's drowning in despair.

She's just a young woman, one of hundreds you see every day. Soon after, she'll be forgotten, her face erased from memory. When she leaves Nedret's boutique, nothing of her will remain behind. After Handan Sarp has ordered her dress, she'll leave. When she comes for the fitting, maybe she won't see "her." Maybe "she" will be working in the back or out on an errand.

Does being forgotten compound the loneliness?

But "she" had stuck in her memory. A shiver had run through her, which she disregarded. A shiver reminiscent of sexual desire. It happens at times, beyond our control. There's nothing you can do.

When the young woman brought the cloth swatch, Handan Sarp involuntarily stood up and approached her: "Excuse me . . ."

Later, much later, whenever she remembers that moment, Handan Sarp will think of the wailing aria from *La Gioconda*, and to drive the song from her mind she will frantically cover her ears, face contorted, and scream: "Suicidio!"

The young woman stopped: "How can I help you?" She was blushing.

The tulle curtains hung slack, and the sky was a deeper evening red and nighttime blue.

"What's your name?" The soprano's heart thudded. She thought to herself, "Have you lost your mind?"

"Elem."

"Elem? Such a sorrowful name."

The young woman smiled for the first time: "Few people know that."

"Know what?"

"That Elem means 'suffering.'"

Handan Sarp tried to smile. Her cheeks were burning. She knew that she had to say something else. The moment dragged on. Her mouth had gone dry. "Can I see the fabric that the other woman didn't like? The brown one."

Just then Nedret said, "Elem!" She was looking at the two of them. "Ah, Handan Hanım!"

"I was thinking of ordering a fall outfit, in brown," Handan said, addressing both Nedret and Elem, "with a beige jacket."

"How about a beige outfit with a brown jacket," Nedret replied dryly.

"Yes . . . I suppose so," Handan said. Had she stammered?

Elem gave the swatch to Nedret.
Handan returned to her seat.

But that's just my sketch of the scene, so who knows what's missing.)

Some nights, when I go into this garden that is hemmed in by tall buildings, I get the urge to flee. But to where, and how? I'd like to leap over the wall, but there's no wall of liberation that leads to an open road. There should be a low garden wall. Perhaps a crumbling garden wall. I'm in darkness. Behind me, apartment buildings loom like specters. But still, the shadows cannot drive me out. Clambering over a fallen wall, I set off down a narrow, earthen path. Suddenly I realize that it is Sakızlı Street and it leads to the sea, the seductive scent of the sea.

Last autumn. Always the pain. Summer and autumn. I'd go into the garden to get some air. I didn't turn on the light in the garden or the lights inside; it was the darkness that would save me. I was thinking that I should plant some lilacs, so that I could remember the garden that I could see from Elem's balcony—a memory like a wound. What were the other flowers? Perhaps a tree over there. An apple tree? And my grandmother. Always my grandmother. The dead grandmother who left me. The living Elem who left me. The two become confused in my mind. My grandmother asked me in Elem's voice: "Çalıkuşu, which flowers would you like planted in the front garden?" That meant it was the garden at the summer house. In the back, vegetables would be planted. Night would become day, and birds would take flight. Wearing a filthy floral-print dress, I ran. If I could make it over the crumbling wall, everything would be fine.

The autumn of last year seemed as if it would never end. I don't know about other people; for them it may have passed quickly. The gardens in my life seemed to merge with one another. The garden in Pendik was a refuge. The garden I dreamed of was the one that adjoined Elem's apartment building. That's where I wept in the dark. I wished that it would be even darker. If only the electricity would go out and the entire city would be buried in darkness. I have no objection to the stars in the sky. This long autumn is still hot and languid; fog obscures the stars.

It's terrifying: the days seem to be shortening. The days in which I took shelter under the crepe myrtle, trying to solve the riddles of the world. The narrow path visible from the collapsing wall passes in front of the summer house and winds into the distance. Somehow it's still there. You walk, running your fingers along the low garden wall which is yellow, or perhaps it's white. You're a child. And you haven't met Elem. None of those things have happened, even those that occurred before Elem came into your life. The windows of the mansion gleam. Summer passes by. The vines have clambered over the walls, and past the mansion there is a laurel tree in the middle of the road, belonging to no one. A few scattered clouds. And finally, the sea.

When I returned to the garden of the summer house, night had fallen. I didn't go in through the gate. I went over the crumbling wall. I don't know why I want to see you in memories of my childhood.

But we need to walk together in this garden. In the only garden that hasn't witnessed our suffering.

I make small changes by embellishing the garden with flowers. I added some clumps of violets—you have to pick them in the cool of the morning, because that's when they won't feel pain—and beyond those, some large-headed margarita flowers, and farther down a single dream-like poplar tree, bare of leaves and shimmering with a silver sheen in the night, an orphan.

"Elem, are you back?"

"Do you remember those two days?"

"Yes, our eyes met in the mirror."

"Now, the moon bathes everything."

"That's how you wanted it. You wanted it that way."

It was Elem. She left me. She left me so that I would miss her soul, not her body. If only it were just her body.

Elem, you'll return to your broken heart. I returned and paid the price. And perhaps saved myself. Now it's your turn.

"You're lying. I never hurt you, not once. But you . . ."

Then she falls silent. In the moonlight, she smiles like she used to smile, only at me.

She says that the memories of our past have taken refuge beneath the leaves of the violets. I ask myself: Is that even possible? I believe you. Under the purple flowers and green leaves there was a bundle of hurt that I inflicted on Elem. It hid there. Come back, I won't hurt you again!

"It was like we were one person. You said that, Handan. But we'll never be like that again."

The moonlight was ashen.

The illusion will soon be over. We'll alight in another garden. You must be cold. Put your arms around me. You'll leave in yet another illusion, until I feel longing for a misty summer morning. Until that morning arrives.

Now I drift off to sleep. Tomorrow, like every morning, disenchanted and radiant—first radiant, and then disenchanted—I'll awake, bidding you farewell, my dear.

("Selim, write a novel. And one day, Elem should read it. Let there be waves and the froth of the sea. My memories are timeless for me. I can squeeze them all down into one moment. And that moment flings me into eternity, but in the end I strike the stones of the shore and am rent to pieces. What can be done?")

I said that clothes are trivial. But if they're full of memories, they can be laden with such significance and power.

Inside, there is a wardrobe. If you'd like, I can show you a brown outfit, the value of which is incalculable. And there is a dark green jacket that goes well with the brown, and the cuffs, pocket lining, and inner collar are the same brown as the dress.

I've had it for years, and it could still be worn for years to come. I wore it but rarely, and it never wrinkled.

I don't normally like brown, but it suited me.

The outfit was made, despite Nedret's objections. It was like a small game between myself and my girl* and Nedret. A game of revenge.

But revenge for what?

Elem was new at Nedret's boutique. Previously she'd worked at a clothes workshop in the district of Zeytinburnu. She'd always been adept at sewing. When she saw Nedret's advertisement, she applied hoping that she might make a little more money. The working conditions at the workshop in Zeytinburnu were appalling, and the workers

---

* When she was speaking about Elem, Handan Sarp suddenly used the expression "my girl," which took me by surprise. I dared ask why she used that expression, but the way that she glared at me defeated my courage to push the issue further. (Sİ)

didn't even have health insurance. It was completely different at Nedret's boutique and working there was a turning point in Elem's life; from a workshop to haute couture, what more could she ask for?

Nedret and I were on good terms. In fact, we could almost be considered friends. She had even confessed to me some of her small libertine adventures, such as her secretive flirtations with the young sales assistants working at the shops on Rumeli Street. Embarrassed and flushed, she said that she'd never gotten very far with them. Of course it didn't go unnoticed that the female owner of a clothes shop was poking around in other boutiques. And the young men were ready to respond in kind to her advances. Nedret knew this, but was still somewhat defeated. At Mudo there was a black-haired, ruddy young man; he had a bit of a paunch, but was quite tall. While talking with his friends one day, he'd mentioned that he liked middle-aged women . . . I listened to her chatter, entertained.

Nedret, who was probably in her sixties, said: "Handan Hanım, being a widow is always difficult. How is it that you, for all these years, have been so alone?"

And with those words, even though there were no bad feelings between us, Nedret and I became enemies.

The poor woman was bringing out beige fabrics, showing me samples for the jacket and insisting on brown.

I noticed that Elem had fallen silent, but was slyly supporting me. It was an instinct, mere intuition.

The fact that she silently supported me gave me an odd sense of pleasure. It was as if Elem felt a kind of compassion, perhaps even a kind of love. And my hunger for love is endless. I show interest even knowing that I'll be unable to love, that I'll be as cold as ice.

Of course, it may not have been love. Perhaps the young seamstress found in me a sense of security. The opportunity had arisen and she wanted to satisfy her hatred of authority through my sway over Nedret. No, that couldn't be it; she didn't even know who I was. In any case, can the owner of a boutique object to a customer's request? In the end, I'm the one who will wear the outfit. Nedret would have to indulge my preferences.

"A green jacket, from that cloth, and a brown dress."

Elem smiled: "We could do the collar and cuffs in brown." She brought a magazine and showed me a design.

"Fine, let's do that."

At that moment I understood why I harbored such secret hostility for Nedret, who at that moment turned to Elem and snapped, "I didn't know you were a designer."

Elem blushed.

I didn't show it, but I was upset. I remember thinking that I hoped Nedret would go after the young man at Mudo and that he would reject and humiliate her. Just as Nedret had mistreated Elem.

"I think," I said to Nedret, "this outfit isn't really your style. With your permission, let's turn it over to our young friend here." I was trying to appear as pleasant and bantering as possible.

Elem's cheeks were still flushed.

"My measurements are at the tailor's," I continued, "so when it's ready for a fitting, let me know."

Needless to say, as I descended the broad, steep steps of the Nişantaşı apartment, I was filled with a strange exuberance. I'd seen that I was able to take vengeance on the world that had so devastated me.

But when I was going to the fashion boutique it had been the complete opposite: I was filled with ennui and heaviness. After a confusing period in my life, an abrupt silence and loneliness had settled in. I'd recently separated from a woman. Actually, it was a relationship in its death throes, a sexual passion that I'd never confessed to myself. I felt cut off from everyone, a sting in my heart. Kaya—God knows if that was her real name—could appear at any moment. I missed her and longed for her body, worrying that my life would be in shambles. That's why I'd gone to the boutique: to while away time and forget my troubles.

But Elem's attention and intimacy had gladdened me, even if just a little. She found courage in me and my position, and in her own way had stood up to her boss. I like that kind of attitude; it is a salve for the demons I carry inside.

Her name is Elem.

"Few people notice that, the suffering in my name."

I was one of the few.

It piqued my interest. But I didn't ask about the story of Elem's name. There probably is a story there. But there was no way I could ask in front of those selfish impertinent snobs.

Even later I didn't ask. The question slumbered on in love, in loneliness. Our pain transcended the story of her name.

Nights were always oppressive. But even more so after Elem was gone. I would awake, vaulted from sleep. It was always the same delusion: everything was going to be fine, something extraordinary was going to happen, and the anguish would disappear, at that very moment.

But nothing happened; that wondrous moment never came. There was no miracle. I would get up, drink a glass of water and from the sitting room look at the garden, which I hadn't watered for days. The garden where we sat in the evenings, summer and fall, and my hand would be clasped in yours as dusk fell. But that was long before the separation.

A spent light blankets the garden. It's neither dusk, dawn, nor night. In a swirl of color, black and blue intermingle. As blue tries to flow in one direction, black bears down from another.

Together, we tried to hold at bay the darkness in my life.

In vain, I hope for a trace of the color of lilac. Elem liked its scent. Such loss! Separation upon separation and loss upon loss, enough to make you numb to your loneliness. I imagine hints of lilac among the flowerless branches of the crepe myrtle adorned by the occasional yellow leaf. I feel the totality of loss, and not just mine but others' as well. You reach a point of suffocation, and take within you the suffering of all existence.

There is a slight lightening of shades in the foliage of the garden. But it's not yet morning; perhaps morning will never arrive. Such things are often said, like "morning will never arrive"—trite commonplaces. I try to calm myself with the mantra that morning will come. The morning inside is the one that will never break over the horizon.

Dawn never broke. I'd wander in the garden in my nightgown, barefoot, so that I could feel the chill and tremble. I needed that because afterward I would get into bed. That bed, where Elem and I made love and slept entwined in each other's arms. It was still warm in those days. Only later that fall did I ask Kadriye Hanım to bring out the winter comforter. But even when I was walking barefoot in the garden I didn't feel the chill so much. To always feel cold: an unsolvable vicious circle.

It was unbearable. I would get up again and collapse into the armchair, far from the garden, and turn on the lamp, mulling over the years. They passed, one by one. We didn't notice as they passed by. But they were all so magnificent, full of meaning, and benevolent! They enveloped my heart, transformed into melodies that echoed lovingly in my ears. But was it the years, or the scent of wildflowers? Elem would appear, and tears filled my eyes.

Love doesn't die. It cares for us, helps us.
(Something else was written here, but it was smudged by tears.)

Then came *La traviata*. At the beginning of the season when roles were being assigned, I was given nothing. Then I found out that I'd been given the main role of the opera, Violetta. I not only love that opera, but worship it. But I was going through one of the worst periods in my life, perhaps with the exception of my current state of despair. I didn't think that I had the strength to play Violetta.

Some people believe that art has the power to remedy the problems in your life. But I don't think so. At least, not exactly. The upheavals in your life can perhaps be an impetus for your art. But that's all. The rest is feelings and discipline. Art needs remedies just as much as you.

I'd fallen to pieces, because of Kaya.

At home I was constantly listening to the sorrowful music of that short overture. I listened to it again and again. The violins drove me to a frenzy. But to truly feel Violetta I needed to bow down before that passion.

The overture starts like an awakening from sleep. Or, like when you're gravely ill, gripped by paroxysms and fever, but for a moment you come around and gingerly arise from bed. But the illness strikes again, and you collapse in a heap. Then, as if from a distance, you can pick out the strains of a melody that speaks of joy, of happiness from times past, and the melody crescendos. But they are all just memories. That is Violetta's music, instilling in you the feeling that everything has come to an end and death has you in its grips. Violetta is infirm and forlorn. Even before the curtain opens, you can sense her presence as the pianissimo notes are driven by the gale of life. Then they fade to silence. Death places the final note.

When the curtain opens, the music and set, the decorations, the costumes and artists, everything seems to be a mockery of the overture. This is Paris, Violetta Valéry's resplendent salon. Violetta, knowing that death is drawing near, lives life rapaciously. On this evening of revelry, she'll be smitten by Alfredo and dream that her life will end happily, blessed by love.

I was thinking to myself, "Violetta, yet again I must take you into my life."

Kaya had brought chaos into my life by always pulling away and leaving, staying out till morning, and calling to tell me that she'd slept with someone else (a woman one night, a man the next), but then she'd surprise me by coming back, timid and disheveled, seeking solace.

I waited for her, feeling both hatred and love for her and her body. She'd come to me, but three days later I was ready for her to leave again. It was impossible for me to keep pace with the intensity of her life.

But when she left, I felt miserable; her absence haunted me. My heart was confused like never before.

One time it seemed she was gone for good. What I needed was time to put my life back in order, not be Violetta.

Or perhaps I'm mistaken, as I often am. If I could believe in that voice of mine which I lost all those years ago, once again I could play Violetta:

Alfred, receive this parting gift,
The form of one who lov'd thee;
When Heav'n hath hence removed me
My image 'twill recall.

But it's no longer possible. I've lost confidence in my voice, and in my age. Never again could I be Violetta. Ten years ago was the last time.

Now I have just one desire: to give Elem a picture of me, so that even for a moment she'll recall my image.

There are a few photographs of us taken together. In one, with Gelengül, the three of us are at Hristo's. In another, we are at a house—but whose? She had a few pictures, and I have a few. And the ones she has? Did she tear them to pieces? Because I couldn't bear to look at them, I hid the pictures, but sometimes I come across them. It happened once, a photograph of her fell out of a book . . . A sudden stab of pain.

("Selim, I can almost hear you saying, 'The banality of all this!' But it just shows that banality and suffering can be one and the same.")

Ali Arkın played Alfredo Germont in our performance of *La traviata*. It was the first time we appeared on stage together. He was a successful young tenor, beginning to garner acclaim. It was rumored that his wife was older than him.

Opera is supposedly a high art, but it's rife with gossip. Ali was a striking young man, and in love with his wife. But in those circles, people were stopping at nothing to break apart their marriage. They all wanted to sleep with him. Even Necmi—our costume designer—was after him. He made no secret of his desires, and was always fluttering about when Ali was around. But nobody was able to break Ali's will. And that's why they began to hold a grudge against the couple.

Even the stage manager thought that Semra, Ali's wife, should play Flora, but the director insisted that she play Annina.

Semra Arkın was much younger than me, and, like her husband, she was at the beginning of her career. We knew of each other, and if I remember correctly, we even sang in the same opera once. She'd once heaped praise on me to the point that it was nauseating. Later we developed a tenuous friendship, but I only found out that she'd married Ali after the fact.

Semra was passionate about being a mezzo-soprano, but in the beginning, she was quite rigid. And when she looked at me, her normally kind eyes took on a bitter gleam. I found it strange, but didn't think much of it. From the first day of rehearsals onward, however, I was unhappy. On top of that, Semra's behavior was getting to me. Ali wasn't like her at all; right from the start we got along well. "What's going on with this woman?" I thought. After three or four rehearsals, her behavior didn't change, so started ignoring her. In any case, I was distracted and unable to shake off my troubles over Kaya.

Later I found out about the Annina situation. Perhaps the poor woman thought I'd played a part in the conspiracy. To make matters worse, as though life were playing some kind of cruel joke on me, she may have been jealous of me and Ali. There was nothing I could do, so I withdrew further into my shell. I was aware of the fact that I was going to be a disastrous Violetta. Ali Arkın was already struggling, and I was dampening his enthusiasm.

But it was Semra who extended her hand in friendship. I think she did it for the sake of her husband. That's love . . . One day she brought me flowers, four or five bouquets of violets, the first of the season.

I was in fine spirits that day. Like a character from one of Muazzez Tahsin Berkand's romance novels, I exclaimed, "Oh, violets!" and was whisked away to the garden of the summer house in Pendik, sitting under a tree reading Berkand's *Young Lady of the House* or *Endless Night*.

And Semra understood: "Your reaction was like something you'd read in a romance novel."

After that day, our friendship grew. Unaware of what the future would bring, I didn't know that Ali and Semra would be just about the only friends with which Elem and I could be open.

It was in the first days of March, but what day, which year? You, chimera of separation, do you remember, my dear? There should be an anniversary for our separation. The day, month and year. As the years pass, I'll write in my agenda, "This was the first day of our separation, which, over the years, I've never once forgotten."

And you, chimera of separation, you should write something as well. You wrote of death for both of us. But I was so hurt. This time it should be something beautiful; death won't suffice. You should write to me of the sea. You should write to me endlessly of the sea.

It was in the first days of March. In a bouquet of white lilies given to Semra Arkın there were a few sprigs of cherry blossoms ablaze with pink flowers, a pink that floats off into the air.

"Sprigs of blossoms," I said to Semra.

"If only Elem had come!" she whispered.

You couldn't have come. Semra knew that as well. We always avoided mingling with that vicious opera crowd.

"Who's that girl with Handan?"

"Don't you know? Have you seen the way they look at each other?"

"They live together, the girl and Handan."

"What? May God strike them down!"

If only they knew . . .

The coward Handan told no one about you.

They left the premiere and went to a meyhane on the backstreets of Beyoğlu. It was known as "Art Meyhanesi." Today all these things strike me as absurd: the opera performers going to an "art" meyhane. I was falling to pieces those days, right in front of everyone's eyes. Dried up. Art—of course not the Art Meyhanesi—had lost its meaning for me. If it hadn't been for Semra, I wouldn't have gone. I curled up into the chair, just wanting to forget about opera; the music itself was painful. You didn't call out to me, "Come back to me, back to your art!" You drag me through the streets. You go out, as if I were by your side, smiling like you did in the past, holding my hand, throwing your arms around my neck. Didn't you have any pity for me?

A young woman asked me, "Are the blossoms in bloom?" The weather was still cold. Spring hadn't yet arrived.

I smiled at her.

She was taken by surprise. Handan Sarp had been silent all night, sulking. Handan Sarp smiled at a woman she didn't know. She was probably a lover of one of the opera performers.

Or was I smiling at your youth? Did I feel the need for a young body? You were young. I had probably quickly become drunk. My standards had slipped. The immediate desire to draw close, to make love. In the morning you'd forget. In the morning you'd be flustered. In the morning you'd miss Elem.

But this longing wasn't the pain of separation. I was driven along by the hope that I would get better and that sooner or later you'd come back. To sleep with all of those bodies, and be repulsed by every single one: that's all it was, nothing more.

"They were probably grown in a greenhouse," I said, smiling again.

She also tried to smile.

Elem, you were jealous. Silly Elem! I can't even remember that woman's face! I can't remember men's and women's faces. I don't remember any of their faces. The people I slept with or attempted to seduce, or the people who rejected me or left me feeling humiliated, none of them.

The sun plunged into the sea. Your lips appear and disappear in the sea; your eyes and skin are in the sea that swallowed up the sun. The sun plunged. And nothing else is left. Like looking at the sun with your heart. I close my eyes tightly; a face of flame appears in the sea, in the sun. Elem, I cannot stop this wheel of fire, it's laying waste to everything in my life.

"A sprig of spring blossoms," I said. My mind swam with ideas, like caressing, kissing and embracing that woman I didn't even know. But at the same time my thoughts drifted to the pinks of spring, and the yellow pollen-dusted stalks at the center of the pink flowers; I was slipping back to the first summers of my childhood and youth.

Somehow it's always the 23rd of April, the day of celebrating national sovereignty, snare-drummed 23rd of April: a Girl Scout, knowing nothing of the life ahead of her, not even thinking of the future; a Girl Scout filled with the enthusiasm of youth but probably feeling the rat-tat-tat of the snare drum differently than everyone else, the secret of music throbbing within her. And there's the day of the picnic when we gathered deadnettle, but that was long before I became a Girl Scout. Eating the deadnettle gave me a deep pleasure; the droplets of honey at the tips of their small flowers were beyond my comprehension. Just as I couldn't understand life or my trust in you; and despite my trust, how you could leave me? I've never understood, my dear, never.

I try to stop it. Which night is this? Elem, am I with you? One of the nights when your skin began to seem unfamiliar? I was saddened, but trying not to show it, and even though your skin seemed so distant from me, I kissed you—kissing you despite the howls building within me—I kissed you in the night knotted around us . . . Enough!

Can you ever understand my tenderness? I find myself falling in love with you, not just with your body, but you.

No, not so many years have passed; I'm with my school friends. Elem, you haven't been born yet, how many years will pass, how many, and as the years pass you'll be born and more years will pass me by. But where should I seek you out now, in what period of my life?

"Well done!" says my teacher Hanife, straightening the strap of my snare drum. Aside from Hanife and Handan, no one is left. I've lost my friends as well. Hanife died; I saw the obituary in the newspaper, but I didn't attend the funeral. There would be no one there for me to remember. My teacher . . . Poor lost drum, where did I leave you, where were you stowed away?

The first days of March. Early spring always blossoms like this. I go out into the garden; I'm deceived yet again by the sprigs of buds. In the long evenings, always imbued with loneliness, the pink and white flowers tell me that I'll pay the price for so much more and be pulled under by the undertow of life.

I can see that, in the unkempt garden adjoining your apartment, purple lilies have begun to bloom. But the cherry tree of my imagination has stopped blossoming. Its stunning sprays of flowers last but two weeks; then, as the flowers wilt, love withers and skin wrinkles. And there is a flurry of green leaves after the flowers have begun to brown.

With the arrival of summer, cherries flicker red among the lightly dusted leaves.

Elem, hear my call.

The cherries go un-harvested. There are just sparrows and ashen clouds piled into peaks only to be scattered yet again.

Perhaps I really had given up on living. My pores dissolve in the ashen clouds as my cage of skin falls to pieces.

When I'm in that state, there are moments when I'm unfurled to my beloved unkempt gardens, where plum, mulberry and Judas trees blossom one after the other. Every year I worry over the lilacs. Elem, my only close friend, my dear old friend, I'm no longer worried. But the two of us used to fret over the lilac in the garden, wondering if it would flower in the summer.

I told you, didn't I, that when I bought this apartment it was the lilac in the garden that swayed my heart. I hadn't even noticed the crepe myrtle, and Kaya's laurel tree came later.

The purple lilacs would bloom every June to keep us happy. "They blossomed!" you'd exclaim. I wanted to cut a few to put in a vase but you never let me.

When I saw the sprigs of buds in Semra's bouquet, I thought of our lilacs and a flush of fear ran through me. It was that young woman again. I should get up and call you, because your voice will save me. I was agitated, and the woman could sense it. We chatted: spring flowers, opera, Semra's successes. After two glasses, my hands were in hers. Revolting!

But now, I'm silent, my head bowed forward.

How quickly it passed and faded.

I'm puzzled over whether I really saw that cloudburst of wisteria. It exists somewhere. In the garden of Şem-i Dede's tomb. Wisteria, draped from one end of the tomb to the other, a cloud of lavender.

How would I be able to call you anyway? You were sleeping and would go to work in the morning. The young woman observes Handan Sarp's weakness for alcohol. I stood, saying that I needed to go. "Stay a little longer," they said. They were enjoying themselves, laughing together, and it all looked so lovely. Including the young woman. I don't remember her face, I swear. But I slept with so many people, uncountable people, not even remembering their faces.

Every year, every Saturday, when the wisteria are in bloom, we pass by Şem-i Dede's tomb. The bees are humming about. My insides sink: that's where I left my friend, my lover. Where I lost her. But still, it never really happened. I've lost everyone, and everyone has lost me.

"You've fallen into a daze."

"I was looking at the blossoms."

"They must have taken you somewhere . . ."

"It happens sometimes. You slip into sorrow."

"Are you lonely, Handan? We women are often lonely."

"Yes, I am. And you?"

She was provoking me. Do you understand? She was trying to seduce me. Her smile seemed to be intimate, but it was haughty. The hour when I lose myself must have arrived, that time when my eyes go blank, when I'm undone. Elem, that's how life has been.

She rose, and sat next to one of the men. Probably her lover. As though to show that she wasn't alone.

Elem, it often happened that people were trying to show me that they weren't lonely. Both before you and when we were together. I once knew a slender woman named Elem, and she never once mocked me for my loneliness. Here, I'd like to thank you. Here . . . and where? Where am I? A glass was overturned; the glass and the musical score on the table are wet. Just throw them away Handan, throw them out.

It was the first days of March. It was the night of the premiere, a night when I didn't know that other separations would happen; as we left the meyhane, Semra Arkın gave me one of the sprigs of buds.

"But I couldn't," I protested.

"Thank you for your friendship," she said.

I was surprised.

"And you, for your kindness. Always."

I took the sprig. All through the night the sprig stayed awake out of fear. I put it in water and placed it on the doorstep of the garden. What did it mean, except for being wrenched from home and exiled? Days and weeks passed. The pink flowers dried up, shriveled, and fell away, the color of clotted blood. But I didn't have the heart to take the sprigs out of the vase and throw them away. And then something strange happened: the branch sprouted leaves and two pink buds appeared. I was astounded. I kept looking at the branch, bringing it inside and then back outside. They took shelter in the sitting room on those stormy days. We spoke, and I talked of you, of my "Elemishka." The trees in my garden were slowly coming into bloom, and the sprig had sprouted leaves along its length. That branch of the earth continued to thrive in nothing but water.

I was in the midst of a searing spell of loneliness. Every morning I rushed to the garden; don't let it die, don't let there be yet another separation . . .

It goes on living! In the middle of April, with its young childlike leaves.

I don't want to believe that one day it will leave me. Who knows, perhaps that branch goes on living just for the sake of my heart. Just because my heart wants it so.

Elem, I wasn't able to keep you alive; I couldn't keep the sprig of blossoms alive.*

On some mornings, the sea seems so near. In the center of the city, despite the roar of traffic and polluted air, I can hear it. The sound of the waves has a spellbinding effect.

This morning, the jellyfish are so close. A ferry could stop and whisk us away to the isle of Elem's childhood. We'd gone to Zeytin Island, two or three summers in a row. When I awake some mornings feeling that the sea is nearby, those distant memories come, soothing me.

"Why don't we go to Zeytin Island? Nobody would know you there."

"But won't the people there find it strange?"

---

* In Handan Sarp's somniloquies, time is always disjointed. In this somniloquy, she writes at first as though it were a night before the separation from Elem, but then she writes, " . . . don't let there be another separation." I could have made corrections. But in the end, this is the documentation of a state of the spirit. For that reason, I decided to leave it as is. And I similarly decided not to try to smooth over the tedious repetitions about separation, loneliness, longing, loss and her desire for Elem to return. (Sİ)

You smiled like a partner in crime: "They wouldn't say anything to you. They wouldn't dare."

But how long could I stay on an island? The way is long to the distant sea and from there, on toward the island; there is no returning. On its shores there are the cries of children and other people. The memories await; no, I can't. The seashore is not the place for you. Let the memories wait there, even the pleasant memories. We were happy—it was the two of us, and for the first time we were together for days.

But still I was counting the days, hours and seconds until we would return from the island. I missed my time alone, my gowns. How could I have known that I left behind happy memories? But I did. Kisses given, kisses received, our embraces . . . I left them all behind. The barren room of a run-down hotel whispers down the years.

But there are no colors, none at all: not the olive greens of the island's knolls; nor the white, blue and green of the cheap cloth canopies; not the multihued clothing of the women and children, or the colors of the summer fruit and vegetables; not the salt-burned blues, whites and greens of the ferry approaching the dock, the boat's colors faded by the sea . . .

You're consumed by the fire of pining for Elem.

To be Violetta yet again—I was enchanted by the idea. Kaya and my inner darkness no longer mattered. Breaking free of life's bonds, I found refuge in art.

Ali and I were a good duet. True, I may have been a little old for the role. I showed Ali and Semra the pictures of when I played Violetta in my youth. Then, to their astonishment, I tore up the pictures: "They should all be destroyed," I exclaimed, "so that I can make a new start."

The second act was trying for me. There is a scene in which they describe Germont's daughter. Violetta is told that the daughter is as pure-hearted as an angel. Alfredo's father is concerned about being able to marry off his daughter. In my opinion, the lyrics are rather trite, a mere family affair, but they are set to extraordinary music. The father fears that his daughter will be left without a future. Violetta takes pity on the daughter, not wanting to see her fall victim to the same fate that forced her into the life of a courtesan.

In my first performance, I'd looked down on Germont. But this time, I was revolted by the scene and the lyrics. Of course you can make a sacrifice for someone you love; however, that act shouldn't contradict your views on life. Because Violetta was a courtesan, Alfredo's sister would be unable to marry, as Violetta's presence would bring shame on the family. That was the situation. But what of my suffering . . . Violetta's suffering! Alfredo appears, as I await death.

Why should Violetta sacrifice her life for a domestic little brat? In any case, her life was already spent. I was searching for another way of rendering her voice and character. In the end, I decided to merely disregard Giorgio Germont and his words. For me, our duet was not really a duet; it couldn't be. I sang as though I were trying to drain the words of meaning. A peculiar coldness came over me, chilling my words, everything.

At first the stage director objected. The person playing Giorgio Germont—I won't mention any names, but anyone who is curious can look it up in the Istanbul City Opera's magazine or reviews of the opera—said, and rightly so, that our duet was never shared between us. But I remained indifferent to this critique, and also to the praise that others heaped on me.

Tell the girl, so beautiful and pure,
That I'm sacrificing myself for her.

Those were the words, but I sang them with ice in my voice, bewailing the crimes that life commits. Without mercy I rejected Giorgio Germont and Alfredo's "pure" sister, that family girl in pursuit of a bright future in marriage.

Soon after, everyone was moved—with the exception of Giorgio.

As I was basking in the glow of my success, I received a phone call from the boutique. A young woman by the name of Elem had left a message on the answering machine, saying that she wanted to set a date for the fitting of my outfit.

Semra and I went to the boutique together.

She wanted Nedret to come up with some new fashion designs for her. Semra had confided in me that she was unnerved by all of the women around Ali, and believed that a few new dresses, a new hairstyle (she had lovely hair, what they used to call "downy locks"), stylish makeup and a firm body would be able to save her.

Love leads to vanity.

Fear of losing Ali drove her to seek out such childish tactics.

"Ali loves you," I told her. "Nothing else matters. He simply loves you. And he always will."

None of it mattered, neither her youth nor her age.

She was overjoyed and insisted on buying me a sachet of lavender from a gypsy street vendor on the corner. Brushing aside my objections, she tried to change the subject, asking, "Why isn't *Carmen* part of the repertory?"

Carmen isn't one of my favorite operas; our new star had faltered, perhaps because she was too much of a woman. Of course, I didn't tell Semra that.

The gypsy, who was wearing a faded red scarf over her hair, asked if we wanted her to read our fortunes.

"Why not?" Semra asked.

I just smiled in reply. A weary smile. The idea of having my fortune read in the middle of the street stirred nothing in me.

Thoughts of Elem floated at the edge of my mind.

But I was thinking more about how loves fade over time. I hadn't lied to Semra; Ali would always be in love with her. He was a sensitive young man and dedicated to her. But that love would fade, dwindling into a meaningless, monotonous habit. And in the process, Semra Arkın's concerns would grow ever more deeply rooted. The fear of losing Ali would gradually replace love, and Semra would think that her obsession was love.

I was the fortune-teller, not the gypsy woman.

The sharp smell of lavender burned my nostrils.

Strangely, Elem didn't appear in the fortune. I couldn't even remember her face.

That evening the three of us left the boutique together. I didn't notice that, while the other girls were working, our young seamstress had left work early. As dusk fell, a coolness settled in. Crowds thronged on Rumeli Street. Nişantaşı, as always, had an air of frivolity. ("Selim, that was the word Elem used. She said, "Even if I work there, Nişantaşı will always be foreign for people like me. It's frivolous.")

We walked for a while, and our ways were about to part. "Where do you live?" I asked Elem.

"In Kocamustafapaşa."

"If you have time, would you like to join us for a drink?"

The question caught her off guard and she blushed. I noticed that she had full cheeks, a broad forehead and dimples when she smiled. She was sweet, shy.

"My family would worry about me."

"You could call them."

My insistence took Semra by surprise. My private life—what did she know of my "sexual preferences"? But she kindly tried to persuade Elem, and said, "We won't stay for long."

My Munise gave in.

Sexual preference? At that moment, was I feeling sexuality? I don't think so; no, not at all. Kaya had hurt me so deeply in body and soul that it would've been impossible for me to feel anything sexual. I was just very taken by Elem's sincerity, warmth, goodness, youth and beauty. But it was an attraction tinged with sorrow. When she said she was from Kocamustâpaşa, my attention was roused; what could we suggest or offer for someone from that rather impoverished district, aside from shabby advice to climb the social ladder? My attitude betrayed a bitter mockery.

Semra and I had initially been unsure about having a drink after leaving the boutique. But Nedret's coldness toward Semra, her curtness, had shaken my nerves. I decided that a drink would be the best medicine.

Nedret had looked at the dresses that Semra liked, and said, "It wouldn't be right for you. You're too short." It was out of character for her. In the end, Semra was forced to try on a few dresses that ill-suited her figure. Cocking an eyebrow, Nedret raised the hems of the skirts, and impatiently tossed them down.

I couldn't help but say, "Why not have the dress tailored for her?" but Nedret cut me short: "No. I'll have to make the pattern myself."

She dashed off a few sketches. I don't know if Semra liked the designs. But she sulked like a frightened child and ordered two dresses in the end. They didn't even talk about the price. I was vexed by Nedret's behavior.

And something else put me off that evening: Elem had to drop off some fabric with the shoemaker for a bride's white satin shoes. I hadn't noticed the bag she was carrying.

In front of the cafe-bar, she said timidly, "I'll be right back."

It was as though an abyss opened up before me.

Where had we gone? We weren't on Rumeli Street. We must've walked down from Valikonağı Street. My mind was hazy. The sudden disappearance of Kaya, the nervousness of being on stage, the falling out with Giorgio Germont . . . The only pleasant thing was my new outfit, the brown dress and green jacket. Even though I don't like brown, I was happy with the results. Then I realized that I'd forgotten the sachet of lavender at the boutique, and I stopped. But, not wanting Semra to know, I continued walking. Gifts, and the respect we feel for them, have always been important to me.

I remember the place as being dimly lit, reminiscent of a British pub. Semra and I sat across from each other. I thought of ordering whiskey, but not knowing why, I changed my mind. Perhaps I thought that it would be inappropriate to drink whiskey in front of Elem. Then I had an even more distasteful idea: I would order rakı. More than anything, I wanted to escape.

Semra asked, "How about having some wine?"

It was like a lifeline, and I decided against rakı.

We ordered wine; there was an open bottle, and we were brought two glasses.

After a long while, Elem returned. Her wavy hair was dampened ever so slightly by sweat.

"You said you were going to call your family," I said. I wanted everything sorted out so that she could sit down and join us. Beside us, that young woman, much younger than me, or for that matter even Semra, would stand out in all of her modesty. Yet again a protective urge had come over me, a maternal instinct.

"I called from the shoemaker's," she said.

Doubts crept into my thoughts. Maybe the issue of calling home had just been a ruse, an unnecessary precaution to protect herself from my advances. Perhaps no one cared what time she'd return home, perhaps no one would even notice. I was torn between the instinct to protect and the paranoia born of attraction.

As I struggled with those feelings, Elem mentioned that she didn't drink alcohol. She ordered a Nescafé with milk.

"Yes, you're quite young," I said, stealing glances at her. "Quite young to start drinking. But you're such a sensitive type, one day you may well need a drink." Unable to bite my tongue, I was babbling.

"The bride wants jeweled buckles for her shoes," Elem said. She too was obviously ranting. I almost laughed.

But then, forgetting our young seamstress, Semra and I began talking about *La traviata*. I remember that we were talking about the costumes.

I'd had an argument with Necmi, the costume designer. The outfits he designed were a memorial to tackiness. In the fourth scene, in which Violetta dies, I was wearing a shocking nightdress, the collar of which was emblazoned with monstrous red camellias and parrot-green leaves. Verdi, however, had set that opera in his own day and age, when it was written and composed. That was, as regards costumes, new for opera. At the very least, I needed sufficiently modest costumes that would reflect that innovation—something with plain lines, carried over from the nineteenth century to the present day, a modern day interpretation of nineteenth-century style. If I could only explain that to Necmi. When I saw the nightdress, I shouted: "What are you trying to do, dress me up in the cast-offs from your own wardrobe?"

What I said was cruel. And of course, I regretted saying it. But I wasn't about to let myself be dressed up like a fool.

Semra said, "You should be thankful, at the very least, your costumes have some pomp. What about my servant's outfit!"

Elem suddenly asked, "Why did you say that I'm sensitive?"

"But aren't you?" I was trying to turn it into a joke. My feelings were inscrutable. Why had we brought her along? What did I expect from her? This attractive, tall young woman, with blond hair—no, it was light brown—would soon enough put on weight, especially after she got married. Were her eyes hazel or green? I couldn't tell in the dim light. Inviting her had been foolish. She fell silent, and didn't answer.

Then she gravely said, as though it were the most natural comment, "In fact, it's you who are sensitive. You thought of my feelings, and cared for someone as insignificant as me."

I nearly knocked over my glass. Her self-deprecation was dervishlike; I was completely taken aback. I looked around at the gaudily dressed women, corpulent men and spoiled girls around us. I turned to Elem. She was probably wearing the same skirt and blouse as the day we'd met. I stammered, "Everyone who works deserves to be valued."

On my return home, I was bewildered.

Elem, I'm writing this to you.

Because I didn't know that we'd lose each other, it never occurred to me that one day I'd write to you. I had thought that we, the two of us, would be together until the end. Every moment, we'd talk face to face. But now, there is no other choice but to write.

Little by little, Elem, I'm losing you. I write to you of death. You'll live one last time through my writing. And when I finish, that will be the end. I'll no longer write to you, but to death.

But there is always Reşat Nuri Güntekin. The last bridge between us. A bridge of literature. And so I write to you of Reşat Nuri Güntekin.

I first learned about Reşat Nuri Güntekin in a primary school textbook. It was a short story: "The Cherries." You never read it; the story wasn't in your textbooks.

Elem, when I tell you about "The Cherries," it will echo in your ears. When the day comes. When that day comes, my utterances of the heart will echo with their roaring of the sea, and sorrow will flood you. You'll resent yourself. You'll take that resentment, exiled and alone, because you hurt someone who opened her heart to you.

This is the story of "The Cherries." It was a tale of such grief that I wept, unable to stop myself. I thought the world had come to an end. But which world? A small world, the land of children. The grief of that story is enough to destroy the world.

Futilely, my mother told me, "Don't cry, please don't cry." My poor mother. Her plea cut deeper day by day, settling into my heart. When she said that, I saw my mother, that woman who I thought cared only about the fact that her husband had abandoned her, in an entirely new way. More of a child than me. Weaker than me and sulky. My mother, an emptied woman.

Zehra, too, did not have a father. She lost her mother as well. Zehra: the girl in the cherry tree.

My mother and father were alive, but I had no one. There was only my grandmother, who I visited all summer long, the only person I thought loved me. Just like Zehra's grandmother.

More than forty years have passed. I still remember "The Cherries." And I probably will until the day I die. I'd wanted to read it to you, but I couldn't find the book. If one day I find it, I'll remember that I didn't read it to you.

Among my hazy recollections is a memory of Reşat Nuri Güntekin's death. Aunt Nadire had pressed a copy of his novel "From Word to Heart" to her chest and burst into tears. She'd read that Reşat Nuri Güntekin had died in London, where he'd gone for cancer treatment. "From Word to Heart!" she wailed in a fit of hysteria.

I don't know if the news of his death saddened me as much as "The Cherries." In those times, death was something far from my life.

I hugged Aunt Nadire, murmuring, "The Cherries." Breaking into tears yet again, she said, "What cherries, girl?" and shook her head in grief. For a moment I was repulsed by her silky hair that trembled as she sobbed. Aunt Nadire, doomed to be a spinster, knew only "From Word to Heart."

As though I hadn't read "From Word to Heart, Evening Sun" or "The Wren."

Elem, I learned about death from Reşat Nuri Güntekin. But not from Zehra. One day I read "The Wren"; Munise died in the novel. Zehra's death never moved me as much as Munise's.

It was Zehra's poverty that pulled at my heart. A young migrant girl, driven from her homeland in the name of religion and nation.

Munise, the village girl, was just about to find happiness when death struck. The innocent happiness of being home, reunited with Feride.

She dies, leaving Feride clutching at an infinite separation. If Feride lives a hundred years, maybe two hundred years more, if by a miracle she could live that long, she'll still never see Munise again. To never see someone you love ever again . . . That's how I came to understand the separation death brings.

But what separation isn't forever?

For a few days I stopped reading "The Wren." Feride's adventures had begun to pale for me. I grieved for Munise.

I even wanted to die. But no one loved me like Feride was loved! I flipped through the pages, wanting to read about Munise's death one more time, one last time. And what happens after that? I couldn't read on; for me, the novel ended with Munise's death.

My mother had read "The Cherries" to me from my textbook. That's why she saw me cry. But later, I hid my sorrow for Munise from her, from everyone.

I hid my sorrow from you too, Elem, and so you thought I was cold. But what could I have done? If it all could've been stopped, it would have been on a hot August day. But Munise dies, and Feride gravely kneels before death with no cries of defiance. Isn't that how suffering goes?

Elem, true suffering cannot be spoken of. It cannot be shared. We simply learn to endure it. Try as you may to share the pain, it doesn't subside; on the contrary, it grows, driving us to loneliness. What happened when, after years of silence, I told you of my sorrow? And isn't that what you'll think: that because I told you of my sufferings, that it's time for our final farewell?

That's how it seems to me. In the sweltering heat of that August day, Munise died one more time. Ever since the novel was written, she's died again and again for thousands, hundreds of thousands of people. But for me, it wasn't just another August day. It was the day of a child who didn't know that Munise would live on through you. I had run to the dry well, and spoke to it of Munise's death. I stroked its roughly hewn stones. With Munise's death, I was left with no one. That's probably how I began to feel such an intimacy with the sea; I was in need of a sea that was vast, endless.

I stopped writing for a while. I went inside, into the kitchen. Then to the bedroom, where I crawled into bed and wept. No, it was just a few sobs. I stopped myself; I didn't want to cry. I didn't want to cry for you, or for anyone.

I poured a glass of vodka. The liquor table was covered in dust, as was the maroon velvet tablecloth you sewed. Why hadn't Kadriye Hanım dusted the table and shaken out the cloth? Because, my dear, of a need to forget; that's all. I'd like to be able to blame Kadriye Hanım. How many times did I tell her: "Please don't touch the bottles, they'll break." Vodka with no cherries. I left the glass untouched.

I went back into the sitting room. On the bookshelf I found a copy of "The Wren," as though I'd placed it there intentionally. But you were the last person to organize the books. And after that, the separation. Never again did I touch them.

"The Wren," and the glass; I went back into the kitchen for ice and a slice of lemon.

I must've read "The Wren" three or four times. I can tell because of the markings in the book: fountain pen, pencil, ballpoint pen. Those are from the last reading, when I was working with Fikret Bey on "The Opera of the Wren," my grandest idea ever. But the project has long since been put aside. Just like the others, never to be revived.*

Elem, I wasn't going to write anything more to you. It's impossible to write to the dead. But on the thirteenth page . . . Read!

"But I knew fully well; when the time came for this separation it would be a calamity that, despite any precautions I took, was as inevitable as the setting of the sun and the falling of rain."

I had underlined that sentence with a green felt pen.

"When the time came for this separation . . ."

How uncanny. Had it been a premonition? Why had I underlined it?

No, I'd felt nothing, understood nothing, knew nothing. How could I know that one day, just as Feride lost Munise, there would be bitter separations in my life, that I would suffer losses perhaps more painful than death?

---

* As will become clear later, it's doubtful that Handan Sarp ever worked on the *Opera of the Wren*. She said that the project never got beyond the planning stage. Perhaps the narrative is incomplete; she may have worked with the composer at a later time. It's not quite clear what she wanted to say on that point in this somniloquy. (Sİ)

Those other sentences I'd underlined with a fountain pen; the ink was faded. Tremulous lines, drawn in my youth. Later, the lines become heavier in my books, in my librettos, as I became surer of my role.

That means that I'd separated from the tremulous lines of my youth as well. Had the time come? I don't know, but I do know that I was unable to endure separation. I'd like to forget "The Wren."

And yet a feeling reminiscent of sympathy gnaws at me. Everything speaks to me of such a sentiment. As though you'd written me a letter. Your writing was always small; like that of a child's, miniscule capital letters. All I have of your writing is a few sentences, written on the music tapes you made for me of songs that you liked and wanted me to like. And the dates you wrote below the newspaper clippings that mentioned me. Your writing carries the curves of a gentle tenderness.*

Elem, I'm so tired. Come, embrace me.

You wrote with small letters, the handwriting of a child. So touching, but who would understand? Look at your writing—it's still yours. And what I have is a memento of heartbreak. I have no one to share it with.

It doesn't matter, Elem, whether or not there is anyone in your life. Even when you have someone, nothing changes: the same silence, the same lull, the same turning inward. Always turning inward. Withdrawn: that is the only way I can describe myself. I should have explained myself to you, but didn't.

When you try to explain something, the poetry gets lost. In silence, the poem thrives on mystery.

That's what I'd thought. That we understood each other in silence.

But we were always an "other" to each other. Other, even when we were closest. Other, when we grew closer. We were alone and had no one. That was the only way. For me, there was no other choice.

---

* The tapes mentioned here will later be recalled as recordings of a performance by Handan Sarp. (Sİ)

I thought that you'd changed. That you'd found someone.

Once you wrote out the names of songs. And she, Handan Sarp, merely thanked you, blind to your small uppercase letters.

Never mind; go your way.

I close my eyes to set myself free. When I close my eyes you say to me at an old-fashioned restaurant on the Bosphorus: "When I was in middle school our teacher had us read 'The Night of Fire.'" Wasn't it "The Night of Fire"? Everything aside from that is over: love. Love, even now the word sticks in my throat. You were in love. When you spoke those words, "The Night of Fire," your eyes blazed with love. On the yellowed page of a diary, everything is in place. In place, perhaps, but on its own. Who knows where it has all gone. Years have passed: the chairs, table, our voices, our gazes. And I'm gone as well. Without mercy, you, my dear, tossed it all aside. Elem, writing to you, pleading with you, is painful for me.

Just as I was about to sneer at this rotten thing called life and scoff at Feride and Munise's quivers of compassion . . . Boomerang!

"That girl moved me as much as the sunshine of a warm autumn day."

On what page? My eyes are blurring, I can no longer read.

A boomerang from me to you as well, Munise.

There are some things that I only now understand ten years after the fact. Ten years have passed. Even more. The years flow past, and I can no longer keep track of them.

Snow is falling.

The lilac and the crepe myrtle are mere outlines in the snow. The laurel has been completely buried.

The garden is blanketed in white. Later, flecks of blue will flicker across the immaculate white of the snow. But still, in one corner of the garden, the shriveled, dry branches of autumn have shaken off their tufts of white.

Elem is gone. I lost her. I must accept that.

It never occurred to me to win her heart. I was feeling suffocated. Toward the end of our intimacy, and even afterward, it felt like a nightmare. My Munise was enveloped in silence and sadness. And I was irritable, lashing out in anger. But I never left her. Not once did it cross my mind. She had no pity for me.

The days of *The Night of Fire* were different. Often we went to Hristo's. It had been renovated and looked like the other restaurants in Tarabya. My girl was embarrassed that she hadn't read any other novels than *The Night of Fire*, but I pushed her, asking questions, not thinking that one day I'd suffer from her torment.

If it weren't for those memories, perhaps I could forget Elem.

A snowstorm rages outside.

Insistently, the snow buries again the bare branches struggling to return to autumn. The garden is pleased with its whites and blues.

I've always wondered what happens to the things we leave behind; the chairs at Hristo's, the tables upon which I leaned my elbows, and time . . . Where does the past go? Does my voice, which brought to life so many songs, not echo somewhere? What about her words of love? And my salacious moans?

I can't orgasm without those obscenities.

For three days, the snow has been falling. The storm began suddenly. It's the first snow since we separated. When it snowed, she was afraid that we wouldn't be able to see each other on the weekend. Now, she probably doesn't even remember, or that fear has slipped from her thoughts. Contentedly she watches the snowy night from the window.

Night. My garden is like a huge white ship plunging toward me, as though it will crash through the glass door. The snow falls like bird feathers, obscuring the sky. I try to imagine that the snowflakes are white flowers. But in vain. The snow falls, along with flowers of mourning. As I watch the snow falling, I notice that my hands have balled into fists and a strange feeling of dread washes over me: even at night, it seems that this infinite whiteness will go on forever. The bluish white illuminates my life, a life worn thin and nearing its end. I'm able to look at my life more ruthlessly than ever.

The mounds of snow are ringed in fire, drawing outward into a dreary, motionless plain. Soon it will be utterly desolate, and then fade away. A shudder runs through me, because I have no fear of that. I wanted everything to fade away to nothing. Months have passed since we separated, and I haven't been able to release myself from the grip of a longing for death.

The wind whips the white rose that we bought from the Spice Bazaar and planted together. Small and delicate, its leaves are covered in snow. There were days when I hated that plant, as though it were the symbol of our separation. We bought it thinking it would bloom pink, but instead, like a sign of what was destined, white roses blossomed.

The next day, she brought the sachet of lavender I'd forgotten at the boutique to the opera house. "I'll bring it to you in the evening," she'd said. I'd told her in such a way that Semra wouldn't understand what I meant. After leaving the cafe-bar, Elem went back to the boutique and found the sachet just as someone was about to be thrown away.

As I was preparing to leave in the morning, she called. "You can keep it," I told her, but she insisted that she would "deliver" it, in her words. She emphasized the word "deliver."

But perhaps she was merely curious about opera. By the afternoon, I'd convinced myself that was the case. As fate would have it, we weren't having a dress rehearsal that day. Either Necmi's preposterous costumes would pique her interest and she'd think that opera was a garish carnival, or she'd be petrified by the tastelessness of it all. In any case, there would've been a topic of conversation.

I got permission from the director and notified the door staff; when she arrived, they were to let her in. However, I didn't know her last name. It didn't really matter, because the doorman was already perplexed by the name "Elem."

That night we didn't get to talk. I saw her bundled into her seat all the way in the rear. Finally we took a break, and I approached her. The color had drained from her face. She looked like a wildcat caught in a trap, overwhelmed and stunned: the orchestra, the chorus, the bustle of people and Necmi, who was a crowd on his own, was shouting at someone who had put on the wrong costume. She didn't say anything, but I sensed her unease.

I could tell that she wanted to leave as soon as she could.

"You'll get home late because of me. Just like last night."

"I told them I was coming to see you."

I didn't ask, but I wondered: Did her family know who I was?

The writer Yahya Kemal once described Istanbul as "remote" and "destitute." Like the word *remotus*, from the root *removeo*. Neighborhoods that are removed, inaccessible, isolated, forlorn. In such a remote neighborhood, why would they have heard of an opera singer like me?

I never found out if her family had ever heard my name. There had been a few news pieces on television and a few photographs in the papers, but would her family have even noticed? I mean, before I became involved in Elem's life. Of course later they heard about me, after we met; Handan Hanım was in the papers, Handan Hanım was on television. But in the beginning, it was different.

Such mysteries remain. Even though I'd been to Elem's parent's house three or four times, I never learned the way. If I were to try now, I wouldn't be able to find it.

I can only describe the atmosphere of Kocamustâpaşa. And the tomb of Şem-i Dede. I remember where the tomb is, because it left such a mark on my life.

To get to her house, you have to make a number of left and right turns after passing the tomb.

The first time I went there, Elem was the only person at home. She'd invited Semra and me over for dinner, and her family had gone to her grandmother's, the funeral for whom would be held at the small mosque designed by the architect Sinan. That's what her grandmother had requested; I think I mentioned it in one of my somniloquies.

Why had Elem invited us? That too is a mystery.

Semra asked, "Are we going to go?"

I said that we would. You can never turn down the invitations of people poorer than yourself. Even if it means long, tedious hours. I simply cannot bring myself to hurt anyone who holds me in high regard. If sins exist, then that would certainly be counted among them.

La traviata had begun, and Semra invited Elem, Hüseyin and İnci—their older sister—to attend a Sunday matinee performance. Semra has always been quite talkative, so who knows what she may have asked them that day.

That invitation had been completely unnecessary.

"They came when you invited them," I told Semra. "Now we have to go."

Inexplicable things were happening in my life. At the very least, I thought that Hüseyin and İnci might be at home, especially since Ali had been invited. Had I been worried about how much all it would cost? If so, why was I so indifferent?

Three young people, to avoid hurting our feelings, had been flung into the alien world of opera, and we had to pay the price. We went.

Dusk had settled. We took a taxi and Elem was waiting for us in front of the Funda Patisserie. In the shop window, cakes made of cheap chocolate were on display, decorated with sugar roses. In a long tray, there were pastries left over from the morning. In the mornings, my Munise buys pastries fresh from the oven before getting on the bus at the stop nearby. Over time, I would find out about things like that.

Elem joined us in the taxi. Out of nervousness and excitement, she asked, "Have you been waiting long?" She didn't even know what she was saying. Semra laughed, and replied, "You probably waited a long time for us." Ah, such a strange thing, this past, and remembering it: her flushed cheeks, her nostrils twitching—such a timid creature.

We turned right.

As soon as we rounded the corner, the tomb of Şem-i Dede loomed into view. The season was well into autumn, and the courtyard of the tomb was filled with leaves. The wall was crumbling in disrepair. There were stubs of melted candles along the windowsill. A radiance spilled outward.

"What's that?" I asked. The tomb had moved me immensely.

"The tomb of our grandfather," she said. That's what they always say: the neighborhood grandfather. Şem-i Dede are always in poor, forlorn neighborhoods.

We passed the tomb.

Maybe I'm confused about the season. It was winter. The courtyard couldn't have been filled with autumn leaves. The night was bitterly cold, and we were shivering. I was afraid that I'd fall ill, and I kept pulling my cashmere scarf tightly around my neck.

Elem had sat in the front seat. She turned and asked Semra, "Why didn't your husband come?"

Semra stammered that there had been some confusion; her husband had promised his friends, old military friends, that he would meet up with them.

We'd debated over whether or not Ali should come. If Elem's family were religiously conservative, we thought, the presence of a young man they didn't know could disturb them. We had mixed feelings about going, and in any case, Ali wasn't enthusiastic about the idea.

My thoughts were still on Şem-i Dede: "Elem, one day I'd like to visit the tomb."

"Sure, Handan Hanım."

As we proceeded deeper into the neighborhood, the narrowing streets became darker, and the houses, whether made of wood or masonry, were falling into disrepair; the hastily built apartment buildings nestled up against one another. I peered into the darkness: there, probably a school, and there, a road leading up a hill. There were just a few scraggly trees, their branches bare. "Coming here was a preposterous idea," I remember thinking to myself. Light glowed faintly through closed curtains, and the flicker of televisions illuminated nearly every window. Night had fallen. It was Saturday, and that night, there was no *La traviata*.

We got out of the taxi. Semra wanted to pay the taxi fare, but I insisted. Elem showed us the way, leading us into—if I remember correctly—a four-story apartment building, the exterior tiling falling away in places. The entry door stood ajar, its glass cracked from top to bottom. We slipped through the doorway. The threshold of poverty.

A narrow corridor led to the stairs and a bare bulb hung from the ceiling. The narrow, slippery steps may have been scrubbed hundreds of times but they still looked grimy, stained with the dregs of destitution. I could now envision the life that Elem lived; this was the horrific rift between Kocamustâpaşa and the glitz of Nişantaşı.

There was a clear disjuncture between her life there and what she saw in Nişantaşı. Every day was the same, every day the same contrast between your life and the magnificence and pomp of the lives of others. Wouldn't it slowly eat away at your spirit?

"Be careful, the third landing is cracked," Elem said.

We climbed gingerly. Semra clutched the balustrade.

The paint on the walls was puffed up in places, peeling away, and the walls seemed to be leaning in toward each other like the walls of a pyramid. There were thousands of apartments like that in her neighborhood. Walls upon walls closing in on each other. Lives upon lives caving in on one another. Everything worn bare, like the shoes in disarray on the doorsteps of the apartments.

I fell silent, withdrawing into myself. I felt suffocated by something that had wearied my heart for as long as I can remember. Reality, the facts of life that I had tried to escape from, save myself from. After having seen those lives and knowing that there is even worse, how can you return to your own life? How would we go back, in just a few hours?

There were two flats on each floor. We approached the one at the end of the corridor, and Elem opened the door. I can't recall, but I don't think there was an entryway, and we walked straight into the sitting room. The memories of my other visits are blank as well in that regard. Maybe there was a kind of entry hall, with a shoe rack closed off with a piece of printed cloth. There was no heap of shoes on the doorstep of Elem's family's flat. A decorum of delicacy.

There was a large room with a balcony at the far end. At first, she didn't turn on the light. For a moment. As if she couldn't find the switch. I tried to sense what moved through her soul. As if she didn't want us to see her family's house; perhaps she regretted inviting us over. She'd never seen our homes, but she may as well have; she'd seen how we live and how we dress.

A streetlight illuminated the balcony, which was filled with flower-pots. The plants clung to life in the cold of winter. There was a wax plant that bloomed every year, weeping tears of wax. That evening, we went out onto the balcony and she told us that growing plants and flowers was a family hobby.

She finally turned on the light. The house was spotless. ("Selim, cleanliness in the midst of poverty is a torment for me.")

There were two armchairs, and a few other chairs. The back of the sofa rested against the wall of the balcony. The dining table was in the center of the room. It had been set for four people, as Elem had expected that Ali would come. A few pillows were scattered on the sofa, and there were plastic flowers in cheap vases on the end tables along with family pictures in faux silver frames. I scanned the room, taking it in like a camera, and tried to smile. I felt like a complete stranger. As always, a stranger.

After our separation, which I've always dreaded discussing, my memories of that room and the wax plants on the balcony became a nightmare for me. When I close my eyes, I see the room, but it has changed; the décor is no longer the same.

Among my memories is this: it's evening, any winter evening. A blue light begins to seep in, its source unknown, bathing the room in a light reminiscent of the last light of day, trying to envelop the tremulous furnishings in the apartment. The chairs, sofa, and table become drawn out, warped and twisted, transformed into something else. The furnishings seem to have been tastefully chosen but are sparse, perhaps because of a lack of means. The tapestry fabric, which had obviously been selected with great pleasure, is nonetheless of the cheapest kind. As the blue light shifts, a gossamer shadow is cast over the fabric. There are three globe lamps, and although the flowers on the globes seem to have been painstakingly painted, the paint is flaking away. The chairs come alive and fidget, as though it was now time to express their inner joy. Elem and I step out onto the balcony, and she removes the perforated plastic sheet covering the flowers; as she said, they are weeping.

At that moment, night bears down and the blue light fades. I can no longer see anything. The room disappears.

I'll likely never visit that house again. Why would I? When I had put on my perfume at home, its scent had filled the room: Amazone, by Hermès. After climbing those three flights of stairs, however, little probably remained of its scent. A wave of irritation washed over me. The perfume was expensive, an extravagance for me.

When we entered the flat, I caught the smell of tangerines. My immediate observation: a handful of tangerine peels had been tossed on top of the coal-burning stove. The exhaust pipe of the stove was deep green, almost black. The stove didn't burn with a roar, but merely sputtered. With dismay I realized that the apartment would never warm up.

As I took in the room, I heard Semra's idle chatter: "I just adore houses that have coal-burning stoves. It's been years since I've seen one . . ."

"The house where I was born had a stove," I said, and went on to tell about the stove at the summer house. My grandmother stayed at the Pendik house all year, and when autumn came, the living space dwindled to just a few rooms near the stove. That was when I'd return to my mother's apartment in Istanbul.

We sat down at the table. The scent of my Amazone perfume revived, overpowering the smell of tangerines. When Elem went into the kitchen, Semra and I looked at each other: "It's good that we came," she whispered. I felt an affection for her, the same as the day she'd brought me a bouquet of violets.

I looked at Elem, thinking, "How old could this girl be? Is she even in her twenties?" She kept going back and forth to the kitchen and would stop and look at the table as if she had forgotten something, not wanting anything to be missing. I thought, "She's still but a child. She couldn't even be out of her teens yet."

"You'll have wine, won't you?"

"Won't your family be upset if we drink?"

"No, they're not conservative like that. I bought some wine."

"Let's have wine, then."

"My father drinks," Elem said. "Every night he has a few glasses of rakı."

Fragments of our conversations from that night . . . I can't remember what we had for dinner. Semra spoke the most, and Elem listened. As I sat there, my thoughts kept drifting back to the times when I was her age.

In those years, my imagination soared. At the conservatory, as I was studying under my rather well-known teachers who told me that my voice was "flawless," I dreamed that one day I'd be the most famous soprano in the world. I tried to dress fashionably and flirted with the boys my age. When we danced and they put their arms around me, deep inside I burned with loathing for them. My thoughts were of Nilüfer—I was enamored only of her. In those days, my flights of fancy were my sole refuge. But Elem had no such dreams. Perhaps it's better that way if day by day your dreams will simply crumble into disappointment.

That's how mine were; I was like Norma—life withheld from me as much as it gave, and I went to the pyre and burned everything. I played the role of Norma, which was my greatest desire. But the stage and spectators weren't enough for me. I understood that being Norma would not lead to happiness.

In the end, it was a wasted life. Nothing more. But then Kaya and I came together. And what did she do? Raze those years to the ground as well.

The evening drew to a close. We rose from the dining table, still unsure why Elem had invited us. She called a taxi for us; thank God there was a taxi stand nearby. Elem walked us out, and we shook hands. I fell silent, withdrawing into myself. Semra said, "She's such a nice girl."

Who? Elem?

If only the lights would shine upon me again and I were in the opera!

This separation is like an unending symphony. Actually, an opera. Longing, ceaseless longing. I'm under the lights, and Norma throws herself into the flames; the fire is her savior.

Just yesterday I wanted to call you. But you haven't called for so many days, so many months. You didn't call, you never called. Perhaps tonight, or tomorrow. Who could know? No one, none of us. You didn't call; you plucked me from your life and tossed me aside. My face is concealed by a black veil of mourning, and I walk toward the raging pyre. But no one walks beside me. No Roman commander, nor Elem. The flames leap, and soon the curtain will fall. Ah, Norma, why did you love so much!

But who of us can understand another person's love? Or Norma's passion and jealousy? My only companion is alcohol, because my life is eternal but in this place, there is neither life nor eternity. Here and now, never to return to you, here in this house you visited hundreds of times, I call out to you my dear, one last time, the last night. My life has always been yours, but there wasn't a single day that you understood me. Or perhaps it was the passing time that took you from me. Time stole you away. I walk toward the lights. I'm in a state of rapture; there, the temple of the goddess of war, and I walk through the forest among the trees, and this night I leave Norma forever, but my home is now surrounded by boulders and I'm as alone as Norma.

As alone as Norma. An oak tree in a thicket. I'm trying to listen: this voice, used up and exhausted, as flames envelop my voice, this song that I murmur, my voice. Elem, you believed that after the blaze we'd start life anew; you believed in life after death, and on those nights when I rose up in drunken defiance, like Norma who renounced her sinner's pledge but then sought nothing but to be consumed in the flames, you told me that God exists and the day of judgment will come. Grabbing a spear, I run for the oak tree and strike the shield three times. If we meet again in another life, you'll see that I was ruined for eternity when you left. Surrounded by others, but the loneliest of all. You'll say to me, I never was able to understand how lonely you were. And when you lift the black veil of mourning, you'll see Norma and hear the song "Casta diva" that we listened to together— you asked me, "Do you always shout like that? You're always shouting . . ." It was a howl.[*]

Elem died. It was I who killed her. All through that night in those hours when the furnishings were shrouded in shadow, when they withdrew into themselves and, plunging into darkness, refused to speak to me, I repeated to myself again and again: Elem is dead.

But she denied it, saying, "That's impossible, you would never do such a wicked thing." There were mimosas in the vase; I'd bought them that day, the early blooming mimosas of spring, from the flower seller on the corner of Mim Kemal Öke Street. What I spoke of today took place years and years ago. So, you didn't die. You've come to me. Together, just you and I are here at this house where the furniture fills with darkness, listening to that opera that I'd come to despise performing onstage. Next, when "Casta diva" began to play, you embraced me, Elem. "Don't be sad," you tell me. "Nobody killed me, I'm still alive. Could you ever do such a thing? Could you, Handan Sarp, ever kill me?"

---

[*] In some of her somniloquies, Handan Sarp disregarded grammatical rules. I've left her sentences as they are, although it's not always clear what she intended to say. (Sİ)

How can it be that here, at this house, as I look at the ghost of the vase of mimosas that arose from the past, I find myself running to that familiar beach. People turn and look at me. But I don't care. I no longer have a life to hide from anyone. I destroyed Elem, and the price has been paid.

In the beginning, the sea is calm, blanketed in mist in the distance. "Good," I said, "today we are at peace. Today they won't come. You've shrouded the way in mist, and they won't be able to find it."

They come so often! Though their time came to an end long before, you look and there they are; you can see and smell them. They're there in body, in the flesh, and you can reach out and touch them. But I find them unbearable. I kiss Elem and am seared by my longing. And then I find myself in Kaya's arms, and I don't know from who or what debauched way of life she learned this, but she transforms this pain into a frenzy of sexuality, from woman to woman, man to man. I never dreamed that I would miss making love so much! I'm tormented by a desire to return to Elem. No, that can't be right. In this life, Elem comes later.

When I couldn't be rejoined with Elem, a wind began to blow; a ship drew near, and they told me that they would take my girl from me. Once again I was swept into that famous aria from "Madame Butterfly," and my entreaties crescendo into wails—the orchestra must not keep pace with me! You, my dear, my everything, they are going to take you from me.

When my voice fades—no, it doesn't fade—when my voice goes unheard in the third act, I've already taken refuge in the roar of the sea. I no longer have a reason to flee or to rise up in revolt. There's nothing on the wave-pounded shore except for my memories and seashells. It's as though Elem smiles as each wave crashes over me: Handan, you didn't hurt me.

If that's the case, Elem, why am I sobbing?

(As I struggle to weave Handan Sarp's somniloquies and narratives into a "novel," life has begun to feel oppressive. I awoke this morning exhausted, even though I'd gone to bed rather early. Until morning, I kept having dreams, one after the other, which is unusual for me because I rarely dream.

My dreams last night were disjointed, strange and sorrowful.

Perhaps it was the effect of Handan Sarp's repeated utterances of "loss" and "separation," but in my dream I was confronted with people who had disappeared from my life, whom I'd lost through death. I dreamed of my relatives and acquaintances from the neighborhoods where I grew up. The faces in my dream belonged to people that I hadn't thought about for years, that I'd assumed had been erased from memory.

Everyone was leaving Istanbul. Why? It was unclear. The houses and rooms may have been different but they all contained suitcases and large bags. The hour of the day differed as well. For some, the hour of parting was early in the morning, before the break of dawn. For others it was in the evening. Despite the hour, the lights hadn't been turned on, and the darkness suffused the scene of parting with even greater sorrow. With their suitcases and bags they went, leaving behind empty rooms and homes.

Next came the trains and stations. Some of them were large, like Haydarpaşa, and there were small, forlorn stations by riversides that seemed to be lost among the trees. And then the relentless, piercing train whistle. Why did they always go by train? It's a mystery.

Handan Sarp said to me: "Travel always speaks to me of separation. But trains pain me the most. When I was a child I would go to the train station in Pendik and wait for the long-distance trains to pass through. Some were on time, others were late. As they came and went, I felt like breaking down in tears."

Everyone was leaving, but I felt like I was the one leaving them. I forced myself awake, trying to escape from the dream. What time is it? Is it morning yet? But my eyelids were heavy as lead; my eyes closed, and I drifted back to sleep. An unending nightmare.

In my last dream I was going into the Emek Cinema, in the Beyoğlu of my adolescence, along with a group of people I didn't know. A film began. It was about the life of Chopin and how he died from tuberculosis. In the film, George Sand, the female novelist with whom he'd fallen in love, dressed in men's clothing, smoked a pipe and constantly berated Chopin.

Hadn't I had seen that film years before, at the very same theater? After watching the film, I'd decided I would become a composer.

I remember the end of the film: Chopin vomits blood as he plays the piano, and the keys are washed bright red. George Sand runs toward him.

But before my dream got to that scene, I awoke with a start. At first, there was a powerful sense of weightlessness and a feeling of youth, a return to my childhood. But that passed quickly, replaced with a sense of being in a state of exile, weighed down by exhaustion. I decided to turn back to Handan Sarp's novel. To the novel

I couldn't write. To the novel that refused to bring itself into the world.

Handan Sarp, that woman who wearies my soul.)

Kaya. A girl of the streets.

She was young then. Sometimes I wonder how she's doing. After having separated time and time again, I saw her one evening on the street; she'd put on a lot of weight. We pretended not to know each other. At the time, Elem and I were still seeing each other. Kaya had meant separation for me, but I tried to push that from my thoughts. It was in Beyoğlu that I saw her, on a street lined with bars. Purple light from a sign flashed across her face. We ignored one another. But was it really her? It had to have been Kaya. Separation was everything. If it were Kaya, what would change? I saw her tug at her purple beret. A bitter pain was left behind.

Had we separated?

It was I who left her.

Kaya.

("Selim Bey, I told Elem about Kaya. If I hadn't, maybe I could've changed the course of destiny. Sometimes the power to change fate truly is in our hands. Or, at least you think it is.

Those were the days when opera, *La traviata*, was taking its toll on me. If your art is unknown to most people, if it's seen as an absurd luxury, a cipher, then you too would carry that burden. Your initial enthusiasm begins to fade. You fail to achieve what you seek. You stumble yet again. If it hadn't been for Semra and her husband, I would've been mired in misery.

On opening night, the sight of the half-empty opera house was like a crushing blow. At that moment, the ideals and dreams of my youth collapsed. I'd dreamed that, under the stage lights, I would see the crowd in the dark. A flood of people. And the roar of applause. When you hear the word "diva," what else comes to mind? Indeed, I was called a diva. A diva of emptiness. For most people, the word signifies nothing at all.

That's how my life was passing by. Playing Violetta yet again meant nothing to me. You want to sing with a vengeance, drawing on all your might; but you also know that you've dedicated yourself to Violetta for nothing.

I was at home, alone. Again it was dusk, with its fragile melancholy brought on by the setting sun and the dying of the light. It was winter in my garden. Like a wounded animal, I paced back and forth.

I tried to console myself with thoughts of gardens: still pools, crumbling walls, lavender, wild hyacinth and gilliflowers. And there was always that sharp, enchanting smell of dried-out flower beds. My life was like that: a bed of dried-out flowers.

That's how it had always been.

I could bear it no longer.

So what did I do? I called Elem at the boutique. Trying to change my voice so they wouldn't recognize me, I asked: "Can I speak with Elem, please?" Fear and adrenaline. I was fleeing from myself, but also from the judgments of society—a double escape.

A long while had passed since we went to Elem's for dinner that night. I'd seen her, however, when I went to pick up my dress. I kept a cool distance, and my Munise was silent, sulky.

She picked up the phone.

"Elem, this is Handan Sarp."

"Yes, Handan Hanım?"

"Can we meet tonight, after you finish work? At the cafe we went to before, the first time we went out. Just for an hour or so . . ."

"Yes, sure."

"Good-bye for now, Elem."

"Good-bye, Handan Hanım."

I looked at the clock; it was almost five o'clock, which meant I had two and a half more hours to wait. What else could I do? Naturally, I'd drink! There was no other way I could meet up with Elem. And it had been the same with Kaya. Ever since alcohol came into my life it has been like that. Despite the terrifying thought of losing my voice, which had held out so far, I sought refuge in alcohol.

For a moment I hesitated, thinking that it might be expensive for Elem to go to that cafe, but I decided that since I'd invited her, it would only be right if I paid. And then I turned to whiskey to assuage my fears. I still had to get dressed and do my makeup. But instead, I put some ice in a glass. Even two sips helped; I felt myself relax as the alcohol flowed through my veins. The sharp scent of rotting plants in flower beds gave way to lavender. Soon, I would smell of Amazone. I laughed.

But with the second glass, worry set in. I thought, "Was I crazy, why had I invited that girl, what could possibly happen between us?" I wasn't in love with her. I knew quite well that I didn't love her. Then it struck me: I wanted to forget Kaya's absence. I wanted an accomplice in forgetfulness.

Selim Bey, when people have gone to ruin, they don't take into account whether or not their accomplice committed the same transgression as themselves. But you must always have an accomplice.")

I didn't put on any makeup or perfume and threw on a dress, wrapping a shawl over my shoulders. It was black with blue flowers. Some people think that light blue is a warm color, but they're mistaken; it's cold, indifferent, lacking the yellows and oranges in green. My flowers were the blue of ice. For me, they were a form of protection.

By the time I left my apartment, I'd had a few drinks. The cold air was refreshing, a bitter cold that promised snow. Although I'd dressed in a hurry, I wasn't so disheveled that people on the street took note of me. Even if one or two did turn and look at me, I merely glared at them and moved on.

Elem hadn't yet arrived and the cafe was nearly empty. I slipped into a booth in a corner and ordered a whiskey. But then I was gripped by fear: what if she doesn't come?

She arrived. That day she was livelier than before, more sociable.

"I'm sorry for being late. There was something I had to . . ."

I cut her off: "That doesn't matter. What matters is that you came." For the first time, I addressed her with the informal form of "you." That's how I remember it now: that was the night when I addressed Elem so casually.

And that was the night she told me one of the most beautiful things I have ever heard: "On the way here, I was really cold. But now that I'm with you, I don't feel the chill."

I smiled. But I was filled with an odd feeling of compassion, almost like an ache. At the time, I didn't realize that the feeling would never recede, as though it had come into being for all time. That realization would only come much later.

And at the same time I felt joy, but it was elation tempered with fear. I asked myself, "What will you talk about with this girl? Why did you invite her out?"

That evening, Elem was in bright spirits and more talkative than usual. She told me about her short life, which was unremarkable, unmarked by dreams. She said that she'd started working after finishing middle school. Hüseyin, her younger brother, was attending high school, and she wanted him to go on to study at university. İnci, her elder sister, stayed at home to help her mother. One day, she'd get married.

"And you?" I asked.

As she talked, she seemed lost in thought. But when I asked that question, she looked into my eyes. I saw flecks of green in her amber eyes, as well as indecisiveness, hesitance. Quickly she turned her gaze away, as though it was unbearable for her.

I insisted: "Why don't you answer my question?"

"Why did you ask that, Handan Hanım?"

"Aren't you going to get married too?"

"Have you ever been married, Handan Hanım? Are you married?"

I recall feeling my cheeks burn, but I don't know if it was because I felt angry for suddenly being cornered or embarrassed that she'd seen through me. My body was flushed with heat, but at the same time a chill ran through me. I ordered another whiskey. There were still a few shreds of hope: perhaps Elem was trying to tell me that she was someone like me? Regardless of what she was trying to say, something was changing. The secret Handan, the "other" me, was coming to life—and I've always been her slave. Alcohol, whether it's whiskey, cognac or vodka, always has the same effect: after a certain point, the "other" rises up, and I'm powerless before her. For all appearances, everything seems normal; my attitude doesn't change, nor does my voice. The only difference is that my eyes become ever so slightly fogged over. I once tried to see this transformation by looking in a mirror. It seemed that at any moment, tears would gather in the corners of my eyes.

Now that the other had risen, what would she talk about? She obviously wasn't interested in hearing about Elem's bleak life in Kocamustâpaşa, nor about İnci's desire for a husband, Hüseyin's struggle to get an education, her father's labors, or family dinners. The other Handan, grieved by Handan Sarp's own personal story, was indifferent to the tragedies of other people.

She knew she wouldn't be able to restrain herself and would talk about Kaya. The pain of separation. Longing for Kaya. If Kaya were to show up, the other Handan would consent to that scandalous relationship yet again. Her gaze drifts to the ice-blue flowers adorning her shawl, and she begins talking about Kaya. She wasn't aware at the moment that she was sealing her fate. No, she wasn't trying to put Elem in Kaya's place. Could Elem even be a confidante? Perhaps. But Handan wasn't even aware of what she was doing. She thought that by talking, the pain might die down. Blue is a cold color; and as she spoke, her language was inflected with the coldness of blue.

I met Kaya at Cafe Diken.

("You know Cafe Diken, in Beyoğlu. It's on the street where Kaya and I last saw each other. That's the street where it all started, and that's where we saw each other for the last time.")

I told Elem that there was a place called Cafe Diken in Beyoğlu which was quite similar to the place where we were sitting. They served tea and coffee, and alcohol as well. About two years before that I had gone there with some friends from the opera after the opening night of a performance. The opening night for what? I remembered at the time, and I told Elem about it.

Years have passed. Kaya has faded away. Perhaps it was *Aida*, but I'm not sure. It could have been *Aida*; Kaya had watched it, and wept. That's what she said. But what's it worth? *Aida* means nothing. Nor do tears.

In any case, let's say it was *Aida*. After the performance, we went to Diken. There were two young women sitting at a narrow table, drinking beer. They were wearing cheap imitations of the latest fashions. Both wore makeup, and they both seemed at ease, maybe even a little too at ease.

That's not quite true. At first I didn't see them, nor did I notice what they were wearing. When I'm in a crowd, rather than walking tall and proud, I tend to merely stare straight ahead. I wouldn't have noticed anyone.

But I'd felt Kaya's gaze on me. I turned and looked: her brown eyes, thickly lined with mascara, were both inviting and unnerving. She greeted me. Soon after, she approached our table: "You're Handan Sarp, aren't you?" Occasionally it does happen; true aficionados of opera recognize you, and, expressing their admiration, ask for your autograph. Such people usually aren't trying to show off. If they are, they manage to do it tastefully. But Kaya wasn't like that.

"My name is Kaya," she said. "I'm a fan of yours."

The women and men who approach me are always well-off educated types, and while they may offer praise, no one had ever said to me, "I'm a fan of yours." I don't have the popularity of a pop singer or film star. Obviously, Kaya was lying; she'd never set foot in the opera and had no idea who I was. It was a lie, but still, I found myself smiling like a fool.

Kaya caused quite a stir at our table. I'm sure my friends were gawking at me as I talked to Kaya. But it was preposterous of course that they'd be so envious just because they thought that this street girl's admiration was real!

And just then, Kaya said, pointing out a small table, "Can we sit here and talk?"

I should have been irritated by her brazenness, but I wasn't. I turned, and noticed that her friend was getting ready to leave. Kaya was petite. And young to be out at that hour of the night.

"Your friend is leaving," I said.

Kaya smiled: "She's going to work."

Cafe Diken is always rather dark. Even during the day, the light of the sun barely filters through cafe's dark windows. And at night, with the dim lights, there's a strange intimacy to the atmosphere. In the midst of the crowd, you feel as though you can be completely alone with someone. There's a neon tinge to the darkness. Most likely I'd fallen under its spell: my body was sapped by lethargy and my inner world had long been nothing more than a skeleton of memories. The neon dark whispered to me. She was still standing, and although she was no longer smiling, there was a devious glint in her eyes. The intimate setting seemed to incite our bodies; but would we share our loneliness, or would it simply congeal? But it didn't matter if it were fake. I needed some tenderness, even the compassion of a street girl, and I would've been willing to pay for it.

I'd never slept with anyone for money. Well, that's not entirely true. It's difficult to explain. I mean, giving money to someone, or giving a gift . . . But it happens; there are prostitutes who sleep with lesbians for money.

I stood up. My head spun and nausea churned my stomach. I was afraid that my friends would find it odd if I went off with Kaya. But no one said anything. In any case, they all had their own lives. I was playing Cinderella: "I don't have much time. Tell me what you want to say, but make it quick." I was trying to put up my guard.

Sitting down, she took a pack of cigarettes from the small purse slung over her shoulder. In those days, unlike now, I hardly ever smoked. But for some reason, I accepted when she offered me a cigarette. As she lit it for me, I could feel the hot skin of her hand, and I knew that I would be lured along. I was at the precipice and would give in to that remorseless desire. And I wanted it, immediately. I was terrified, but that's how it always happens. I lose myself: art, pride, my reputation—it all vanishes.

I pulled my hand away, and looked at her face, which was barely visible in the dim light. Actually, she wasn't that young at all; she'd probably had a difficult life.

Although I'd asked her to be brief, Kaya settled in, taking her time. She said she was out of a job but used to work as a dealer at a fancy hotel's casino. That was before all the casinos in Istanbul were shut down.

As she talked, I gazed blankly at her. I was perplexed. Her face seemed to blur but her eyes glimmered, and I was surprised to see in their dark depths the warm glow of compassion. Or was I making it up?

"At the casinos," she was saying, "we deal the cards, and in the process, lives are ruined. We spin the roulette wheel, and when I collect the losers' chips, my heart goes out to them. They've lost everything. You hear the shouts of winning numbers and the bells of slot machines as the lights flash around you. My friend was also a dealer. Later she found a job as a night receptionist at a small hotel. She was actually the one who recognized you. 'That's Handan Sarp,' she said. I didn't know who you were. I lied to you. So, you do opera . . ."

Kaya: my friend, caught between good and evil. Always up, then down. She would tell a thousand lies and then confess her deceit. A street girl, she'd run away from home and her family. She told me one night that her father, or maybe it was her brother, had raped her. She was drunk and crying, clinging on to me, but too ashamed to say who had done it. She fell asleep in my arms, her cold nose pressed against my skin.

Like a madwoman, I told Elem everything.

"Things like that happen all the time," she said.

I was stunned by her calm demeanor. Kaya's experiences, as I witnessed them, seemed so singular that I thought they could only be hers. It was as if she was the only person in the world who had run away from home, as if no other woman except for her had spent nights roaming the dingy bars of Beyoğlu.

With an air of solemnity unbefitting her youth, Elem said, "And the other girl, Kaya Hanım's friend, I suppose she'd never been to the opera either. People like them, like us, know nothing of opera." She pulled a newspaper clipping from her coat pocket: "Did you read this?"

It was a news piece about *La traviata* and there were pictures of me as well. It was a photograph of the final scene. Ali and I were in an embrace, and my face looked like a mask of death.

"When I saw it was about you, I cut it out."

Ah, Elem! From that day on, you started cutting out every article and photograph of me that you came across, and pasted them into an album. I can't help but wonder: do you still do that?

I looked at the close-up photo of myself. It was from a pleasant period in Violetta and Alfredo's lives. Still, my smile was bitter. And the look in my eyes was frighteningly pained.

But Elem remained calm and collected, as though she'd heard time and again the kinds of things I told her. The story of Kaya's life saddened her, but she was unperturbed by the relationship that had unfolded between me and Kaya. She was silent as I talked. I clearly remember how she looked that night. Her lips were fixed in a line, and her eyes were a motley hazel, filled with caring and compassion. But now that compassion is gone. Never again will she look at me in that way. Just like her compassion, Elem is dead.

Cafe Diken was closing. It was nearly dawn as we stepped out into the streets, which were empty except for a few stumbling drunks. My friends had left long before. Kaya and I walked together. It was unsettling for me, but she didn't find it strange that two women would be walking in Beyoğlu at that hour. And it seemed strange to me that the people around us took no notice.

I wanted to take a taxi. Where would our ways part, and how? But the devil inside me urged me to wait. "No," the voice cooed, "don't get into a taxi just yet." In the end, I heeded my devil's word.

I went with Kaya to an all-night diner in Sıraselviler that sold soup, flatbread and grilled meat. I'd passed places like that hundreds of times but had never gone in. I ordered a bowl of lentil soup. Kaya had soup and cheese-topped flatbread. I paid the bill.

When I stopped a taxi, she climbed in with me. She'd stopped talking. "Nişantaşı," I told the driver, not knowing what to do. I felt ashamed. Wave upon wave of regret crashed over me as I wondered, "What had possessed me to sit with this little strumpet? What could we possibly talk about?" But I was so exhausted that the shame and worry were falling away bit by bit, replaced by a cool flush of numbness.

As if it were the most natural thing in the world, she got out of the taxi with me. Day had broken. My face must have been a wreck. Was this girl a blessing or a thief? Gelengül had once told me, "Be careful! Those murex who sleep with you for money are all thieves." I laughed haughtily: "And just what is a murex?!"

I opened the front door. And something unexpected happened: Kaya began weeping. "I'm cold," she said. Warm air wafted from my apartment. She asked, "Where am I going to sleep?"

"Kaya, why are you crying?"

"Don't ask. When I'm with you, I feel like I can cry. Just don't ask anything."

I held her against me, hugging her tightly. But it wasn't sexual desire; I felt no attraction. It was just an urge to protect her.

But had it been like that in Diken Cafe? I'd felt as though I were aflame with desire.

Our fingers entwine, and, minds lightened by drink, control falls away as our bodies fiendishly press together in a tight embrace. As we kiss, we pull off each other's clothes, piece by piece. When we're both completely naked, I pull her face to my breasts and my nipples stiffen, and we both tremble . . .

But that's not what happened: we slept in our clothes on my single bed. That "single" bed which perhaps is a means of protecting me from myself, from the true essence of myself.

We slept in our clothes. That's a significant detail. Kaya would eventually bring her vagabond ways she'd picked up from the streets into my flat, into my life. For two years she would turn my home and the order in my life upside down: no restraint, no rules, no responsibility. It was pure anarchy. She'd ask for money, but whenever she got a little money herself, she'd give it to me. After spinning lie upon lie and heaping deceit upon deceit, she would be wracked by regret, and tell the truth with tears in her eyes. For days on end she would disappear just to spite me, sleeping with other women and even men; but then she would return, weary and repentant, offering to introduce me to the people she'd seduced.

And I would go. Was it out of curiosity? Or was I basking in the victory of Kaya coming back to me? It was always late at night when we met up with her flings. Me, Handan Sarp: the soprano, the diva who appeared occasionally on television and in the newspapers, the reclusive and cowardly lesbian, always toeing the line of society's rules!

I agreed a few times to meet those vile women. For Kaya it didn't matter if they were fat, thin, tall, short or even masculine, behaving for all the world like what I call "old-fashioned lesbians." In the dim light they'd eye me from head to toe, glaring all the while at Kaya, and in the end they'd sweep us from their lives. Most of them were married and wealthy but had never heard of Handan Sarp. It meant nothing to me that they thought that I was married, had children and had found myself a lesbian lover with my husband's money. I said "a few times." But it was more than that. Some of them were Kaya's on-and-off lovers. With husky voices they spoke of their husbands and in-laws and blathered about their sons and daughters. Many of them were gamblers that Kaya had met in her days as a card dealer. But some of them were new.

I went and met those men who came to Istanbul from Izmir, Bursa or Germany to take care of business, whatever that could've been. And at first, even though I'm by no means unattractive, they'd brush me off as just some woman in her thirties; but then, the attempts at seduction would begin. Shamelessly they'd propose threesomes: "Girls, I'm man enough for the both of you!" And then opera would begin echoing in my ears.

That all came later. Eventually I told Elem everything, thinking the time had come. But in the beginning, I only told her about my separation from Kaya. As for the rest, that came after Elem and I had become close and I could open my heart to her.

We slept in our clothes. As Kaya slept, I held her in my arms. And as I held her, I saw that she was washed clean of the streets and her youth and innocence blossomed. I was pleased that I'd brought her home. With me, she would forget the streets, the casinos and all the trying times she'd been through. That would be my gift to her.

I was given the gift of music, of opera.

Cemil Sahir Bey, his fingers decked in rings, was playing the piano. It must've been 1968. So many years have passed, and as I aged, my voice was left behind. Cemil Sahir Bey passed away. But what of his rings? Flashing with rubies, diamonds and turquoise as his fingers flitted across the keys. "Sing, Handan!" And I began with the first notes. What was the song? It was an autumn day and I can still remember my nervousness. Behind the piano there was a large window, through which I could see the sun-dappled sea and the Istanbul skyline.

The song ended. Cemil Sahir Bey rose and approached me. I was terrified that he might say, "You're a failure."

He kissed my forehead. "Handan, I bequeath upon you the gift of music, the gift of opera—all of it!" His ringed fingers stroked my cheek. His fingers were warm, but the stones on his rings felt cold against my skin.

We slept in our clothes. Though I was afraid of waking her, I gently stroked her hair and cheeks, and traced my fingertip across her eyelashes. Her cheek twitched. In her sleep, she hugged me.

It was morning and Kaya was sleeping.

It was morning. I was thinking of a summer morning. Though I'll never be able to remember the day, or the month, I know it was 1968. A young woman sings an aria, impatient for life to begin. Sitting at the piano is an elderly man. Istanbul smells of the sea. When the song is finished, Cemil Sahir Bey opens the window, flooding the room with the scent of the sea. The sea!

We smelled of cigarettes, alcohol and cheap food.

Kaya slept peacefully. After traipsing through the streets, she'd found a warm room. She was used to finding people she could sleep with. And now on her list was Handan Sarp. "So, you do opera . . ."

"Do" opera!

She's dead, I was saying. She had another attack. The woman who "does" opera is dead, dead! But I can always sense her corpse nearby. They don't bury that corpse. It follows me constantly.

I think about her death. She put a bullet through her temple. Cut her wrists. Threw herself from the eighth floor. Drowned herself like Virginia Woolf. Turned on the gas like Şevkiye May. My thoughts are filled with lonely, despondent women. Drowned in the sea.

But the sea is calm. The sun is setting, and the water is pulling away from the mossy stones. First, I'll see the evening star. The sea whispers . . .

It was you who killed the woman who "does" opera!

Cemil Sahir Bey abruptly takes back all the music, all the opera. The skyline of Istanbul fades away, and so does the sea. I put my arms around Kaya; in our sleep, we begin kissing, and I pull Kaya toward me, close to this body in the throes of death.

Now and then, you stop and look back. It is good; it makes your mistakes, your faults, visible.

The occasional flight of fancy. Who could object? We all need dreams. Through them, we distract ourselves from our drab, dry lives. When our dreams collapse in ruin, we keep on going.

For me it's an obsession: I go to sleep thinking of Elem and awake with her in my thoughts. Am I merely looking back? I don't think so. I'm trying to bring back to life the times I spent with Elem, conjuring up what was lived. I know it's impossible, but the temptation is irresistible.

I spoke of Kaya because of an aching desire to relive the beginnings of my intimacy with Elem.

Desire? Do I truly want back the first days that Elem and I spent together?

I'm at the cafe in Nişantaşı with Elem: she's sitting across from me, and my shawl with ice-blue flowers falls off the chair. Elem picks it up and folds it. I was probably crying this morning. I revealed my secret to Elem: I fall in love with women. Is that something that women say? That they fall in love with women? Elem listens to me with concealed compassion. She takes my hands in hers: "Don't be sad."

With that moment, the memory of those days weighs on my heart. I want to live that lie again. I should flee from those days, flee far away!

I told Elem:

When she awoke the next day around noon, Kaya went out into the garden. She was surprised: "It's like a small forest hiding among all these buildings. The Handan Sarp Forest."

The weather was still cold, but it was a sunny day. "Kaya, you'll get to see this small forest in the spring," I promised.

"Do you have breakfast here?" She was standing beneath the crepe myrtle.

I leaned against the garden door. "I mostly come out here in the evenings. Lonely evenings. Just me, by myself."

"What kind of tree is this?"

"Crepe myrtle. It's also called lagerstroemia and acerola."

"It has so many names!"

"Originally, they grew in India. But the Chinese started growing them too. It's a kind of shrub."

"It's like a sculpture."

"At the end of June it blooms, purple-pink and lavender flowers. Thin, delicate blossoms. I've always been fond of it." I turned to go back inside.

Kaya said, "Your garden is just like you."

I took it as a compliment; I was still young.

Soon our formal forms of address turned to the familiar form of "you."

As I remember it today, the month of June seemed achingly far away. That may be a small detail, but it is reflective of me. I wanted to get away from the stranger in my home and take refuge in a time when she'd be gone from my life. Much, much sooner than June, when the flowers would bloom.

But Kaya acted as though she had no intention of leaving. She smoked cigarettes in the garden, walked around, yawned and stretched, looked up at the balconies, gazed out the windows. She did every possible thing to get on my nerves.

Taking her to lunch seemed to be the best way of getting her out of my house. If she tried to come back again, I'd tell her that I had work to do at the opera.

With a small brush she pulled from her purse, she tugged at her long hair in the mirror. Then she put on lipstick and mascara. In the daytime, she put it on even more thickly.

In those days there was a restaurant across from the American Hospital run by a woman who made home-cooked meals, and that's where we went. We ordered crepes, joking about the fact that we'd just been talking about crepe myrtle. It was past lunchtime and just a few tables were full.

In my memory, that afternoon comes to life in all of its details. Sunlight shines through the window, illuminating Kaya. It's almost as if I can't see her for the light.

"You should plant a laurel tree in your garden," she says.

The stunted laurel in the garden is a memento of Kaya.

She spoke of laurel trees. I was surprised at how much she knew. New sprouts, she said, are covered in green and red down, and from a distance they look black. She said that she liked them because they don't lose their leaves in the winter. The yellow-green flowers give way to deep blue fruit. But if you break off its leaves or branches, the laurel will turn sullen.

Kaya also told me the story of Daphne, who had vowed to never belong to a man, but one day Apollo fell in love with her. He approached Daphne but she refused his advances. Again and again he tried to seduce her, so she begged Zeus for help. Just as Apollo caught her in his arms, Daphne turned into a laurel tree.

As she spoke, my thoughts turned to the leaves of the laurel. Or maybe that's how I remember it. Memories, feelings and time are all jumbled together in my mind. After all that pain, my memory has begun to weaken. I'm afraid.

But there were laurel leaves in the opera *Norma* as well, in which Maria Callas played Norma. I first saw her on a page of the magazine *Hayat*: Maria Callas was wearing a crown adorned with golden laurel leaves. She was walking, hands held out in front. It struck me as odd that someone would pose like that in a photograph. I could see the stage and the soprano with her crown of golden leaves. That was the first time I saw the word "soprano." My first soprano. My memory latched onto that word and the image. I kept going back to that page. My mother said, "We're late, this isn't the time for reading." I went outside. On the street, thoughts of Norma, sopranos and laurel leaves swirled in my mind.

"Are you going to plant a laurel tree?" Kaya asked, smiling.

I merely nodded.

Her smile faded. When our eyes met, she asked, "Can I see you again? Once in a while, when I feel lonely, like you on your long evenings . . ."

I sensed that a new grief was entering my life. I borrowed the waiter's pen and wrote my number on a napkin: "You can call me."

Where had she found that miniscule laurel? We planted it in the garden. Kaya was as ecstatic as a little girl: "My own laurel! My laurel, growing in your garden!"

I share so much of Kaya's loneliness in that way. Home, garden, clothes . . . "Things that belong that to you." They were all so removed from her. Her only taste of the feeling of ownership came from a tiny laurel tree. And it never really grew.

Kaya. Who was she?

There's no need to conceal it: I fell in love with Kaya. It was probably sexual love, more like passion. But the feeling changed over time, and I began to despise her. Often, she would disappear for days, even though I'd opened up my home to her and even given her a key. What terrified me, however, was that even though I hated her, I couldn't let her go. I felt as though life would be unbearable without her. She once watched me perform *La traviata*, and later that night, she held me and wept. "Why are you crying" I asked. "Because," she replied, "my body is also for sale." A shudder ran through me. When she was gone, I missed her. It never occurred to me to flee, or try to push her away. It drove me mad that I was bowing down before love. I was overwhelmed by an oppressive feeling of sorrow.

I'd said that we'd just talk for an hour, but it was already nine in the evening. I was getting tipsy, and Elem was late getting home. But she listened to me pensively.

As though we were very close. Too close. We were accomplices. I understood why she had come so recklessly, why she didn't hesitate when I expressed my desire to see her: we shared the same secret. She'd realized that long before.

My Munise was demure. She'd never say that she was running late or speak of her worries, disappointment or pain. In her relationship with me, she was always withdrawn and silent.

It was my turn to be concerned: "You shouldn't make your family worry about you."

"Would you like me to stay with you tonight? That way, I could also see Kaya's tiny laurel," she said.

I looked into her eyes. I'd never dreamed she would say something like that.

She was calm and determined. In the light, her eyes appeared green. Without awaiting my reply, she rose to make a phone call. I stopped her, and called to the waiter, "Can you bring the telephone?"

But her family refused to let her stay out. I didn't hear what Elem said on the phone. While gazing at her face, so beautiful and yet heavy with sorrow, I noticed that when she was upset, she tended to blink her eyes. She hung up the phone, head bowed: "I have to go home now," she murmured. "They told me I have to go home."

God knows how overjoyed I was that night, thinking that she might stay with me. Perhaps it was just the alcohol.

We left together. Despite her objections, I dropped her off at home and took the same taxi to my place. On both trips, I saw Şem-i Dede's tomb. On the return trip, I asked the driver to stop, and I opened the window. "Here," I thought to myself, "in this misty, bluish light, is where that saint of the poor sleeps for eternity."

What is it, my dear?

I'm thinking of our first days together; no, all of them, all of the days we were together. Yet again, it is evening. I don't know how many nights have passed since our separation.

Is this love, or compassion?

For a long time, those were one and the same for me. But it was never reciprocated. Except for those moments when you were my Munise. Dusk falls. You're probably leaving work now. If I were to rush to the boutique and wait there, I'd see Elem from a distance. Elem, with no Handan in her life. Where will you go? Didn't we always call each other as the day came to a close to say where we were going?

How strange; without an ounce of fear I'm thinking of my Munise, as though we hadn't parted. Undeterred by regret, I smoke cigarettes one after the other, enough to bring on death. Handan Sarp has lost her voice; she'll never sing again. She has lost the most beautiful gift that God granted her.

In the dark blue light of evening, I doubled up, sitting in front of the window, my mind a blur of thoughts: a new despondency, new ordeals, a new hopelessness. The old grandmother explains which reed bed it came from, and where it wants to return; her eyes well with tears. She tells which reed became a *ney* flute. *You became a ney for me, my one and only, and you never spoke bitterly of separation.* The grandmother murmurs, "Mevlana, was it a lie?"

The ney speaks of longing, the grief of distance and separation. *You didn't listen; ears deaf to the song, you left.* This evening, wracked by yearning, I long to escape this cage of flesh. Hasn't the time come yet, the time of eternal love born of compassion?

As though you had returned, again and again I listen to the same song, a song awash in a flood of joy: "Casta diva." *You liked that song. That night you and I turned the volume all the way up and listened to the song in the garden, heedless of the fact that the neighbors might think I'd lost my mind. It was the first time that you enjoyed opera.*

The old grandmother knew nothing of opera, of "Casta diva." She knew nothing of Çalıkuşu and her granddaughter, or the sound of a distant ney.

It is night again and I'm listening to the same music. The furniture is the same, the armchair in which you always shyly sat. No one is home, and you're in a home I've never been to. Evening falls. Did you turn on the lights?

What about the connection between Norma and Mevlana? I say to you: "It's the human desire to rise up toward God." I say that, and a slight tremor runs through you. Even though my words may not express it, a moment occurs in which both of us feel as though we've drawn closer to God, and those people who mocked and scorned our love are damned and driven away. And I say to you: only love can heal, only music and art.

But now, we've become estranged.

(Parts of the next section were smudged by tears and were unreadable. Sİ)

I listen to the same song so that you won't be so far from me. That song, always the same song.

Midnight. After midnight. Those novels that, in my youth, I read and loved. I understand now that I read them so that I could write these somniloquies . . .

I was drunk during the day, but I'm okay now. I vomited. It was dreadful, and embarrassing. What agony is this? What are these regrets? What has happened to me? Why do I feel so humiliated?

In the distance, dogs howl. They are afraid of the night. But cats prowl quietly through the darkness . . .

In Pendik, summer came last to that old narrow lane, perhaps because it didn't get any sunlight. But it would come all at once. Every morning I would run and look at our lane, and one morning, summer would have arrived. Leaves burst forth, flowers bloomed in a splash of color and the earth gave morning the gift of mist. The reddish brown branches of the strawberry tree would be adorned with bright green buds. In the fall, the tree's fruit would become a fiery red. Everything was suffused with color and light.

Elem, if only we'd spoken more. If only our life together hadn't ended. In my imagination, we spoke. Just for a few minutes. Your voice whisked me away from the banality of this world. Just a moment ago we spoke. You brought a poem.

I'm trying to remember what we spoke about, but my imaginary conversations with you fade quickly from memory.

My love, sister of my heart, you came to me with all of your compassion. In my somniloquies, I want to tell you these things. One day I could die, without having expressed my feelings to you. I had been afraid to love.

Just now, I saw that person I was afraid to love on the lane with the strawberry tree. It was a summer morning, a day from my childhood. She was leaning against the trunk of the tree. Elem. She was there. Always with me . . .

Rather than feeling like a separation, it seems as though you've simply gone on a long trip. You'll return and put your arms around me. You'll say, "I'm back, Handan. The pain is gone now."

You hide behind the tree. You're picking the fiery red fruit, and popping them into your mouth: "They're sour, Handan, just like sour cherries!" But no, that's impossible. We'd never talked about that shadowed lane, nor about the strawberry tree that caught the summer light. Autumn meant leaving Pendik and returning to the city. We didn't talk. You hid behind the tree, just to hurt me.

Then, Elem fades from sight. There's no tree, no fruit, no leaves. Just darkness. In the morning, I'll wake up exhausted.

You sleep. Your eyelids are closed, and I cannot see your beautiful hazel eyes. I awake, and gaze upon your face. I see your innocence, as though painted by a Flemish artist, your purity—you know nothing of evil. You gave yourself over to me, sleeping by my side.

Housewives have always frightened me. Women who marry, take on the burden of children and lay waste to their lives with their husbands. I'm also afraid of divorcées and widows, but not as much as women with families; they aren't as judgmental.

To sweep the tedium of their lives under the rug, to sweep aside their unhappiness and loveless marriages, housewives always meddle in the lives of others. Especially when such women get together.

I remember that when I was a child, my mother and I went to visit one of her friends in Maçka. The details are vague, but that day was burned into my memory. I can remember the scene in all of its repugnance as if it were yesterday.

It was women's tea day. That's why we'd gone to that plump woman's apartment. There were end tables covered in lace, a sideboard, tacky knick-knacks and wedding pictures in silver frames.

Standing by the window, the plump woman said, "Come quick!" Everyone, including my mother, rushed to the window. The tulle curtains were drawn, and they stood there, peering outside. Something compelled me to approach as well. "There they are!" she said, pointing.

Across the street there was a tree, perhaps an acacia, with clusters of white flowers like a shimmer of silver rain. Under the tree there were two women, one middle-aged and the other much younger. They were probably saying good-bye and had just embraced. The young woman turned and began walking up the street. The other woman stood there watching her. The young woman turned a few times and they waved to each other. The silvery rain of the white acacia flowers.

Our host, the plump woman, exclaimed, "My God, what a disgrace! Right out in public, without a thought for what others may think."

The women moved away from the window. "Really?" they asked, raising their eyebrows.

"Don't believe what you've heard. They really are living like husband and wife."

I didn't know what it meant to live as husband and wife.

"Come now, you shouldn't gossip like that."

"What gossip? They left the curtains open once, and I saw them kiss each other on the lips."

Kissing on the lips. That was also unknown to me.

Then there was a heated conversation, punctuated by shrieks and coarse laughter. Only my mother remained silent, perhaps trying to force a smile.

I found myself pulling at the curtains.

They had forgotten about me, or simply didn't care. Their voices died down to a whisper, and they sounded like conspirators.

That day, I learned a new word when one woman said, "Are they sapphists?"

"What's a sapphist?" I wondered.

Kaya and I also had farewells like that, in the middle of the night under acacia trees. Those partings pained me, but I kept my silence and even smiled as I waved. When and where did I tell Elem about those partings? I told her everything.

A Saturday evening, winter. Kaya unexpectedly came over. She wanted to have a drink. In those days, I didn't keep alcohol at home. I drank occasionally, but if I had a heavy night of drinking, I wouldn't touch a drop for days. I called the corner shop, asking for a bottle of vodka.

"Don't you have a performance tonight?" she asked.

"No, not for another two weeks."

A despondency came over her, as though she regretted she'd come. She took her eyeliner from the small purse that was always slung over her shoulder and went to the mirror, freshening her makeup.

I don't like unexpected visitors, but I was pleased that Kaya had come. A few drinks would warm us up, helping me cast off my inhibitions. Drawn together, my lonely Saturday evening would be warmed by human touch.

But as she put her eyeliner back into her purse, Kaya said, "I'll stay for one drink, but then I have to go. My friends are waiting for me." My hopes for the evening crumpled.

"Whatever the hell she wants, let her do it," I thought. I gave the delivery boy a tip and brought the vodka into the kitchen. My hands were shaking as I prepared the glasses, lemon juice and ice. Kaya hugged me from behind. But I realized that we could be seen through the kitchen window.

Memories of that plump woman from my childhood flashed through my mind. The same nightmare as she howled, "They were kissing on the lips! Are they sapphists?" I tried to slip from Kaya's arms. She held me tightly; even without a single sip of vodka her body was warm, and I could feel her heat pressed against me, her femininity brushing up against my thigh. She kissed the back of my neck, and I trembled. "Don't," I said.

"Fine," she answered, and, without looking at me, took her vodka and left the kitchen. I swallowed down half of my drink.

That was the night of acacia trees. Later, I would follow Kaya onto the streets.

Despite what she said, she stayed for a while, drinking in careful measures and looking out into the garden. I'd always thought that girls who grew up on the streets don't know how to handle their liquor. I told her this, and irritably she said, "In the casino, no one ever dared try to get me drunk." That's not what I'd meant. But if she were to get tipsy, I thought I could persuade her to stay. But I didn't have the courage to say that out loud. And in any case, Handan Sarp was the one having drink after drink.

I must have looked forlorn, because she said to me, yet again, "Being with you makes me want to cry. Your eyes are filled with such pain." Letting your guard down always brings on loneliness.

She felt pity for me. The day had dwindled into darkness, and she suggested, "You should come too. I'm going to meet up with two of my friends." The thought of refusing never crossed my mind; it was Saturday, and I had no heart to bear the loneliness I felt. I got dressed, and even put on a little makeup.

I didn't know who she was going to meet. What kind of people were they? Could it be the girl from Diken Cafe? But I was in no position to ask.

We went to a small bar on Valikonağı Street. It's a clothing shop now, but in those days it was a standing-only bar. I was surprised that I'd passed the place so many times but had never noticed it. It was packed with couples, the usual Saturday evening crowd of young people. They were the young working type, scraping by in life, but on Saturday night they would get dressed up and go out on the town. Music was playing in the background as they ate sandwiches and drank beer.

Kaya's friends came, two young women. I can't remember the other one, but Bedia stands out in my memory. Despite her heavy makeup and flashy dress, she looked disturbingly like a man. I've never seen such a masculine woman. At first glance, you might think she were a transvestite. But a transvestite would never want to look so manly! With her shoulder-length hair, she moved like a gladiator, and when she shook my hand, she nearly crushed my fingers. She seemed to know me: "I've heard of you. Were you interviewed in one of the newspapers?" No, it was probably the magazine *Rhapsody*.

I guessed that Kaya had told them about me. Bedia eyed me up and down, and said, "You're an attractive woman." I remember blushing hotly. The effects of the alcohol had worn off. The other girl had a cheap, sleazy look about her. "What a fine mess," I thought. What had I gotten myself into? What had Kaya told them about me? That we sleep together, that I'd taken her into my arms and offered my bed to her? Alcohol was my only solace. After sitting there for a few hours, even though it was quite late, they decided to go to Master Bey's. I looked at them blankly. Bedia sidled up to me: "Don't you know what that is?" she cooed. "Tell me, what does it sound like?" She laughed gruffly, and tried again: "Do you understand now where we're going?"

I glared at her condescendingly. It may have seemed that I was in control of the situation, but that was far from the truth.

What a coarse creature! She brought you down to her own level. I didn't understand why she behaved as though we had a common past. Soon enough, I would understand why.

Where were we going? At first I couldn't figure out what she'd meant. Moment by moment I was feeling more uneasy, almost to the point of anxiety. "I should go home," I thought. "I should just run out of here."

But I couldn't bring myself to leave Kaya. I thought of how affectionate we'd been at my flat. Saturday night. All those Saturday nights I'd spent utterly alone, nights when I wasn't at the opera.

The relationship between Kaya and that girl perplexed me. They shared a strange intimacy that seemed to be born of repulsion and attraction. A kind of spent passion.

And I was right. Bedia was Kaya's ex-lover. Proudly, Bedia told me about the bond we shared. Kaya would later tell me, "She helped me through some difficult times." Financially. Would I be expected to do the same?

Bedia was cool, indifferent. She was rich to begin with, but now she was making even more money. The reforms introduced under the

Özal government had served her well. As a business woman, she'd scored successes after the coup of 1980, taking out loans and investing in the service sector. Putting on the airs of a proper working lady, she went on and on about how we had to catch up with the times.

Men came around to our table, apparently friends of the young woman with Bedia. They were caught up by Bedia's speech about the new government. Captivated, in fact. The place was crowded with yuppies, the generation of tomorrow. Why not? There was no difference between those men, Bedia and those yuppies, and I had no place among them.

Lines of music drifted through my mind: "Ah, Alfredo! Our love will end, shrouded in darkness."

The rest of the night is a blur. We went to Master Bey's, which looked like a hangar. Music blared from the speakers as young men and women danced under the flashing neon lights. Everything appeared and disappeared again under the lights, and I had a splitting headache.

Of course I didn't dance. Handan Sarp doesn't dance. Occasionally Kaya came to where I was slumped in a corner, and asked, "Are you okay?" I wasn't. My life was being shunted away along with my voice. The music that would save me was drowning in the cigarette smoke that filled the club. Songs thundered in my mind, the songs that I knew and loved. The songs that I sang.

Kaya came again, putting her arms around me. At last, our bodies had come together. "You should leave," she said. The lights pulsed. I tried to pull away, but she hugged me even more tightly. Her makeup had run, her hair was damp with sweat, and her eyes shone. "This isn't the kind of place for you."

"What are you going to do?" I asked. It took all my strength not break down in tears. I was spiritless, ashamed.

"I'm going to stay with the girls. That's what Bedia wants." I could see her shameless desire in the way she smiled. But then she seemed apologetic. I knew that I would never forget her ambivalence. Her attitude changed again; she pressed up against me, resting her head on my shoulder. Under the flashing lights, for some reason I was reminded of a sculpture of Mother Mary cradling her son after the crucifixion.

"Why Bedia?"

"She wants to make love."

"Damn both of you!" I whispered. The horrific music drowned out my words. Kaya took my hand and led me through the crowd toward the door. I was like a sleepwalker. The hulking doormen knew Kaya. I hadn't noticed that when we came in. They opened the creaking iron door. Lightning flashed.

There was a late autumn thunderstorm. I saw a row of bare acacia trees across the street, dotted here and there with bunches of dried flowers illuminated by the silver glow of the lightning. I let go of Kaya's hand and started running. She cried after me, "Handan!" but I didn't look back. I had no idea where I was running to or where I was.

Elem,

We are summoned by water. It was always the water that called out to me. In the distance, I saw a sailboat, a ship; perhaps a ferry. On the sea. Standing on the quay and looking into the distance at the horizon. That happened to me: I stood on the quay, trying to look beyond the horizon. The sea called out to me. The sea summoned me from all of its epochs. The roar of the sea. My face, my skin, my eyes were burned by the salt. How many times did I tell you about the calling of the sea and water? Even in the very beginning. Kaya, the sea, the quay. How I stood paralyzed at the quay, unable to set forth upon the water. Kaya isn't enough. But Elem is. Soon,

*in the sea and the infinite, where her name is found. On the quay, I'll be
saved from this death that is life. Soon.*

That same night toward dawn, the phone on the nightstand rang.
In my dream the phone had been ringing. That happens to me sometimes. I hear sounds in my dreams and then again when I awake. In
my dream I was running after ringing phones in my apartment, at your
parents' apartment and at the house in Pendik. My heart pounding, I
answered the phone. It was Kaya.

Kaya! "Can I come to your place?" she asked.

I couldn't believe my ears. Overjoyed, I tried to find the light
switch. My anger and loneliness vanished. "Come now!"

In the background, I could hear the pounding of music. What
time was it? She was probably calling from the same place.

"I don't have any money," she said. "I can't pay for the taxi."

"I'll pay for it when you get here. Come."

I had awoken from a death-like sleep. I tried to remember how
I'd gotten home. Soaking wet under the acacia trees, I'd stopped, not
knowing what to do, hoping I would see Kaya, hoping she would
leave, unable to bear seeing me go. Aside from the doorman, no one
else would've seen me. He was probably looking at me as I stood there
alone at that late hour, looking for all the world like a washed-up
prostitute. After a while, a taxi approached. Most likely I waved it
down. Did I start to cry? At home, as I put on my nightgown and a
cardigan, I was crying. My feet were cold, and I pulled on some wool
socks. In that state, how could I ever be Violetta! I despised myself,
and the opera was beginning. I was listening to the overture—Violetta
was ill—and now the curtain would rise, revealing Violetta's sitting
room in all its splendor! Nobody should be there. Nobody. Lamenting
Kaya's absence, I drifted into sleep.

But now I was sober and alert, putting on the morning gown that Nedret had given me for New Year's. That might have been the first time I ever wore it. But all that mattered was that Kaya was coming back to me (that time!) and that night of agony was over. She'd left Bedia for me. I rushed to the door of the apartment building in my silk morning gown. The rain was pouring down in torrents on the empty street. I waited, not caring if anyone saw me.

Kaya drunkenly clambered out of the taxi, in a state unfitting a girl of her age. I was happy, but this was tempered by a feeling of resentment. Holding Kaya's hand so she wouldn't topple over, I paid the taxi driver: "Is this enough?" He eyed both of us; God knows what he was thinking: "Sure, that's fine."

I told Elem everything so that she would know that I lose myself at times.

"What happened to Bedia and the others?" I asked Kaya.

"They left me. Bedia found a new girl. If it weren't for you, I wouldn't have had anywhere to go."

I was just beginning to learn about the lives of these half-prostitute, half-lesbian street girls. My entire being wanted to rise up in revolt.

She snuggled up to me. From Bedia she had desired passion, but in the end she brought me compassion. I listened to the sound of the rain.

Bedia. I never saw her again. But I'll never forget her behavior that evening. By what miraculous feat was she able to transform all that femininity—her lush dyed-blond hair, breasts like Anita Ekberg, voluptuous thighs—into something resembling a gladiator? What was she trying to prove?

Bedia wanted intimacy. But her fawning attitude, innuendos and capriciousness revolted me. Once she saw that I wasn't responding to her, she turned on me and grew distant, even ignoring me. Trying to play the queen of the evening, she joked around with those yuppies, bursting into peals of laughter. The fervor of her ambition was astonishing. I'd been erased from the evening, which in any case suited me better. I was just a woman, tagging along with the young crowd. That's the role I'd played. I was desperate.

Bedia wanted to rise up against the world, but that wasn't enough for her. She was determined to take over the world, and everything was hers; everything was for sale and Bedia could buy anything she wanted. As she danced, she rent her life to pieces. Nonchalantly, Bedia made a gift of that strumpet to the men in the bar, and later was quick to remind her that she was her "property." One minute she would be composed and courteous, and the next belligerent, surly and obscene. If you were no longer of use to her, she wouldn't lift a finger to save your life. It was a terrifying experience: I'd met one of the "rising stars" of the day.

I followed the news about her in the papers. Indeed, just as she'd said, she was moving up in the world. We all know the story. She was a successful business woman who started as a partner in foreign investments and moved on to a holding firm, and from there branched out into media industries, ever growing, even becoming a patron of the arts. News about Bedia appeared everywhere: in the economy pages of newspapers, in celebrity reports, on television talk shows. Somehow she'd managed to adorn her gladiator style with an air of aesthetics. The huskiness of her voice seemed shockingly genuine, and her lips were always twisted in a bloodthirsty smile.

A number of scandals broke out, and her name came up in accusations of smuggling historical artifacts and of mafia drug dealing, but she always managed to emerge unscathed. Of course I didn't make a habit of keeping up with her successes. My ideals were different. But we were living in the "age of Bedia's," and in that age, my ideals were doomed.

A few years ago, I was asked to sing in a rather dull and sentimental rendition of the musical *Zeynep of the Seven Villages*. That was the first time I'd ever received such an offer, but I turned it down. The organization sponsoring the production turned out to be a bank, one of the major shareholders of which was Bedia. Perhaps it was just a coincidence.

Nights of sex and nights without sex. Two kinds of nights.

Nights with Kaya seething with sexuality. Nights with Kaya filled with suffering. And many nights in which we were plunged into churning whirlpools of loneliness.

For Kaya, my home was a place of refuge from her men, women and friends. When I say friends, I mean unhappy streetwalkers like her. She called in the middle of the night, her voice trembling: "I sold my body for money and I've started using drugs . . ." But she wouldn't say where she'd been, where she was calling from or why she called.

Please, let it be over! God, let this relationship end!

Then she'd return to my "glass menagerie" and stay for a few days. She wouldn't wear any makeup and would become young again, like a child. The nights of suffering and refuge would begin. I told Elem about one of those nights. Until that day, I'd never shared it with anyone.

That was Kaya before her life on the streets, before the hotels, casinos and Bedia's. Kaya as a child. A distant memory.

It's heartrending, and difficult to tell.

"You're like a mother to me," she said, weeping. Many nights were like that. But I couldn't help her; there was nothing I could do.

"If I'm like a mother, then tell me what happened."

It's all a mystery. In that childhood mired in poverty, what hopes could there be? No school, no toys.

It all came crumbling down. Without having lived out her childhood, she was forced to become a young woman.

She said, "Turn out the light." We sat in the dark. A deathly glow spilled in from the garden. In the dark, like a mother. Her words were jumbled and I couldn't understand everything she said. Occasionally, she'd break into sobs.

"Would you like me to wipe away your tears?"

"No."

It began to sound like a somniloquy. Words hung in the air, disconnected. I held and stroked her, and then showered her with kisses. It was like a children's game. It had been her father or older brother.

"Who did it? Who?!" I shouted. Who!

"Please don't ask."

Her face was a mere shadow. I could make out lines of ashen sorrow, like soot, like mist. It was unbearable.

I thought of my own protected, spoiled childhood and felt ashamed.

Elem listened. I was choked by tears, but I realized she was unmoved. She said, "There are so many girls who've been mistreated like that."

Even in those times, I think my Munise, who was just starting down the path of life, already knew so much about the world.

It was over with Kaya. In the early hours one morning, it was truly over.

I was sleeping. But it wasn't a calm, peaceful sleep. That was probably a few days after I had first met up with Elem. My life, desperate and broken down, had gone to pieces. I avoided people. I didn't see Semra and Ali very often. We only talked at the opera, just a few words before a show or later at night. Kaya's absence was an ache for me. I was at home, completely alone again. The doorbell rang.

I awoke in a fright. I thought: "Am I imagining that someone is ringing the bell? Is it just my fantasy that someone will come?" But then I heard it again, the clipped ring of the doorbell, a light knocking, the tinkle of the bell. I was afraid.

Then I thought I heard a whimper. It sounded like Kaya whispering my name. Perhaps it was a premonition? I went to the door: "Handan, let me in! Please, open the door." I opened the door and there was Kaya, in a terrible state. "Can't I even miss you?" she whimpered. She stepped toward me to hug me, but I backed away. She was swaying, on the verge of collapse.

She reeked of a meyhane, like the foul smell of leftover food and dirty plates. "I slept with some asshole."

I thought she would start crying.

But she didn't.

I looked at her, almost in a state of shock.

"Is there no kindness left between us?" she asked.

She came in and collapsed into a chair. My mind was blank. I had no idea what I should do. It seemed like the right thing to say, so I offered to make some coffee, but she refused. She was talking about kindness and compassion. I turned on the lamp, and she asked me about the laurel. But all I felt was a cavernous emptiness. I felt nothing. None of it seemed real, as though I had made it all up. The men she slept with, the darkness in her life, the days of sorrow that we shared together, it all seemed like a product of my imagination: her suffering, my longing, her grief. At such a moment, what could be as preposterous as a laurel? Tomorrow, actually that morning, after dawn broke, the laurel would be gone.

"Don't worry, I'll leave."

"I'm not worried, Kaya. But I think it's better for both of us this way."

"What is?"

"Knowing that our ways have parted." My voice was firm.

She got to her feet, as though suddenly sober. Her lipstick was smeared and rubbed off, probably from kissing. The zipper on her small purse was half open. Kaya was looking at me, as though she'd seen Handan Sarp as a dead woman. But wasn't it all just a dream, a love fantasy, the impossible dream of love between two women?

In my mind, I was shouting, "You said you'd leave, so go!" but I forced a friendly smile. Kaya saw through it, of course; she'd lost her faith in my love and friendship. Her lack of trust was obvious. Straightening the ashtray, she dabbed her finger into the ashes that had spilled onto the side table and turned to me: "Can I hug you one last time?"

I recalled that she'd wept while watching my performance of *La traviata*. She'd said something like, "I'm just like Violetta." Was it *La traviata*? No, it must have been another opera. Was it when I played Norma? The last time. We embraced one last time. A shudder ran through me, a trembling that was almost orgasmic. If it lasted another second, I'd be defeated, and we'd begin passionately making love. My passion was for Kaya, and Elem meant nothing to me at the time. I had already forgotten her.

"Good-bye," she said. "I'm giving you back your opera."

I could have gone into a fit of rage. How could she say that after sleeping with some man? But pain enveloped everything: the anger, the hatred, the early light of dawn. Soon, I would be in darkness. Pain wouldn't cover the darkness. Pain can never cover the darkness.

At that moment I knew that I needed to prepare for my first morning without Kaya.

(For months I've been working nonstop on Handan Sarp's novel. But what have I achieved?

Handan Sarp's narrations and writings have tired and unsettled me. First, listening to her and then the recordings, again and again, as I work on the text. And her somniloquies! The handwriting at times is an illegible scrawl. Then trying to put the narratives in order, and editing and re-editing . . . At times, I'm moved by her story, but at other times I feel like washing my hands of the whole thing. I could write an apologetic letter telling Handan Sarp that I simply can't write the novel and give her back the cassettes and texts. Liberation! It has become overwhelming.

But at the same time, it has a certain charm. I find myself attracted to the disarray, the uncertainty surrounding events, the rise and fall of characters, the perpetually elliptical sentences.

Waking up to a morning that finally hints at spring . . .

I awake to a morning that finally hints at spring. As though there were a morning that I want to remember, I say over and over, "It was the morning that . . . It was that morning . . ."

In the passionate novels of the past, there were certain words and sentences that evoked the atmosphere of a novel:

"Evening was settling in . . ."

"It was a calm evening . . ."

"In the dark of the evening, she smiled . . ."

It was always evening. I can't really recall any such "morning sentences."

Should novels begin at night, take place at night and end at night? *Evening Sun, One Evening, Last Evening of Summer.*

When you read "Evening was setting in . . ." it brings you back to nights of the past because, as I mentioned just a moment ago, such words ring of those impassioned novels, like an embrace with the romance of bygone times.

Handan Sarp's novel, on the other hand, is relentlessly harsh.

The refuge of evening.

Where would I like to be? At this hour, when Istanbul has been transformed into a wash of color and silhouettes, where will memories take you? Whose memories?

I find myself in one of the neighborhoods mentioned by Handan Sarp as I search for the tomb of Şem-i Dede. Had she described it as a misty blue light? It's strange; even though I've been writing down her narrations, for some reason they don't stick in my memory. I should find the garden with the lilies at that wooden house on Nemli Yufka Lane (not Elem's house—the other one). How am I going to describe the soprano's expression as she looked at the lilies in the garden, all alone? An expression that is now infused with images . . .

I search up and down Rumeli Street but can find no trace of Nedret's boutique, nor of the life on the street that I'm looking for. Everything is shadowy, indistinct. It's concerning.

It was morning. There are those deceptive spring mornings when you wake up feeling invigorated, refreshed and rejuvenated, and flights of fancy fill your mind.

"I've been saved!" I shouted.

Was it a memory or a dream? I, Selim, as a student in the last year of high school. He was armed with hope. It was a day in June—it had to be, because those were the days of final exams—and he was bursting with delight. One of his short stories was going to be published in the magazine *New Horizons* the following month. He'd become a writer! That was many, many years ago.

Disappointment had not yet set in. The drive to write had not yet worn thin. Such ambitions fade over time. Only the dregs are left, and the sufferings of life in society. Ideals crumble and hope breaks apart.

When I shouted "I've been saved!" I meant liberation from Handan Sarp's novel. It burns like acid.

If you start daydreaming of a June morning years ago, it's a reflection of the desire to relive the past. To save something of yours, to make a fresh start. Write a novel that brims with hope and smile at others out of goodness; people should smile at each other out of goodness. Just like you took the ferry to the islands of mimosa.

But Handan Sarp says the opposite. Over time, we lose everything we began with. Let this morning fill with the scent of lilacs; let the mimosas bloom on the island to your heart's content. The enthusiasm of youth has long since faded.

Weren't those the days of the literary magazine? Impatiently, I'd wait for the next month's issue to come out. Poems, stories, essays. I'd sit under a sycamore tree with a fresh bread ring and cheese, reading under the green light filtering down through the leaves.

Those days seem so distant now. It's all gone: the writing, long nights discussing literature, morning breezes. Writing about those things has lost its meaning. They are all, in fact, faded dreams.

Morning. A light breeze. The lilac in the rear garden, like the lilac in Handan Sarp's garden, has begun to bud. Overhead, a clear blue sky. But the words . . . One by one, the words have begun to fall away. Just a few years ago, I would've been intoxicated by such a morning and written about it, like smiling at a memory of a morning or a breakdown. Like confronting your fear of the future.

I went to a seaside cafe in Yeniköy to read over my latest frustrated attempts at editing Handan Sarp's novel. But I couldn't. Although it was quite early, the cafe was crowded, filled with couples, wealthy intellectuals and students skipping school. There was also a group of plump women resting after their morning walk, looking like a fashion parade of tracksuits. It was their fault, I told myself, that I couldn't focus on the text. But that was a lie; I simply didn't want to read it. Sunlight beamed through the windows of the cafe, reminding me of fires I'd seen in my childhood. I was escaping from Handan Sarp's novel.

I had an urge to leave the cafe and take a walk along the seaside like in old times, forgetting Elem and Handan, the novel, and even that spring morning. As I was putting the manuscript into my satchel, a piece of paper slipped out onto the floor. It was a note that Handan Sarp had written to me.

I should probably thank you.

But in the end it doesn't really matter if you write about the story of my separation. Perhaps it isn't even worth it. Nonetheless, the way that you silently listen to my story has touched me. I have a desperate need to open my heart.

As you left this evening, you said, "Handan, you shouldn't stay at home alone so much."

I gave you my word that I wouldn't. But I was frightened by the cold night. Cold and silent. I thought of calling Ali and Semra but changed my mind. Everyone has their own order in their lives. And who would want to spend time with a woman weeping over her lesbian lover?

You know that I try to save myself from this darkness by listening to music and reading, and at times even watching television. Don't worry, it won't happen again; I won't kill myself. Alcohol and cigarettes are all I need. I guess that means that I'm ready to be alone.

While going through my bookshelves I came across a copy of "Hamlet," and I eagerly started rereading it. Such thirst for power, passion and hypocrisy . . . It's terrifying.

Selim Bey, did I ever tell you that in my youth, I read "Hamlet" voraciously? I would come up with twists to the story that would have petrified Shakespeare. Before dying, Ophelia and Hamlet would be reunited. No one would find Ophelia's corpse. Hamlet wouldn't make his speech to the skull of the poor court fool. Wearing a white gown, Ophelia would be held in Hamlet's arms. Ridiculously childish, isn't it? I thought it was.

Selim, have you ever made up fantasies like that? I remember in one of your essays you said that you always prefer the bad characters over the good ones. I found that idea interesting. Is that a way of protecting yourself against life? It would mean that rather than Ophelia and Hamlet, you like the king and Gertrude. I never would have thought that.

As for me, I played the role of the merciless soprano. My life was always filled with longing but I was never able to actually miss anyone. The terrible thing is this: believing that Ophelia and Hamlet were reunited, but never being able to miss anyone in real life.

By the way, please don't think of me as some pedant prattling on about Shakespeare . . .)

I went out for the curtain call and saw you applauding me. I can always pick you out in a crowd.

Kaya wept for Violetta. But you, even though you didn't like opera, wanted people to applaud me. You were nervous because I was singing on stage, perhaps you even sent me your prayers.

Elem, I kept your goodness to myself like a secret of the heart.

Those desolate days dragged on. A long, clingy Istanbul winter. I had withdrawn from everyone.

Ever since we'd spoken that night about Kaya, I hadn't heard a word from Elem. For a while, I was bothered by the fact that she hadn't called. Why had I told her my secret? Just what was that secret? Kaya, or my lesbianism? After a while it fell from my thoughts. I was comforted by the thought that this "young seamstress" wouldn't—no, couldn't—say anything about me. She wasn't in a position to say anything to Nedret.

No, I wasn't comforted.

I never have been.

It wasn't just my life, my desires and my weaknesses that wore me down. I could see the lives of others around me, the society in which we lived: Turkey, a country that was said to be developing day by day. The universe was writing its memories. With its million dollar cigar, it tore through everything. The nouveau riche attended performances at the City Opera, and bedecked with their jewels, furs and perfume, they held aloof, posing for photographs as an army of chauffeurs awaited them in front of the opera house. They said that they "admired" me and my colleagues as they shoved bouquets of flowers into my hands.

I could see that the end had come for opera, and, more importantly, for its authenticity. With a tasteless bouquet of flowers in my hands, I stood awkwardly on the stage.

It seemed that winter would never end. The trees and shivering plants wore snowy garments. No flowers bloomed. I hoped for at least a few snowdrops.

When I was a child, how surprised I was when, on a rare day in the park with my father, I saw a group of blossoming snowdrops, the whites of which were like a rainbow with their fine variations. My father smiled at my excitement. I never saw another snowdrop again.

Snow is falling into my life, which doesn't even feel like my own. Everything merely flashes before my eyes. I can't manage to put events into any kind of order. Just moments ago I was a young girl going to the seaside with my mother, looking at the islands in the distance. Then it is night and we're sitting at a night club on the shore, the islands aglow of lights. But I can't understand why the lights flicker all the time. Aunt Nadire says, "That's how they look in the distance," and she sighs: "Just like life." And with that, childhood is over. My mother is embarrassedly explaining what it means when you become a woman, but little does she know that I'd been through that traumatic experience long before. I was disgusted by the blood, and despite my fear I spoke to no one about it. The girls at school giggled at me. I wonder if every girl is cruelly hurled into life the same way. And my mother, blushing beet red, was trying to explain it to me. Neriman—I'll never forget her name—had asked me, "Have you gotten your period?" and then laughed knowingly, saying, "As soon as you get your period, the other girls will too." But it wasn't like that. Over and over I read *The Wren*, trying to understand Munise. Then *Turandot* starts, and under the full moon on the stage I'm pleading; with my voice and supplication I'll change love, I'll change life. Such ideals suffocate me. Like choosing a picture, I pick out days, years, nights from my life. The first girl I ever fell in love with! She was a school friend. I remember Neriman's name, but not hers. From a distance, she pointed out the person she was seeing, a bow-legged irritable-looking boy. They met secretly and had secret telephone conversations. She asked him to kiss her breasts, and she showed them to me. I was stricken. In those times, I was just learning how to control myself and my feelings and desires. I teased her, saying, "Be careful or you'll pop your cherry!" No, I'm not there anymore, the days of my sexual awakening, the throes of sexual longing. Soon I'll be at the piano, and music will heal me; I imagine that I'll be like everyone else. And that meant flirting with boys. But I started making love with Kaya. The flirting with boys must've just been a slip of time. During the most intense period of rehearsals, when I needed her the most, Kaya left me for a whore, some guy with money, or a society bitch. Which opera? Who was the director? Who was the conductor? I don't know. All that remained was Kaya's cruelty. I went to Master Bey's looking for her. "She hasn't been here," they say, "not for a few nights." Under the white blooms of the acacia trees, I suddenly think of Massenet's *Werther*: "Leave, let me weep a little." Yes, let me weep for Kaya's cruelty, my screams and my resistance against myself. I resisted and didn't break down. Then I see Elem; she's cutting pictures out of magazines and newspapers with her beautiful hands scarred by work but still lovely like a child's. She's cutting out photographs of me and articles that mention my name. "What are you going to do with those?" I ask, and she blushes, avoiding my eyes, and says, "I like them. They make me feel proud." I'll pay for that goodness. I'll have to pay for all of Elem's goodness.

I always lived my life wanting to pay something back.
But I never had anything to give.

It has stopped snowing. Night falls. The snow stretches out like an undulating sea. Everything is bathed in blue light.

The sea has not called to me in a long time.

First I see the magnolia tree in the garden of the villa that looks like a seaside summer house. It's strange, I seem to be walking in Kireçburnu. A sudden hunger comes over me; perhaps I should buy some pastries from the bakery. These past few months have taken their toll on my mind and spirit. Elem and I are practically living together. Some might say that we are a homosexual couple. But I despise that term. How could I transform a wildness like homosexuality, like anarchy, into family life? I'm afraid of hurting Elem. The magnolia blossoms anew. Or am I just secretly happy? There's a young woman who loves me madly, my young seamstress; a happiness that I've tried to conceal even from myself. If only the magnolia blossoms would bloom!

After everything is over with Elem, I'll pass by there again, one morning when I'm feeling claustrophobic at my apartment, which feels like it belongs to a stranger; I'll rush out into the morning. Flowers sprout from behind the wall. The air is heavy with their scent, and I await the sound of the sea. It's such a tranquil morning that even the surly sea is silent. Not even the sea shares in my pain; even it has left me, as the blue waves churn with hope.

She called. She called me. She called that day.

"When are you coming for the fitting?" she asked.

I was surprised. "What fitting, Elem? I haven't ordered anything."

She laughed: "I thought maybe I could trick you into coming."

"Why haven't you stopped by? One evening, after work, you should . . ." I was astounded at my own audacity.

She cut in: "Can I come tonight?"

Later she confessed that she'd calculated the day, knowing that I wouldn't be at the opera, but she said she had been nervous because perhaps I would be busy or wouldn't want her to come. I said just one word: "Come." My flat was a mess, and I set about tidying up, wondering: "What should I prepare? Would she stay for dinner? What should I wear?" Then I did something rather out of character and called Semra. I told her that Elem was coming to visit me. Had I wanted to invite Semra as well, as an escape from the young seamstress? But in the end, I didn't ask Semra and Ali to come. "Send her my regards," she said.

We're in bed. We're making love, shamelessly. That's the only way to describe it: shamelessly. "How did we get to this point?" I wonder, but I cannot pull my thoughts together. We hadn't talked about Kaya, or about sexuality.

Wrinkling her nose, Elem had drunk a glass of whiskey. I had drunk at most two or three, but it went instantly to my head. I think we were criticizing those wealthy women who squander away their money. At one point, I mentioned that I wanted to visit the tomb of Şem-i Dede when the purple clusters of flowers were in bloom.

It had begun with a gesture of kindness. Turning to the bowl of salted almonds on the end table, she said, "You haven't had any." Was her hand shaking, or had I imagined it? But I saw that her lips were quivering, and her nostrils flared.

I felt something, a fiery longing. I took the bowl she offered, and at that moment, kindness was transformed into something savage. I pulled Elem toward me. "Don't!" I thought to myself. "This is a complete mistake! She might reject me, I'd be disgraced. She's just a girl . . ." Immediately I composed myself, but Elem took no notice. She settled in my lap, put her arms around me and closed her eyes.

All rationality vanished. With a sexual passion that verged on fury we began exploring each other's bodies. No vestiges remained of my composure. Driven by my longing for human touch, I kissed her.

But even at such moments I feel an irresistible need to analyze my childhood, my character, my essence. I'm withdrawn; I read novels and listen to the music coming from a house in the distance. And I look out the window, watching the rain, pulling into myself. At one point, I climbed trees, wanting to be one with the sky. They say that if you pass under a rainbow, boys will become girls and girls will become boys. I ran and ran, trying to pass under the rainbow. But it's impossible; it was always faster than me.

In my schooldays, I dreamed of being Norma, even if I didn't know who she was. There was that photograph of Maria Callas with her crown of laurel leaves in the magazine *Hayat*. But another desire, another love, wreaked havoc on my passion. Although I wanted to fall in love with men, I found myself drawn to women. The boys my age were no more than brothers to me. But later, when I saw her, the one whose name I can't bring myself to say, the love that I felt for women with the passion of Norma was ingrained in my heart. I'd given up on the rainbow, but I wished that women would fall in love with women and men would fall in love with men. The incurable pain of life. I'm like a prisoner, caught between men and women, different from them, different from everyone.

Who am I?

Will I never be able to live my own life?

I was perplexed by the young woman lying in my arms. Who was she? What was the attraction between us? Sexual desire? Social pressure? Loneliness? My mind swirled with questions. New questions that could change for both of us. Was it the difference in our ages, or our different lifestyles and financial backgrounds? I was just getting to know Elem. But the old fears nagged at my mind: perhaps she would just use me. Perhaps she didn't like me and just wanted to take advantage of my weaknesses. But she was so young, childlike and innocent.

The unease set in once again, the pestering doubts. She was obviously no stranger to lovemaking. Perhaps she was much more experienced than she appeared. My introversion and questioning tormented me.

She had initiated our lovemaking. Her cheeks burned, and she whispered lasciviously into my ear. In my fantasies, when I brought myself to orgasm alone, I had silently shouted such words. But to hear them from Elem! Could this young woman in my arms be the same Elem as the somber seamstress I'd seen at the boutique, a girl who looked sorrowful even when she smiled? Her lascivious words had startled me; far from pleasing or arousing me, they were hurtful in their coarseness, and I thought of telling her to stop. But just then she pulled back, responding to my kisses and caresses with embarrassment, and as her words softened to expressions of gratitude, I felt that I was with a complete stranger.

Although she made love with a masculine aggressiveness, she preferred giving herself over to me. Under my kisses, she would surrender her body to mine. Little by little she let down her guard. But her compassion always flowed forth, which frightened me. When the sexual fervor has ebbed away in a relationship, regret and coldness take its place. But attachment and compassion never fade. In her embraces and caresses I sensed a search for love.

When we embraced, she'd say such strange things that I was taken aback. What she said seemed meaningless, and it saddened me. "Did you know," she said once, "there is a realm of dreams in your home. The furniture has a certain dignity, a humility, and the dark reddish browns in the living room and the pale blues in here are so unpretentious. Just like you, Handan." (Was that the first time she ever called me by my name?) "Just like you, they are shy. The flowers in the vase look like you picked them in fields after the rain. The jonquils are so humble, and the small red carnations, because of their color, are timid."

Was she trying to charm me?

"I'll never have a home like this," she lamented. "I don't know anything about decorating."

"You will," I told her. "A home as tender as your heart."

I don't think I even knew what I was saying. And today, I laugh bitterly about it. In those days, I was working hard to help my Munise have a home of her own. My friend Gelengül, the woman so proud of her mustache, had told me with a knowing glance that I was making a mistake and no good would come of it. I thought she was just being distasteful.

Elem had her own concerns. She'd been so conditioned to think that a young woman of her class could never leave her family and move into her own home that she couldn't even raise the subject with her parents. But I pushed the issue: "What's so crazy about the idea? A lot of working women live on their own. If some people don't like it, that's their problem."

She often fell into despondency, especially when she had arguments with her mother. Tense and tired, she'd come and answer my persistent questions with silence. The arguments were always about her moving out, which was a bigger issue now that her sister İnci had gotten married.

"Why shouldn't a young working woman start her own life? Don't worry if they disagree. They'll complain and hassle you for a few days, but they'll get used to the idea."

I wanted Elem to have her own home so that she could live her life. I wouldn't always be there for her; she needed to learn how to live. If homosexual women don't learn that their lives will pass in loneliness, and if they don't learn to bear that loneliness, they'll fall prey to that scourge called society, which will torment and scorn them.

I became obsessed with the idea. Even when Elem's home life was going well and her mother had stopped nagging her, I'd tell her about an inexpensive apartment I'd seen. I was saving money for her, buying and selling bonds, and collecting interest on my accounts. So that she could be free.

My own home. Didn't I have difficulties when I began living alone? Hadn't I waited for my mother's death before moving into my own place? My family isn't even working class.

After my mother passed away, Aunt Nadire kept saying, "Let's move in together," even though my grandmother had taught her the freedom of living alone. But I didn't remind her of this, to spare her heart.

When I found this apartment on Sakızlı Street, I was overjoyed.

By moving there, I'd be saved from the house I grew up in, a house full of reminders of my mother. I left everything as it was, except for a few pictures and trinkets. I decorated my apartment, which Elem liked so much, over a long period of time. Money was scarce. I wasn't Leyla Scala, and I didn't perform at La Scala. Although I had a few performances abroad, they paid little. Step by step, over a period of long lonely years, I brought an order to the place that was my own.

My dream house was entirely different. And impossible. I wanted a house near the sea. The balcony door or a window would be left open, and the sea in all its shimmering blue would spread out before me; it would be so close that I could hear the sound of the water. On some days, I'd hear the crashing of waves.

But my dream didn't end there. The balcony door is open, and the tulle curtains blow in the breeze. I probably read about this in a novel, but the scent of jasmine would fill the rooms, and I'd hear the chirping of crickets as the reflection of light from the sea would dance on the ceiling.

But I gave up on my dream house, and tried to create my own world here.

Days have passed, and I'm completely alone. I have no one except for Kadriye Hanım. On most days I see her, but no one else comes. I don't want anyone to come.

I think of Elem. My thoughts verge on savagery; I destroy her, or I destroy myself. I destroy what we lived together. Awaiting news from her, I realize she must be dead because I've heard nothing—the dead don't communicate with the living.

Walking past Nedret's boutique, I want to laugh and shrug my shoulders. But at that moment I notice a small detail, such as scaffolding set up around a building where repairs are being made; that lifeless thing breaks something inside of me. I wonder if, as she passes by, Elem has seen that they are painting the building light yellow and moss green. Rather than simply shrugging as I walk past the boutique, I'm overcome by an inner darkness as the old anxieties and regrets flood through me, and my rage threatens to drive me from sanity.

Kadriye Hanım asks me what's wrong. It seems I'm not the same as I used to be.

I'll never be the same again. Never.

I should focus on her story, and forget my own.

For twenty years now I've known Kadriye Hanım, perhaps longer. At a young age she was widowed and left with five children—three boys and two girls. Her husband had a perforation of the heart, but the doctors didn't realize it. Kadriye Hanım neither wept nor complained; she worked hard and did the cleaning at my flat, but she always broke something, as if she were trying to get revenge. They'd moved to the city from a village. I know little about her family; I've seen her daughters, and just one of her sons. Their story was always remote for me.

Once she was a stranger to me, but now Kadriye Hanım is the closest person I have in my life. I can sense that she wants to protect and look after me. She's much more talkative than she was in the past, and sometimes even talks about her husband. The other day she showed me a picture of him, pulling the tattered photo from her purse. For some reason I found it odd that she kept it. "I always keep it with me," she said, but then seemed embarrassed and stammered, "As a reminder." It was strange to me; it never would have occurred to me that for people who do nothing but slave and toil all their lives such a memento could be so moving. For twenty years I've taken advantage of her labor, and she doesn't even get help from the state. Her children all grew up and she has nothing left. "May God protect you, Handan Hanım," she says.

For years she's been wearing the same black coat. In the summers, she wears a black cardigan and a gray head scarf with black flowers. When I used to give her my old clothes, she'd say, "The girls will be so pleased." But her daughters have grown fat, and neither of them ever married. I think that one of them was engaged once, but the engagement was called off. They no longer fit into my old clothes.

That's all I know about Kadriye Hanım. A summary. A barren, spiritless summary drained of life.

Since she knew nothing about Elem, I don't know why she wants to look after me. She never once saw Elem at my apartment. Occasionally she speaks with Ayşe Hanım, the building custodian, but what could Ayşe Hanım tell her? That there was a young woman who used to come and go, but she doesn't come around anymore? No, it's not interesting enough to be worthy of gossip. Ayşe hadn't paid any attention to Elem. Shrouded in the mystery of my fame, my existence at 27/1 Sakızlı Street goes unnoticed.

Kadriye Hanım must have sensed my loneliness, that bleak loneliness that pervades my life.

On some days, I flee my flat before she comes around to visit. To the sea, the winter sea. Despite the gray skies, the air is clear. The seaside is cold. Where am I going? Standing by the sea, I shiver. Nature heals; perhaps shivering will do me good. What's left of me? I'm just a woman who's been spared the sword, nothing more.

When I return, Kadriye Hanım smiles and says, "Ah, you're back," as though she wants to cheer me up.

Both of us had gotten dressed. She hugged me again. The lascivious words she'd whispered in my ear as we made love still throbbed in my mind.

"Elem," I said, "are you sure that you want to be with a woman?" I had to ask; it was the only ethical choice. "You'll get used to women's bodies. No one should ever shape another person's life."

Her gaze was firm: "I'm no stranger to this. It's good that you told me about Kaya. Our hearts are the same."

The hour had grown late. She refused to let me take her home: "I'll go by myself. You can't come every time."

It was our first lovemaking, and our first parting.

It can happen that two people may never see each other again. It can happen that red candles leave stains. The wax stain on the white table-cloth that Kadriye Hanım could never get out. "Let it be," I told her, "don't bother." Elem, I need to gather my thoughts. I'm feeling unwell again this evening. Today, dusk resisted the coming of night. Winter days sometimes dwindle into strange dusks in which everything seems different, as though reminiscent of our loves. Just when evening appears to have arrived early, cutting the day short, the pale winter sun holds out, refusing to give in; the sky remains light, a yellowish thick light that resists the falling of night as though trying to soothe the pain in my heart.

My heart aches.

I went out into the garden; it was bitterly cold. I asked myself, "Is Elem cold? Does Elem know that I'm cold? Does she think of that?" I asked questions, trying to answer them myself, and I heard voices, our voices. We were talking:

> *when i'm with you handan i don't get cold*
> *where are we elem? we are at the seaside, walking*

When you said that, I began walking. I was afraid, but I wanted to mock my fear. A group of young men and women passed by, joking, laughing and shoving each other. When was that? I walked like this, alone. It was probably in the autumn following our separation. I was walking toward Kireçburnu. Perhaps I would have a glass of tea. They had sealed the windows of the teahouse, so maybe I could get warm. All the flowers had fallen from the magnolia tree. Judas tree!* With the coming of autumn, the fruit of the tree ripened, covered in dark rust-colored fuzz, and the vibrant red seeds burst from their pods. For years we passed by there. In summer there were flowers like white forsythia, and in autumn the fruit that resembled a pinecone. "Fruit? How could that be a fruit?" you asked. "How could a magnolia ever have fruit?"

When the crowd of young people left, I looked in the direction they had gone. The winding lane was empty. That was a road of desolation. In the crisp autumn light, I could make out in the distance the colors of small boats of fishermen at sea: one was red and green, another one teal. It was mackerel season. Elem, I'm so cold. The lane has begun to fade from sight, as well as the shoreline, and with the coming of night the boats chase their reds and greens, and white foam flecks the sea as the waves send up blue-green spray. In the distance a shadow approaches me. Could it be you? Have you returned?

But I'm in the garden, not on the shore; there are no magnolia, no fruits like pinecones bursting with bright reds seeds. Just over there is Kaya's stunted laurel. Kaya faded quickly for me. But you—

my time with kaya isn't over, nothing in my life ever ends
i bore the weight of everyone who came into my life

---

* The Judas tree is also called a redbud. Handan Sarp mistakenly used it here to refer to a magnolia. (Sİ)

In my final moments of that long evening in the garden, you, my one and only, weren't with me. You must've been cold. Since we aren't together any longer, you must always be cold now.

But that time you betrayed me:

Handan, don't you understand, it's over! I'm starting a new life, a life that will never include you! It won't ever be the same, what do you want from me?

i don't want anything from you, nothing at all. i don't expect anything of anyone

I closed the door tightly. Evening was coming on. Trembling, I collapsed into the chair, burning with fever. The phone rang, but I didn't answer it. The magnolia is the Judas tree. I never told you that because I didn't know then. I know it wasn't you calling just a moment ago; that's why I didn't answer the phone. I curled up into the chair. Soon, the evening ritual would begin: a little alcohol, some spirits to stave off death.

But this evening mustn't end in such disarray. Anew, everything anew! I'll set the table, where you and I used to sit together, and as I start life anew I'll raise my glass alone in a toast, Elem!

You were always the one who got the tablecloth from the bottom drawer of the sideboard and you always set the table. Wanting to smoke a cigarette, but knowing that I wouldn't, I quickly prepared dinner.

After clearing off the table, I spread the tablecloth and there was the red candle stain. "It wouldn't come out," I told you. "Kadriye Hanım tried but she couldn't get it out."

"It's better this way, Handan. Now it's a memento of us."

A memento of us . . .

Wax stains can happen. Red wax stains can happen. The lights are out. The unlit darkness of night. The garden lights are like yellow droplets. You freeze, throat knotted up. You can smoke without fear, Handan, there's no longer any need to worry. Now, the candle stain; it stained your life as well, seared in by a hot iron.

Elem, to you I'm a candle stain.

I removed the tablecloth, unable to bear the sight of it. I didn't bother trying to find another one, and gave up on the idea of setting the table.

The lightless dark of night could be a reflection, forever repeated: Has she fallen asleep, is she happy, is she okay?

When you get lost, when you lose yourself, everything dwindles: the regrets, the shame, the desire to defy the world. I understand now that the world is a nothing that should never be challenged, a nothing! My cry of "nothing" will resound through all the streets of the city and Elem will hear it.

Elem didn't hear it—she never will.

I returned from the rainy night. Such a pleasant, yet piercing, autumn rain. The streets were nearly empty, just a few stragglers on Rumeli Street and the traffic lights flashing red.

i returned from the rainy night
when parting from you, rainy saturday nights
is today saturday

I promised myself that I wouldn't drink. Your voice, your voice! Distant, hoarse, choked, but still so near. Listening to your voice is something akin to happiness. I rewind the tape on the answering machine over and over: "Handan, it's Elem." How many nights did I spend listening to the recording of your voice?

What happened? After such a long period of silence and resentment, what is this sleep, weariness and joy? Constantly calling, constantly starting, constantly saying: where is she this morning, this evening? Listen to the rain. Is she troubled? Don't be. Does she miss me? Elem should never be sad.

A deep blue wave rushing in from the sea fills the room. The sea fills the room with darkness; it is the sea of my mind, my refuge. On those Saturdays when I waited for you, I hated this sea. On those Saturdays when I waited for you, this sea was magnificent and the sky was blue. It was always spring. Even if I didn't feel like making love, I would always freshen up as though we were going to. Six o'clock? I must shower! Scented soaps, Amazone perfume. The lovers and love-making is over, it's all over: the shouts of children, the street cats that sneak into the garden. Knowing that we wouldn't, I would still get ready as though we were going to make love. Our bodies had wearied of each other; Elem's expectations bored and repulsed me.

It isn't her body or sex that I miss. It is her heart, the beating of her heart. I used to put my head on her chest and listen.

Do you remember that too?

Ever since that night, no matter where I go or what I gaze upon, I think of that separation that I was powerless against.

Just the other night, there, on the fabric. Red candle stains. In the darkness of night, bathed in candlelight. You can strip your heart bare and examine life. You can pray. You can take refuge in God.

People should die. Happiness comes rarely. Death should have come when I was happy.

I returned from the rainy night and listened to your voice. For days I listened. I thought of your days, but I was afraid of thinking on your nights.

We were in front of the window facing the garden and other

apartments. You wanted to kiss me. "The curtains are open!" I whispered. "Let them see!" you said. Shameless lovemaking. "Close the curtains, they're going to see us." Let them see. Perhaps it was love that made you speak like that, in defiance of everything that forbade us from being together.

With your previous lover, your first (I never asked who she was and you never told me, some young beauty I suppose), you practically made love on the suburban train.

I knew you by that time. I knew that you had a secret life.

Your secret life in the past frightened me. I didn't want to know.

"I want you to take my virginity." Elem, you must be out of your mind.

I go back to the rain and watch it fall, rather than drown in those memories.

"I'm a virgin."

Elem, shush!

Munise and Feride were neither male nor female. When the curtains are closed, society's norms are at peace.

handan i want you to really make love with me
with you, i can share kindness, compassion and love

Turning away, I refused to let you embrace me. I got up; where is my morning gown, Nedret had made a morning gown for me, a gift.

"Handan, won't I be yours forever, until death parts us?"

The mad passion in your voice, which was there just a moment before when you asked for the unaskable, gave way to fear.

They are still candle stains.

The ney always laments separation. Listen. In those days when I didn't know you, it was in the distance, buried in loneliness. My breath passes through the ney, turning into fire.

Your focus on virginity seemed so banal to me. "You'll have a long life, Elem." My voice trembled. I wanted to shout: "Get out of my sight, do you think it's been easy for me? Those lesbian girls screw whomever they want to lose their virginity!"

But I held back and lapsed into silence. A cloudburst of grief. With the courage of old age and impending death, for the first time during my adventures in this world I told myself the truth: Handan was the one who took Handan's virginity. Because she couldn't bear life and the morals of others.

Now you know, Elem. You had always wanted to know.

I walked and walked, and on the empty streets I saw that Munise was by my side. Pain in my heart, I smiled at her.

I'm better now, Elem. Better than before. I don't feel the pain as much. But it persists. I've grown accustomed to it; we have become brethren.

Elem, who wanted to make love with me in front of the window, who wanted to make a gift of her virginity and—how else can I say it?—who left me. I'm fine. There's nothing wrong at all. I'm sober as I write these lines.

I waited until the end, the very end, to make love with you with the curtains open. We were in our small garden. I was aroused and assailed you. The possibility that the neighbors could see us from their windows and balconies excited me, rousing my lust. I undid the buttons of your blouse, which was made from inexpensive cloth. I could because it was over, it had never been—not with you, nor anyone else. Leaning toward you, I caressed your breasts and kissed your chest.

Once you wanted to make love when the curtains were open, and said, "Let them see!" How quickly that passed! Where had that sudden shyness come from, cowardly seamstress? You ruined my life. Everyone ruined my life: women and men, people I slept with and people I didn't sleep with.

It doesn't matter. I'm not going to drink. Ever.

Elem, in that moment when I wanted them to see us, you grew distant and afraid. I take pity on myself, and on you. Deplore the rules that destroy our lives. I'm not going to drink tonight, Elem. The rakı glass sits before me.

I'd made a decision: I thought at the time that I'd never be with a man. But there have been men in my life, after I was thirty-five, forty. I was promiscuous in those days when I'd grown weary of you. I didn't love you when we were together.

It's a lie, my dear! I'm lying to you. My undying compassion for you has never faded. It won't tomorrow, nor the next day.

"No," I said. "No, Elem, not forever. Only until death. If we're together . . . No, that will be your decision in the end."

I slept with men.

The first sip. The smell of anise burns my nostrils. Tonight I'm fine, I can take my memories into my arms with kindness. Tomorrow? Tomorrow I could be drowned in pain again. But tonight I've made my peace with it.

It was difficult to decide. What's expected of men? Men entering you. No, there will be no men in your life. Afterward, I slept. I become drunk quickly; a sudden state of ruin. I slept with men. They probably thought that I'd been "broken in" by a man. There should be a better word than "broken in," something more violent to describe that "fall."

It was during one of my performances and I was walking toward the front of the stage. Which autumn was it? I was playing Lady Macbetto, taking the stairs step by step. Scotland in the Middle Ages. I was wracked by pangs of conscience. If I killed him, then I killed him; nothing more can be done. Just one time Lady Macbetto. I wandered the nights in my sleep. After wandering the night, why would anyone fear anything? I descended the stairs, bellowing, mocking the witches of fate because they thought that they'd shaped my life and my destiny and because the other witches in life had damned me and hurled curses against me. A few opening nights; pure farce! On the premiere night, there were women in evening gowns and men in tuxedos—and I wanted to sing to a young seamstress!—and I descended the stairs down from my life. Out damn spot; red stains on my palms. I would kill on my own but I'd already been killed. And if you consider what the witches said, I'm suffering from the sting of guilt and the blood will never be washed from my hands, never! I won't ever give in to anyone.

There were around ten performances. Lady Macbetto wore a deep blue dress, a blue that I couldn't distinguish from the color of the night sky.

Did Lady Macbetto truly live? Was there a blue dress and a life taken down step by step?

Is separation something to be feared, my dear? For me, there is no separation from you. But there was the suicide of Madame Butterfly . . .

It's all over, Elem: Munise died. Just a few moments ago.

çalıkuşu, ill and sullen
was smiling wasn't she, her teeth like pearls
and munise returns from afar, from suffering, and looks at her,
at çalıkuşu, ill and sullen
the tears in munise's eyes have dried, but there are droplets of tears in
her sleepy lashes

They give Munise and Çalıkuşu a room on the top floor of the summer house facing the sea. The sea! The sea, in a majestic blaze of light.

But mine is dark, my sea is dark and starless.

Far in the distance, guitars at a night club play for the sea's shimmering greens and reds. The two of us, my Munise and I.

Everywhere, everything ended in disappointment.

The bare arm of my dearest one—your arm!—slipped from the silken sleeve.

I held your bare arm. I wanted to kiss you one last time. Memories of you holding my hands and kissing my palms surged through my mind. You didn't know that I would clutch your hands and weep into your palms. Time will pass, Elem, and you will remember. Elem, who is no longer Munise.

"What time is it? It's over, isn't it?"

Death came to Munise as gently as moonlight. Death kissed her with mother's lips. Death didn't frighten Munise, my girl.

I could never be its peer; I couldn't even be death.

Life should signify something, but I had stripped mine of meaning. I was throwing my life into the streets, and I needed to find a way out. For a long time I thought on that. Those were the days, weeks and seasons that I slogged through, the hours passing unnoticed. As though I weren't even alive. I had but one obsession, one fixation: separation! I slept and woke: separation. I forced myself to spend more time with others: separation. Semra and Ali would come and drag me out on trips to the islands, the Bosphorus, Belgrade Forest and the Black Sea coast, but everywhere it was the same: memories swarmed upon me, suffocating me, memories of separation.

I told myself it was sheer folly. Had Elem been my lifeblood? I'm not as helpless as that. But that obsession had sunk its hooks into me, destroying everything. I was on the verge of falling ill—perhaps I was ill—driven to illness by separation, by love. I had based my life on opera and lived through opera. No matter what, Elem was condemned to disappear from my life of opera. Looking back on our years together, I can see that our relationship was exhausted and Elem was but a shadow. The pain I suffered then was in vain, as I hadn't yet lost her.

However, opera had come to an end as well.

Opera has something in common with traditional *alaturka* music:

singing at the top of your lungs, and pleading. It's all about waiting, longing and pleading. But what you expect never comes and you're never united with your object of desire.

I was listening to opera; I was listening to alaturka. I was on the brink of losing my mind. But then I suddenly grasped the value of life. You can be cut off from everything and it can all be severed. But then you must start again, always beginning afresh, never succumbing to defeat. You can leave everything behind. And you should let go of those who leave you.

At times I had such moments of courage, shorn hope and fits of breath. Then crushing defeat, yet again. It would never be possible! I couldn't figure out why those things were happening to me. Waiting and longing. And my cries were all for nothing.

I was forced to start a new life without opera and without Elem.

But I still don't have the strength.

Serene days followed that first night when Elem and I became intimate.

We didn't talk for a while. I told myself it was better that way. It had ended before going anywhere; it started and then came to a close. But I was uneasy because our intimacy seemed meaningless and flawed. And I felt regret.

The fact that she'd whispered those lascivious words meant it wasn't love. No, she wasn't in love with me. In the beginning, love is spoken solely through words of compassion. Only later, after it has become tattered and exhausted, does love need sexual provocations and pathetic games.

In the very beginning I asked her directly: "How could you say such words?"

She said she couldn't remember.

"The words you said when we were making love."

We were sitting in the garden. We couldn't see the evening sun, which had set behind the walls and apartment buildings, but the sky was still bright. The light played across Elem's face, and her hair was set aglow. Her reaction to what I said was immediate; she began to blink. As if to sadden me, the color of her eyes kept changing in the light as her eyelids fluttered: from hazel to moss green, at times glints of star green. Head bowed, she fell silent, as she always did. My child, she always met my harshness with silence.

"Never mind," I said, but there was something sharp in my voice.

I think that was when she told me about her ex-lover. She said that it had become a habit. Her ex had played the male role and said such words. I told Elem what I knew about lovemaking between men and women, what I'd heard from my friends, and that men usually don't say such things, especially those from "good families."

But how could she have spoken such words when they didn't even have a place to make love? I didn't ask; I had no desire to know more about her past lover.

"Are you angry?"

The sun was setting.

"No, Elem. I was just surprised."

But later those words, those lewd words, would be heard coming from my own mouth as my sexual desire for her began to wither away.

Those serene days brought me happiness in the beginning. I'd been rescued from Kaya and the pain she brought me, and in the end, not a trace would remain of Elem. Handan Sarp was returning to her life of seclusion. One morning, I was getting ready to go to the opera to attend a memorial for my teacher, Cemil Sahir Bey. Elem called. I was irritated but didn't show it.

That day she was even shier and more withdrawn, perhaps even despondent.

"What happened?" I asked. When the phone rang, I was putting on my makeup; I had the urge to break the eyeliner pencil that I held in my other hand.

Because I was a coward. Only when I was on stage, when I was singing, was I myself. A change was coming over me.

Aunt Nadire hurriedly put on her holiday outfit and did her makeup like the film coquette Belgin Doruk, even painting a mole on her cheek. But I didn't have the chance to object. In Çemberlitaş everyone stared at her. Aunt Nadire beamed, soaking in the attention, and smiled boldly at everyone, left and right. As we walked that summer morning, she greeted everyone we passed.

We passed through a large door. The wooden building was large but old and sagging. Perhaps it had been a mansion in the past. We went up three or four marble steps. There were columns, and then the door. Royalty of old must have lived there. Aunt Nadire said, "It's just lovely!"

A man in a gray suit came to the door. My aunt asked, "Are we late? Where are the singing auditions?" He pointed the way. I saw other children my own age.

So much time has passed since then.

Double doors. And from behind the double doors comes the sound of a piano and singing. The sounds come to a sudden halt. The door opens and a child timidly emerges. Women reminiscent of Aunt Nadire, or men wearing suits and hats, run over to the children as they enter the room. Aunt Nadire is raising the hem of her gingham skirt, as though wanting to show off her lace underskirt. But to whom?

The singing and piano stop abruptly again. The double doors open and an elderly woman steps in. She's more heavily made up than my aunt. But it's different—her makeup isn't farcical, but rather somber, like a mask. The woman is wearing a mask of makeup, and says, without looking at anyone in particular, "Handan Sarp."

Aunt Nadire's lips are murmuring in prayer, "May God give you success . . ."

First there is the sardonic man playing the piano, his fingers adorned with large gold rings bedecked in jewels. How can he play the piano with such rings? They'll hit the keys. But they don't. I've never seen a man wearing so many rings. The fingers of Cemil Sahir Bey dance across the keys of the piano, and he says, "Sing these notes!"

Sing these notes!

Sing them!

And I sing them.

The woman with the mask of makeup, the mask-like makeup, approaches me: "Now you'll sing a song."

From that day onward, my courage will never fail me and I'll sing.

Courage! My father had come on a rare visit and all hell broke loose: "I'm not going to let my daughter become a singer!" he shouted at my mother. Aunt Nadire cowered. My mother took her revenge: "You should've thought of that before having a child." To my mother, Leyla Mahmure Yönder, and to my father, Şevket Sarp, I said: "I'm not changing my mind."

I asked Elem, "What happened?"

Her answer was unexpected, perhaps even unwanted: "I miss you. I miss you, Handan Hanım."

"We're beyond formalities, Elem. Don't call me 'Hanım.'"

My mind was churning with thoughts: perhaps my Munise thought that I'd used her for her body, that I just wanted to defile her and then toss her aside. That's how it usually happens. But maybe it wasn't just a matter of tossing her aside. That's how it appears to be, but in the heart it's different. There is fear, regret, hatred and disgust for oneself lurking in the heart. We seek out who is truly at fault. And, there is the pressure of that cruel immorality we call morality. And the fear of sharing your sexual secret with someone like yourself, your twin in sexual desire. Becoming two when you're one. Even Gelengül, shedding her masculinity for a moment, said with her ringing laugh, "Are you crazy? She didn't do the same thing for you?" Same *thing*? Thing!

Isn't that enough to pain the heart?

But there are other stings and pricks as well, such as conforming to society's absurd demand for concealment. Behind closed doors, as soon as you hurriedly finish your "business," you have to forget about it all that until the next encounter, until you are driven mad to the point of excruciating sexual loneliness and sexual crises, ignoring the pain of your other, transforming her into an object of sexual desire. It's complicated, and tedious. Long ago the power of disdain drove you cowering into a corner.

Did she think that of me? Is that what she thought I did? Had I corrupted the spirit and mind of such a young woman?

I mentioned fear and regret. She was so much younger than me. But when we make love, such things are forgotten. If it were love, perhaps that regret would've disappeared, driven away by suffering.

("Selim Bey, later, much later, it became a mutual addiction. But it was never love, not for me. An addiction that resembled love. Its twin. I thought it was mutual. Wasn't it? Because it resembled love, it pained me, like the pain of love. And that suffering brought me a new happiness.")

My spirit has left my body and observes in bewilderment what transpired, brooding over what happened between Elem and me.

"When will you come, Elem?"

"Can I come early this evening?" The pleasure in her voice was unmistakable. "I'm going to leave work early."

"I'll be waiting for you after five."

She came. She'd made a blouse for me, my first gift from her: a yellow chiffon blouse. She hadn't noticed that I don't wear colors like pink or yellow.

It was beautiful chiffon and obviously expensive. She must have saved up some money from the little that she made.

("You may be disgusted by me, Selim Bey, but for a moment, just a moment, I thought that maybe it was made with scraps from the boutique. Nedret sometimes gives them to the girls working there, acting as though it were a great act of kindness.")

Brokenhearted gifts. I became the recipient of such broken-hearted gifts.

I wore the blouse one time. Actually, the blouse didn't look bad on me, but it wasn't the kind of thing that Handan Sarp would wear.

Thanking her, I gave Elem a hug: "You didn't need to do that."

"I just wanted to."

But because I was so preoccupied with the color, I was blind to the fact that she'd somehow managed to sew a perfect fit just based on my measurements, without a fitting, using such a difficult fabric as chiffon.

Most of the time, I secretly spurned her other gifts as well. Perhaps, not knowing my tastes, Elem wasn't aware of this.

The second gift she gave me was a black porcelain vase. She bought it from a nearby street vendor when she came to see me one night after work.

I knew because I'd seen the vendors before. They sold vases, sugar bowls, porcelain picture frames with gaudy roses and flowers; cheap, miserable things for the homes of the poor. Why did the sellers even bother coming to Nişantaşı? Surrounded by such wealth and extravagance, it was tragic.

She must have seen my displeasure. How couldn't she? I said something like, "Why did you go to the trouble?" Blushing, she replied, "I saw it on my way here, and thought you could just put it aside somewhere." The whimper in her voice struck at my heart, but at the same time I was thinking to myself, "At least it's black and won't stand out too much." I was incapable of feeling any happiness or joy for her thoughtfulness, incapable of feeling anything at all. Nothing crossed my mind except for the thought that the vase had no place in my home. I made no effort to find a place to put it. Rather, I went out into the garden and cut a bundle of leafy branches, and placed them in the vase; it disappeared beneath the foliage. All the while Elem watched me.

Like poison . . .

Elem is gone. The black vase—just as Elem had said—has been put aside somewhere. On some evenings, I awake to Elem's scent: lemon *kolonya*, the perfume I bought her; the workshop, fabric, cigarettes. Then everything goes black. Her scent is transformed into that black vase. Burying my face in the pillow, I weep.

It was my birthday, probably our second year together. She'd bought me a miniature trinket chest made in India. A vile, petty sense of pride welled up within me; the way that she carried herself, her manner of speaking, her likes and dislikes had all changed. In place of a tacky porcelain vase, she bought me a small chest; it was cheap, but at least in good taste.

Those gifts: a decorative box or two, a few censers. I never expected any gifts from her. But why were they always the same? Didn't that reveal some carelessness or indifference? The same boxes, the same censers; I knew where she bought them. Little by little I began to feel hurt.

But I never showed it.

One day she said to me: "I don't want to come to your opening nights anymore."

She always sat far in the back, alone.

"But I'd like to send a bundle of flowers to you onstage. Like the others do."

"Stop with this nonsense," I said. But in fact I was secretly smitten by those flowers, bouquets and massive wreathes adorned with blossoms that are no longer a part of my life. For me, they symbolized victory. In that false world of opera, I needed the solace they offered. I've said again and again that most people feel nothing for opera but just want to be seen listening, watching and applauding. All the same, they should offer up flowers; there should be a price for the moments you spend in the presence of art.

That box, adorned with brass, saddens me now. I was blind to what it meant. Pay. It's my turn now to pay. For that censer, for everything.

"For the love of God, what flowers would you send onstage?"

"All the flowers in the world."

I laughed. I laughed at her. But now I'm silent.

Later she made some flowers and gave them to me; they weren't all the flowers in the world, but she made them herself, hoping that I'd pin one on my lapel. I wore that yellow chiffon blouse but grew increasingly indifferent to the fake roses, tiny bunches of violets and over-starched freesias. The flowers must be somewhere in a drawer in the wardrobe, tossed aside, wrinkled and torn, faded by time, stained and smelling of the mothballs that Kadriye Hanım puts in my drawers. Elem's flowers.

The gifts continued: a glass candleholder with blue-purple feet, a hair dryer, a rechargeable vacuum cleaner. I'd given her a bronze candleholder, one of a pair, and the other is still here, with me.* I was always telling her the same thing: "What need is there for such gifts?" And she'd hold out the small vacuum cleaner, expecting me to understand, hoping I'd love it.

I can't use the hair dryer anymore. In the past, I did. Mine had broken. But now I can't bear to touch it, that device of fire.

If only she hadn't given me those gifts year after year, time after time.

She once gave me a handmade silver box embellished with roses. Yet again I asked, "Why did you do go to the trouble?" But what did I mean? Perhaps it was subconscious. I asked her why she was spending the money she'd saved up on gifts for me.

("Is that the box?" I asked Handan Sarp. If I'm not mistaken, I believe it was Persian. Indeed, that was the box Elem had given her. Unlike the other gifts, it was out in the open in plain sight. It was a fine piece of craftsmanship. The night-blue velvet lining gave it an even greater air of refinement.

Asking about the box was probably a mistake. Handan Hanım's state of mind quickly deteriorated. I could tell that she'd gotten dressed up in anticipation of my arrival. But after I asked about the box she began to wither, drawing away and pulling into herself, as though she'd begun to disappear before my very eyes, fading away.

And afterward there was defiance, anger and the refuge of alcohol. I'd seen it happen before. First she would stop talking and withdraw; then she would regret her silence, and launch into an attack, her words running together.

More or less the same thing happened that time. Handan Sarp rose

---

* I'm not sure why, but throughout her memoirs Handan Sarp repeatedly referred to the bronze candle-holder she gave to Elem; she mentioned it at least three or four times. (Sİ)

and although she hadn't had a drink, tottered as she walked. It was a pleasant spring day, sunny, marred only by a bitter wind. The buds on the branches reflected the beauty of spring. Handan Hanım showed me the buds, saying, "Spring has come again." Later she said, "I've told you so much . . . All the grandeur and the dismalness of my life."

I knew what would follow, having seen such paroxysms before, along with moments of self-glory, self-hate and even jealousy.

"A long time . . . I've been speaking to you for such a long time. I've spoken to you of times long ago. I've told you that my life was full of failings. Failure! An utter failure in every sense of the word. Will you be able to write the book?"

It was almost contemptuous. In fact, it was contemptuous. I could've told her that, until then, I'd never written a novel "on order." But I opted to keep my silence.

In any case, the second act was starting. Every fit started defiantly, but by the second act her defiance subsided and Handan Sarp would fall back to reminiscing on the past and her suffering.

From a room somewhere in the apartment she brought out a small cardboard box. She reached into the box and pulled out a yellow chick. I wanted to laugh so badly that it was difficult to contain myself. Such toy chicks have always seemed strange to me, rather pathetic in fact, and the word "chick," especially when spoken aloud, strikes me as preposterous.

Perhaps we're incapable of understanding pain. We cannot grasp the suffering of others; for Handan Hanım, that toy chick was devastating, the ultimate torment.)

We were nearing the end, but neither of us knew it. An exhaustion, a darkening of the heart.

It was autumn. We left Elem's place and were walking toward

Beşiktaş to the ferry terminal. Were we crossing to the other side of the city? At some point, I'm sure they've caught your eye, those peddlers in the underpass on the way to the terminal, selling everything under the sun. Elem saw that one of the peddlers was selling toy chicks on the sheet he had spread over the ground; tiny yellow and white chicks with fluffy feathers.

For me they don't mean much, but Elem has a weak spot for soft, furry things. And she was enraptured by those toy chicks. No matter what price the seller offered, she bargained still more, but I just wanted to leave. I would've paid for them, but I didn't want to hurt her pride.

Elem bought three chicks, two yellow and one white. She gave me one of the yellow ones. That was the most touching gift she ever gave me. But I didn't realize it at the time. That day, I just tried to make sure that it didn't get crushed. When I got home, I forgot to take it out of my purse. When I finally did notice, the toy chick had been flattened, and I was unable to fix the wire feet bent out of shape. It stood there lopsided, no matter where I put it.

After our separation, the chick took on a whole new meaning. I could no longer even bear to look at it. My tears flowed. She'd bought me a tiny toy chick. She had such a desire to share things with me!

I was wracked by fits of weeping because that strange toy spoke to me incessantly of the purity of Elem's heart and her kindness, her guilelessness.

The thought occurred to me that when she saw those chicks, she forgot about me. She was buying them for herself. Then she remembered old Handan, the friend by her side. Out of shame, she bought three of them.

("It's not coming across in words. When you write the book, put some spirit into it.")

Slowly it washes them away; the water washes them away. The waves gather them up, taking them away.

But whose are they?

Not mine, not yours; the warm summer wind.

It stole them and took them away.

Sometimes I think of Zeytin Island: the summer celebrations and its emptiness in autumn. Drowned by the sea. With the coming of autumn, the island empties as the summer crowds leave. The year-round residents withdraw into their homes. The yellow blossoms on Çalı Island shrivel and dry out. The sea becomes insolent. The wind howls through the empty streets.

I think of Zeytin Island, and my heart sinks in my chest.

Three or four summers there, with you.

Tonight I want to write of the island. But, as always: where should I begin?

All at once. Memories. There is a terrifying darkness because they are memories. Memories are loss. And everything we lose brings suffering.

What if I were to go there now, at the beginning of winter, and meet up with the specters of summers past. Horse-drawn carriages pass by.

How I'd love to be able to go back in time. The acrid taste of wild olives in my mouth. It could bring me back to life. "You're not supposed to eat those!" you said to me. "You're a grown woman, Handan, but you're acting like a child."

I left those olives behind. I no longer want them.

If it weren't for the olives trees bristling over the entire island, it would be barren. Zeytin Island, Olive Island. Barren island: I rode its carriages, wandered its streets, stayed in its cheap hotels and pensions with white sheets. I doubt I'll ever see you again, or my footprints in your sand.

How I'd love to be able to relive the last days of my youth on

Zeytin Island. I wasn't a grown woman yet. But you said, "Grown woman." Even then you thought I was old. At that moment, "grown" became embedded in the vocabulary of my life.

It was the end of my youth. A week, ten days on Zeytin Island. A few summers, in a row. Horse-drawn carriages pass by.

I should begin with the ferry dock. I should begin somewhere on the island.

It was an island of the middle class, of the poor. Workers, lives spent toiling in sweat. Just mention opera, and they'd probably blanch with fear.

I'm Handan Sarp, a soprano at the Istanbul City Opera. Gelengül gave me a bikini, but I couldn't bring myself to wear it. In the morning, standing before the mirror, I put it on and took it off time and time again. Handan Sarp doesn't wear bikinis. You smile; laughter, our laughter. Island of the middle class, the poor. Drowsy, free, you get up from bed and put your arms around me: "Who cares? Just put it on."

An opulent brilliance fills the sky. That's how evening begins. The skies of the island's sea are a deep blue. The sea darkens. That's how it is; first, the sea goes dark. The sky is smeared by pinks, oranges and turquoise, and a last faint bluish white line fades away. In the distance, the lights on another island, a desolate island, flicker on and off.

Flickering.

Zeytin Island, the island of Elem's childhood.

I'd heard its name, but knew nothing about it.

When summer came, Elem's family would go to the island. When her father had the time and the means. But they went almost every year. "It's not like Bodrum. Poor people like us go there." That's how she described the island.

At first, I was irritated. Then I realized she was right. It had never occurred to us, not in my childhood or youth, to go to Zeytin Island. Neither my mother, Aunt Nadire, nor later, me. Years later, when I told Aunt Nadire that I was going to Zeytin Island, she screeched over the phone: "Have you lost your mind?! That's where smiths and seamstresses go!"

It was beyond her comprehension.

But Zeytin Island remained faithful to Aunt Nadire's memories and longings.

Even the first summer we went.

Elem had been obsessed with the idea: "Let's go to Zeytin Island." Together. The two of us. Far, far away. The idea wasn't unattractive. And I needed a vacation. The sea, sunshine. Elem wanted to spend her vacation—which Nedret would grudgingly give the girls, fifteen days a year, as if it weren't their right by law, and she'd always remind them that she'd paid their holiday wages—with me. I was undecided. Where could we go together? Bodrum? That would be impossible. I might run into people I know. Semra and Ali were going to Kaş; but there was the danger that the same thing could happen there. They knew of my friendship with Elem. I told them that Elem had mentioned Zeytin Island. But they were thinking of buying a summer house in Kaş. They left. The days of summer were passing by. If Elem didn't take her vacation soon, the busy season would start and Nedret would make her wait until the next year for her time off. "Fine," I said, "let's go to Zeytin Island."

But Elem paused in a moment of panic: "What if you don't like it?" The large families, children running about; beaches packed with people; the hotels, pensions, fifteen-day rental houses, restaurants, everything so hastily built . . . "Promise you won't get mad at me when we get there."

The first summer we went.

Night and day the streets all looked the same. They were all side streets that ran down to the main strip which stretched the length of the shore. The wind blew. Almost all of the houses were two stories, built facing each other in rows. Small gardens in the back. Summer flowers always in bloom. Olive groves abruptly rising up the slopes of the hills.

It was evening, and Elem and I were eating at Yakamoz Restaurant on the shoreline street. When we first arrived on the island, I saw it there among the slovenly diners, beer halls and grilled meat sellers: "Tonight let's eat there," I told Elem. Children were running around and I noticed that the girls and women were all heading down one street.

"Where are they going?"

"To the open air cinema."

I looked at her blankly.

"There's a summer cinema here," she continued. "We always used to go." Movies were shown on an empty plot of land. Summer cinema: Pendik, my mother, grandmother . . . I closed my eyes. Elem was saying that everyone went, eating sunflower seeds, whistling during the kissing scenes, buying cold drinks from the vendors. Her eyes glistened with the joy of being on holiday, of being free.

But I was thrown off by memories of lost youth: "What's playing?" I stammered.

Her answer was even more painful for my memories.

"Classic Turkish films. Sometimes they even show old black and white movies. Garden of Nostalgia—that's what it's called. The cinema is called Garden of Nostalgia."

I attempted to soothe myself with feelings of contempt. What did they mean, "Garden of Nostalgia"? But still, a flutter of delight ran through me.

She told me that every night they show a different film.

Our dinner half-finished, we got up. We were off to the cinema, to the Garden of Nostalgia. I couldn't hold back my tears. In my mind's eye, I saw three women: my mother, grandmother and Aunt Nadire, driven mad by her dreams for the future. Feverishly, I told Elem that two of them had passed away, but Aunt Nadire's dreams were as vivacious as ever.

And something unexpected happened: a time warp, right there in the bustling outdoor cinema! There's no other way to explain it. Time shifted and I was suddenly back in my childhood. How could I not recognize that elderly woman holding a cushion, with her summer coat and headscarf? My grandmother! She'd just become a little poorer, a little slumped and stooped, more timorous.

Perhaps after a while she'll light a cigarette, saying, "It whisks away the sorrow," the glow of her slender Gelincik cigarette like a firefly in the night.

Then I hear the voices. How can it be expressed in words? The women and men on the screen, the faces of the actors and actresses, their laughter and their weeping, all change—but the voices are the same. The women are different but they all speak in the same voice, the men are different but their voices are the same. I was stunned into silence by shame. I was hearing those voices once again, such nasal voices, and even the village girl had a voice that belied an Istanbul grace. That was the voice of Adalet Cimcoz, once a renowned dubbing artist.

And that familiar music; regardless of the film, the same melody always plays for the lovers' scenes. After a long while I raise my head as though "looking" at the music, and on the screen I see Belgin Doruk and Göksel Arsoy. But the child Handan doesn't return; that elderly girl feels Aunt Nadire surge through her like never before, and suddenly she understands all that has ached in Aunt Nadire's heart. And isn't that glum woman in fact Aunt Nadire? What a coincidence! In the desolate district of Kireçburnu she runs toward Belgin Doruk and Göksel Arsoy on the shoreline road, the fishing nets spread out like tulle curtains.

It was a poor copy of an old film, *The Time of Love*. Belgin Doruk and Göksel Arsoy love one another. Çolpan İlhan comes onto the scene. Then Belgin becomes pregnant with Göksel's child. But she'll end up marrying Dr. Avni Dilligil. In the meantime Çolpan and Göksel go to Europe to continue their education. We know that because of a still shot of a postcard: was it Paris? London? Her husband calls her downstairs to meet some guests. Of course this is in Istanbul, set in a mansion. When she sees that the guests are in fact Göksel and Çolpan, she faints, falling to the floor.

Throughout the film there are disturbances. Just as Elem said, there are whistles and hoots, young men make jokes and children shout and scream, but the married women there, the mothers my age, made me think of two lines from a poem I can't remember very well:

Here, the actors in the film
Eyes wide, forget their own lives.*

I turned and said to Elem, "Ah, my Aunt Nadire!" But I cannot recall the rest.

"I bought the ferry tickets," Elem told me. It was her first vacation without her family.

The day before, Kadriye Hanım and I had prepared my suitcase. She didn't quite believe that I was going to Zeytin Island. The truth of the matter was that she didn't think I was capable of going anywhere for a vacation.

---

* The poem that Handan Sarp couldn't remember is "Summerhouse Garden" by Behçet Necatigil. (SİL)

Aside from concerts abroad, I hadn't been anywhere in years. When I was younger, I'd gone on vacation with some friends from the opera, and with Nilüfer when I was quite young. Then I gave up on summer vacations, even on winter vacations. I closed that chapter in my book.

Kadriye Hanım asked, "How will you go?"

I acted as though I didn't understand: "By ferry . . . It's actually a small ship."

"Do you think you can handle it?"

"Kadriye Hanım, I'm not going on a trip around the world!"

We laughed.

On Saturday morning, my heart pounding—I hate setting out on trips—I went to the ferry terminal in Kadıköy. It'd been a long time since I'd been to that waterfront. When I was thirteen or fourteen, I'd gone on a Mediterranean cruise with my father. It was a horrible trip; my father's new lover had come along, but they acted as though they'd met on the ship: there were "surprise" encounters at the same dining table and on the ship's deck, and it pained my child's heart which went out to my mother, seeing them dance together, hearing loud and clear the words of love and passion they whispered to one another. At one point I was about to tell Elem, but she was speaking of such innocent matters that I drove it from my thoughts.

When I arrived, Elem was waiting for me. We boarded the tiny run-down ship. Our seats were unnumbered, on the upper deck—because she bought the tickets. The ship was swarming with passengers. What would we do for four or five hours?

Elem was brimming with the excitement of a child. The people setting off on a trip that Saturday seemed to think they were the happiest people in the world. At first I didn't understand. Elem explained that the people who go to Zeytin Island always knew beforehand when they would go: "Our vacation was always short because my father didn't have so many days off, and so we knew what day we'd go and when we'd come back."

And those families, those children, saw each other year in and year out like that, on the ferry, on the island.

The darkness of my memories and my nervousness began to fade. Once again my father was just a distant stranger.

We were far out at sea. The horizon stretched out, uninterrupted. It felt as though that open sea would wrench my heart. Vast, infinite sea.

Patiently, I tried to clear my mind of everything: the children running around and stumbling on the deck, the shouting mothers and their thermoses, cola bottles, homemade sandwiches, imitation brand-name blouses and faded summer outfits, as well as the Armenian madams puffing away on cigarettes and blowing smoke in my face, and the group of young women in one corner who were pointing at me but couldn't quite figure out where they'd seen me before. I was wearing dark sunglasses and no makeup, and I was sleepless—and smitten with the horizon.

The seagulls began heading back toward shore. At times, in hotels I come across cargo ships, or perhaps they are ferries or fishing boats, in watercolor paintings as they sail across directionless seas.

The next time we went, we sought refuge in the restaurant on the rear deck of the ship. Elem and her family had never been there before. A brisk sea breeze blew in across the tables where tea and alcohol were served, far from the poverty of the upper deck; there was feta cheese, sliced tomatoes and cucumbers, cold beer, and fried potato wedges. It was a pleasant way to spend three or four hours at sea, but perhaps a bit melancholic for those on the return trip.

"You should've told me this place was here!" I said to Elem.

She smiled bitterly: "How could I tell you when I didn't even know?"

The ship sailed on.

I was always enchanted by the sea; to venture into the infinite, to lose myself in its vastness . . . I carried within me an unrelenting desire for the infinite. And then suddenly Zeytin Island appeared, far in the distance but still breaking the line of the horizon. It was like the mapmakers of old who would place an imaginary island in the middle of the sea for their loved ones, an island named after their beloved. Elem's cheeks flushed as I told her that, and, squinting in the light of the sun, she said, "Handan Island . . ."

Elem, where is that Handan Island now?

The island appeared tiny, but little by little it drew near—but it was unclear, were we approaching the island or was it coming toward us? Children clapped their hands in excitement, and people began to exclaim, "There's the island!" Just a while ago it was but a smudge on the horizon, and now it loomed larger and larger. Olive trees dotted the brownish hills and whitewashed homes and shops lined the coastline. I could make out horse-drawn carriages that looked like toys in the distance. Then the night clubs on the shore came into view. And the awnings, striped blue and white, green and white . . .

Those awnings are so lovely the whole of summer. Still clean, the fabric unsullied by the salt of the sea, their colors not yet bleached by the sun, the awnings billow and flutter in the breeze, as though speaking lightheartedly of joys to come.

That summer, the summer we went to the island . . . . The coast road, which they called an avenue, ran the length of the shore, bordered to the front by an endless beach. I saw it as the ship drew near. I saw boats painted in blues, greens, reds and white, their colors faded by the sea. And there were barges and fishing boats. I saw people selling watermelon from boats and watermelon sliced in half and into wedges like still-life paintings. Little by little, the island was growing on me. Elem watched me, with a mixture of concern and pleasure in her eyes.

I even became friends with the madam who kept blowing smoke in my face. "Ah, why haven't you been to our island before?" she sighed. But the expression "our island" would come to haunt me later; the island was mine and Elem's. Four or five, maybe six summers . . .

We set about finding a hotel. Sellers lined the road: jars of olives, large tins of olive oil, natural olive oil soap from the island's groves. Right away I started buying things, asking questions like, "Is this pressed olive oil?" Elem laughed, asking me why I was in such a hurry. For years I hadn't gone on vacation and I'd forgotten how long we were going to stay on Zeytin Island. There were large seashells that glistened pink inside and sea sponges of all sizes. On the south of the island there were vineyards as well, where they made red wine, the island specialty. The women of the island, with their wizened jovial faces, sold their handmade lacework, embroidery, trinkets and prayer beads made from olive seeds.

Why do I remember all this? Down to the smallest detail. And, above all, on this winter day! Is it summer and warmth that I long for? Or Elem, Elem's friendship, how she worried that I wouldn't like the island?

As we walked, she asked if my suitcase was heavy. "Why, are you going to carry it?" I asked. "Would a young girl carry her older sister's suitcase?" We'd assumed the role of being sisters.

But it was impossible: the "older sister" had brown eyes and her hair was dyed black, while the other had blondish-brown hair and beautiful eyes that flashed from hazel to green. She was one of the island's summer girls. But not me, her "sister." No matter what I did, I'd always be a stranger to Zeytin Island, forever an outsider.

The diners, cafes, tea gardens, night clubs, beer halls and Bodrum-style bars had opened for the season. I saw a place called Yakamoz Lokantası: "Let's eat there tonight," I said.

"That's the most expensive restaurant on the island," she said. "My family and I have never been there before."

The way she insisted on using the word "restaurant" instead of *lokanta* set my nerves on edge.

That night we went to Yakamoz. I ordered grilled prawns, "with a little olive oil drizzled on top." I explained to her that the word "restaurant" was a recent French import, whereas "lokanta" was Italian. "We're used to using the word 'lokanta,'" I explained. "It just sounds better: lokanta, Yakamoz Lokantası."

She blushed in embarrassment.

I said that, not knowing that my words would come back to sting my heart on this chill winter night as the snow begins to fall.

That summer we stayed at the Mercan Hotel. In the same room.

The following summer, again we shared a room.

But the summers after that, I decided we should stay in separate rooms. I couldn't bear the thought that even subconsciously others were judging us. And one summer, Elem came with her family. That year I didn't stay at the Mercan Hotel; I booked a room at the Hotel Kermen, a more expensive and luxurious place that ill-suited the island's modest atmosphere.

It was probably the last two summers that I stayed at the Hotel Kermen.

New places have the effect of seducing and leading you astray.

The sheets at the Mercan Hotel had been patched but the beds were impeccably clean. A lamp stood on a shabby nightstand between the two beds. The walls were painted mint green and the windows were covered by curtains of thick gray cloth.

I opened the curtains. New places always liberate me from myself. Fearless, I can let my desires run free, especially if I know that the woman I'm with is fond of me. I smiled at Elem: "Our room gets a lot of sunlight."

When I pulled the curtains shut, the room fell into darkness, but a few beams of light filtered through, flickering on the ceiling. It was as if we were in an aquarium. The heat was heavy with humidity, and I began undressing. I've never been ashamed of my body, nor of my desires. I wanted Elem to see my body in that mottled, undersea light.

That was the first time she'd seen me behave so brazenly, and she didn't understand what I was doing or why I'd gotten undressed.

"It's so hot," I told her.

"Yes," she stammered, her lips trembling ever so slightly, like the lightest of breezes.

"There's no mirror," I told her. I was completely naked.

"There should be one in the bathroom."

I traced the fingers of my left hand over my right breast. My nipples had stiffened.

I thought that she'd draw near and put her arms around me, but she held herself back. She'd learned that I always made the first move.

But at that moment on Zeytin Island, in that room in the Mercan Hotel, I was no longer Handan Sarp. I didn't even recognize myself. That which had devastated me my entire life and brought me to despair was suddenly gone, and I found that my sexual desires brought me no shame at all—we were alone in that aquarium-like room and I didn't care what anyone would say. Elem, this time you're not going to make love with Handan Sarp! You'll make love with another woman. Istanbul, my life and my name had all been left behind, far over the sea.

She fidgeted with her bag, trying to open it.

I stood, watching her.

"Are you going to take a shower?" she asked.

"No . . ."

She loved me, but she also loved my body. This is difficult to explain, because in a way the two have never been one and the same. Perhaps only when I'd been with Nilüfer when I was young, all those years ago. The first time that I felt the pain of not being able to make love!

It wasn't just my body, the heat of my skin or my hands that caressed her. Of course Elem liked those. But she also wanted that which passed through my heart. This young woman, who swore salaciously during lovemaking, had long been in love. And she expected me to return that passion. She'd say, "Handan, I'm more in love with you. I'm the one who loves the most." And in my eyes she'd become a child.

Her kisses were filled with emotion, as were her embraces, caresses and desire to be touched.

I, on the other hand, thought of nothing except my own satisfaction. I wanted it again and again, especially on that summer afternoon in that aquarium-like room with mint green walls.

Love was lost to me. Kissing, embracing and making love were all a game for me. To give yourself over to pleasure—that was everything. Do other people feel the same way? "Normal" people? "Normal" couples? What about people "like us"?

At times when I was alone—and I usually was—those questions would run through my mind. And I couldn't share my anguish with anyone. Not once have I ever spoken with Semra about matters of sex. Did I say sex? I meant to say sexual loneliness. I never spoke with Semra or Ali about the loneliness of sexuality.

But then later, placing my faith in our years of intimacy, I once tried to explain it to Elem: love doesn't exist. I'm not in love with anyone. It's all fears and phobias. I'd grown tired of the fact that sex always left me feeling defiled afterward.

Her agitation was unmistakable. "And do I defile you as well?"

"No, of course not."

She didn't understand that because she didn't defile me, because she couldn't, satisfaction always eluded me. First there was desire, passion, the ache of the flesh; and then mutual defilement, a shedding of humanity and the castigation and scorning of feminine sensibilities. There have been men in my life who wanted to take on the women's role in bed! I have nothing against them. But we were both like wild animals. Later would come the regret. A vicious cycle of anxious misery.

My sexuality was based on that: it stripped people of their humanity.

The first summer we went together.

And the summers afterward.

Zeytin Island. Horse-drawn buggies pass along the length of the shore.

I should return and find some peace so that these dark memories will let me go.

We were walking as evening approached. The sun was setting, an explosion of pinks and oranges, and then the blues and purples of night, yellowed whites and flaming red. And finally evening settled in.

A light breeze blew, in sharp contrast to the searing heat of July: "Is there a breeze every night?" I asked.

"Yes, but the weather on the island can change quickly."

It was evening. The beaches emptied as sun-weary vacationers returned to their hotels and summer houses. Barbecues were lit in the yards and the scent of grilling eggplant filled the night air. Children played ball in the narrow streets. Then we turned onto the seaside lane again, faced by the vast expanse of the beach, now completely empty.

Having returned from the beach, showered and hung our swimsuits on the rooftop terrace, we got dressed up for the evening. Elem had made a special point of asking me to wear something nice and put on makeup. I applied some eye shadow; if the mirror in the bathroom wasn't deceiving me, I still looked quite young.

That night we planned to have some drinks: "I'm free and I want to get drunk," she whispered to me. People looking at us could have thought we were just two friends or relatives. Eyes that truly saw, however, may have recognized us as lovers.

But that young woman walking beside me was an enigma. Elem and I had made love, and the island sent my senses reeling. I was in search of love, driven mad for the love that eluded me; Elem was a stranger to me. I didn't know her, that young woman by my side—I'd never seen her face before, or tasted of her body. She could have been one of Michelangelo's youths—that's how frenzied my mind was. And it has always been that way.

Elem was captivated by dreams and mystery; she told me that since her childhood she'd been fascinated by islands, and that as soon as she set foot on Zeytin Island she felt as though she'd returned home. There were no snobby rich women, no Nedret, no family "trying to keep us apart"; but still, of course, she loved her grandmother, brothers and sisters, and they knew that one day we'd be here on this island of hers, walking toward the sea together.

I felt something inside me hardening to stone.

The exhaustion of days, weeks and months of waking up early and rushing off to work after a hasty breakfast, or no breakfast at all . . .

Crowded buses shuttling from the old textures of the city to the new . . . The old was marked by poverty, backwardness and having been left behind, while the new was all about vulgarity, coldheartedness, coarseness, ambition and greed. That was the life of my youthful Munise. Years of weariness weighed her down, and during those two weeks of vacation, she was unable to awake early in the morning.

And I didn't have the heart to wake her.

Silently I'd get dressed and slip from the room, momentarily stung by a pang of worry because I was leaving the door unlocked.

I padded downstairs, saying "good morning" to the receptionist.

He hadn't recognized me yet: "Good morning, Handan Hanım." The name Handan Sarp meant nothing to that young man from the island.

Perhaps opera was a cipher, a zero. That which I desired to share with people through opera was met with silence. Or perhaps opera had always been foreign to them.

I rushed from the hotel into the morning, a foreigner among those people.

There was a morning breeze and the island was completely empty. That's how I best liked the island: the sandy beach not yet sizzling under the heat of sun and there were the seabirds, the expanse of morning and salty tang of the sea, the scent of freshly baked pastries, the fishermen heading out in their boats. Those things pleased the foreigner. She walked to the other side of the island, where the hotels, pensions and nightclubs give way to summer houses surrounded by yards with white, pink and bright red oleanders. Bursts of passion flowers bloomed from the walls of the houses, most of which were whitewashed and adorned by green and red window shutters.

A silence always hung over the morning. But it wasn't exactly silence. The sounds of the sea and the morning breeze were transformed minute by minute, wave by wave.

Elem was weary of working life. The foreigner was trying to cast off the weariness of her soul. Emotion weighed upon her. And the sounds were a fresh welcome—the morning breeze caressed her while the sea beckoned. All along the shoreline could be heard the hum of the wind and the patter of waves tamed into quiescence by summer.

On her return to the hotel, the beach would begin to gleam as the sun rose a little higher in the sky, sprinkling the sand with flecks of gold. And as the morning breeze retreated, the waves subsided as well.

Even though morning was drawing on, the beach remained empty. Where were the island-goers? Why weren't they coming out for the sea and sun? It struck me as odd how much the vacationers and year-round residents slept.

But then at a certain hour, say ten o'clock, or five till ten, you look up and see that people are flooding from their homes and pensions toward the beach, and in a single moment the seaside is filled with people, like a military camp drill. It made no sense to me at all.

I asked Elem, and she said: "They're watching *Wild Rose*. Nobody leaves home before it's over."

"What's *Wild Rose*?"

She said it was a television series.

Those were the days when there was just one state-run channel. At least I don't think there were any other channels at the time.

It was a Brazilian program, she explained. Wild Rose was a character who always found herself in heartrending situations. Even Nedret let the girls working at the fashion boutique have time off to watch it. But, I wondered, would Wild Rose be happy in the end?

I began to laugh at myself, at how foreign I was to it all.

Elem laughed along with me.

Cemil Sahir Bey repeats a line of poetry, tears in his eyes:

I weep as memories of our laughter
Wash over me, again and again.

The next morning I decided to watch *Wild Rose* at the hotel rather than go for a walk. Breakfast had been served. Nobody spoke, not even a whisper. There was just the sound of the languorous, over-dubbed voices of the program.

It was preposterous. Wild Rose was a pint-sized woman with fake lashes and porcelain-capped teeth. The men in the show were wild about her. That poor coquette made everyone feel they were the apple of her eye, and then she'd go off and start bawling somewhere. The women watching the program were all jealous of her. But I couldn't figure it out—was she someone's adopted daughter?

Everyone around the television wept along with her. They swore at the ill-intentioned women who did her wrong. The sighs, the tears, the sniffles . . . what a fiasco!

Wild Rose was supposed to be in her mid-thirties, but she was played by a girl who couldn't have been more than twenty.

It was infuriating.

At the same time, now that I think on it, was it really different from the Nostalgic Garden films that I used to watch? Why had I been so upset? I remember being deeply touched by *Hour of Love*. So why had *Wild Rose* left me so cold? And why didn't those men, women, and children take those old Turkish films seriously when they were so enraptured by that Brazilian rose?

To be able to turn back the hands of time, to be able to laugh till my sides hurt for that "foreign woman" who had never heard of *Wild Rose* . . . If only I could.

We swam in the sea and sunbathed on the endless expanse of beach. One summer, perhaps the first one, Gelengül had bought me a ridiculous red bikini which struck me as absurd. But everyone lolled about in the sand without a care in the world. Cruelty had no place there: the women in bikinis, the people who splashed in the sea fully clothed, families, the young prostitutes, the old gay men. For ten or fifteen days life was able to smile. No one was looked upon with contempt, or judged or labeled.

Elem said that was the miracle of poverty. To live, to enjoy, to be happy for a few short days. There was no time to think about what others were doing.

Perhaps she was right.

It must have been two or three summers later, because a number of bars like those in Istanbul and Bodrum had sprung up at the end of the shore road. They'd been "decorated" with items left over from the old Greek homes on the island.

After discovering Yakamoz Lokantası, I found those bars as well. Although I complained about and belittled them, I was able to feel more at ease there. Before dinner, we would stop by for the sunset. I loved those sunsets on the island. The light would linger in the western sky. Soon, a single band of light would remain, poised just above the horizon. The island would quiet down (of course, later on it would pick back up), but just for a while a hush would fall over everything. Despite its name, we were sitting at a place that served terrible martinis: The Martini Bar.

The young bartender seemed to recognize me. "You're an actress, aren't you?" he asked.

"That depends on how you look at it," I replied. I was having a good day, and I smiled at him.

"You're a theater artist, right?"

"Whatever that means," I thought . . .

I could see that Elem was afraid I was getting upset.

The young man looked at me, waiting for an answer.

"Something like that," I finally said.

"You must be a theater actress. I've seen you on television."

I retreated into silence. But Elem cut in, and told him that I was a soprano at the Istanbul City Opera. I'm not sure if he knew what a soprano was, but his friendliness and curiosity were undaunted; he offered both of us martinis, "on the house."

"It's none of his business who I am or what I do," I said to Elem. I despise being left out in the open like a sacrifice for the slaughter.

Elem's retort was harsh that evening: "Don't you see that he was impressed because of who you are? He recognized you from somewhere and respects you. Just because you're an artist he puts you on a pedestal. Is it so important whether or not he knows what opera is?"

Then she fell silent, as though regretful of what she'd said.

I have no art. I have nothing.

Elem, that dear child of mine—I tried to take her side. Being an opera singer gives me no right to gloat over other people. But the society in which I live would like to be rid of me, and that's precisely why I must disappear.

True, but if someone else had been in my place, even Semra or Ali, do you know what they would have done, Elem? They would have sat down and talked for hours, going on about how opera is such a "high art."

Which of those is "gloating?"

The bartender made dry martinis for us:
Four ounces gin.

One ounce vermouth.

Combined into a mixing glass, and garnished with a green olive . . .

A green olive from the island.

As I said, it was a terrible martini. Either that, or my mind was in a state of confusion.

And that's how we became regulars at the Martini Bar. At least, that's how I became a regular; Elem just went along with my desires. But there I felt the most at ease, and if you counted all the people who took shelter there because they couldn't adjust to life on the crowded island, there would've been no more than thirty of us.

After dinner we'd drop by for a few drinks. The second time we went, the bartender offered us sweet martinis, using sweet vermouth in place of the regular, and he garnished them with a lemon slice. It was even worse than the other.

But there was one night . . .

I think that is the night I really want to talk about.

There was a small tea garden next to the Martini Bar; probably by now it has been turned into a bar as well, but in those days it was like a remnant from the past. It was a tiny place squeezed into a niche. Two steps down and you were on the beach, and then there was the sea. They still served tea in samovars. There were seven or eight tables, with samovars for each.

I didn't enjoy going to the Martini Bar because it was nestled up against the tea garden, but still I did enjoy watching the samovar tea gatherings.

In the house where I grew up we had a giant samovar which, according to the stories I was told, was from Czarist Russia. It was Russian silver, and what an alloy it was: if left in the sun it would start yellowing and become spotted with tarnish spots of reddish brown. My mother would polish and polish it, but the gleaming samovar was never used a single time.

One night, people were crowded around the tables in the tea garden. There were only women and children. The older women were wearing head scarves and summer overcoats. Children dashed about, running along the beach.

"Where are the men . . .? Where are their husbands and fathers?" I asked.

"The fathers only come on the weekends," Elem told me. "They take the eight o'clock evening ferry on Fridays after they finish work in Istanbul."

"Is that what your father did as well?" I asked.

"No, he used to come with us."

A group of gypsies arrived with their reed horns, *darbuka* drums, and tambourines, and then the carousing began.

There was a woman in the tea garden who had caught my eye. She was young, attractive, somehow different from the others; she sat silently, gazing into space, and eventually she nodded off. But when the gypsy music started, she bolted awake as though set free from a dream.

As she watched the gypsies, I observed her. She was wearing a long black dress decorated with white flowers, and the collar and sleeves were embellished with white lace.

Rising from her seat, she signaled to the gypsies and the waiter. The music began, and the waiter brought a beer. As the woman drank her beer standing in the tea garden, the older women wearing head scarves looked at her and the gypsies with expressions of surprise and unease.

In a single gulp she finished her beer and set the glass on the table. In the dark of dusk her eyes gleamed like dapples of light.

Normally I'm repulsed by belly dancing. But her way of dancing was so harmonious it reminded me of a religious rite, sending chills up and down my spine.

"Enough, sit down!" one of the older women snapped.

"Mother, leave me alone . . . The whole winter I dreamed of this night!"

That moment left an indelible mark on my mind.

The image of that slumped, sluggish young woman kept creeping into my thoughts: her dress with lace and white flowers, her slumberous expression . . . And then how her eyes snapped open as the lively music began to play, the gypsies' overture to joy.

But what did she see when she opened her eyes?

Dreaming of that night for the whole winter . . .

It pained me.

But I wondered, was the woman she spoke to really her mother? Perhaps it was her husband's mother. And then there were the other somber young women, who were they?

Did her eyes open onto a free world, the nomadic world of the gypsies?

I'd forgotten that night, that entrancing dance, that unhappy—was it unhappy?—life. Just today it arose from the depths of my memory as I talked about Zeytin Island.

The thought of dreaming of that night for an entire winter isn't as heartrending as it would've been before. At the very least, she had something to dream of.

In my dreams, I don't see that island which belonged to me and Elem.

These recollections are not from my somniloquies. I had taken notes at some point, during one of our trips to the island. Island memoirs. Memoirs of summer.

Their happiness lasts but ten or fifteen days.

Those who have summer houses, the island's elite, stay until the schools open.

People sending off loved ones wait at the ferry dock until the boat departs, tears in their eyes. "Until next summer!" they say. Why don't they see each other in Istanbul? Nearly everyone who comes to Zeytin Island is from Istanbul.

It was as though they were traveling far abroad.

A local woman said: "It's summer now. Life here is so lovely. Why are you leaving?"

On the day the ferry departs, I sit alone at a cafe and watch the farewells. But perhaps they find this solitary woman strange.

As the ferry departs, people gather on the upper deck, watching us and the island fade into the distance.

The sky above the sea is distant, a desolate blue. I love the color of the sky there. And then there are the seagulls, and all of the other birds of the open sea whose names I don't know.

As I was passing down a small lane, a woman called out to me from her garden, "Would you like to have some grape sherbet?" I thanked her, but declined. She insisted: "This is the right of every passerby." Some fresh mint had been added to the chilled drink, the green leaves floating on the surface. It was tempting, and I accepted—it was exquisite.

"Elem," I said, "it's too windy to be at the seaside today." But she said it was only like that in front of the hotel, and that there were other beaches and coves sheltered from the wind.

The owner of the Mercan hotel is an elderly man, a local from the island. His wife passed away the year before. My second summer there, he realized who I was and told me about his wife: "She loved opera. But never once in her life did she go." It seemed incomprehensible. Apparently she'd seen an opera on television once or twice in which "men, foreign men" were singing. Perhaps it was a performance by the tenors Carreras, Pavarotti and Domingo. The woman was instantly smitten: "This is what I've lived my life for," she said. Or was the old man making it up?

That was the longest memoir I wrote: the owner of the Mercan Hotel, his wife, and opera. I can no longer even remember his face. Perhaps he has passed away. The last few summers I didn't stay at his hotel. In the evenings he'd drink a glass of rakı at the hotel entrance: "After a long, tiring day, I like to enjoy a glass of rakı," he said to me.

Why hadn't I thrown away those scraps of memoirs?

All around me, summer was in full swing.

And now, winter. Endless winter days without Elem, without even a chance of seeing her.

Elem and I got into arguments. One of them happened on Zeytin Island. But why?

Handan, don't lie to yourself. You know why it started.

I dislike arguments. For as long as I can, I try to avoid them. Falling silent, I turn a blind eye. I hear nothing, and sink into indifference. But once I explode, my blind anger knows no end.

That one time Elem and I quarreled on the island.

And later as well, when we were on the verge of separating. It was vile, horrifying. As we drew nearer to the brink of separation, we fought a number of times. I'd like to erase those bitter moments from my memory.

We were at Yakamoz Lokantası. It was a beautiful night and the sky was full of stars. Every night on Zeytin Island is beautiful.

Just think: on such a beautiful night, you were arguing with a young woman who truly loved you.

The rest of the island was enveloped in peace. There were young people strolling about and couples were at the restaurants. There was a seller of iced almonds, and the scent of roasting eggplant drifted across the island.

I was telling Elem that, in opera, the stage manager is actually not that important. I didn't mean that the stage manager is entirely insignificant, of course, but just that the conductor of the orchestra is the one who breathes life into an opera. In every performance, the work is brought to life through the guidance and direction of the conductor. Most likely she'd asked me a question about it, because normally I wouldn't broach the subject of opera with her.

But she kept comparing it to theater. "In theater, isn't the stage manager important?" she asked. "In film, isn't the director important?" There were film stars who went to Nedret's boutique, people admired by society. They were all attractive, alluring women. And skilled in their own way. But they insisted on remaining ignorant. Somehow, whenever the issue of cinema or theater came up, they gushed about the importance of the stage manager or director. "Without him, nothing could be done," they said. All empty words. And Elem had probably listened to their discussions. Even I got caught in them at times. But as she tried to sell me the arguments of those women who swore on the importance of the stage manager, I was becoming increasingly irritated.

I explained to her again about the maestro of opera.

A strange stubbornness, unlike anything I'd seen in her before, had overtaken Elem. "What's the maestro?" she asked.

"The conductor, the one who leads the orchestra."

But my words fell on deaf ears.

In my mind's eye, I saw the conductors I'd worked with in the past. They were somber men, most of them Turks who'd returned to Turkey after having studied abroad only to find upon their return that society thought nothing of opera; and then there were the foreigner maestros, spoiled, young and haughty. As those thoughts drifted through my mind, a weariness came over me.

"But don't they just direct the orchestra?" Elem asked.

Then the gypsies showed up. Usually the people dining at the Yakamoz wouldn't invite them to play music, but that night there was a particularly rambunctious table—I had noticed them when we came in—who had asked them to play a song. The carousing began.

As the musicians played, passersby stopped to watch. One of the men at that table suddenly leapt to his feet and with his shirt unbuttoned to his waist began dancing, arms extended, fingers snapping. Not even an amateur belly dancer could have flopped her belly about like him. Others in the restaurant began clapping, driving the already impassioned musicians to an even greater frenzy.

I turned back to Elem. She was watching the musicians. It seemed to me that she was smiling, as though ironically pleased. There was no more talk of maestros and stage managers.

"Why are you smiling?" I asked.

She winced.

Ignoring the way she pulled back, I continued, "This is more familiar to you, isn't it?"

"You're drunk," she said.

And that pushed me over the edge.

"These gypsies, these scoundrels and bastards . . . *They* are what you know. That's what you understand of art. Why are you asking about opera? What do you want from it? From me? What do any of you want?!" I'd lost myself. My eyes blurred over, and everything appeared in waves and jittery streaks: the red, blue, green and yellow light bulbs strung around the restaurant, the people, the tables, the road, the sea, the night . . .

She sat in silence.

"It's true!" I said, as a second wave of anger boiled within me. "What's the point? Who will say if an opera is good or not—the stage manager, the conductor, us? What good will it do? Aren't these gypsies enough for you?"

Tears trickled from Elem's eyes, and I could see the clear outlines of the small blue, green and red light bulbs. The sea and night no longer trembled.

She was glaring at me: "You," she said. "It's always about you, just you. Elegance, fineness, art—it's all yours. We're nothing to you." Her voice caught and faltered.

Thank God for the gypsy musicians. I may have been shouting, but it was drowned out by the music and no one noticed us. I tried to compose myself.

Lowering her voice, she said, "I know who I am," and rose to her feet. I thought that she was leaving me. Her voice seemed to be full of hatred. In a moment I'd say, "Don't go . . ." She turned and walked away, but I didn't watch her.

Sipping my glass of vinegary island wine, I tried to seek solace in the horizon of the night sky.

When she returned, her eyes were bloodshot. I'd never seen the pupils of her eyes such a light shade, almost golden yellow.

The remainder of the night we sat in silence. At one point, I asked, "Would you like to have coffee?" My anger had subsided, and I pitied her.

"I don't want coffee. Thank you," she replied.

"Let's go then."

"Whatever you want."

I asked for the bill, and like always, I paid. Yakamoz Lokantası was quite far from the hotel, and we had to pass by the island's cafes, teahouses, nightclubs and beer halls on our way back. Narrow passageways opened sporadically onto the sea, and then the beach spread out before us. There were times we'd walked down that road half-drunk, leaning on one another, childlike and content. Moments when we meant something to each other. But that night, a gulf opened up between us.

Sometimes we'd stop at a cafe on the way home. But not that night. Other nights we would walk the other way and have a last drink at the Martini Bar.

That night we went back to the hotel. Everything seemed to throb in pain.

Thankfully there was no one at the entrance. As Elem got the key from the reception desk, I went up the stairs without waiting for her. She came, opened the door and we entered the dark room.

Weeping, she put her arms around me: "Let's not fight ever again."

Outside, the music of the island played on, our enemy of night.

"Let's not ever fight again."

What did those words carry within them? Nothing. Everything. But they were said with such sincerity, and it was such a heartfelt desire that it carried you away with all of its innocence and purity to a moment in which you felt truly human.

And every time I remembered those words, my heart would sink. That's what weighed on me the most: every time I remembered them, I felt that no one had ever loved me enough to say those words, and I was left with the ache of knowing that they were lost forever and nobody would ever say them to me again.

Elem, you won't love again either. Not me, nor anyone else.

For two summers I took the risk of staying in the same room as Elem. During the second summer, however, when the owner of the hotel began calling me "Handan Hanım," I started feeling uneasy and my discomfort continued to grow.

What would the owner think of me staying in the same room with a girl who practically could've been my daughter? But it wasn't just what he thought; perhaps he was gossiping with others, with the young man working at the reception desk or the cleaning woman. That thought was unbearable.

I decided: from that summer onward, we'd stay in different rooms.

But there are memories from the two summers in which we shared a room together.

She always slept late in the morning. I'd wake up and watch her. Even when asleep she was somber, curled into a ball. Although she was in the flower of her youth, there were faint traces of pain and sorrow in her still face marked by loneliness. I couldn't solve the mystery of her unhappiness, nor could I overcome it, and that pained me.

I'd get an urge to stroke her face, but my fingers would pause in uncertainty, and I'd pull back. Tossing aside my nightgown, I'd leave my bed unmade and go out for a walk. When I returned, my bed would be made and my nightgown neatly folded. One time, I entered the room without knocking and found Elem tenderly caressing my nightgown. She immediately pulled away her hand. I pretended not to have noticed.

As evening fell, we'd return from the sea and sunbathing, our limbs heavy with weariness. Sitting on the bed, she'd awkwardly smoke a cigarette, waiting for me to get out of the shower. I knew that she had a habit of slipping into reverie. What was she thinking about? Why was she so silent? Why wouldn't she tell me? When she noticed my presence, she'd quickly pull herself together and smile.

Dusk would settle and we'd go out. Somehow I just never found the courage to ask her.

But sometimes, in the early hours of evening, I could tell that she was in need of compassion. One time she even said, "I miss home." She said that she missed Hüseyin and İnci, as well as her grandmother and grandfather. "Didn't you call this morning and talk to them?" I asked.

Her desire for compassion would shade into melancholy, and she'd slip into silence, smiling. It felt as though something were breaking inside me, and when I took her into my arms, she would hug me tightly. Then the smile would fade from her lips. I could taste the salt of the sea on her eyelids, forehead and earlobes. Because the sea still clung to her a secret flush of pleasure would run through me.

Sea and salt. But the sea clings to her no longer.

Elem, Elemishka, if only we'd talked, if only we'd told each other of our worries and fears. Both of us were too withdrawn. If we only could have spoken.

That song is somewhere on a cassette tape. And on the tape is your handwriting. You recorded it for me. The handwriting was meticulous, as if for a homework assignment—because you were writing for Handan Sarp. A cassette, with that song and your writing. I can't bear to look upon it.

Inside this apartment, seas and seas distant from Zeytin Island, here on Sakızlı Street. Somewhere . . . How could I have known that one day I'd be wracked by such sobs?

It's a distant echo, nothing more, just an echo resounding from afar.

Elem, memories, our life together . . . My mind is a blur. If only I could break free: it was a song, the sound of waves breaking in my mind.

There's a man on this shore—now, he's alone. A man with a young voice. Elemishka, on the cassette that you gave me there is your handwriting, penned with the meticulousness of a young girl; but I can no longer bear to look upon it. Yet again I can hear the sound of the waves crashing and pulling back to sea.

This woman, a stranger, is alone, utterly alone on this shore to which she'll never return, never again see. Elem, hadn't we promised each other?

Words. There should be words. The words of songs. I've become lost in a haze.

For me, the words of the song have wilted and fallen like flowers that are no more, the flowers of the coralbells. That's why I cannot remember; and there is the sound of the waves and the rush of water as it is pulled back to sea.

Let half of it remain.

Yet another August like this, years ago. Evening.

Wasn't it yet another August evening like this, all those years ago?

Why August, why always August?

August, August, on these shores.

This shore! You, my one and only, when we went back to the cafe at that hour of the night, just you and me, the men were playing backgammon and the families and men looked at us. "Let them stare," you said

But one day we will separate, Elem.

Now you are sad. That's why you don't call. You never forgot that you love me. And you know that I still love you. Elemishka, my every-thing. Perhaps it means nothing to you, but that's how it is: you're my everything.

That song . . . I buried it, the cassette, under the coralbells, I buried the song. The dead must be buried, they cannot go on living among ghosts and corpses.

The song says: Yet another August evening, years ago.
You said that we too should promise one another.
"We too should promise each other. Handan, let's keep our promise."

I live among ghosts and corpses. I arrive from fiords and terrifying surging storms, entering the bay on a black-masted ship with sails the color of blood, the ship of Fliegender Holländer. But this time the storm won't break. The Norwegian sailors should silence their joyful songs. In this blood-red opera even corpses can fall in love.

What does it mean to you that I slip between life and death?

I swear, this time I'll keep my word. The dead in love—are you there, Elem—the dead in love have come, the black-masted ship silently drops anchor, slips into port after braving the terrifying storm.

Who knows where it is now, on which horizon.

Elem, everyone forgets. You forgot. And I did as well.

I forgot.

There's a ghost ship in my life. I'm like the Flying Dutchman.

The sound of waves, the rush of water. Once we walked this shore and promised each other: we will never separate! Your hand clasped mine, enveloping my life and my loneliness in its warmth.

But I no longer know . . .

It seemed to me that a young man was singing the song.

"Yes, he was young when he composed it," you said.

To compose a song . . . Tonight, this idea doesn't upset me.

You admired him. You went to one of his concerts, a "public concert," you said. I understood, my dear, a public concert. I wondered, but didn't ask: do you need to pay, to buy a ticket, for such concerts?

With carnations in your hands, you approached the stage. "Young girl, did you bring those for me?" he asked, picking you up. Together you waved at the audience with carnations in your hands; you were embarrassed and ecstatic at the same time. Such scenes are so endearing, moments when artists and the people are brought together.

Children bearing carnations never came to the opera. Nobody came to the opera. I sang for myself alone.

I am a diva.

We listened to that song over and over. He was a well-known singer, and it was one of his early works.

Elem asked, "Do you like it?" She wanted me to like the song.

"It's kind of like opera," I stammered. It was an emotional song, but rather gloomy.

The singer passed away at a relatively young age of a heart attack. I played the song for Elem, but still she couldn't cry. It was always the same scene: at the public concert her mother hands Elem a bundle of carnations, and she wants to give them to the singer. Or she wants to give them to him but can't; she stands, frightened, at the side of the stage. Then he sees her and approaches, picking her up. It seemed pitifully absurd to me, that show of affection. A show!

I was left cold.

"You never really liked him," she said.

I didn't reply.

There was a line in the song which went something like, "But when we go our separate ways . . ."

How could I have known that we were rehearsing for our eternal separation! How many more August evenings were to pass.

Which morning would we part ways—was it in August? The thought of it never crossed our minds.

That summer and the ones that followed, I was surprised that I wasn't disturbed by the crowds, the kind of people who would attend public concerts. Even though I was a stranger among them, I somehow managed to remain detached.

The streets, the shore road and the beaches were always noisy and packed with people, but it didn't disturb me.

Even on the ferry, the shouting children and Armenian woman who offered me stuffed bell peppers from a plastic container and whose son was a jeweler in the Grand Bazaar were tolerable for me.

Little by little, however, it was changing: the island, Zeytin Island, was changing even if we didn't notice.

That woman, and the young women like her who enjoyed themselves dancing to the music of the gypsies, had disappeared.

The memory is like an obsession:

One night on Zeytin Island we were sitting at a bar, and there were groups of women and children, and on the tables were glasses of tea, soda and beer. A young woman had nodded off. And then the gypsy musicians came and the music started.

The young woman suddenly awoke, and as she drank more, she began singing loudly along with the gypsies, and one of the women wearing a head scarf and summer coat tried a few times to pull her away. The older woman was ashamed.

"Leave me alone," the young woman said. "All winter long I dreamed of this night." And then she got up, and started dancing again.

Why did I find that scene so memorable, so captivating? Was it her openness? Candidness? Naturalness? The fact that she enjoyed herself but a few nights a year? I don't know. But somehow the memory of that night has always stayed with me.

The island started to change. People with a little more money to spend started going to the island. And from dusk to dawn, a ruckus of music and voices filled the streets.

Elem and I were staying in separate rooms. I'd see her light go off and know that she had gone to sleep. Until three or four in the morning I'd sit on my balcony, waiting for the noise to die down so that I too could sleep. Echoes from discos, which had opened in the previous few years, thudded across the island. Pointless laughter rang shrill in the night. Below my balcony, people would drunkenly chat before going into the hotel.

I find that rising new class of people revolting. There is a shocking coarseness about them, and if it spreads to you, you're finished. I'd begun to despise Elem's summer vacations and spending them with her.

Those vulgar hordes filled the restaurants, and the gypsy musicians would move from table to table of revelers. But none of them danced with the grace of that woman from my memories.

The festivities of the coarse and greedy lorded over the days as well. On the beach in front of the hotel, there was a sea scooter, or sea cycle—whatever it was called, it was some kind of sea monster awaiting the curious. Putting on life jackets, people would get on and launch into the sea at top speed, terrifying the people who were swimming. Like an ancient beast, water squirted from its maw, and I referred to it as the dinosaur of the twentieth century.

And then Elem turned to me and said, "Shall we try it, too?"

I suppose she was young and wanted to experience new things. But it was absolutely ridiculous for me. I snapped at her with biting cruelty.

Zeytin Island had become an enemy for both of us.

Who knows what absurd fates will befall us? There, on Zeytin Island, who could have guessed that I'd see Nilüfer?

Nilüfer, my first love.

In the story of Elem, she may never have appeared.

When Elem and I were together, I kept alive the memories of my life before her. I told her about many things, including my relationship with Kaya. But I never told her about Nilüfer, meaning that all traces of her had been erased.

("Selim Bey, in my life after Elem, the past—what my grandmother would refer to as yesteryear—has become enveloped in a dense fog. My grandmother used to say that yesteryear is nothing but a fountainhead of pain. And now Elem is that source of suffering, just her: at times my girl, my Munise, my young seamstress. But she too has become murky and shrouded in darkness. More than anything she has become a hurtful past, the colors of which are fading. Soon it will be swallowed entirely in darkness.")

I'd like to speak about Nilüfer, because she plays a part in the story of Elem. And I'll have to go back to that fountainhead of pain and delve into the torment of memories.

But I don't want to dig too deeply.

Is that possible? Nilüfer is like a character in a novel. Or perhaps characters from a few different novels. For example, although she might be the lead character in the first novel, in the second and third she appears in a secondary role and then vanishes. Over time, her role diminishes, just as her power to impact others fades away. In the story of Zeytin Island, she'll show up in a few pages and then disappear.

In the past, I was such an avid reader of novels! Perhaps what I have to say about Nilüfer was actually inspired by what I read.

Just to give an example, I read the novel *Handan*. I was quite captivated by Handan's memories and somniloquies.

She was attracted to men, to what today would be called the "opposite sex." But even today, in the name of morality there is this hypocritical belief which denies that women can love more than one man at the same time or that women could want to make love with those men: the scandal, the utter depravity—she could be nothing but a whore!

Handan, even back then in the era of Sultan Abdul Hamid, wrote in her memoirs and somniloquies of her longings not just for her husband but also for her cousin's husband, probably for her doctor, for Nâzım, and likely for other men as well, longings tremulous with sexual desire. It didn't strike me as strange at all. Replacing the male characters with women and girls, I felt like I was reading the novel of my soul. Even if I hadn't tasted their pleasures yet, those were feelings and desires that I knew one day I'd experience.

But Handan was dying.

A few years later, I read the novel *The Clown and His Daughter*, which was written by the same female author, Halide Edip Adıvar. The storms of passion in *Handan* had died down in that later work. In fact they had died down so much that you wondered if Halide Edip was truly the author. *The Clown and His Daughter* is a banal fairy tale. The plot is quite simple: Rabia and Peregrini, having passed all the tests of morality and tradition, pull themselves into the dullness of their lives and false pretenses, and they come together in a way that creaks of civility. Peregrini even becomes Muslim, and they get married. The triteness of the novel is mind-numbing.

But there is one scene in the novel in which Handan appears.

I was stunned! It never would have occurred to me that someone who had died in one novel could be resurrected and live on in another. But there she was. And just why shouldn't she continue on in Rabia's day and age?

In that scene, Peregrini and Rabia had taken the Tünel up to Beyoğlu, the fashionable district of the time. Rabia despised earrings, rings and everything that was ostentatious in the world. Two fancily dressed young women were greeting their piano instructor; their gowns hugged their bodies, their mantles were cut quite short, and their face veils were sheer as gossamer—in short, two young Westernized women: Handan and her cousin, or maybe her sister, who later would marry Refik Cemal.

("By turning Neriman into Handan's cousin I'm trying to return to that 'morality' I disclaimed; if you fall in love with your sister's husband, you're deemed depraved, but if it's your cousin's husband, then there's more room for forgiveness.")*

Peregrini refers to Handan as "Hüsnü Pasha's wife." Most likely Neriman hadn't yet married Refik Cemal, and Handan hadn't yet fallen in love with him.

For days I reenacted that scene in my mind.

You go back in time:

And when you go back, everything else pulls away as well—the future sorrows, the sexual longings slandered by false morality, the paroxysms of fever, death . . .

Over time, however, that scene weighed on me. Handan, whom the novelist had once defended, was belittled in Rabia's eyes. He saw Handan and Neriman as diabolical women. Rigidified by morality, the author had succumbed to defeat.

Just like Handan had done, Nilüfer suddenly appeared in my life. And I was anything but a Rabia.

She appeared from out of the past with her astonishing beauty and youth, as always enveloped in an air of mystique. But it wasn't the same Nilüfer.

What should I say about her?

---

* Handan Sarp was mistaken. In Halide Edip Adıvar's *Handan*, the two women were step-relatives. (Sİ)

After studying for a few years at the conservatory, she went on to study theater, but in the end she abandoned everything: art, her beloved Ibsen—she had always wanted to play Hedda Gabler—and studied medicine.

Hedda Gabler, Nora, The Wild Duck. They would all be forgotten.

She'd been a friend of mine at the conservatory. And now she was Dr. Nilüfer Çangal, specialist of internal medicine.

Perhaps it was just me, but she seemed to have a strange beauty; you couldn't bring yourself to gaze upon her for long, nor could you approach her. She'd come to you, granting the gift of her friendship. Her beauty was like a summer morning enshrouded in mist.

We were at one of the cafes where we used to gather: a community of enthusiastic young men and women who were convinced that theater and fame—in other words, art—would save the world. Her laughing blue eyes were fixed upon me, and she smiled. Or perhaps I was mistaken. "We don't even know each other, so why is she smiling?" I wondered. Two years younger than me and passionate about Ibsen, she was determined to be an actress.

That tall, slender girl with shoulder-length hair asked, "Why aren't we friends?" She told me that she lived in the district of Ataköy and had graduated from the German high school, and that, like me, she was a single child. She'd read all of Ibsen's work in German.

I began reading Ibsen with a passion: Hedda, who wanted to rip the vestiges of her era up by the roots; Nora, who returned to her childhood home to find the identity that she'd lost; the destitute wild duck, fuming with rebellion against life. Nilüfer told me about the other works that hadn't been translated into Turkish. But was it Ibsen or Nilüfer that I was in love with? Most of the time, Ibsen would fade into the background.

We spoke of Hedda Gabler. With her body, Nilüfer would've played a perfect Hedda, that unhappy woman back from her honeymoon. In my mind, Nilüfer was always a novel, a scene from a play—she was Hedda herself: aloof and cold, becoming intimate only when she wanted, and then shutting you out again on a whim. Perhaps later in my life I began to imitate her.

Both of us were just setting out in life, buoyed by the excitement of youth. But she would only glow with enthusiasm when speaking of theater. Our conversations, our walks, our voyages of the imagination would last until evening. Always theater, always poetry. She set herself above me; we never spoke of opera. And I never said a word; I was in love. With her malicious heart, she knew that but pretended not to notice and used it to her advantage. She'd play cool, and then suddenly embrace my mother, addressing her as "Aunt Leyla Mahmure!" When we were alone together, she'd mock my mother, laughing at the fact that she had two names. And my mother adored her: "Nilüfer is so smart, such a levelheaded girl . . ."

She was nothing but a traitor.

I was in love but couldn't bring myself to confess it. As soon as her blue eyes fixed on me, the mist dissipated. I can't recall how many times I was flushed with hope and desire when I thought I caught a glimpse of attraction in her smile, when she seemed to have fallen silent in expectation. Then the smile would fall away: "Good-bye, Handan, I'm leaving now."

One day my mother had gone out and we were alone. With the grandeur of a queen, Nilüfer sat perched on the armchair beside the telephone and we spoke of nothing, not Ibsen, not opera, and the blue of her eyes was a piercing light. My heart was set aflame, and I took her hand in mine and began kissing her graceful fingers. She didn't pull away at first, and I wept as I kissed her hand, but then she said brusquely, "What are you doing? Handan, have you lost your mind?" Her gaze, which just a moment ago seemed so inviting, was now filled with derision. Glancing at the tears in my eyes, she burst into laughter.

I was in love.

Night after night of loneliness. Until night fell, during those long days it seemed that I could feel the Nilüfer of my imagination by my side, and as I drifted asleep after all that longing it felt as though we'd slipped into each other's arms. In the morning my heart was clenched by the coldest despondency.

In their twenties, people are unable to cope with love. It's something terrifying, unreciprocated love. Life is terrifying. You have no one, neither father nor mother. I could share that love with no one but myself. But Nilüfer knew, and she stoked my desire only to use it in the most malevolent way. Playing the role of Hedda, she took pride in this unrequited love even though she'd given up on theater. If she hadn't, she would've cut off our friendship, but our ways had begun parting. However, her best friend was Handan.

Nobody tried to save me from Nilüfer.

Rushing off to Ataköy, I'd find myself hesitating among those towering blocks of apartments. Wavering for minute upon minute at the door, uncertain.

Coldly she'd open the door as though for a stranger, her face blank. Only her mother would welcome me, whisking me warmly into the living room with its plants and flowers. It's difficult to believe but when Nilüfer was a child, her mother dressed her in boys' clothes when they went out. Nilüfer would go out of her way to show me her childhood photographs, leaning over beside me: "Handan, just look at what I'm wearing in this picture!"

Even then, such things weighed on my heart and repulsed me; somehow, however, Nilüfer thought I'd be enraptured. But I simply found Nilüfer's mother strange, that woman who went on and on describing her blossoms and fuchsias.

As far as I can remember, her father was quite distant. An evening drinker. The dining table would be laid, along with his drinks, and the world faded from his eyes. Who knows, perhaps after the drinks had softened his mind, he thought that Nilüfer dressed in her sailor's suit was actually his son.

Such cruelty!

We went on summer trips together, always to the Mediterranean, to the Aegean. Anxiously my mother would send me off at the bus terminal, and if it weren't for my grandmother's insistence, I never would've been able to go on vacation by myself.

Those Aegean nights, the sky of the open sea filled with stars. It was the first time I had ever seen the heavens filled with such light: I couldn't get enough! Reach out and you could grasp a handful of stars, even the entire Milky Way. It was then that I started drinking, with the stars and Nilüfer; just as I'd teach Elem, I started with beer, and some of the young men from Nilüfer's university would drink pungent glasses of rakı, though a few dull girls hanging out with the crowd wouldn't drink a drop.

Nilüfer said to me: "Handan, they like you so much! They told me so. 'Ah, those dark eyes,' they said. They were entranced by your eyes." Or: "Don't be such a bore, the boys have invited us out. Let's go have a good time."

But I just wanted to be alone with Nilüfer. Just the two of us. For the rest of my life, just the two of us, for as long as we live!

In the end we'd go out with them. And I always wondered: "Why was it always her friends? Why wasn't anyone from the conservatory invited?" All of them, even those glum girls who didn't drink, were from the medical faculty. The answer was obvious: I didn't have any friends! As I danced with one of the young men, I saw Nilüfer in the arms of another man and she winked at me—I laughed, but my heart flushed with poison.

But she never flirted with the men from her faculty; she never flirted with anyone. They would drop us off at the entrance of the pension. As they walked away, she would say suggestively, "Idiots! They don't realize what's happening between you and me." And then she'd crawl into bed and drift off to sleep.

But I was left sleepless, pondering over what had happened that night: in those years after the coup of 1971, how could those leftists (and all of Nilüfer's friends were leftists) be here? Hadn't they all been hung? After a few drinks, they'd sing revolutionist folk songs, and Nilüfer was the lead singer: "The hung remain with the hung, and those who were murdered brave the bullets . . ." Was I really thinking about that? Is that how I interpreted it, placing her body on an autopsy table? I doubt it. The image flickered and faded.

Sleepless. Between our beds there was an old battered nightstand. Nilüfer slept on the other bed, and outside the stars would soon give way to the break of dawn. It felt like summer paled in comparison to Nilüfer's radiant heat.

One day it ended. Little by little my feelings subsided, and we saw each other but rarely. In the last few years, we didn't see each other at all.

When the fresco was old . . .

It was a fresco of an island, Zeytin Island.

Frescos are painted when the plaster is still wet.

A voice called out and it was unlike anything from the past: "Handan!"

I turned. Immediately I recognized her, but she'd changed dramatically. Her voice sounded as foreign as she looked. The Hedda Gabler she'd once carried within had vanished, and a cloying conformist had replaced the rebel. What I saw was a plump, doughy woman wearing heavy makeup and a tight chemise-like dress of bottle green.

Elem and I were just entering Yakamoz Lokantası. Octopus, shrimp, sea asparagus with walnut, garlic and yogurt sauce, and perhaps grilled swordfish or bluefish: I was thinking that the dinner, the night, would be like all the others. After two double vodkas, I'd be getting drunk, trying to forget about Elem.

"Handan!"

I turned, not recognizing the voice.

Years ago, probably in Bodrum, we'd stayed at a pension adorned with bright red geraniums. She emerged from the shower bundled in a towel: "Would you leave the room, Handan? I'd like to get dressed in private." The woman calling out to me hardly resembled the young woman who'd once spoken those words.

I walked out the door of our room, jaw clenched in frustration. There were brilliant red geraniums planted in olive oil tins in front of the pension. Tins, rust, that was all—nothing but rust and decay! She was toying with me, with my rebellious sense of independence. And there I was, tossed into the courtyard. "Tomorrow," I thought to myself, "I should just go back home tomorrow."

I walked toward Nilüfer with those hurtful, malicious memories that always seemed to envelop my life. I was probably smiling: as the years go by, the effect of rejected love fades and withers. The wounded pride falls away, and you flash an indifferent smile.

"Of all the places," she said, "after all of our vacations together, who would've thought we would run into each other here!"

Such a strange coincidence: behind Nilüfer, on the low wall that separated the restaurant from the beach, bright red geraniums were in bloom, planted in tasteless plastic pots.

"I remember your mother, Aunt Leyla Mahmure!" she said, her voice ringing out in peals of laughter. She embraced me.

"My mother died," I said. "I lost my mother years ago."

After my grandmother passed away, for some reason my mother and I went out there, to the summer house in Pendik, for one or two more summers, and then it was abandoned—the rooms stood empty, the windows were broken, and then the demolishers came. That overgrown garden where I used to read *The Wren*. Could the banal woman standing before me actually be the same girl who used to stroll that garden? No, aging hadn't changed her. It was her coarseness that was disconcerting.

The man sitting beside her rose to his feet. He was dark-skinned and mustached, and wore shorts and a T-shirt that did nothing to conceal his belly and sagging chest. Later I noticed a ring on his pinkie with a large single stone set in the center.

Extending her hand to Elem, my old love introduced herself: "Doctor Nilüfer Çangal." But the love had disappeared long ago. Or perhaps it never existed.

"This is my friend, Elem."

Her laughter still filling the air like the ringing of bells, Nilüfer said, "This is Semih. He's a construction engineer." As she introduced her friend, I caught her gazing at Elem, an unexpected gleam in her pinched blue eyes: "Let's sit together."

I tried to refuse.

But she wouldn't listen. She prattled all sorts of nonsense to Semih about how Handan Sarp was a prima donna of the stage and beloved of opera aficionados. Then she said, "But what would this brute know about opera!" and wrapped her arms around him. She seemed happy, satisfied and content with her life, as though she recalled not a single line of Ibsen. So that's how it was: art would save nothing in the end! Ibsen had written all that for nothing, and Nora would never return to her childhood home.

Resigned, we accepted her invitation. Nilüfer had Elem sit beside her, and Semih Bey pulled up a chair for me.

Elem appeared shrunken; she had withdrawn so deeply into her shell that she resembled a small child, if she was there at all.

The conversation turned to memories, and Nilüfer spoke of the "deep" friendship we had all those years ago. Everything she said was a blatant lie. She talked as if we'd traveled the entire coastline of the Mediterranean and Aegean. She said that I'd "fallen in love" with the indigo blue of the Aegean Sea where I "swam like a fish"; all the young men in the medical faculty—they were all well-known physicians now—had been "smitten" by me, but she'd "never once" gotten jealous. All the men jostled to "line up" for a chance to dance with me.

Nilüfer was completely drunk.

Unable to bear it, I said, "You've been drinking."

"Semih and I started in the afternoon. You two should hurry and catch up with us!" she laughed. As the waiter approached with octopus salad, she turned to him and said, "Bring the rakı first, and be quick about it!"

The waiter said that we don't drink rakı: "Handan Hanım drinks vodka. And Elem Hanım sometimes drinks beer, or wine."

"Vodka?" she said, taken aback. "In the past you always drank rakı. And as a young woman, you drank your fill!"

The only way out was to turn it into a mockery: "Of course, in the old days I used to drink glass after glass of rakı." We laughed—but not Elem.

Semih asked, "But isn't it bad for your voice, hanımefendi?" And turning to Nilüfer, he said, "And you thought I knew nothing of opera!"

Yes, rakı soothes my voice.

Alcohol, cigarettes and separation, but above all, separation: my voice is gone!

It was a vile evening. And melancholic. But the melancholy didn't hurt.

Then Semih Bey called over the musicians. He got up and spoke with them about something, but I paid no attention. Just then a darbuka and tambourine launched into a wedding march version of "La cumparsita," and Semih staggered back to our table. The tambourine player leapt into a dance, and everyone at Yakamoz Lokantası turned to each other, smiling. I knew that everyone was staring at our table, and I kept my head bowed.

Semih looked at Nilüfer, and asked, "Will you marry me?"

I heard him.

They began kissing. Elem sat rigid in her chair. And as quickly as it started, the cumparsita ended, but the air of revelry continued with a new song. Semih Bey danced and the horn player trailed behind him, and as the construction engineer shook his belly left and right, his double chin quivered. Nilüfer was in paroxysms of laughter, and I think she was singing along. The evening had become an abomination.

The waiters gathered around our table. People passing by on the street stopped and watched. My head spun, and I tried to light a cigarette. Back then, I'd go days without smoking. But the lighter slipped from my fingers, and I saw that Nilüfer had started dancing too.

"Nilüfer, marry me!"

The crowd applauded. But why were they applauding?

I fled, seeking refuge in the restroom.

When I came out, Nilüfer was standing near the door. She seemed more sober.

"Do you think he's good for me?" she asked. "Could it work? A man like that, and me?"

I tried to smile, and an insidious shudder of joy ran through me.

"I really like Semih," she said.

But my joy turned cold: "Do you remember *Hedda Gabler*?" I asked. "Is that girl your lover?"

"Which girl?"

"Esma . . . Is that her name, Esma?"

"Don't be ridiculous, Nilüfer. You're disgusting."

"Once upon a time . . . if you'd wanted, we could've slept together. If only you hadn't taken everything so seriously."

I was stunned. More than anything else I wanted to flee from that conversation, but she held me by the arm. Our reflection in the cracked full-length mirror of the restroom looked warped and distorted. Perhaps it was a projection of our inner selves.

"If you'd passed it off as a joke, I would've slept with you. Once, maybe twice." She fell silent, but still held tightly onto my arm. Then she said, "I'm going to marry Semih."

I think it was that summer, a few nights later: I lost my way.

I felt as though I couldn't breathe. It was nearly midnight, and Elem had gone back to her room. Her light went off. I thought that if I went for a walk, I might be able to get some sleep. For a long while I sat on the balcony, listening to the sounds of the sea, trying to ignore the noise, music and laughter. I thought that the rush of the waves would calm me, but it only pulled away farther into the distance. After a while, the music and laughter began grating on my nerves, and I decided to take a walk.

I turned off of the shore road, away from the nightclubs, tavernas, pop music, and glittering "stars of Zeytin Island," away from all the noise that filled the night. The narrow lane was dark and secluded.

There was nothing but olive trees, what they call "immortal" trees. The wild ones are known as "delirium." Their gnarled trunks gave off a silvery shimmer. With my heart plunged in darkness, I touched the gnarled trunks with my fingertips and kissed them.

The olive groves began thinning out. I must have walked quite far from the seaside, as the sounds had died away, and there was nothing but darkness. I walked toward the hills, alone. Fear had fallen away. The path took me wherever it willed. I knew I was lost, and this gave me a strange satisfaction—I needed to be lost. To drop everything and go. But where to? The faint light of the July moon showed me the way, leading me to the cemetery, to the hills. I was content.

There were cypress trees and humble gravestones all around. "Life is fleeting, but death is here to stay." Is that what was written on the gravestones? In the moonlight the letters were hard to read. Maybe I'd made it up. But life indeed is fleeting.

In the distance, lights flickered, as though winking.

There in the middle of the cemetery, I remembered the delicate jasmine blossoms. My childhood. I prayed for my grandmother; it was on such a summer night that she had lamented that the jasmine hadn't bloomed.

A sentence arose in my mind, repeating over and over:

Last night, Handan Sarp committed suicide!
Last night, Handan Sarp committed suicide!
Handan Sarp . . .
Committed suicide . . .
Suicide!

Those final summers . . .

In those final summers I decided not to go to Zeytin Island. The last two summers.

A feeling of nothingness was consuming me. My life, opera, Elem. That nothingness grew more oppressive day by day. I felt as though, in the end, there would be nothing else left.

Before going to the island, I told Gelengül about my feelings. Speaking with the confidence of experience, she said, "This is normal. We're at a dangerous age!" She warned me not to say anything to Elem. Rubbing her hands with their close-cropped nails, she said, "Every woman goes through this in the autumn of their lives. Sadly, it will happen to us as well."

Was I really in the autumn of my life? I felt like I'd fallen into an odd delirium that was pulling me toward some unknown destination.

"This summer I can't come to the island," I said to Elem. I told her that Ali had bought a house in Kaş and that I'd be going there with Semra and the others. "You should come too, if you'd like," I added. But my coldness drove her away; she didn't want to come. A pang of sorrow ran through my heart for her, my child, my Munise. But then that coldness clamped down again, shutting her out more than ever. Elem said she would go to Zeytin Island with her family that summer, just like the old times before we met, before we fell in love, before we came together. "Fine, Elem, if that's how you want it," I told her.

I knew it wasn't what she wanted. But there was nothing I could do. Dwelling on her silence and helplessness, I tried to place the blame on her.

Blame?

But was there any blame, was there a culprit?

At the last moment I changed my mind about going to Kaş. Elem was already on Zeytin Island with her family. I called and told Elem that I was coming. Surprise in her voice, she asked how I'd get there. But what was it that drew me to the island? Was it the seagulls, the cormorants and the other seabirds whose names I didn't know? Was it my longing for the sea, that unwavering longing? The oleanders were in bloom on the island: white, pink, deep crimson. You pass through the olive groves. The morning breeze coming from the sea blows across the tiny yellow blossoms of the ancient linden trees, filling the island with their scent. The island always smells of linden.

She met me at the ferry dock. From a distance I saw her waiting; she had matured, and was trying to find her own way in the depths of a bitter loneliness, but she knew that I wasn't helping her. Despite her youth, creases of sorrow had begun to form under her eyes, and as I approached, I could see her forehead creased in concern, furrowed by worries that she kept bundled inside. As though nothing were amiss, I greeted her, "Hello, friend!" but instantly despised myself for what I'd said. The word "friend" echoed the distance driven between us.

Her family had rented a house that summer, so Elem reserved a room for me at the Hotel Kermen. As we walked to the hotel, which was on the promontory of the island, we passed through the market with its sea sponges, bottles of wine and trinkets. The same sellers, the same things. Both of us were thirsty. All those details that once seemed so charming had suddenly lost their attraction. She said that there weren't as many carriages anymore because people weren't using them.

She prattled on about the unemployed coachmen and the city bus drivers, but I wasn't listening. I was put off by the fact that rather than thinking of me, she was lamenting all those horse carriages parked idly in the yards of homes.

We were carrying my duffel bag between us. Suddenly I let go of my strap: "Gelengül thinks that I'm going through menopause."

She stood there in silence, holding the bag by herself.

As soon as we entered the hotel, I was filled with regret; the luxuriousness of the hotel stood in sharp contrast with the rest of the island. A young man with gel-slathered hair and a T-shirt bearing the letters "H" and "K" took my bag from Elem and have her the key. It seemed so incongruous: a hotel with an elevator on such an island. As we rode the elevator up, I looked out onto the sea, thinking: "My God, the sea looks so stagnant! What happened to my wild churning waves?"

Why these memories? Why have I been through this? Why these ordeals?

Why have our lives become like this, like a dried flower that suddenly drops from between the yellowed pages of a book, a faded violet perhaps, a gladiola with a broken stem, or a brittle sycamore leaf? Why has life become so sorrowful?

Why don't you call out to me? Weren't we together? Elem, my Elemishka, together we used to walk together down the shore road! Evening would fall, and we'd return to the Mercan Hotel. That first summer: how we laughed at the red bikini that Gelengül had given me. That first summer: how we laughed after I watched that Brazilian television show. That first summer: Elem, how I misunderstood you. Elem, I've lost everything that I could say to you in this world. I need to despise you. But I don't.

Ah, Elem, I'm slipping away, my mind is folding in on itself; I hate my country, I hate this country that taught me the habits that have made me who I am. I remember how your clothes smelled of cheap laundry detergent, and when you undressed you smelled of cheap soap; that oily smell had seeped into your skin. When we went to Zeytin Island, we always used expensive detergent with exotic scents. When we made love I was repulsed by the smell of cheap soap. I was repulsed by your body!

Elem, listen to me: I bear no malice. There is a slight breeze. And always the scent of linden. Snapdragons and gillyflowers in the flowerbed. Luscious passionflowers bursting in bloom over the wall on the corner when we come and when we go. Prosaic life. Island life.

Why didn't Nedret give her employees gifts of perfume and deodorant? Not for the stench of sweat, but to cover the smell of cheap soap and detergent. It was unbearable.

Call out to me, Elem, come to me with your scent of cheap soap! I swear to you, I won't think of expensive perfumes, of Amazone. To cover the smell, I bathed everything in perfume. Forgive me, Elem.

We walked, two people in the night. There was jasmine, the island, people separating and coming together; in a song that you loved, the island smiled and wept with us. With a voice of youth that singer sang of August, and now it is another August evening. Elem, the two of us are here together. We left life behind unknowingly, without calculation.

Elem,
This letter will never reach you. It will never be sent.

Do you remember Zeytin Island?

I told you about my life there. We were at a restaurant. It was Yakamoz, or maybe it was Gümüşselvi; I can never remember names.

I told you about my life. The life of a stranger. You, I said, were so much younger than me and yet fearless in your choices and desires. In the candlelight at Yakamoz Lokantası I told you that I'm always afraid because the greatest human fear is to be unable to carry yourself through life. And I failed in that. This weary Handan Sarp, unknown star. There is a form of art called opera and all of its stars are unknown.

I told you everything: about the excitement of a young girl, the crashing of waves on the shore just like in your song, Pendik and the summer house which was like a mansion, the well in the garden; Çalıkuşu would climb the trees and she was completely lonely! So lonely that no one dared draw near.

I was drunk, wasn't I? "Don't tell me any more," you said. "All these memories just make you sad, Handan." Tell me that again! I was drunk . . .

Horse carriages were going down the road. I must have lost my mind: "Coachman!" I called out, "What are the names of your horses?" Shepherdson, Sorrel Girl, Night, Halfblood, Fateless . . . It's all like a fairy tale when these names of horses live on in the past like this from summers long ago. In my past, this is our fairy tale: Zeytin Island, roads, the patisserie where we ate Napoleon pastries, Belgin Doruk's wry smile, the Garden of Nostalgia, the yards filled with oleander.

Years ago, an August night. Like a dream.

August: this night. Nişantaşı, Mastic Street. Winter.

Who said to whom, "I will never forget!"?

Had we walked on the shore road? Not holding hands. In that song, they hold hands. In our lives, our hands merely grazed each other. And now, such a burning longing! The sound of waves whispering ceaselessly from broken seashells. You didn't believe it. The sound of waves. Every broken seashell whispers of them.

My dear, a little more alcohol. It's the only thing that can save me. I began vomiting in the elevator of the Hotel Kerman. I was wearing the red bikini Gelengül gave me but it would inspire no longing, nor would that low-cut dress: menopause—my fertility dwindles away like a mockery.

I stand before the holy tomb of Şem-i Dede and kiss the ice-cold iron bars of the windows.

Don't be sad; we never promised each other anything, not on this beach nor on any other. Don't be sad, and don't be afraid: I never promised anything. It was Elem who made the promise.

The sad old homes on the island resemble us in so many ways; they utter not a single word. Mired in despair, they've fallen into silence and no longer speak of the adventures of times before.

We pass along a deserted road. Up ahead is an abandoned vineyard house overlooking an olive grove; it has crumbled into ruins. But on the top floor, through an empty window frame I can see an old wardrobe.

I stop in my tracks, entranced. I can see the wardrobe's mirror. But that aged mirror won't speak of who dressed themselves before it nor of what they wore. There, across from the olive grove, sometime in the past, a young woman stood looking into the mirror, gazing at her reflection on this old island that refuses to speak to me of its secrets.

Old island . . .

We were alone in a garishly decorated room at the Hotel Kermen.

There was nothing left for us to say to each other. It even seemed pointless for me to say that I didn't like the room or the hotel. It was the end of island adventures. Never again would the island bring us joy and happiness.

We sat, looking at one another. Elem was tanned, darker than I'd ever seen. I knew that I needed to let go of those summer days of the past on the island, days we spent in a different hotel room. It felt like my hand belonged to someone else when I approached her and began stroking her back and kissing her shoulders. She turned, wanting to kiss me on the lips. But who was that young woman? Elem seemed like a stranger to me. If only she were a whore and I could throw her out after paying her . . . We kissed briefly, but I turned my lips away and kissed her neck. Pulling down her skirt, I began to kiss her bronzed skin. I wanted to hear her sharp cries of pleasure. That's all she was capable of: small, timid cries that she couldn't hold back.

And then her cries began.

"She's still in love with me," I remember thinking to myself.

From the balcony of my room, Çalı Island was visible in the distance. It was a desolate island of yellow-blooming heath and a stony shoreline. Nobody lived there. At night, the lights warning of the island's rocky shoals speak of its desolation.

The girl at the reception desk had said, "The moon rises from behind Çalı Island." She told me there would be a full moon that night. Elem was with her family, and I was alone on the balcony. I'd bought a bottle of whiskey; in the morning, the cleaning women would see the bottle. I thought about the full moon and the bottle I'd snuck into the hotel. Side by side, the two seemed so incongruent. The whiskey would last me a night or two . . .

The moon hadn't risen yet.

They call the plant that grows on Çalı Island "golden bell." At

279

night, it is as though the flowers await the light and the island's beacon is swallowed by the darkness.

I recall a false moon. It bled in oranges, pinks and golden gilding. Where had I seen it? From where did it rise? It didn't ascend for fields of golden bell waiting in the dark.

The island's beacons weren't there to illuminate the darkness; no, their purpose was to hint of darkness and the night.

Filled with hope, a young woman watched the false moon rise. In a moment, she would begin singing songs of love and melancholy. A prince . . . She was probably in love with a prince, and his name was something like Prince Calàf. But I cannot remember the name of the young woman.

The moon rose, setting the golden bell flowers agleam. It ascended with dizzying swiftness as vermillion bled into pinks and burst into shades of orange as though set ablaze.

The moon rises but once. Then it grows cold, and disappears.

You gazed upon me and smiled: that's probably how the song went. That was it. The prince smiled. The young hopeful woman remembered and told the prince. But the prince won't see her; he'll dash her hopes, for he had smiled into a void.

The moon rose.

"Handan," I said to myself, "how many years ago was that?" From a great distance, a chorus joins in, along with a mournful flute.

Could that young woman smitten by a false moon be the same weary woman standing on that balcony flushed in ecstasy? Perhaps. Yes, Handan, that is her. But what about the moon? Why has it changed so? Why did she lead such a life? She hasn't achieved a single thing. The young woman who sang with such hope fell silent, and turned her back to life.

The beacons in the middle of the sea are there to bring light to the darkness. But the dark can never be illuminated. The moon rises for nothing.

You should seek out that young woman whose heart was set ablaze by a false moon in the underworld; now, filled with the darkness of the sea and sapped of spirit, she idly watches the rising moon as it bids farewell to the island of golden bell flowers.

When will the moon set?

Let the moon be gone.

I joined Elem and her family for early evening tea.

We sat in a flower-filled yard. Flowers of all colors. But I was pensive; if they had asked what kind of flowers, I couldn't have said. I didn't even notice.

I couldn't be sure if they liked me or not. In fact, I didn't even really know them. Altogether I'd seen them three or four times. The first time I went to their place in Kocamustâpaşa I'd brought perfume for İnci and Elem, but was distraught when I realized I had nothing for Hüseyin. And the other times I went there, I brought things like chocolate and cakes.

We sat in the yard of that house on Zeytin Island that they had rented for fifteen days. The owner of the house joined us; she was an elderly local woman, a widow with two daughters who'd married and moved to Istanbul. She complained to me of her loneliness.

İnci must also have been married by that time, because I don't remember her being there that evening. I'd gone to her wedding; if the occasion arises, I'll describe it.

Hüseyin met me at my hotel. I always liked him. He was a somber young man. And just as Elem, his older sister, had wanted, he continued his studies and would probably go on to work as a manager. He was tall, light-haired and had fine features. We chatted as we walked, and I told him how much the island had changed: "Do you go to the discos?" I asked. He blushed. Like Elem, he too had a shy side.

We arrived at the house, and their father was sitting in the yard. He greeted me: "Welcome, Handan Hanım." But I didn't know his name. Hadn't I asked? Hadn't Elem told me? Perhaps she had, but I couldn't remember. I didn't know her mother's name either. At that point, what difference would it have made?

Elem's father seemed old for his age, broken down and spent, out of breath. Just taking a few steps was a struggle. Despite that, he still worked, and would probably do so until he died. But I couldn't remember what kind of work he did.

Later Elem's mother joined us. She was cheerful but in a flurry, wringing her hands. She'd made *börek* to go along with the tea, but complained that they hadn't been baked long enough. I smiled, but knew that I was complete stranger to this woman. I couldn't help but wonder: was she being sincere? Later, after the rupture between Elem and me, I felt a grudge against that woman, even though, thankfully, our lives would never cross again. In my mind, she was one of the people who'd destroyed my life. And I wonder, one day will I be set free of this bitterness and pain?

"The yard is lovely," I said.

"You should have stayed on this side of the island. It's much quieter." She was wearing a floral-print dress that buttoned down the front, and she adjusted the sash around her waist. She was plump and had badly dyed hair—she probably did it herself at home. "I wish I had," I stammered. "My hotel is so noisy."

"I told Elem. But she said, 'Mother, Handan Abla wouldn't like this part of the island.'"

When at home, did Elem refer to me as Handan Abla? I don't think she did. Not long ago, she'd called me just "Handan" in front

of them. So was her mother simply being respectful? Or was it a blatant way of showing that she found her daughter's relationship with
Handan Sarp strange? My mind was a jumble.

I'm uncomfortable with family life. With the exception of summers, I'd always lived alone with my mother, a lonely and unhappy
woman. And we weren't the typical mother and daughter. She was
always in her own world. Sometimes hours would pass without a
word spoken between us. I grew up on my own.

I never had a family; no parents in the traditional sense, no brothers
or sisters. No father who came home after work. No mother who made
börek for teatime. Elem had a family. She had İnci and Hüseyin. With
gardening shears, Elem was clipping roses to put on the table. She
wanted to please me. I had a sudden urge to leap up and shout, "We
make love!" and lay waste to that innocent, naive family setting.

"Handan Abla wouldn't like this part of the island." What had
Elem meant? Did she think that I looked down on people, scoffing
at their lives and where they lived because of their poverty? It was
infuriating.

But now, at this moment, just as I've always done after our separation, time and time again I envision Elem in that yard on the island:

In my memory, the yard is suffused with swathes of flowers of
every color. My Munise clips roses from the flower beds.

A cheap vase from the market with a chipped corner, filled with roses.
Tea has been set.

As I imagine the scene, it feels as though we were bound by a deep
friendship, by trust.

Handan Sarp is a soprano visiting the young seamstress she met at
Nedret's boutique. They visit the family of the young seamstress at a
summer house they rented on that summery island. But being with
them means little to her.

As for the family, they'd boasted to the owner of the house that Handan Sarp would be coming to evening tea, taking pride in knowing Handan Sarp.

The owner of the house, of course, knew nothing about Handan Sarp. They explained to her that there was a kind of art called opera; interviews with the soprano appeared in newspapers and magazines; hadn't she heard of Handan Sarp? And the owner is swept off her feet by the idea that a famous artist would grace her home. But no one knew of her fame. It was a riddle.

The only person who understood and loved me in the midst of that painful farce was Elem. She knew my heart. She was my friend, my everything. But I didn't understand her or what she felt; I hurt her, and now it was thrown back in my face.

We drank tea and ate cheese pastries. There was rose jam in a glass jar. Elem was happy I was there with her family. As we talked, the initial silence and awkwardness subsided. The old landlady lamented that the olive industry on the island was drying up: "It's become nothing more than an amusement park."

After tea, Elem's mother began working on a piece of cross-stitch: a basket adorned with grapes, pears, and peaches overflowing with plums and cherries. It was lovely with its patterns of marbled yarn.

I looked at that poor woman who'd given up her life for her three children. What did I want? Why did I feel such anger toward her? She was a mother, living out her life as she'd been taught. That was her world, nothing more. Never had she imagined infinite horizons; she was incapable of it.

But with thread, a keen eye for detail, cross-stitch and embroidery she was bringing to life a basket of fruit. She'd become lost in her work, just like an artist.

I couldn't restrain myself: "It's very beautiful."

"Do you really like it?" She was moved by my compliment.

"Yes, it's quite lovely."

That was our first and last moment of emotional connection. She set aside her thread and needle and looked at me, her wrinkled face glowing. She sat there as though listening to the whirring of the cicadas, and as we gazed at each other I thought, "Why does she look so beaten down, so withered?" And for a second, I had an urge to weep.

"I'd like you to have it."

A shudder ran through me. "But all the work you've put into it . . ."

She beamed with pleasure. "You've done so much for Elem." With the contentment of a mother she smiled, looking at Elem and me.

We were enveloped in something sublime that transcended the self, there in the yard of that humble house on Zeytin Island: with the empty tea glasses, the pink and white roses in the vase, and the buzz of the cicadas' song, it seemed as though we were starting a new life, a new world, as the plums, cherries and dappled peaches spilled from the basket in that strange silence punctuated by the raspy breathing of Elem's father. And there was that lonely old woman to whom we'd bid farewell, and Elem and Hüseyin, and soon that cross-stitch that would quickly be completed; for just the briefest of moments we'd saved humanity. We realized that it could be saved.

I wish that island would be plunged into the depths of the sea.

The last summer.

For me, it was the last summer of my life.

Elem would go back to Zeytin Island. In our tale, the page about Zeytin Island wouldn't be turned. Most likely I'll tell that story, because it's our experiences that hint at what our futures will bring. Without talking about it, I cannot move on.

But now it's the last summer.

Despite my complaints, I stayed at the Hotel Kermen. The usual groups of snobs trying to look rich were nowhere to be seen.

Elem and I came together. We had separate rooms.

The island was deserted.

The season was over by the time we arrived at the end of August. Nedret had postponed Elem's yearly holiday, because the boutique had been busy: wedding upon wedding, bridal gowns, suits and dresses.

The season was over and the sea had gone cold. With the coming of August, summer on Zeytin Island comes to a close. Autumn blows in from the open sea. The cusp of autumn.

But I didn't care.

I was working on *Manon Lescaut*. I needed to work. I'd gone to the island to listen to my art and to myself.

Puccini, one more time. But my dreams had been drained of life. I knew that I was struggling for nothing and that all my efforts were in vain.

I was too old to play Manon. But even if I'd been young, it wouldn't have mattered. I had been young in *La bohème* . . .

Opera felt more distant than ever.

But in opera, being along has its own bittersweet pleasure.

I had doubts about my voice. It was fatigued, and I'd pushed its limits. I tried to avoid drinking and smoking, but it was too late. I'd destroyed my life. But I wasn't afraid—with one last heave of resistance, I swore that I would succeed.

On Çalı Island, the bright yellow golden bell flowers were withering. And the wind, especially at night, whipped across the island. The clouds would gather, thick cumulous rain clouds, bringing downpours nothing like summer rain.

I was pleased with the season. It was an autumn I'd never seen before. I felt that the storm I carried within would quiet down, and the torrents would wash everything clean.

The golden bell blossoms may have been fading, but on Zeytin Island there were still bursts of color. It seemed odd to me that people would pack up and leave, missing out on that show of blossoms. The wealthy vacationers had left the island, finishing out the season somewhere warmer.

Some of the flowers had wilted and fallen from their stems, but tiny wild blossoms dotted the yellowing hillsides. They were the island's fall flowers, something akin to sweet william.

Then came the citrus in their festive glory: tight buds of fruit on the lemon, orange and tangerine trees in the island's gardens. Slowly, they began to show their colors. The lemons shaded into yellow, the tangerines became lighter and lighter green, and the blood oranges were flecked with red.

And then the leaves—they were stunning! Seared by the flame of August—a dying flame—the red leaves faded to rust and brown, while some held out, shimmering green. And yellow leaves fluttered down from the trees like showers of rain.

The olive trees, however, stubbornly refused to shed their dark gray-green leaves. The desolation of olive groves is the true harbinger of the coming of autumn.

In the evenings, Elem and I were practically the only people at Yakamoz Lokantası. The summertime waiters had all returned home. And in a way, we weren't there either as we sat in silence, withdrawn into ourselves.

"Did you swim today?"

"Yes."

"Was it cold?"

"Quite. But I couldn't resist."

That was it.

In fact, I knew that Elem had gone swimming. From my balcony I can see the beach, the empty shore, the sea. I just didn't know what to talk about.

But Elem's expression said, "I've lived and found happiness, and tasted joy." She loved the years that we spent together. She matured with me, and loved and suffered. She was content with what would come, even if it was torturous. That's why I was so bound to my Munise. Together we faced the tomorrows.

The weather was warm, as though summer had returned to the island.

But shriveled and parched leaves rustled in the breeze, speaking day and night of the passing of summer.

Elem went to visit the owner of the house they'd rented the summer before. On her return, an air of sadness hung over her.

"Her oldest daughter had to have one of her breasts removed."

There are some things that you don't want to hear.

"Last winter she had surgery at Cerrahpaşa Hospital. She'd been so kind to us."

"Who?"

"The owner of the house." She looked at my face, and saw that my thoughts were elsewhere.

"If they removed the breast, then she should be fine."

"The cancer spread."

"It's a shame."

"She has three children. The youngest is only four."

I wondered if I'd begun to lose my mind; I was completely indifferent, untouched. The fact that a young woman was going to die of cancer moved nothing inside me. My only desire was for Elem to stop talking. And she did.

Manon Lescaut was going to be staged for the first time in more than a hundred years in a country where opera was largely unknown.

Life sometimes seems so strange; when Puccini was composing that opera, it never would've occurred to him that someone with a destiny such as mine would become part of the plot: more than a hundred years later, in Istanbul, a lesbian would play Manon! A soprano afraid of her own lesbian nature, hiding her sexuality from everyone. Living as though stricken with the plague.

We hadn't started working on the music yet. There, all alone, I was trying to grasp the soul of Manon Lescaut.

I wasn't satisfied with just reading the libretto, and after much searching, I found a copy of the novel. I wondered if I'd be able to manage with my weak French, but in the end I got through the book.

The first thing that struck me was the length of the author's name: L'Abbé Antoine François Prévost. He'd been born three hundred years before, in the very month of August. It sent a shudder down my spine; you read a novel on an island at the end of summer, and in that silence broken only by the sound of the sea, you open to a page that speaks of that same time of year—August!

Prévost could never have known that I'd read his work in a place called Zeytin Island in the same month he was born. The metaphysics of life can be terrifying.

Had he really gone to America, to the New World, to that newly discovered continent? Where did he write *Manon Lescaut*? Not much is known. It's a masterpiece among sentimental novels written in the eighteenth century, and Puccini transformed it into a powerful musical piece. Of course, the French never forgot about Massenet's *Manon*, and they knew its place in the annals of opera.

In other sources, neither *Manon* nor *Manon Lescaut* are given much creed; *Manon* has practically been forgotten, while the other work is mentioned solely in reference to the fact that Puccini contracted tuberculosis when he was young.

("I know that my work is of no interest to you or anyone else. But I find myself in a strange state of longing. I miss opera. Just as I miss Elem.

No, I miss it even more then her. I'll always miss opera the most. But I've forgotten my destiny. The characters in operas have an air of the tragedian, of grandiloquence; and this created for me a second life.")

It's unclear whether or not Abbé Prévost ever went to America.

But why was Puccini so interested in America? *Manon Lescaut*, *Madame Butterfly*, and *The Girl of the Golden West*—all three deal with America. And perhaps there are others that I don't know about.

The end of *Manon Lescaut* is like the beginning of *The Girl of the Golden West*: the gold rush in America!

The Gold Rush was my childhood film; I laughed as we watched the jittery silent film in the screening room at school, but it left me with a feeling of melancholy—in the end, *The Gold Rush* is a tragedy.

In those days, adolescent Handan daydreamed about Maria Callas. If it hadn't been for the feature stories in the magazine *Hayat* about Callas and Onassis, the Metropolitan, the Scala, Leyla Gencer and the Ankara State Opera, what dreams could she have had? What ideals could she hold onto?

Her whole life was spread out before her. I miss that Handan. She truly believed that, while on stage, she'd save the world as she sang the world's most beautiful songs, reaching out with her voice to the defeated in life and to all the oppressed and all the heartbreak. And as she fantasized, losing herself in her dreams, she'd fall into a trance, filled with hope.

I tried to understand Manon from a different perspective: flight in the name of love, perhaps flight from love itself. From the monastery in Amiens to Paris, and in Paris toward the arms of a new lover—but always that old love persists! Branded as a criminal and thief, she ventures with her lover to a ship departing from the port of Havre, and from there on to America, where she dies of hunger and thirst in the arms of her first love.

It grieves me that Manon Lescaut, filled with hope for a new life in America and such passion to survive, dies in the arms of Des Grieux.

I'm untouched by the suffering of that woman Elem told me about, that young mother whose body was ravaged by cancer, while I'm wracked by sorrow over those operatic lovers dreaming of becoming citizens of gold rush America.

I'm told that the stage director is Italian. What kind of atmosphere does he want to create?

A barren stage appears before my eyes. It is swathed in the colors of the steppe under the harsh light of the sun, a light that blinds; a stony landscape stretches into the distance and there is Manon, wearing a gown that has been torn to shreds. She'll drag herself across the ground, ragged and weary, but don't let her die in anyone's arms—she must die alone, we always die alone!

In the early hours of morning I was unexpectedly hounded by memories of my youth. A young Nilüfer appeared, graceful as a gazelle, but imbued with the coldness and distance of Hedda Gabler. "Would you leave the room, Handan" she says. "I want to get dressed in private." Withdrawing from the room, I felt like I'd been slapped. With greater desperation than ever before, I thought of her naked body, her form stripped completely bare, and those red geraniums, all of those red geraniums, seemed to be a symbol of my pain. One by one they were transformed by the tears in my eyes into images of Nilüfer and me, two people who missed each other and longed for each other's bodies with mad passion, but there I was, alone in the courtyard of the pension.

Nilüfer came out of the room: "Aren't you going to lock the door?" she asked.

"The key's inside."

"Why don't you get it then, sweetie." She laughed, straightening the straps of her bikini, but her voice was tinged with cruelty.

"You go ahead," I told her. "I'll come in a while."

She shrugged.

I entered the room and lay down on her bed. Overcome by frenzy, wracked by the chasms between us, I pulled off my bikini . . .

What was the meaning of those persistent memories, of thinking about Nilüfer after all that time?

In the mornings I got up early. Soon, the holiday would be over. I wanted to savor every moment.

I set out on a walk, down to the shore road as usual, but the season was different. The beaches were completely empty and the birds seemed ill at ease; cormorants nestled up against one another, no longer stitching the sea with their sharp beaks.

Walking to the other side of the island, I took in the scent of morning mist. Sometimes the shoreline would be enveloped in fog, making it difficult to find your way.

At times the island smelled of rotting leaves, permeated by loneliness.

"After eight years . . ." she said.

Perhaps she said, "seven years" or "nine years." Seven, eight, nine years . . .

In the dim light, I couldn't make out the expression on her face.

They no longer turned on the strings of colored lights at Yakamoz Lokantası. Only a few tables were full, altogether about five or six people. The waiter brought candles to the tables, but the glass holders were useless against the wind and the candles constantly blew out.

"To our friendship," I think I said, out of bitter reproach for my life. I wanted to see her reaction.

Her voice trembled. "Aside from loving you, I was good for nothing else—isn't that true?" she asked.

At the moment I didn't understand. But now that seven or eight years have passed, I understand what she meant. That night I gave her a blank smile, waving my hand in the space between us as though brushing aside a pointless topic.

"If only I'd read books other than *The Night of Fire*," she said. "If only I'd watched operas . . . But that's not how it was. No matter how much I'd like that, you can't change the past. With you, I'm a stranger."

Zeytin Island was nearing curtain call.

It was a summer after that.

One or two years later. After I abandoned Zeytin Island. My life had fallen into the grips of a profound monotony.

Neither I nor Elem went on vacation in those years. Elem didn't even take her yearly leave. Her family was probably in need of money, just as Nedret needed Elem. And İnci was preparing her dowry.*

I think those were the years I joined the festivals with Semra and Ali. Concerts, theater performances, operas. Far from Elem. Far from memories of her. From city to city, believing in nothing. Art disgorging itself, emptying itself out. No sincerity, no authenticity. Excitement, feeling and meaning were all swept away.

I watched some of those ridiculous "new" operas: the baritone playing the king approached the orchestra pit and smashed the instrument of the lead violinist against the violinist's head. Grand finale! Grand opera is finished in this world. The audience rose up in roars of applause.

Accompanying that monotony was a despair that laid waste to everything in its path.

---

* I decided to ask Handan Sarp about this discrepancy. She claimed that İnci had gotten married during the years when she had gone to Zeytin Island, but here she states that İnci was saving money for her dowry. Like always, she merely smiled at me wryly and said, "Of what importance is that?" (Sİ)

It was a summer evening, stiflingly hot and humid.

We were sitting in the garden. Not a single leaf stirred. The flowers of the coralbells drooped in the heat.

Elem said that she was going on vacation. Yes, again to Zeytin Island.

"But of course. However you like."

"Aren't you going to come?"

"No," I said, "I'm not. Are you going with your family?"

"Yes."

A few leaves had fallen on the table. Dried and crumbling, they'd already become leaves of autumn.

They had decided to go on vacation as a family. We'd be far apart. Elem was being stubborn. And her mother? She was probably gloating over the fact that she'd saved her daughter from me.

I cut her off: "Elem, it's over, isn't it?"

"What's over?"

"Us. We're through."

She said nothing.

"Elem, it's over. You're young, you should have your own life. And I'm getting older. It's finished. My life is finished." It was unbearably painful. I murmured to myself, "The chasms between us."

Images of her mother came to mind: badly dyed hair; ungainly, weary body; smeared, carelessly applied lipstick. I imagined her on the island, complaining about the oven as she served börek, her heart secretly set against me. In the yard on the island, colorful flowers in bloom. This year, "Handan Hanım" won't be coming to evening tea. A sigh of relief, that "opera woman" isn't after your daughter . . .

I laughed bitterly: "It's over!"

After tea, they'll water the flowers. It will be a quiet evening. The dark sky will be filled with stars, and while trying to count the points of light in the Milky Way, they'll suddenly burst into laughter—and nothing will seem banal to them.

Elem said, "I don't understand what you mean."

"You'll have your own life. A new life without me. But, of course, we'll stay friends."

For a long time she looked into my eyes. "Meaning, all that's left will be a sweet friendship," I said.

Normally she'd blush, fluttering her eyelids, and bow her head. But she continued to look at me, as though studying this "damned" thing called life, my silence, and my reticence, trying to find the reasons why I was pulling away from her.

Memories of our past together raced through my mind. At the boutique, we agreed on the brown and green outfit, irritating Nedret. Not wanting to hurt my feelings, Elem drank some beer with vodka at Hristo's. But then the memories splinter and fly apart, only to fade away.

She clenched the tablecloth, glowering, perhaps thinking that I'd betrayed her with another woman.

My heart raced: "Let's not drag this out. Both of us will move on with our lives."

If only the sun would let us be!

A few days later she came with her blue folder filled with clippings about me: articles, the occasional news story, photos.

Feigning ignorance, I asked, "What's this?"

My ears rang and I felt faint. It occurred to me that all the furniture in the flat was dark. I'd chosen such dark colors for my home, where Elem and I had once spent time together.

A betrayal! Of what? Our flesh.

Among all of the dark-hued furniture, she spoke of how she'd always been faithful to me. Of the loyalty of flesh.

Meaning that the heart had never loved.

Taking the folder, I thanked her. I was filled with hatred. It was over. We lapsed into silence.

Today I cannot bear to look at that folder. At Elem's handwriting. The clothes she sewed as gifts pain me. Just like everything else she did for me.

But that summer night, I felt nothing but anger. I was angry with Elem because I wanted to be set free. The furniture infuriated me: the reddish browns, the purple and blue glass vases. I was surrounded by shades of mourning.

Can the flesh betray? Can the body betray? The betrayal of the body is based on a bestial desire. That's what I wanted: the freedom of animal desire.

I sighed. We'd never loved one another. "Would you like some whiskey?" I asked.

"No. You have some."

"I will. But I was just asking if you want any." I stood up, setting aside the folder, and went into the kitchen.

She was frightened. Following me, she picked up a glass. "Beer and vodka. Do you have vodka? Like the old times."

Had she somehow sensed the memories that had flashed through my mind? I answered coolly, "Of course. There's always vodka. It's in the fridge."

She poured a little vodka into the glass and then filled it with beer.

I smiled: "Cheers."

I could sense that she wanted to embrace me.

Pulling away, I said, "To our new lives," and poured myself a glass of whiskey.

"Handan, what do you want me to do? What am I supposed to do?"

I went into the other room and got my spare keys, and gave them to my Munise. "This is your home. For as long as I live. Take the keys! But we're separating. You . . . I . . . We're finished. Over. Love fades. It dies away." I had no idea what I was saying. Just like my sentences that broke apart, I sobbed in quick heaves.

"Love doesn't die," she said. "My love didn't die." She was desperate, completely shaken.

But it was unbearable for me, and my sole desire was for her to leave. To be without you, Elem!

And she, that child of mine, began to cry, her olive green eyes flooded with tears.

Pulling myself together, I said, "Elem, this is how life is. Sooner or later, love fades away. You know this, I always told you that I don't believe in love."

"You never believed in love? When you hugged me, when you held me in your arms . . . When we were everything to each other, when we kissed . . . When we kissed on the lips . . ." She was trembling.

From the very beginning, when she wanted to give up her virginity to me, it was the idea of the purity of the body, the faithfulness of the flesh, which had led her astray. For her, our kisses, our lovemaking, was a way of being true to each other—not an act of rebellion. Those were things that couldn't be done with someone else. Our sins could only be forgiven through betrayal. She could neither understand nor feel what loyalty of the soul meant.

But at the time, neither could I.

So long as we didn't "betray" one another, there was no sin. And that "sin" could only be brought about by another person.

Elem's way of thinking about betrayal disgusted me.

Abruptly she asked, "Do you find it disgusting?"

I was startled. My inner turmoil at that moment was indescribable.

A crisis of terrifying proportions. I should've told Elem about the insignificance of the body. Even if we sleep with hundreds of people, if there is love, loyalty, a spiritual connection, sympathy, intimacy, compassion, then it doesn't matter.

"Elem, enough!"

"We're leaving this weekend. Good-bye." Putting her glass of beer and vodka on the kitchen counter, she turned and left, slamming the door on her way out.

I did something strange: I poured out the beer, and kissed the faint trace of lipstick on the rim of the glass. Yes, I kissed it. A sudden, irresistible moment of tenderness.

But it was short-lived. An image of her mother, that belittling woman who took such pride in her child—my child—stuck in my mind like a bone in a throat. I drove that imaginary mother from my thoughts. Create whatever life you want for your daughter: a woman of virtue, a mother of three children.

Wasn't there another woman just like that, being treated for cancer at Cerrahpaşa Hospital?

Cancer spread through me as well, with my cigarettes and alcohol.

I took a gulp of whiskey and opened the folder. There was an article about my success in *Manon Lescaut*. It said that I'd stirred interest in opera. Particularly in the last act, I "sang of the flutterings of the heart and soul." The stage manager, Lorenzo Cella, said that I was "a world-class soprano." But Lorenzo Cella would never again see me, nor hear my voice. They wrote that I "ran circles around" the younger generation of opera singers. I'd said that my career was in its "final throes," but they wrote that this was my "final rose."

So with that "final rose" I left my Munise to the innocent Feride of novels. And the true Çalıkuşu desires that nothing be left at all and nothing more be lost.

In those days a young woman had appeared in my life, a girl with glistening dark eyes and a "tight body." as she herself said; but where had we met? I walked to the telephone on the rosewood end table. There, among the pages of the phone book, I would find the business card she'd given me. She worked as a representative for a cosmetics firm.

Probably dating from 1947, there was a photograph of my mother set in a silver frame; she looked melancholic in the picture. No longer would she frighten me; she no longer had that power over me. My father, Şevket Sarp, was still alive, and I didn't have a photograph of him.

I called her that night. For the first time. "Handan Hanım, I'm such an admirer of yours. I'd like to get to know you better." Okay then, where are you, hard-bodied slut? Dirty lesbian whore!

Within an hour she arrived, and we sat in the wicker chairs beneath the coralbells.

In a rush, I prepared some nuts, feta cheese in olive oil sprinkled with oregano and red pepper flakes, and slices of tomato and cucumber. I dashed about, getting myself ready: I took a shower and combed my hair, then put on a sky-blue chiffon dress that Elem had made for me, and did my makeup; it felt as though I were flying, but I wasn't really myself.

I was taking revenge. But why? And against whom? Against life! My Munise had died in the moonlight, and the light from the moon shone on her lifeless face, and a little ways off, a gramophone played and a moth fluttered.

Smiling, polite Handan Sarp. Smiling, polite admirer. Soon I'd notice that the glimmer of her eyes was actually caused by her colored contact lenses. But it didn't matter. A powerful sexuality surged between us but we spoke of opera, art, *Manon Lescaut*, Puccini, Manon's second lover, the problems that arise when people fall in love, how I prepared for *Manon Lescaut* on Zeytin Island. Have you ever heard of Abbé Prévost? What do you think of American politics today?

That's as far as it went. In her game of courtesy and forced familiarity, I knew she was after something else. Yes, there was that powerful sexuality—let's sleep together now! But at the same time I also sensed that something rang false about her sexuality. It was a lie. Everyone has their own repertoire: mine was *Manon Lescaut*, and hers was Handan Sarp.

Had I wanted to sleep with her, to make love?

A moment comes when you suddenly fall to pieces: in her arms, my Munise would appear—in the dark, in that piercing loneliness. We always make the same mistake, seeking in another person the one who left us or the one we abandoned. With Elem, didn't I find myself longing for Kaya? And with Kaya, the one before her?

There, in the garden at night: the stunted laurel and the white rose that Elem hoped would be purple.

I was flooded with desire, a repulsive desire that humiliates and torments. With my polite guest, we were transformed into vampires.

Following me into the kitchen, she said: "Your apartment is just lovely, especially the garden."

"The white roses didn't bloom this year," I told her, thinking of my grandmother saying that the jasmine hadn't bloomed. Her granddaughter, that young girl, Çalıkuşu, knew nothing of that night, nor of the apartment on Sakızlı Street, the kitchen, the garden dappled in light. She didn't know that in her future life, she would be perpetually defiled by sexual longing. There should be a medical term for that: a disease of sexual defilement.

I was going to refill our drinks. Thoughts of her body swirled through my mind. I had never had a lover who was so fit. But I'm vile— because after that rush of desire, my mind turned to Elem's matronly body, her breasts that had aged before my own, her matronly hips.

Before going out into the garden, I left her for a moment and turned around that silver frame on the end table so that my mother wouldn't see us. It may seem childish. But, until the end of my days, until the curtains close for the last time, I'll always be a child.

As I stepped out into the garden, the telephone rang. I answered, but no one replied. I spoke into the silence: "Hello? Hello?" Could it be Elem? "Elem, come back! Elem, call me." There was no one there. The line went dead.

Coolly, diva Handan Sarp held to her role as she entered the garden. The young woman, whose eyes glittered through her colored contact lenses, was standing beside the lilac. "What kind of tree is this?" she asked. "It's losing its leaves."

"It's a lilac. And it's just like me."

"Handan, are you a lilac?" Her laughter tinkled. "Do you smell of lilac?"

I'd meant the falling leaves. She approached me, and I could feel her breath on the back of my neck.

That Hollywood scene revolted me. "Leave!" That was the first time I raised my voice in the garden; I'd never dared, for fear of attracting the attention of the neighbors.

But she didn't. She pulled me toward her and kissed me on the lips. Elem!

I was filled with shame. But it wasn't the shame of betrayal of a virtuous woman, or a virtuous lesbian, or a housewife.

Don't be misled: I didn't sleep with her.

I'd believed that the animal freedom of the body was something easy, that it would liberate me from myself.

But a feeling of loneliness washed over me, more poignant than ever. And loathing, followed by anxiety and wounded pride.

"Leave!"

No matter how hard it might be, I decided to resist until she left.

She apologized. Standing in a dark corner of the garden, we were shrouded in shadows. She stepped into the light; I remained in the darkness. Although she tried to smile, her face was crossed by lines of disappointment and fear. I'd spoken harshly, and felt myself being pulled down into a futile trap of pity: I smiled. Immediately she was put at ease, and sat back down as though nothing had happened. Clearly I was to blame; I'd invited her to my place and given her false signals.

Again she launched into a discussion of opera, Puccini, and my successes in *Madame Butterfly* and *Manon Lescaut*. She told me that in her monotonous work life, opera and art were the sole glimmers of joy; she was a very lonely young woman, she said. She went to concerts and painting exhibitions and read books at home. And then abruptly she said, "You misunderstood me. Who would know that I . . ."

"I understand you. I respect you and your feelings."

"Handan Hanım, it's just admiration."

"Yes. Thank you."

Taking my hand in her own, she said that she wanted to apologize. And then she made another attempt to kiss me, but I didn't respond. With laughter that rang out like a bell, she tittered: "You've wasted my whole night, you wrinkled up lesbo!"

Regret caught hold of me. I'd thought it would be easy to leave my body aside; as though our bodies were budding flowers, the moment that our damp mounds brushed against one another, our mounds and the erect points of our breasts, then I'd be set free of Elem.

That "wrinkled-up lesbo" went straight to sleep, probably out of fear.

Elem had left for Zeytin Island. She must have—the weekend passed, and I heard nothing from her.

I struggled to breathe. It wasn't longing; I didn't miss her. Just the pain of her absence. The pain of knowing that I made her suffer.

But maybe she moved on without a second thought, letting it all go with greater ease than I could. Perhaps she just erased the past, our past together. She left without calling, and never called from Zeytin Island.

Not to think, not to feel . . . If only I could do the same. If only I had a family that would take me in and comfort me. I cannot bear my father. Nor Aunt Nadire. Before me, time stretches out—time to think, to feel.

She didn't call.

Had they rented the same house? The young woman with cancer, was she still alive? Her elderly mother—we'd spoken but an hour or two—was she still on the island? There was a telephone somewhere in that house.

("I didn't call, Selim Bey, I didn't call out of stubbornness.

I found things to occupy myself. The *Çalıkuşu* project came up: *Çalıkuşu Opera*. I'll tell you about it. The scenario enchanted me. With the *Çalıkuşu Opera*, I could have concluded my career")

Nothing pains me. I cast Elem from my thoughts. I shall start life anew as though I had many long years ahead of me. Looking into the mirror brings no discomfort: the bags under my eyes, the sallow purple of my lips, the sharp creases on each side of my nose. I pay them no heed. My youth had been long-lived, isn't that enough? Isn't the suffering it brought enough as well? Those agonies stripped away my youth. Tears are meaningless. When I learned how to keep my feelings inside, I also learned to hold back my tears.

She didn't call.

The idea of separation frightens me.

I should recount what followed next. It's a point of shame for me, among the secret aches I carry. This ache is tenuous, not always tangible. But it will always be there, a constant throb concealing a twinge of operatic sentiment.

Elem and her family came back. She didn't call on the night she returned, but the next day she called from work. The holiday had gone well, she said; it was relaxing. It had been good for her father as well—his cough seemed to have quieted down.

I pulled away my mask: "I've missed you," I told her. "I'd hoped you would call. Thank you . . ."

When I said "thank you," something flickered through her voice, an anxiety that I can't put into words; a distance, a flight, a shying away.

As though I hadn't noticed, I mentioned the *Çalıkuşu Opera*: "I'll tell you about it tonight."

We embraced when we met up, but she was rigid, distant. We'd agreed to meet somewhere, a restaurant probably, but the place isn't important; just as now, Elem's coldness sent a tremor of pain through me. I thought she was just being resentful.

But before I even mentioned Fikret Bey's idea for the opera, she said, "During the holiday—on Zeytin Island—I met someone."

"Who?"

"A very nice person," said.

"I'm happy for you," I managed to say. But a storm howled within me. That wild, strange sea I carry within. I've always been a stranger in this world, a stranger to life. Only in that dark sea can I exist, so I can drown in infinitude. "What kind of person is she?"

"She's never been married. Her family is well-off. She doesn't work now, but she knows how to sew."

"How old is she?" In fact, I wanted to ask if she were beautiful. It was a surprisingly womanly question.

"She's forty-two."

I laughed, cruelly. "Elem, are you sure you aren't looking for a mother, or a father?"

She was lost in thought, her gaze turned inward.

"Why someone older than you? Why don't you find someone your own age? And I can't believe how quickly you found someone else." My voice was beginning to crack at the edges.

"Handan, you told me, 'It's over, we're finished.'"

I was discovering a new Elem. Here was a woman who, on a two-week vacation, could leave behind all we'd been through together and shrug it off with indifference. I was astounded at my own stupidity; while I thought she was all alone, pining away on that island, she'd found someone, an unmarried woman who knew how to sew.

Life suddenly seemed so banal and common.

It felt as though we were rehearsing for our true separation.

Panic struck me. Panic at the thought of being alone. "Let's be like we were before," I said. That itch of rebellion I carry within had long since quieted down.

My Munise didn't object.

We went home . . . to my home.

After work that Saturday, she met up with the woman she'd met on the island. She was tense as she told me about it: "It was just a summer fling," she said.

Summer fling! That expression was so poignant—where had Elem picked it up? It echoed down over the years: summer fling, summer romance, summer . . .

"Elem, was it a summer fling that you wanted?"

She wasn't listening to me.

The woman had been heartbroken, and wept. As she told me about it, Elem also cried. Elem doesn't cry easily. I'll never forget her tears that day. Was it the breakup that had upset her?

"Poor creature . . ." she said.

But which of us did she mean?

Everything was calm. Just like before. Our relationship was a steady monotony.

In those days, I thought that life had settled down. You can disappear in the tumult of this sprawling city. People don't look you in the eye. Your life, your preferences, your choices may differ from theirs, but you don't suffer for it. A kind of civility. That's how I thought—for a short while, anyway. My relationship with Elem didn't tear at my life. Sometimes we met up with Semra and Ali, the four of us, and went out. We went out with others as well. Elem had become a part of my life. "It's good that we are together," I told myself.

Only occasionally did I think about that woman, the one Elem slept with on Zeytin Island.

But later, my conscience began to torment me. That faded flower of a weeping woman—she knew how to sew, just like Elem. Perhaps they dreamed of a future together: opening a dress shop, living in the same home, a few tabby cats . . .

A stab of conscience. Everyone has their own life, and loneliness is my destiny. You can never go back, Handan—your path will always lead you deeper into loneliness.

No one ever dies from being alone. You simply get used to it. And in the end, loneliness becomes a comfort. You've donned the flaming shirt of Nessus, choosing loneliness as your destiny. But you drove them apart.

Who was she? How did they meet? The first touch, the first passionate kiss . . . I was sure that poor woman had fallen in love; and Elem had been suffering because of me, so of course she would open her heart to another's passion.

I thought that woman would become like the soul mate of my Aunt Nadire. Soul mate—what a bitter expression. And because of me, Elem was never to be. Nothing was to be. Your fate is shaped by time, by place.

Fate. If that woman and Elem had had a life together . . . Who was she? And what happened to her? Is she living out the destiny of Aunt Nadire? Is that how life ends for a woman who likes other women? Who never marries and doesn't have a man in her life? Is it true that she wasn't sexually interested in men?

For years her memory has stayed with me. But Elem and I never spoke of her again. The thought of that aging woman's pain, and perhaps Elem's unhappiness as well, lurked in the back of my mind.

To be alone until the very end, until death comes for you—and then to feel pricks of conscience no longer. You find yourself huddled in an armchair, unable to move, and the echoes of the hundreds of songs you once knew fade away; looking outside, all you hear is the sound of rain lashing against the window. The rain speaks to you of the people who have brought you suffering and those whose hearts you've broken. Then you take a few weak steps toward the window, wanting to feel the rain sting your face. And then you're faced with your loneliness.

The same chorus rings in your ears, always the same line from *Macbeth*: "Patria oppressa!"

This is my land of bitter exile, my corner of reclusion. Always the same withdrawal into solitude. Once, it could've been a sprawling empire.

("Have you noticed how absentminded I am? You finished your drink, but I didn't even notice. Let me get you another.

These days I'm always like this. When I'm talking about Elem and our separation, when I'm alone or walking outside, when I awake in the morning, or am reading the newspaper. My thoughts always wander.

Like now, I start thinking about my unkempt garden. I don't want to tend it anymore. Let it become overgrown and wild, it suits me better.

And maybe when the garden gets that way I'll change my mind about telling you all this.

Time seems to slip: I find myself thinking about the garden of the house where we used to go in the summer. In that old garden, the sky seemed to go on forever—it was nothing like this small garden here—there was an infinite blue sky streaked by the rays of the sun. In that broad summer landscape there is a crumbling stone wall, fruit trees in full leaf, and wild white roses bursting into bloom, spilling over from the neighbor's garden.

Fine, but why? I don't stop there, because of the Handan of my childhood—she doesn't know where these memories will take her, where they will pick up and leave from. It is that childhood Handan who interests me. And now, I fall into reverie about her, that young girl who doesn't yet know what adventures await her.

Everything is a jumble.")

The friends we had . . .

In the midst of this confusion, exhaustion and scattered musing, that's what comes to mind: the friends we had.

During that long, heartrending period of time, neither of us had many friends. And certainly no common friends. I suppose we preferred just being alone together.

Is it always like this for loves that are rejected by society's false morality? Just the two of you—but actually you're alone.

There was practically no one else. Perhaps we weren't even friends.

And in any case, I'm not a very sociable person.

No, we weren't friends. She wasn't my confidante, nor was I hers.

Elem had her own friends, her own social circle. I'd never even met them, and I don't think I was interested in getting to know them.

Did they know about me?

Sometimes Elem would talk about her friends, but with embarrassment. A lull would settle into our conversations, an awkward rift—maybe she told me about them just to break the silence.

But I couldn't relate to these distant events, these people I'd never meet. In the end, they would never be a part of our life together.

She spoke as though one day those people would be of interest to me. And eventually I did become curious about who they were, what they talked about, their passions, ideals, and dreams for the future, because in all of those desires and longings I hoped to discover Elem's own secrets.

If I wasn't her confidante, then they probably were. She may not have spoken to them about Handan Sarp, but she might have told them things she didn't tell me.

It wasn't just indifference that I felt, but also jealousy.

Beyond jealousy, I wanted to meet them and hear what they had to say about the days of the past and the present.

I remember one evening: autumn was settling into the city in grays, yellows and pale reds. Elem, Gelengül and I were sitting in the garden. It was either a Saturday or a Sunday.

In those days, Elem and I would meet up on the weekends because she had to work late most evenings. Actually, that's not true; leaving work late was just an excuse for me. I was trying to build a new life for myself, staying out until the early hours of the morning with Gelengül in the dingy bars that she frequented. And Elem was no longer a mere seamstress; she was now one of Nedret's top employees, a young career woman who had set her life in order.

As we sat in the garden, I was feeling so miserable that I wasn't paying any attention to what Gelengül was talking about. My life seemed like a nightmare. I no longer felt any intimacy with Elem and just wanted to live my life. But it wasn't clear what that life was.

As Gelengül told her unending stories, they both laughed.

Their laughter soothed me. It was like a distant, drab stirring of life. I began listening: when Gelengül was a teenager, there was a neighbor's wife she used to make love with. There was no end to their fooling around, kissing and tumbling in bed, but then the wife would come over to visit Gelengül's parents and call her "dear sweet girl." Gelengül began cornering the woman anywhere she wanted, not caring if anyone might see them.

No, their laughter repulsed me. That drab stirring of life quickly faded. What stirring? I was disgusted by life, by the weakness and desperation of those creatures called human beings.

Gelengül said, "How could my mother know what was going on? She and my father hardly every screwed—what would she know about that kind of thing?!" and then burst into laughter, swilling from her glass of rakı. Then she took a drag from her cigarette, and the smoke swirled around her.

I looked at her, as if for the first time in my life: just above her purplish lips, a thin line of a mustache stood there as a challenge to the world. She had straight, graying hair, which was combed back, and since the first day we met it always reminded me of a fairy tale witch's flying broom. I looked at her bloodshot eyes, which see the world in shades of red.

Why was she at my home? It's pointless to ask: I needed a third person, because if Elem and I were alone together, the silence would bear down on us. So I invited Gelengül to join us, but hinted that she should be careful about not being seen when she came. She knew that her appearance struck others as strange, but she took great pleasure in that.

Elem said, "Yes, everyone has their own separate life."

"What do you mean, 'separate life'?" I asked, frowning.

"A life that's different from what it appears to be."

"Is that what your life is like?"

Elem, as though sensing that a storm was about to break loose, hesitated for a moment: "I do."

"And you?" I asked Gelengül.

"Maybe in the past. But now I don't care. I don't give a damn about any of you."

Elem looked away from both of us. "I have to. In my life, I have to pretend. I'm not like you. I'm not as free as you."

Gelengül's attitude suddenly changed. "Ah, Elem! All of us are like that." With that deep voice of hers, all of those feminine "my dears" and "ahs" were absurd and a little pathetic. First she'd come across as masculine, but then something rather feminine would slip out in the things she said. Poor Gelengül, who was so proud of her masculinity, would slip from being the perfect man into a sleazy gay queen—and then the game was up, the role was over. Or, she'd start a new game and take on a new role.

A storm didn't break out. That night, the way that Gelengül could shift from being a housewife to a neighborhood brute and then a gay whore, struck a painful chord within me, driving everything else away: Who are we? Why are we like this? Did nature create this piti-ful farce? Our instincts? Are we all the same? A thousand questions swirled in my mind.

At times, I'd catch a glimpse of that "life" in which Elem had to appear different than she was.

Her social circle included the other young women who worked at the fashion boutique. More or less I knew who they were, and Elem wasn't close with any of them.

At İnci's wedding, there was a table of young men and women. Maybe those were Elem's friends—she kept going to their table, and they would talk and laugh.

I don't know.

Today I'm feeling unwell. Perhaps it is just fatigue brought on by the coming of spring.

Gazing at the ruby on his ring, my teacher Cemil Sahir said, "The power to change life is in our hands." He said that often: "We have the power to change life."

But I didn't. Only later did I have that desire. I could've severed the ties that bind me; but I gave in to a lust for hollow fame, and was led astray by my arrogance and pomposity.

I was unable to become close with anyone.

I never let anyone see the "true" Handan Sarp, fearing that they wouldn't like her. That fear always weighed heavy on me, lording over and tyrannizing my life. I hid beneath it. Hiding was easy for me, and that's why I lived a life bereft of friends. I was a castaway in my internal exile. As soon as I left the shelter of my shell, I scampered back to the "morals" of society that I rejected. My existence had long been cleft in two. But was it just two? Perhaps three, four, or five.

In the end I had no one.

And I thought it was better that way.

What about Cemil Sahir? Was he able to change life? Everything about him was enveloped in an air of pitiable melancholy: his piano, rococo-style home, bejeweled rings, thin fragile laughter. Only among us did he command respect.

I'll never forget when, as a student, I went to visit Cemil Sahir for the first time. I asked the way, and a young boy, cocky even at his age, said: "So, you're going to see Mother Ghost?" as he pointed out the apartment building. Of course, I didn't understand what he meant, so I said nothing. Later it struck me, like a bolt of lightning: Mother Ghost!

If changing life meant being a mother ghost . . .

Full of dreams, Handan Sarp had no time for mother ghosts, or father ghosts—the whole world was going to hear her voice! At the time, I didn't realize that I would need his guidance.

And I was unaware that I was striking roots at the edge of the abyss.

When Elem and I had become close, I told her that we were on the brink of that abyss and that we'd always live on that precipice. I held my personal morals above all else. I didn't call that young woman to my thorny path. She came of her own will, out of love. And that love pained me.

Sifting through the past, I think of the times when Elem was deeply in love with me, her days of youth when she believed that our relationship would never end.

I try to welcome spring with its crisp, chill evenings. The daytime sky is a bright broad blue that darkens with the falling of night. Stubbornly I sit in the garden, shivering from the cold, until the day comes to a close. I rummage through my memories of the garden like an archaeologist, searching for traces of our shared loves. We both loved that garden, and would be filled with a childlike joy when the lilac bloomed.

At the beginning of every summer the lilac blooms again.

It's not me, but the rain that waters the garden now.

There were so few things that we both loved. She never liked opera; she merely put up with it, and tried to appear interested. For me she listened to it, and for me she attended my performances. And now I'm far from my Munise who didn't like opera; knowing that she didn't like it pains me even more.

In the garden, my hands clench into fists. Awaiting remembrances of her, I dream that she'll come. But she won't. Last spring I waited as well.

I have the feeling that I'll never sit in this garden again. It's not an obsession with suicide; I've gotten over that. It's probably more about aging and becoming filled with doubt. Will I see the next spring? Just as we worried about the blooming of the lilac.

The blue drains from the sky. And then the faint traces of stars appear, becoming larger and brighter. At one time in my life, I used to look upon the stars and pray. When? It was the child Handan Sarp who prayed.

The lights burn in the other apartments.

Those are such negative verbs: "burn," "go out." My grandmother always said, "Put the light to rest." All that negativity, as though the hearth went out. "Wake up the light," my grandmother would say. She had a heart of pure grace.

I observe the lives in the other apartments. The thought won't leave my mind: how many others live alone? In this apartment there's only Handan Sarp. In the surrounding flats there are a few elderly people living alone, but in the past they had someone; they lost a husband, or a wife. Probably their children or grandchildren come to visit them.

The families are about to sit down to dinner. A woman closes a curtain, and a young girl waters plants on a balcony; but I have no children.

The green of the leaves darkens, and soon darkness will fall. The sparrows have gone. It's a feeling of unease that drives me forth in life. But the greatest pain is the fact that I no longer have my voice, a fact that I always try to conceal.

I was able to get along in life without friends because I had the stage. Onstage, you have no need for friends—liberation is your accompaniment. Wild liberation. And the more you taste of it, the more it pleases you.

The rehearsals are exhausting, and the performances are a strain. But a few rounds of sincere, genuine applause fill you with joy. Your worries fall away. Slowly, you're brought back to life. Late at night in a taxi, the tension drains from your muscles. People say, "Let me take you home," but you brush aside their offers with a nod of thanks. Most of the time you are alone. That wild liberation!

When you feel that way, you begin to distance yourself from others because they strip the meaning from that sensation. And there you are, with your sense of being as dark as a Flying Dutchman, with your absence.

Things happen around you but they appear commonplace. Dry, insipid lives sapped of vitality. You'd been on stage, singing. That feeling of confidence is nearly impossible to describe. It happens only there, onstage under that flood of lights that wraps you in its embrace, and your heart glows. You're spared all of humanity. Spared the reality of life. And as you become purified of life's taint, your art consoles you with its own truth. That grand longing fades, and there is only music, only opera.

Elem had her own friends. What difference does it make?

There were moments when I was in the presence of the Creator.

The early days of our separation were filled with such sorrow that I didn't know what to do with myself or how I'd be able to keep going on. The past months and years opened up before me—hours, minutes and seconds. On some nights, when it seemed that my heart was engulfed in flames, I tried to dash off my thoughts in writing. But they always fell short, those somniloquies of mine.

What I write are just rambling deliria. I pour out my heart though those scribbles, things that I'd never speak to another person: broken hearts, misunderstandings—our life. That's what I wrote about. But as I said, they were despicable writings. I was just defiling the pure surface of the paper; I had defiled my life.

I erased all thoughts of night from my mind. That's how I rose up against the cruelty of night. Nearly everything I wrote, all of my somniloquies, were to Elem. They were a sort of apology, a confession of sins, a sum total of loss. Pages and pages that Elem would never read.

I wrote on and on, only to find myself falling to pieces yet again in the morning.

I don't have a single friend. I never had friends. But at the same time there were people I secretly considered to be friends, though I kept them at a distance. Recluses afflicted with melancholy, living a bohemian lifestyle—they were the only ones close to me.

And I thought of Elem that way, as though she were one of them.

I think of Elem more and more often. More than I ever thought of her when we were together. I can even say that she's always on my mind. An ache that threatens to verge on madness—there's no pride, no arrogance. Anguish has no need of pride; it speaks silently to you of your suffering.

They say to me: you're in the love story of Majnun. The time when he won't meet Leyla is upon us. Majnun was a "man," Leyla, a woman. In love, they say, we've been rescued from womanhood and manhood. Elem, Judgment Day looms near, and you too will understand.

Life is passing by and in the aftermath, you say nothing to that haggard woman . . . You speak no words of hope to haughty, cold Handan who hid behind her mask.

Thinking of Elem just aggravates the pain. Her and me. In the story of Majnun. Each of us strangers. Each of us? No, just the two of us, together. As I write, the pain grows sharper.

I could've been kinder, but it struck me as so common. Elem, rather than belittling your friends I could've gotten to know them; and now, I find myself desperate for human compassion but that desire shames me. How banal! I long for that Handan of the past, that woman who held her head high.

This will pass, I promise.

Handan will be saved. She needs no one.

No one!

(I found those lines on a crumpled piece of paper among her writings. Sİ)

Gelengül: She was one of our friends.

There are photographs of us together, each of them telling their own tale. In a souvenir photo taken at Hristo's old restaurant the three of us are smiling. That was easily three or four years ago. My smile was forced. Elem's was innocent. And Gelengül was in the midst of one of her explosive, roaring laughs.

She roared when she laughed.

She always urged me toward lust. When dressed in men's clothes, she thought of herself as a kind of Pan. True lust, stripped of sentiment and thrust into the open, with no lovers' games.

Her intent wasn't to seduce me; rather, she wanted to lead me off the "straight and narrow" path, even on my most dolorous days. In all that intimacy, she truly believed that lust would cure the pain.

This photograph was taken at her place. I never liked her home. Generally I don't like other people's homes, especially not hers. Elem and I often went there.

She howled in laughter that verged on the orgasmic. It was frightening.

In any case, I was afraid.

"Taking her between my arms, I pulled her toward me, Handan. She began to moan. No, she it was more like sharp cries. And I cried out too! Do you know what she said to me? 'I'll never go to bed with a man again, never!' But damn! Aren't I a man?!"

People called her Clark Gable, perhaps because of her thin mustache which she darkened with eyeliner. Or maybe it was because of the way she gazed seductively like Clark Gable at any woman who approached her. And you can never forget those ears of hers that stood out like sails.

She was legendary for her behavior: she denied her female side and was doomed to live out life through borrowed masculinity.

A remnant of the past, she was like the mannish lesbians of yesteryear.

She had picked apart her character, destroying it, and then she created her own moral values.

" . . . and she wanted something perverse: a relationship, woman to woman. 'You sick tramp!' I said to her, 'Go find yourself a woman then!'"

When I say character, I mean her sexual identity. Ever since the first day she took on a male role, she couldn't bear it when people broached the issue of her femininity.

That first day will always remain a mystery. Clark Gable Gelengül occasionally alludes to that day. She's different from us; there, in the midst of humanity, she differs from everyone else, having found a place of her own among "us creatures." Constantly she rants about how we need to tear down the idea of womanhood. Strutting like a fighting cock, she's always ready to cause an uproar to make sure people recognize her masculinity.

A cloud of ashen smoke envelops her in bluish white; as soon as she puts out one cigarette, she lights another.

" . . .Those men before me would just climb on top of her and then come and roll off. Come and then roll off, that's it. The poor woman knew nothing of orgasms. She tasted the joy of her first with me, and it drove her wild! If you're a real man, you always look after the pleasure of the woman you shag."

Unheard of insults constantly rolled off her tongue concerning members of her "own gender"—in other words, at men. When she was twelve or thirteen, she began sleeping with the woman next door. Casting all morals aside, she was shamelessly passionate about her perversions.

For Gelengül, the concept of shame is preposterous.

Her stories had no end: "I was a real womanizer back then," she'd say. The neighbor's wife had fallen in love with her, and strapping young Gelengül was teaching her the pleasures of the flesh. "And there had been other men as well."

"That's enough, please don't go on."

"Handan Hanım, why are you so afraid?"

It may seem ridiculous, but we both addressed each other formally, despite the blunt openness of our conversations.

She was right though; I was afraid.

"You're such a moral hypocrite," she'd say, and her pendulous ears would wag as she shook her head in disgust, her straight hair pulled up into a bun like a cock's comb. "It happens to the best of us! Every young woman has been through it." And then she'd burst into laughter.

I was powerless. There was nothing I could do to stop her from talking and my frustration only mounted as she subjected me to her tales.

She wasn't content with stopping there: "She'd come visit our place. When she saw me, she'd blush bright red, asking 'Ah, how are you, my dear?' She thought my mother would figure out what was happening. But how? My mom had sex with my dad just a few times a year. The poor woman had forgotten all about sex. How would she catch on to her son's womanizing?"

She told that story again and again. And now as I tell it, I have an urge to disgorge all the memories that have gathered in my mind, and purify myself in the process. But it's impossible. That neighbor's wife always comes back to haunt me:

" . . . and that other one of mine—I'd corner her even in my own home and she'd panic: 'Don't! They'll see us!'" Then another round of chuckles.

Her explosive laughter was so crass that it swept away all your values. Perhaps it was sensitive only to lust.

She loved using feminine expressions in a macho way. She thought that by doing so she was ridiculing effeminate men, those "queens," as she called them.

Her repertory was filled only with stories of the bedroom. But most of the time, there wasn't even time to make it to the bedroom—everything started and ended in a doorway. Try as you might to stop listening or silence her, in the blink of an eye launches into another tale about a lover or sexual encounter.

She believed with all her heart that there isn't a single woman who can hold back her "sexual desires," as she said, in the presence of Gelengül.

"Sweetie," she said, "you're still young. You still have your health. For the love of God, stop living like a nun. Let's find you a fresh young woman. Elem won't hear a thing about it. Why not, let's even make a chirruping little harem for you."

Sometimes she'd say "priest" instead of "nun."

But for me, the lust that Gelengül worshipped was a call in the distance, growing fainter day by day. I knew what a dangerous precipice lust could be.

Back then, when Elem and I were together, I had inflicted a wound on my lust. It wasn't killed completely, just deeply wounded and in the throes of death.

I had to, or else it would have driven me to the brink of my own precipice.

Maybe it did and I'd already been led astray. But what I went through brought me a different kind of pain. For me, lust was transformed into suffering. ("Just like Ayhan's mother in your novel. I can't remember her name now. Ayhan was tormenting his mother because she was sleeping around with different men. It can be interpreted that way, can't it? Everybody judged her for that, because they know nothing of pain. Actually, it's like a mad desire to share with another person.")*

To share, madly! We imagine that all the things we can't share in the world can be found in another person's body. We want to share all of them through a single body. But it's a hopeless undertaking. The devil deceives you; he's impatient, and leaves you no time to think. At full speed, panting for breath, you pursue lust, thinking: "This time the miracle will happen!" That is, until the bodies tumble into an embrace and you see the golden laurel leaves for what they are: sea moss washed ashore. Moss, feces and vomit.

It never ceases, and you're left writhing in anguish.

Before I ruined my voice, singing was the only thing that set me free. As I fell into a strange trance, that precipice would fade away,

---

* Handan Sarp was describing the character Sevim Hanım in my novel *The First Summer of Separation*. (Sİ)

the devil would bow before me, and the desperation would recede. The body is forgotten. Your sole focus is on singing beautifully. But then the music ends; lust is rekindled, and it goads you on. You're driven forth, knowing that it will end in misery. The devil that stirred that passion in you then falls into repose and slumbers.

I used to try to explain this. But Gelengül was never interested, and it broke Elem's heart.

Those were long, tedious evenings.

Either we went to Gelengül's pretentious apartment for a gypsy evening of feasting, or she came to my place where we sat in the garden and later at the dining table. It was always the three of us. In those days, on the weekends, the only days when Elem and I met, I tried to stop thinking about the fate of our relationship. Wherever we went, Gelengül was in the seat of honor, playing Clark Gable.

The three of us. Why did I try to explain that to them? That I was trying to escape, and that things frightened me so much that I was seeking haven? I know: I wanted to escape from our relationship, but I didn't know how.

I told them that lust was useless, and that in the end it would pull you down into the abyss, inflicting upon you the anguish of vanity. Lust and desire, for as long as the passion lives on—but it's a deceptive satisfaction. Afterward, you find yourself on the brink.

When I said that, Gelengül burst out laughing. Then she stared at me blankly for a moment, and tried to mock me. Then she shrugged her shoulders as though fed up with the subject.

"It's all about sexuality." I said. "Perhaps when you're young you can give yourself over to it. It's beyond your control even. But as the years pass, you begin to realize that what you thought was liberation has turned out to be regret."

Elem fell silent during these conversations.

I'd turn to her, and say, "You're young, so much younger than us." She should have had her own life. No one had to think the way I do. And if my tale ended in regret, Elem's could end in happiness. I shouldn't have been a hindrance to her life.

Hurt, she'd fall into silence.

One time she asked, "Why do you talk about our relationship in front of Gelengül? It's none of her business."

I couldn't tell her the truth: it was over, worn out, finished. A mere habit. That's how it seemed to me, that our relationship had become a habit. Both of us had faded in the eyes of the other. The flesh and the spirit had faded. We'd become strangers. But my hands were tied by a painful sense of mercy, while Elem was left with an odd love.

If only I'd been able to share Elem's love and pain, if only I hadn't thought that pain was hell. But it was. I couldn't bear that she loved me.

Elem, my Munise, wanted me to hide my feelings from Gelengül, from everyone. For her, there was hope; the next day, our relationship would right itself, Handan would get better, and we'd return to those beautiful days, to love and friendship.

Perhaps this is a confession: because of Gelengül's prodding, one last time I tried to seek out lust and sex—those words do not come easily to me—with another person. It was a period in my life marked by mistakes. And it truly was hell.

In the dark hours of the morning, the phone rang. It was Gelengül; she said that she'd met "two sexy Russian whores" the night before at a meyhane in Kumkapı. They'd been sitting with some "boorish brute of a guy." And what's more, one of them knew all about opera; she was blond and had slanted green eyes, like a "forest green kissed by a hint of gray fog." Such descriptions! Clark Gable was on the prowl. The blond one was actually a music teacher. "Sweetie, tonight both of them are at our beck and call. Elem won't hear a thing about it."

"Don't be ridiculous," I said. It was unfathomable to me how she dared speak to me like that.

Brashly she said, "Forget that Handan Sarp—forget about *being* Handan Sarp! You can't live life always running away."

Her crassness struck me as terribly coarse. "You have no right . . .to speak to me that way," I managed to stammer.

But the strange thing was the desire I felt, which I didn't dare even admit to myself. I tried to pass it off as curiosity. Indeed I was curious—somewhere, in the darkness of night, things would happen, testimony of Gelengül's maverick life. But it wasn't just that; it was a furtive desire. I found myself dreaming about that "forest green kissed by a hint of gray fog."

You find yourself with a music teacher, the remnant of a collapsed regime that shattered people's lives at a time when there was hope that humanity would be saved, and you make love speaking of Borodin, Mussorgsky and Tchaikovsky, and then there is the price of lust, the haggling over dollars, probably at the same meyhane in Kumkapı, and then the conversation turns to the opera *Queen of Spades*, *Prince Igor* . . . The dregs!

I was being dragged through life, to the edge of the precipice.

I despised Gelengül, but couldn't show it. All I could do was ridicule her, but secretly.

Start with her name: Gelengül, "budding rose." Can you imagine her parents carefully choosing that name, dreaming that a rose was coming into the world. But such a rose!

And the way she dressed, trying to look like a man. She may have worn men's clothes, but nature was cruel: it bestowed her with broad hips and voluminous breasts that she could never conceal. But she paid no heed, strutting with a manly gait belied by her plump thighs and jostling breasts.

If you proposed that she change the way she dressed, all hell would break loose: "What do you mean? Do you want me be a laughing-stock and go out in public wearing such womanly clothes?"

In her youth, on the streets men would shout out catcalls and whistle at her. Mortified, she'd say: "Those jerks are all perverts! This city is full of perverts!" Her diagnosis was clear. And because she had diagnosed the problem, her heart was at ease.

She claimed to be against homosexuality and went out of her way to tell this to the girls she slept with; but she never heard their giggles in response.

Disturbed, Elem once asked, "Who's going to set her right?"

No one. It's impossible.

On rare occasions she'd visit her parents—both of them were alive at the time—and Clark Gable would undergo a painful, shameful transformation into a woman. She'd put on a dress, one that Nedret had made for her as an ironic jest. There was no other choice; her parents knew nothing of her private life. Gelengül was quite wealthy, but all the money came from her parents. It was a mysterious fortune and no one knew how they'd gotten so rich.

My mocking hatred for her began to fade and be forgotten. Just who was that woman? I don't think I ever asked or tried to find out.

The three of us were always together, especially in the final days. When I was alone with Elem, time seemed to stand still. Gelengül had become part of our loneliness, as well as my confidante.

But could someone really open her heart to Gelengül? Did I? There was no need to conceal anything from her, because her brazenness simply plowed through everything. Before her, you stood completely naked, unable to hide anything. And Clark Gable wasn't a very good listener—as soon as you told her something, she forgot it. I needed that; it was therapeutic.

At the same time, my loneliness had overwhelmed me to the point that I was powerless against her will. I was content with her existence; it sufficed for me. I needed someone, a third person, and anyone would do.

There was no one else in our lives. That's how it was. We rarely saw Ali and Semra. Hikmet had passed away. If I don't count Clark Gable, Elem and I had no one else in the world.

It seemed that Clark Gable would help me pass the time. I was in a haze, as though I'd even forgotten about opera. I think that two seasons passed and I didn't sing in a single piece. Opera had forgotten me as well. Little by little all that I had was disappearing.

From evening to evening to the weekends, everything was the same, a droll monotony.

Much later, I asked myself: Why didn't I try building a friendship with Elem? As a friend and confidante. Couldn't she have been my friend? Wasn't she my friend anyway? I told her my secrets—my desires, my deaths!—and they saddened her, weighing on her spirit. There was no place for my fantasies in an orderly life of hard work.

The two of us were far removed from the world of others. Always. It could have been possible, just the two of us, far away. Perhaps I wouldn't have lost myself. My Munise wouldn't have died. Who knows?

To exist beyond the bounds of society . . .

Our relationship was an embarrassment for me; because of our intimacy and romance, I secretly blamed Elem. I felt as though the people who saw us together would see the bare truth of what we did in private, in our secret life, and they would judge us. But people who saw me alone would never brand me as a lesbian and I'd be impervious to their slander. Because of this strange logic, I was driving myself from Elem.

It was unbearable for me to be lovers with her in the gaze of society. It was too much for me: their condemnations, scathing tirades and slander.

We were floundering forth on a journey across a terrifying ocean. In that vastness there were just two weary ships, two separate people, sending distress signals to each other. That's society's nature, that's what it is: an ocean.

Around Gelengül, there was no need for us to hide anything because despite her masculinity and Clark Gable role, she was one of the most lesbian of women the world has ever seen; and it was beyond her control. She despised both women and men. If all the men were removed from society and she could turn all the women into lesbians, maybe then she would find some peace of mind. Even her closest friends were lesbians.

When Elem met Gelengül, she couldn't understand what I saw in her. At first she used to ask me why I spent time with her, but eventually gave up. Most likely she was repulsed by Gelengül but never said anything.

Gelengül took possession of our lives.

One time she even went to Elem's home and had her chauffer bring up bottles of Château Margaux, expensive cheeses, pâté and pork chops. Gelengül strolled around the flat and struck a Clark Gable pose as she looked around from the balcony.

I'd thought Elem would be uneasy, but she seemed indifferent.

Gelengül laughed and said to me, "Let's get you a neighboring apartment and fix it up."

The next day, she had a huge washing machine sent to Elem's place. The attached note read, "Enjoy! A keepsake from your Uncle Gelengül."

I met "uncle" Gelengül at Nedret's boutique. With her typical pretentious airs, Nedret praised Gelengül to the skies, saying that she was an aficionado of classical music. The term "classical music" always irritates me. It shows that you are ignorant about the art of music, just as it gave away Nedret's ignorance.

Nedret told me that Gelengül came from a refined family and was the granddaughter of a member of the Democratic Party who'd been a parliamentarian. The family was wealthy, she said, and quite cultured.

And the strange creature to whom I was introduced said, "I'm a great admirer of Handan Sarp," and then stared into my eyes. I could have scoffed at her, that "admirer" of mine. She shook my hand; her palm was moist with sweat, like it always is.

They admire you. Suddenly they are transformed from zeroes into scholars of opera and start saying the most asinine things about your art. Their comments are trite, uninformed, absurd. And you listen with a bowed head.

She said that she had an "extraordinary" collection of albums. Her collection of classical music had, in her own words, "suddenly come together." When I asked if she listened to them, she replied: "My entire collection is at your disposal." Who listened to those albums with her. The poor girls she seduces? First they listen to classical music, and then the Clark Gable performance begins . . .

At her home, all the great operas and singers would be sent to the grave by that explosive laughter of hers.

Nedret was eyeing the both of us.

She was like a hyena waiting in ambush, ears pricked up with suspicion. She'd once proposed that I order a tuxedo. With her fake smile, she showered us with offers: were we hungry? She offered to order us a sandwich and a cola, or perhaps orange juice . . . She even invited us into her private room, insisting that we at least have tea and a fresh-baked *simit*.

Then she launched into a detailed account of Gelengül's wealth: she came from a large prominent family whose refinement had been passed down through the generations. Gelengül had traveled the whole world. Her mother was a respected lady, and her clothes were all designed by Nedret. As for Gelengül's father, who was a businessman, he was friends with the president of the country but had never gotten involved in politics. The source of their wealth? Hard work, sweat of the brow . . . For a moment, I thought that Nedret was making a mockery of the family.

"But such culture!" she exclaimed, saying that I'd see for myself when I got to know her better.

Gelengül sat listening, burning with shame.

She invited me to her home. And I went—it was utter foolishness on my behalf, a meaningless mishap.

The guests had been invited in my honor. Pretentiously and tastelessly decorated, the living room had windows with a view over the opposite shore of the Bosphorus. Her refinement was the kind that makes you sneer. Their wealth, however, was indeed formidable; but they were right-wing in a way that had long been out of fashion. The servant girls were too prim and proper. That basically sums up the whole evening.

In front of her guests, Gelengül was content to let Clark Gable's feminine side shine forth; she wore a plain purple gown and a pearl choker. And although she'd put on pink lipstick, her mustache was still in place. She spoke in alto tones, drinking her rakı without water.

The guests were much like herself and her home. At first, our common topic of discussion was opera. Tritely they spoke of memories of operas, performances at the Scala, the splendor of the Metropolitan. They asked, "Why haven't any great works been produced in the twentieth century? Do you have a career overseas? Who was the better singer, Callas or Leyla Gencer?" Finally they forgot about me, and the conversation moved on.

Speaking of opera made me uneasy, and I retired to a corner of the room. They spoke among themselves, glasses of wine in their hands, smiling: "Are you going to the States this year? Apparently their daughter was studying there. So-and-so bought a house in Nice, and, oh, weren't the cutlery sets at the Musée Bouilhet-Christofle simply delightful? And your winter garden, my dear, is just to die for, can I borrow your gardener for a while? And I lost seventeen kilos in just two months with my new diet . . ." My ears were ringing and I felt faint. What was I doing there? I asked myself that question again and again, feeling as though I were falling apart at the edges.

Who were those people? The women all looked identical, as though designed by the same surgeon. They seemed to have leapt from the pages of fashion magazines and newspaper supplements. They were insensitive, selfish dull-witted. In a country where famine was knocking down the door, the men proudly flaunted their money, their bodies and souls fattened on wealth to the point that each of them deigned themselves lords of the world while the rest of us were slaves. Will no one ever give those kinds of people the answer they deserve?

One of those lords of the earth approached and said, "You're a very beautiful woman."

I thanked him.

Midnight came and went, and word was being sent to the front door. Who was going to leave and who would stay? I watched as cars were brought up to the entrance, all of them the latest models; the chauffeurs leapt out and opened back doors, while the guards of the complex stood practically in salute. In the midst of that pestilent affluence I was exhausted, a complete stranger.

I didn't belong there. Had they no compassion? The banal topics, the clothes they spent thousands on, the absurd things that saddened them . . . And how they envied one another, unaware of the covetousness they were drowning in, as they went through life blind to the plights of others, completely indifferent.

Gelengül scrutinized her guests with bloodshot eyes. For a brief moment I felt that we could be close. At the very least, there was something contrary about her that I found appealing.

"Can you call me a taxi, Gelengül?" I asked.

And in a flurry of gallantry everyone offered to take me home. The proprietress of the home offered her car and chauffeur: "At your service," she said, her femininity slipping back into her voice. The others were adamant about dropping me off. I knew what they were thinking; the next day, they'd boast, "I took Handan Sarp to her home." As though I were famous! My home, a ground floor apartment on a street in Nişantaşı, surrounded by run-down apartment buildings. For me, even that is a luxury.

I insisted: I came by taxi and would leave by taxi. "No, I don't have a car." As I got into the cab, I shrugged off the scornful, pitying glances of the guards.

After watching me perform one night, Gelengül sent me an enormous bouquet of calla lilies.

The card read: "I know that you'll never attain the stars."

I'd pitied her. Most of the time I take pity on such human wrecks.

But something else was occupying my mind; there was something about her that constantly pulled my thoughts in a certain direction.

At times I try to conceal from myself the cavernous depths. But I can't. I do feel lust, but I've suppressed it, tried to destroy it. It was my demon. And that lust was inflamed solely by depravity and dissolution. And that's the true reason I despised Gelengül. Deep down I was becoming more and more addicted to debauchery. In your art you may howl human suffering, but in your bedroom fantasies . . . No, it wasn't easy.

And the tales she told, even if she made half of them up, were always seductively alluring. Because of my fear for myself, I tried to silence her. We don't know where madness may lead us.

And after my pointless objections, I was forced to bow my head and listen.

She saw Elem and me at Hristo's and immediately understood. Leaving her friends—an elderly couple—she joined us at our table. But she said nothing about our intimacy. Not a single word. Just, at one point in the conversation, she said, "You should bring Elem for a visit to my place sometime."

Elem was terrified that we'd been found out.

"There's nothing to be afraid of," I told her. "Those of us on this path know how to keep a secret."

"Make yourselves at home, my dears. This is your home. Elem, this is your home now. Why are you sitting so far from Handan?"

She was depraved enough to want to watch Elem and me make love. Something only needed to be dark and hidden for her to find it alluring. There was nothing in her life except for sex, and her sexuality was of the most debauched kind. She had dedicated her life to it, and deviance was her sole sustenance. Finally I figured that out.

Passion would strike me deeply. And the things I imagined . . . I won't deny that I imagined her desires and sought to enter her world. With Elem, in front of her. Or others, with many others.

Our illnesses were different. But we were on the same path to deviance. She wanted to "observe" people, particularly women. And I wanted to raze to the ground the world's lies that had been created in the name of morality; I wanted to break them apart and scatter them to the wind.

I even told Elem about Gelengül's desire to "observe" us. The idea of it stoked my desire.

Elem didn't understand and because of that she didn't pity Gelengül.

But the one who needed to be pitied was Handan Sarp, who only felt sexual desire in the annihilation of her inner self.

After work on Saturdays, Elem would come to my place around six in the evening—summers, autumns, dismal winter evenings. If we were going to Gelengül's place, I liked to go at eight-thirty or nine: "At the latest we'll be there at nine," I'd tell her. Preparations took hours as I got myself ready for Elem, preparing myself for our lovemaking; it was pathetic. I would shower, dress and put on makeup and perfume: Amazone, and later, other perfumes. Even before six o'clock, Gelengül would start calling to say she'd done this or prepared that, and I was secretly dreading the possibility that Elem and I were becoming estranged, so I'd start drinking before Elem came, usually whiskey.

Every time Elem would arrive, only to find a wreck of a woman. When drunk, I have a swaying, ambling way of walking. With a drunken smile, I'd say, "You should drink too. What would you like? Vodka?" My life had gone to pieces and was as scarred as my sexual inclinations. And my Munise would look at me with resentment.

I didn't want Elem's sexuality, and it was because of her sex that I'd been driven from my Munise.

Be led astray and you'll never know where that path will lead you. Toward the end of my tale with Munise, I began a descent into the world of Gelengül. I was swept along. Strange bars, strange places, and always when I'd been drinking. I imagined that when everyone was debased, they were actually exalted. But they weren't. Then I'd get the urge to plummet even further. I truly believed that the further we fell, the more exalted we'd become. But no one rises from that pit. And that's all it is—a pit, a swamp. I thought that I'd destroyed Handan Sarp. That, however, was not the case; the truth was that no one even knew her. In those places, in the dark of night, we're all nameless; flesh and the call of flesh suffice—there's no need for names. Being Handan Sarp changes nothing. She's just the response to a crying out for flesh, and nothing more.

I sought out life in the bodies of strangers.

And wasn't Elem's body a stranger to me as well? From the first day to the last.

Weren't all bodies strangers to Handan Sarp?

Just as evening fell and the day was slipping into darkness, at that hour when we're most vulnerable to our weaknesses, she called, telling me that she was sending her chauffeur. He arrived, all grace and respect. "If you haven't any previous engagements, my madam would like to see you." It made no sense to me; why this sudden intimacy? No one ever comes to my door without letting me know first. But Gelengül knows nothing of such niceties; she calls again and again, or suddenly her chauffeur comes knocking at my door.

It's strange, but when it was just the two of us, an awkward shyness would come over her. Her swaggering cockiness needed the presence of others to emerge—even Elem was enough for that. But when just she and I were together, she took on the role of the bashful libertine.

Was it loneliness, or was I powerless against her queenly airs? In any case, I'd go to her home, assenting to her deep voice on the phone when she said, "Come to my place." Gelengül would speak to me of her new loves.

She was constantly falling in love. Swilling her rakı, she'd tell me one by one how she'd seduced her "girls," practically swooning in the glory of her new victories. I say love, but that's not quite the truth; it was lust. Gelengül knew nothing of love. Lust had never come as a consequence of love—it was sheer pleasure, the passion of flesh.

Her large veined hands on her knees, she would prattle on like a teenager about her lusts. And every time I tried to transform that carnality into a tale of love. Perhaps, even if ever so slightly, I was able to veil the crassness of her stories. She didn't object. A tremor would run across her lips, and she'd give in to the idea of love:

"Handan, if you'd seen the glow of her curly hair! It wasn't hair I was stroking—it was a burning flame! She gave herself over to me, lying across my bed, eyes closed. If that's what love is . . . even if just for one time, I've longed for that."

Pulling her fingernails along her knees, she laughed. But behind her laughter there was a sound like a sob. At first I couldn't hear it. Later it became more clear, as though she were choking.

In the beginning, she struck me as rather peculiar. I was disturbed by the way she described her tales of lust that were tinged with the pangs of suffering of a young man. Over time that passed, and I accepted Gelengül for what she is.

"Handan, ah, Handan! Making love is the purpose of life, making love as much as you can! Tasting the nectar of every flower. What's love? Don't believe in love, especially love's pain. Live for lust, and you'll never long for anyone. No one will ever leave you. No one will ever hurt you. Find yourself a new broad to replace the one who left!"

After the third or fourth glass of rakı, however, even though she'd still talk about girls, her mannishness, lewdness and debauchery would begin to fade, and she was left with the ruins of an unloved person; her gender no longer mattered. I mentioned it before: she always drank her rakı straight. Ruefully. Her explosive laughter turned into showers of sobs.

"Gelengül, are you okay?"

"No," she said, "I'm not." She's ill. No one pities her. Her wealth, her fortune, have brought her nothing.

But she's a heroine in a novel, she said. Yes—"a heroine." In an effort to appear spry, she leapt up from her seat and pulled a few books from the large hutch where she keeps all her albums and books.

She said that she's both the woman in the novel and the young girl in the poem. Flipping through the book, she found the poem and hesitantly began to read. It was probably a long-winded poem but she randomly skipped through it.

"A famous novelist and a famous poet were inspired by Gelengül," she said with pride. The poet was her friend. They met the novelist, and Clark Gable immediately became the center of attention. "He called me again and again while writing his novel, asking all sorts of questions."

The only thing that surprised her was that both the poet and novelist had depicted her as "female."

"That's what happens," I said, trying not to laugh. "In art, these kinds of transformations happen."

In all earnestness she asked, "Really? Like what?" And then she asked if I'd ever read the book.

I had. It was a tragic novel. But the lonely heroine, surrounded by impassioned, suffering people, bore absolutely no resemblance to Gelengül. Of course I didn't tell her that.

She handed the book to Elem: "You can read about me in this novel." Then she returned to the poem; as I mentioned, it was quite long. The narrator was a lonely young girl speaking to herself, and there was a table covered in green broadcloth and women playing conquian as trams passed by on the street. It was a beautiful poem.

"Don't read it out loud," I protested. "I can't understand it when you read it."

It really was a lovely poem. The young girl didn't want to grow up, and the world of adults frightened her; but at the same time, she didn't want to remain a child—no, all she wanted was for death to swoop down and take her away.

The urge to laugh had passed. Again I was lost at sea. I didn't want to return to shore, because memories awaited me there. They were unbearable. Rapidly I was pulled out to sea, far from Elem and Gelengül.

In that large living room, Gelengül had turned on just a single lamp. Night had fallen, and the three of us were sitting in the dim light. In the shadows, we withdrew into ourselves. I looked at the paintings on the wall across from me; they were all hung crooked.

They were precious works, but their value went unheeded in her home—they were just conversation pieces, and the pain the artists suffered as they brought them to life had long been forgotten in the living room of Gelengül the heroine. There were also a few worthless paintings. I had the desire to get up and straighten the frames.

The sound of rain. That was the only sound in the room. Was it autumn rain, or spring showers? After all this time I can't remember. Leaves flitted through the air, yellow, or perhaps green, young leaves plucked by the wind. The last light of evening, which faded.

Would Elem read the novel?

Suddenly I was cast ashore, to a land of bitter memories. Both of our pasts were bleeding like wounds, and at that moment, for the very first time, the novel *The Night of Fire* took hold of me. My Munise had told me that of the thousands of books that existed, she'd only read *The Night of Fire*. We were at a restaurant on the shores of the Bosphorus. In all my pedantry I told her that she should read more books.

And Gelengül, the heroine of a novel, was saying, "Here, read this book."

We vile people, we human disasters, were recommending novels to Elem.

In that silence, Gelengül sat there, head bowed forward like a plump servant girl, and I was brought face to face with another side of her social deviance. All at once I felt the hopelessness of everything about her: the Clark Gable legends, the boasts about being a heroine in a novel and the inspirational muse for a poem, and—although she tried to play it off as trivial—her flaunting of wealth and mannish swaggering. For a moment, I felt as though I'd practically become Gelengül.

Is that how she appeared to the poet? Had she truly always wanted to stay a child? Because as a child, she'd known nothing of masculinity or femininity. Because as a child, she had no idea that one day she would grow up and be forced to masquerade as a man.

Beyond a doubt the novelist hadn't based his character on Gelengül. In the novel, the author wrote about a life-weary nymphomaniac whose hopes had been dashed time and time again.

Being at her place frightened me. Not even the sound of the rain, which normally soothed me, could dispel my fears.

One morning she came to my place in a panic. I hadn't seen her in a while, as she hadn't joined my weekend gatherings with Elem. Apparently she'd met a girl and was mad about her. She kept asking for the four of us to spend time together, but I had no interest in meeting the girl.

She told me she'd been robbed. All of her jewelry . . .

"Jewelry? Gelengül, you have jewelry?" I had to ask. Aside from the pearl choker, I couldn't remember her wearing jewelry of any kind.

"Yes, but I never wore it. It doesn't suit a man. They took it all. My rings, bracelets, watches . . . Some of them were family heirlooms, like my grandmother's diamond bridal crown."

"The girl robbed you?"

"Yes, with her boyfriend. They tied me up!" Her voice was hoarse, and tears rolled down her cheeks. "I'd started sending the servants home at night so we could be alone."

She said that the doorbell had rung, and the girl said, "I'll get it." The girl let her boyfriend in, and then both of them attacked Clark Gable.

"And what about the guards?" I asked, remembering the way those country bumpkins had sneered at Handan Sarp for not having a car, chauffeur or wealth.

"Nobody heard a sound. Somehow they got into the apartment complex. I should be grateful they didn't kill me! They held a knife to my neck."

She said that she wouldn't go to the police because a scandal could break out. Everyone would hear about the incident, including her family. She started babbling, "They'll lock me away and won't let anyone see me!"

Apparently she'd trusted that "whore" so much that she'd shown off her jewelry and even given her a Rolex, " . . . even if it was a bit outdated." Gelengül had asked the girl to put on the jewelry because she wanted to see her bejeweled, but the girl had refused. "She wanted me," Gelengül said. "She said she wanted to be alone with me at night."

Soon enough she recovered but continued to rain curses upon the girl. Aside from the jewelry and watches, they'd also stolen all the cash from the safe, "a large amount of dollars," but she didn't know exactly how much. "When they held the knife to my throat," she said, "I gave them the combination to the safe." A few times she told me about what happened and just as quickly dropped the issue. "Don't let Elem hear of this. I haven't told anyone except for you."

And then she went back to frequenting the places where she'd met the girl.

Slowly I began to understand: Gelengül was indifferent to pain. She paid no heed to suffering, whether it was her own or someone else's. She simply didn't feel it; she'd forgotten how to. Perhaps she'd never even felt pain.

She had no interest in the "true" story of that girl she'd picked up on the street, and it never crossed her mind to try and find out. It was as though she'd never met her.

"People don't just suddenly become thieves," I told her.

Laughing, she shrugged as if to say I couldn't understand.

I was beginning to realize that I'd let a negative influence into our lives by becoming so close with Gelengül. For four or five years we were inseparable. But we should never have had a friend like that.

I felt confused; but to be honest, I was secretly pleased that the girl and her boyfriend wouldn't be caught. I told Elem: "This isn't a case of theft—it's revenge. The revenge of so many girls, boys and street children."

I don't think Elem said anything in reply.

We also started haunting those bars, night clubs and dens of debauchery—whatever you want to call them.

I brought Elem along; she probably liked it in the beginning. It was something different for her. The people at those places liked her because she was young and attractive. And she liked their attentions. The young men who slept around with aging homosexuals for money liked her, even fell in love with her, and Elem smiled, a permanent blank smile that spoke of the abyss. They wanted to dance with her. They whispered to her, asking if they could meet up, asking for her phone number. And as I said, Elem just smiled. But what was she smiling at? Something unknown to me, something beyond me.

I was taken aback by it all: the young men who sold their bodies to other men but then fell madly in love with Elem; the hatred that those coquettish older men, who for all the world resembled aging women obsessed with youth, felt for her; and the way they glared at me. It left me feeling dirty inside.

("Didn't anyone ever recognize you?"

"I don't know. They may have pretended not to. It was better that way. And I wasn't really paying attention. But I wasn't the same person then. The Handan then and the Handan now aren't the same person. In those days, I was caught up in a maelstrom. And now, my corpse has washed ashore . . .")

Gelengül told me, "You shouldn't have gotten that apartment for her. She needs to learn how to do things alone, free from the pressure of her family and your control."

Elem's home. I had so wanted her to move out, to be independent and free.

"You don't understand Elem," I replied. I thought that Gelengül could never truly understand her. All those people and the noisy rush of life. The distance in Elem's heart, so reminiscent of my own. It seemed to me that we'd survive all the trials of life, and, taking shelter in each other, find compassion and in the end become an elderly couple as close as sisters—always separate, but more closely bound to one another, more intimate.

No matter where we went or where we were.

That's why I was never able to leave Elem, why I'm still bound to my Munise even though I'd had the urge to pull away and flee. Gelengül could never understand that!

In a way, I'm drawing near the end of the saga of Clark Gable Gelengül.

There's no need to give long explanations. For anyone. For anything. In the beginning, I was enchanted with the idea of explaining everything. But what can it change? Forget enchantment; it's preposterous. Explanations are futile.*

---

* It will become clear that during our meetings, which drew on for months, Handan Sarp began to withdraw from me, just as she had from life. Sometimes she was cold, even hostile; at times it seemed that she even despised me. "If you want, we can stop," I told her. "You were the one who suggested we do this." But she refused to give up. I think it was her pride—that deadly pride—that would never let her give in. (Sİ)

It was the end of summer. Practically the end of everything. Evenings when the refrain, "The end of summer, again" rang in my ears. "It's the end of summer again, isn't it?" Emptiness.

It was one of those countless evenings with Gelengül. Night.

We were sitting in the garden. No, not in the garden—Gelengül didn't have one. We must have been on the large veranda. Maybe it wasn't night. Lights glimmered on the Anatolian shores of the Bosphorus. She was weeping. As she spoke of the infinite loneliness of her life, she said, "Who said that men don't cry!" She was unhappy, she said, always lonely, without a single friend or companion. Just me. If it hadn't been for me . . .

It may have seemed like I was gazing at the opposite shoreline, but I was torn by that familiar pain. I searched for words of condolence. On the sea, there was a rickety Bosphorus ferry. Money, pretty girls, making love—none of those could save her; she was living in a hell of her own making. A hell of not being loved.

She knocked over her rakı glass and it fell to the floor and shattered. She tried to get to her feet, but was unable to stand.

"I'll clean it up," I said. Shards of glass. In those shards of glass I saw her life.

She asked for more rakı. "You've had enough," I said. But she insisted. When I came back into the room, she was even worse. Drunker, half mad. She'd stopped crying, but her cheeks were wet and her mustache was beaded with sweat. Her voice was hoarse, swinging from masculine to effeminate.

She said something that stunned me. At first I didn't realize that she might truly be losing her mind. She wasn't even talking to me. It was a whisper. She said, "Elem! I want Elem. I want to make love with Elem. She longs for me . . . let me have her!" The whisper became a scream: "She's mine! Mine! Elem's mine!"

It was a disgrace. Everyone in the apartment complex could have heard her shrieks, even the guards.

"Elem isn't here, Gelengül," I said. I stood there in shocked silence.

But she didn't hear me. She was lost in her own world. Above all else, she wanted Elem; as she rambled, she mentioned a "perverse woman."

I'd never seen anyone in such a state of hysteria.

"I'll put floral-print garters on her. I'll stroke them, I'll kiss them!"

A strange detachment came over me. I was unmoved by the words, desires and convulsions of that poor creature before me. I simply observed her for a while.

Then there was rain, and a cemetery. Or am I making up the rain? The cemetery was real. I left Clark Gable. I left her home and began walking. The guard at the gate of the complex had nodded off on a chair in front of the sentry box, but he must have seen me from behind as I walked toward the steep road leading downhill. The cemetery is on your left as you go down the slope, an ancient cemetery on the hilly shores of the Bosphorus.

In my memory at least, it began raining. I entered the cemetery. Occasionally I wander through cemeteries, hoping for salvation from the graves of the unknown dead.

An autumn rain began to fall, the kind that ushers in autumn. Fall leaves, narrow dirt paths, my heels sinking into the mud, thick darkness . . . "This is the darkness of death," I thought—I felt at peace. Rain, gravestones, me.

She saw us at Hristo's restaurant: Elem, the young seamstress from Nedret's boutique together with soprano Handan Sarp.

One time we had a photograph taken of the three of us at Hristo's.

Am I making up the rain? The rain might be a lie. Rain was falling.

(After the day she told me about Clark Gable Gelengül, Handan Sarp didn't call me for the whole summer. Although we hadn't been meeting every day, I usually saw her two or three times a week.

As I mentioned before, Handan Sarp's novel had begun to exhaust me, so it was a relief when she didn't call. I wanted to be free of that leaden weight. Everything about the project was cloyingly depressive, jumbled and pained: our interviews, the texts she wrote, my transcriptions of our discussions, the revisions . . . At times I even felt angry.

But still, curiosity won out in the end. What would happen next? How did this series of events that had devastated Handan Sarp conclude?

I called her. She said that she hadn't been feeling well. "These days I don't have the energy to go on. At first I was enthusiastic about the idea. But I think that I've already told you so much. More than I should have. I opened up my heart. But it's all so meaningless." She apologized for having troubled me, and hung up the phone with a curt "thank you."

There was nothing I could do. I gathered together my recordings, transcriptions and her somniloquies, and stowed them away. I even thought of burning them. But I couldn't bring myself to do it. Still, from time to time, the urge to get rid of everything would come over me, but I never had the heart to go through with it.

In all honesty, I was quite irritated; I'd wasted so much time working on the book.

Then this letter came in the mail:

Dear Selim,

Do you sometimes think of me and wonder what has come of my life? Now, as September comes to a close, I find myself confined to a wicker chair as though bedridden, writing to you.

I think that I've given up on my somniloquies. Weren't the things I told you also somniloquies in a way? It seems that I've given up writing to Elem.

But I still see her sometimes; she suddenly appears in my dreams, in my imagination, bringing pangs of conscience.

For example, she's there in the garden with me. She lets her hair down, and as it flutters in the breeze, she smiles. Did you know that she only smiled for me?

But then her smile is transformed from an expression of love and compassion to cruelty. Unable to comprehend why she wants revenge, I whisper: "Go away, leave me be!" and the apparition fades and disappears.

The days have become monotonous. Every day I wait for evening to fall. When you have nothing left to lose, you can spend your time however you please. I'm merely whiling away the time. Dusk settles heavy on my heart. I never knew it could be so heavy. The colors fade ever so slowly. When the northeast winds scour the sky so brilliantly sharp, the final color lingering in the heavens always stings my heart. It's a strange and wild beauty.

Even though summer has passed, Elem's white rose bush is still blooming. In the past, other such bitter miracles occurred; in the second autumn after our separation, the flowers of the coralbells stubbornly clung to life.

And now, September is nearly over. A September like a distant lover. For a long time, ever since our separation, I've become entwined with September, entangled in its layers.

Among the things I haven't told you there was a certain period of time after Elem and I separated, after the death of my Munise; those were bitter, oppressive days, in the month of September. How I wanted to speak of those days! But what good would it do? At first, I thought that the novel of my life would bring me some kind of salvation. But that hope has faded. I realized that it will merely increase the pain.

For as long as I can remember, in September I feel not the onset of autumn but its end. The weather suddenly turns vicious. It seems as though everything is imbued with a longing for one last embrace with summer. If you ask me, autumn actually begins in August. September and August, those two months that drive me toward madness.

In one of those lost months of August, Elem and I had gone to Yıldız Park. We followed the earthen path down to the greenhouses and caught a glimpse of the sea below. The opposite shore of the Bosphorus was set aglow by the sharp light of the setting sun. I told Elem, "Even in August the summer mists begin to disappear." She paused in contemplation, and then said, "Mist is good. Sometimes I don't want to see reality stripped bare." Nearby were clusters of dahlia blooming in whites, yellows and fiery reds. But that first rain . . .

Septembers always swoop down upon me with fallen leaves, rain and stone pools filled with water gone stagnant over the summer. For me, the pool in the novel "The Wren" is a symbol of September.

You know, I once could have performed in an opera of "The Wren." That was also in September, filled with the rotting leaves of fall.

September is a month of endings. Always onyx, topaz yellows and ruby reds. As for the greens, they struggle one last time with the coming rains to glimmer and set the motley colors aglow—but their efforts are in vain.

September also speaks untruths. We feel the coming of autumn as August draws to a close, but in September it seems to retreat. The season lies to us yet again, saying, "September promises many summery days and nights."

That's how it is now, as sunlight streams through the window onto this letter. For a moment, you think it's the summer sun. But it will quickly fade. The sun will not warm our memories.

I'm overcome by a strange sense of delusion. The first rains come, and September is over. Yet another summer in which I did nothing slips past, and I console myself with dreams of the Indian summer days of September. For example, Elem and I could go somewhere. There are no operas await-ing me, there's nothing. We could go to the south; isn't the summer waiting for us there? Elem, what about our plane tickets . . .

Strange delusions. Elem and I never went to the south. But my Munise will come back this Indian summer. What does it matter if she died in a novel titled "The Wren"?

Painful delusions. The falling of leaves. As October draws closer, the final days of Indian summer—this year!—will come to an end, leaving me doubled over in pain, silent and exhausted; I'll have only my lament for consolation.

Taunting us with "countless" days of sunshine, the season will grow heavy, as though weary of its beauty, and be transformed into a mummy, a cadaver.

That's why I'm writing to you. Selim Bey, a voice spoke to you of many things, but it wasn't Handan Sarp's. It wasn't her voice, and yet it tried to describe her. And what of the rest? Don't people who withdraw into themselves need to fall silent?

That roar of the sea—you know what I speak of—that roar has not died down.

I end the letter here. I can no longer stand the roaring. Call me.)

From among all my scattered memories, why did I choose to describe Gelengül? In fact, I'd like to erase her from my memory. But I haven't quite sketched her character; it's impossible, she's beyond description.

Not all of our friends were like Gelengül. We knew some good people as well; it would be truer to say that I introduced Elem to some good people. I'd like to speak of them.

Elem, however, never introduced me to her friends. I didn't know any of them.

Semra and Ali had a special place for us. They knew of our love and our loneliness.

One day Semra and I went to Nedret's boutique. That's where Semra first saw Elem. That was in the beginning, which now seems to be drawing so quickly away. That was the second time I saw Elem. In such a distant past.

When I spoke to you of my memories, they too were distant. But that's not how I felt. The wound was bleeding, and then it probably scabbed over. There will be a scar.

It was evening . . . But I probably talked about this already. I told you my memories of the beginning of our separation, and asked you to write them down. I asked you to write that life had come to an end even before I died. And now, by retelling everything, perhaps I'm trying to distort the past, to create a new relationship between Elem and me. So many memories. Trying to relive them in my imagination. To make them happier, kinder. But it's useless. Impossible even.

I thought I could bring those memories to life by retelling them, but day by day they are disappearing. One day, all that will be left is the shell of a person who has no memories.

Semra. If I had to sum her up in a few words: good-hearted, idealistic, passionate about her art. To the extent that she believed one day everyone would love opera. She awaited an obscure tomorrow that we would never see. And if you asked her, "Will that day come?" she would launch into a manifesto of revolution.

Semra didn't show her sensitivity and kept it trapped inside most of the time. She was so hopeful that she was prone to sadness, fragility and disappointment. But without that hope, she would've been unable to stand her ground.

At the same time, however, that murmuring she carried inside brought her to her knees.

I wanted to tell her that the murmuring voice was defeating her. But I was afraid of hurting her. She'd already been hurt enough. She could only open herself up to a few people and share her belief that opera would save humanity.

"Will that day come? Do you really believe that?" I asked her.

She believed it. We debated the idea, and when I told her that, particularly in this miserable society, opera was doomed to fall on deaf ears, her hopes would be crushed, one by one. She listened glumly as I insisted on that point. But then she took shelter in opera, driven to lament by her withdrawal from the world.

She was always withdrawn.

Of course, when she was younger, she wasn't like that. She wanted to share her enthusiasm with others. She believed in her ideas, just as she believed in opera. She used to fall in love with her teachers at the conservatory; they were idols for her. In a veiled way, she told me about this.

One of those teachers had been my instructor as well. With his lechery, so reminiscent of Gelengül's, he defiled the admiration and love of his female students. He was Semra's first disappointment. As a cultured virtuoso musician, he quickly inspired admiration; but that was followed by sudden disappointment if you spent time alone with him. He'd invite you out for an evening, usually to a restaurant, and tell you about his unhappy marriage and how he didn't get along with his wife. Music would be forgotten, and by the second drink, he'd devolve into vulgarity and start telling dirty jokes. Leaning in, he'd try to whisper into your ear.

Of course, our society that referred to Cemil Sahir as Mother Ghost was fine with this womanizer. The male students called him "Zozik," a man whose lecherousness knows no bounds.

Disappointment after disappointment lay in store for Semra. Deception tainted all of her loves and friendships. That is, until her relationship with Ali. She turned back from the threshold of melancholy.

Semra and I worked together once. There were just a few

performances and they didn't go very well. After that, we more or less went our separate ways, only occasionally seeing each other.

She had large beautiful eyes that that revealed her compassion. She'd never taken a course from Zozik, but her admiration was as sincere as ever. "You're extraordinary," she'd tell me.

I trusted her. Because of that trust, after we'd performed together again in *La traviata*, I went with her to visit Elem's family for the first time.

The weeping wax plant on the balcony; it was as though it sensed that there was a shattered love story. Perhaps in the end, all that will remain is that wax plant. The balcony of an apartment in Kocamustâpaşa. Semra asked, "Does it feel pain when it weeps?"

But at the time, the friendship between the four of us had not yet started.

Elem often asked about Semra, saying that she wanted to spend more time with her. She would ask after her health, her marriage, her happiness and whether or not I'd seen her.

"Yes, we've met up."

"She's a good person. She even invited me and my brother and sister to the opera."

Gathering my courage, I invited Ali and Semra over for a soiree in my garden on a night when Elem was coming. They found nothing odd about my Munise being there. And they didn't ask any questions; not that night, nor any other time. Not the smallest mention was ever made about my private life. They liked Elem.

That night we didn't speak of opera.

With the enthusiasm of a child, Elem had decorated the garden: party hats, paper lamps, strings of flashing lights. And Semra and Ali were quite pleased. "Elem did it," I told them. "She decorated the garden for you." For me, those paper lamps stir up memories of fairy tales and legends.

That night I found out that Ali had been born and raised in Samatya, and that he'd attended Davutpaşa High School. He was maybe three or four years older than Elem. That night they spoke of Samatya and Kocamustâpaşa, and the gardens in Langa where Elem and her mother used to pick their own vegetables. Ali said that he remembered the vegetable seller.

I recall glancing at Elem and Ali; they were so young! They went on and on, reminiscing about the past. The candles in the colorful paper lanterns began going out, one by one.

Even though Semra, Ali and I always stayed friends, Elem never met up with them without me. This morning I was thinking about that.

We were always together during our trips. But Elem never called Semra or Ali without telling me first. One year Semra called Elem to wish her a happy New Year—Elem was so surprised that she called to tell me about it.

This morning I awoke with the pain of that memory. As though all of those things were hidden away in a secret drawer, and when I open it, everything pours out. Lurking there among many painful others, the memory of the fact that even though Elem had liked them, she never got close with Semra and Ali.

Opera had also driven a wedge between Elem and the couple. Opera, which Semra dreamed will be beloved by all one day.

A cool, humid October morning. This year, the coralbell blossoms withered early, falling to the ground. The garden has grown unkempt. I don't have the heart to look after it. Never again will Elem hang colorful paper lanterns around the garden; there will be no more pleasant evening parties.

Even if she was never close with Ali, I think Elem felt some kind of intimate connection with Semra. At the very least, an intimacy of the oppressed. It seems to me that Elem felt distanced from us because Ali and I were always in lead roles. One time she asked, "Hasn't a lead ever been written for a mezzo soprano?" The question struck me as odd and I brushed it aside. If only I hadn't . . .

Over the years we'd become accustomed to being together. That's not quite right—we'd become bound to each other, as though we shared the same pain and suffered the same trials. But if you asked me to describe that pain, I would be at a loss for words. Some people are destined for suffering; the world's agonies course through their veins. That's how we were. We understood each other.

Perhaps I was the one always holding back.

When we were with them, Elem was herself: Handan Sarp's intimate partner, her lover even. Semra was herself: she didn't differentiate between Elem and me, and always spoke of her kindness and refinement. Ali was himself as well: like a younger sibling to me, and a big brother to Elem.

But Handan Sarp always held back, withdrawing herself. She wasn't concerned about their intimacy being known as long as "that topic" was never discussed. To no avail she tried to be herself.

I say "to no avail" because she'd fly into a rage if Semra asked something like, "You're going to bring Elem, aren't you?" or if Ali said, "You're so lonely. It's good that you have Elem in your life."

To no avail. Because whenever they went out, Handan Sarp was always careful not to sit next to Elem. She wanted people to think that Elem was a relative or a friend of Ali or Semra. They should never be seen sitting side by side; that's what she thought. The image of Handan Sarp and Elem seated opposite each other clinking glasses at Hristo's was but a distant memory that had long faded from Handan's mind. If she did think of it, she was taken aback by her blitheness in those days. The stench of a meyhane had seeped into that memory. Elem was always seated beside Ali or Semra, and Handan was even careful not to sit across from her.

Semra sensed it immediately. There was an unspoken agreement, and no one said a word. Enshrouding the topic in silence, they probably attributed it to my being Handan Sarp. Everywhere we went, I behaved as though I'd just met Elem.

Between us, we actually joked about it: Elem as Ali's cousin. Elem as Semra's classmate. But the age difference between them was clear as day. I laughed, unaware I had hurt Semra's feelings: "Which high school? The Ataturk High School for Girls?" Elem had only finished middle school.

I knew nothing about what Elem was feeling. In those days, I didn't even think of it.

Her mind was burdened with worries. "They love each other, don't they?" she'd ask, again and again. She wanted them to be in love; she wanted Ali to be passionately in love with Semra.

"Why don't they have children? Don't they want any?" She asked questions like that. "Children are what bind two hearts together . . ."

At first, I was irritated by her mention of children. "How do you know that? How can you be sure that children bring people together?"

She blushed and bowed her head.

Bitterly I laughed and said, "Maybe they hate children too, just like me."

She looked up and searched my expression. Her gaze was green as the sea. "Don't lie to me," she said. "I know you take pity on children."

I looked away.

I asked her if she thought that one day young, handsome Ali would take to flirting with other woman, and eventually betray and abandon Semra. Smiling wryly, Elem answered, "Life is heartless already. The world is full of enough cruelty." Her words rang in my ears. Full of enough cruelty . . .

But as time went by, she began drifting away from Ali and Semra, as she did with everything else in her life, although she felt close to them when we were together. As we saw them less and less frequently, she no longer asked after Semra's happiness or Ali's love for his wife. Never again did she broach the subject of children.

And I was aware of her silence. Handan Sarp should've felt it. Elem's timidity was limitless, as was her fear. But Handan Sarp was blind to that. Each of those incidents was a warning, a sign that I needed to heed if I didn't want to lose her. But I was cold and jaded, and took no notice of Elem. It was the autumn of my life and I was in the grips of menopause. The only comfort was the thought of my own destruction. And for a long while I'd been doing exactly that.

Unlike Gelengül, Semra agreed with me that Elem should get a place of her own.

When we were chatting in the kitchen, or, later when we'd occasionally talk on the phone, Semra would say, "She should have her own life." Semra told me about how, before she married Ali, she'd moved out and lived alone.

Elem had said of her family, "I just want them to leave me alone, that's all." When Semra told me her thoughts about Elem, I had listened coldly. I was in no mood to talk about why Elem's family put so much pressure on her. Nor was I interested in debating the issue with Elem. Everyone has their own private hell.

Semra asked me whether Elem and I would live together. What an idea! "She's a good person, and cares for you a lot," she said. Living together, she said, would bring us "closer together."

"What?" I snapped.

"Like . . . a family . . ." she stammered.

Or perhaps it was Elem:

At her flat on Nemli Yufka Lane. Night. We were watching television. It was an old film, starring Lana Turner, about a woman who rejects a man's love, and out of spite and pride she marries a wealthy man she cares nothing for. As expected, her life turns out to be miserable. And to make matters worse, Lana Turner's character is diagnosed with cancer. It was a production from the 1950s; cancer was a common theme in those days. At the end of the film, Lana Turner is in her hospital room and she summons her ex-lover—who is still in love with her—to her deathbed, so she can see him one last time. She mutters a few broken sentences about love, lost love. She says that her love for him is as strong as ever . . . Why did I think of that? Then, as now, I thought it was a foolish film, but it stayed in my mind.

I told Elem about that worthless movie; as Lana Turner uttered her final words, I'd been unable to hold back my tears. And now the film was on television, and we started watching it. Elem had a sofa and two small armchairs. Penny by penny she'd saved up some money and bought them at a secondhand store. Elem was curled up on the sofa and I was sitting in one of the chairs. Yet again the film affected me deeply. Unable to bear seeing me sad, she said, "Come sit by me."

"What do you mean by that?" I said rather curtly.

"I don't know . . . Like a family. The closeness of a family." And then she turned back to the film.

It doesn't hurt like it used to. Later, I began to recall more and more often the words my Munise had said to me. That particular moment had wounded me deeply. But time wears things down. The pain ages, withers and shrivels, and lingers on, becoming a throbbing wound that festers.

If I had sat next to her—if we'd become "like a family"—would the pain have gone away? And why did everyone want a family? Semra, Hikmet and Mustafa, Elem . . . Rather than making odd families that society would scoff at, wouldn't it be better to rise up against that society and embrace a deathly loneliness? Perhaps. It's a difficult choice. And I was trying to stake out my preference.

But we had pleasant days together as well. I remember the four of us in Beyoğlu and at Büyükada. A deep friendship had grown between us. It's strange, however, that two of those pleasant days were in the fall. Unending autumn, seeming to last a lifetime. Two autumn days, evenings, nights. For Elem, Semra and Ali, they may have long ago faded to nothingness.

In Beyoğlu, walking at night. That may be the most straightfor-ward description. We walked at night, and ghosts and memories of the past suddenly appeared, singly or in groups, people from our pasts: sopranos, Italian tenors, and conductors. There, in the city of empires.

Sometimes that's how it happens. Gathering up a few scraps of information and their attendant specters, I try to create a new world.

It was one of the most pleasant autumn evenings I can recall. We'd met up at my place. The weather was balmy. It was one of those rare fall days unsullied by Gelengül's weekends and Saturday nights.

They'd wanted to sit in the garden. Kadriye Hanım had prepared the dinner table. "When it gets cold, we'll move to the living room," they said. In that cemetery of old apartment buildings in Nişantaşı in the middle of the city, my garden was particularly enchanting.

We laughed about the rosebush that Elem and I had bought, recalling our surprise when white rather than pink roses bloomed. At the time the rosebush was bare of flowers. But we were talking about the roses of summer.

I picked a laurel leaf for Semra from Kaya's stunted tree. Day by day it seemed to be shrinking further into itself.

"You once brought me a bouquet of violets," I said.

"And you brought one of Muazzez Tahsin Berkand's 'violets' from her novel," Semra replied. She was telling the story to Ali and Elem.

It was probably Ali who got hung up on the idea, but we ended up going to Beyoğlu instead of eating at home. The swarming crowds were overwhelming. It seemed that all of the denizens of the city had spilled into the streets and were traipsing up and down İstiklal Street. What hopes did they have for that Saturday night?

I needed to take refuge somewhere, so I burrowed into my dreams and memories. The teeming crowd vanished as I nudged aside that Saturday evening which promised nothing but sorrow. I emptied the street of people and cleared the restaurant where we were sitting of customers. I silenced the roar of noises: the laughter, the clattering of forks on plates, the music of the gypsy street performers.

"*Opare*," I told them. I was randomly flipping through the pages of an Ottoman ambassador's travelogue about Europe.

They laughed at the word "opare."

But that's how it was written in that old travelogue. And sometimes, "opere."

A garden suddenly appeared, filled with lemon and bergamot

trees. And that's when the "opare" began. Of course it was a love story. Opera always speaks of grand tales of passion.

Who knows which piece it was? The author of the travelogue didn't say. But that was how my Ottoman ancestors had first learned about opera. Caught up by the story, my friends stopped laughing.

Such travelogues were given to the padishah so he could know what was happening in the West. How had he imagined opera to be?

Perhaps Semra would be saddened when I said it, but from the very beginning opera had been treated as something strange in our society. The privy secretary of Sultan Selim III wrote of how they'd gone to Topkapı one Wednesday and watched a rather "trying" foreign performance called "opera," and afterward spent an "enjoyable" evening mocking the performers.

Semra's face had gone ashen as she listened. I had no intention of hurting her feelings, but what could opera save? She said that in a brighter future, people would be able to discover the secrets of music. She was trying to tell something about the enthusiasm of her youth. But what I recalled were the days of the military coup of September 12 and those well-known politicians and commanders—now lost to obscurity—who tried to hastily push the country into the modern age. And if I were to give myself over to those memories, I felt that I'd fall defeated before the carousing at the restaurants of Nevizade Street.

It was fortuitous that the Italian opera troupe went to Istanbul. Bu who were they? What adventures awaited them? Verdi in all his splendor had been brought to life at the theaters of Basko and Naum, even the Gedik Pasha Theater: *Rigoletto*, *Ernani*, and of course *La traviata*!

But enough of Verdi. I took my friends to the grave of Giuseppe Donizetti. I took them to Feride's school, and to the vault of the church in the courtyard. They didn't know that Giuseppe Donizetti had been slumbering there for eternity.

Sultan Abdülmecid suddenly appeared at a performance of *Il trovatore* and the audience rose to their feet. At the end of the performance, the Sultan congratulated the performers. It was here, just a few steps away, probably at the Naum Theater. Who knows when I'd read that book, or even why, but those lines of description were springing to my memory: the building, salon and decor. The people who breathed life into opera and the spectators.

But I knew that those images of mine, those symbols, would eventually be scattered to the winds and driven away, only to fade into the reality of daily life. "This is where it was," I told them; Basko's theater, across from Galatasaray High School. Who will play the role of Violetta tonight? But the glint and glimmer suddenly turns dark. The soprano disappears.

Macar Tevfik Bey's desire to turn the play *Tezer* into an opera dwindles and fades away. That was less than a hundred years ago. The chorus disappeared, even as it was being written. But I think my thoughts had begun to wander. Yet again I was in search of hope.

Elem uttered the most beautiful words said that night: "You truly do love opera." Ali and Semra had been listening attentively as I spoke. They said that I'd been smiling.

Later that evening we walked down to Galata. The buildings from the past were ghosts, speaking nothing of opera.

We'd been overpowered by a strange acceptance, or perhaps a better word would be resignation. To me it seemed we were just four wounded souls.

Elem: future uncertain, her love for me was futile. It suddenly

---

* *Tezer* is probably the play written by Abdülhak Hamid Tarhan at the end of the nineteenth century. I was unable, however, to identify the man Handan Sarp referred to as Macar Tevfik Bey. (Sİ)

dawned on me that she had no life ahead of her. Days of stress, misery and desperation: working for Nedret, seeing me but once or twice a week, dealing with her family's probing and pressure. I should've helped her.

But there, on my open sea, I didn't have the strength. I was nothing more than a strange sea, where Elem would lose her way. I'd been shaken to the point of paralysis. What calm shores can a strange sea promise to a mariner? Elem was alone. Just as she was yesterday, and would be tomorrow. What change could the evening's capricious zeal bring about?

The days, months and years of our friendship, love and intimacy had, for time immemorial, seemed but a distant mirage. That strange sea could only wash Elem upon the shores of a remote island. There, where the sea's thundering waves pounded the island's beaches, there was just sorrow, desolation and misery; I had abandoned Elem there and withdrawn with all the cruelty of the open sea.

Four wounded souls. One evening, hadn't dreamy-eyed Semra, who wanted to embrace life, once said that she was afraid of getting older? Probably. She sought hope in the predictions of gypsy fortune-tellers. There they were beside me, husband and wife. Ali had aged quickly into a plump tenor. He'd been fattened by a love that no one else would ever understand. An ache of love had settled in his bulk. At that time too I'd thought that, in their unhappy love, they'd be consumed. And in the end, they were.

Their lives were so different from my own. They chose to run the risks of dependency, loyalty and gratitude, and that was utterly alien to my approach to life, which sought rebellion. I was possessed by a wry, sick pleasure because soon we would part ways and the evening would come to an end.

Perhaps it was afterward, perhaps before. Our trip to Büyükada, the largest of the Princes' Islands.

I remember much. But all of it's in tatters. Even the pleasant memories were tainted by the separation, tarnished forever.

It was a clear autumn day. A Sunday. Because school had started, the island was fairly empty. I hadn't been there for years. We were going to a house in the Maden neighborhood of the island. It was owned by Semra's friend, but she'd moved back to the city for the winter.

Ali picked us up and we drove to Bostancı. We'd planned on taking the last ferry back to Bostancı in the evening. Leaving the car there, we boarded the ferry, which was more crowded than I'd expected. Even on Saturday and Sunday people still went to the islands, despite the season.

We sat on the upper deck. The autumn breeze tossed Elem's wavy hair, which glowed in the crisp sunlight. For the first time I noticed strands of gray in her hair. At her age! It would be years before she turned thirty. Instinctually I stroked her hair. It had started turning gray for me. Because of me. "That's probably how mothers feel," I thought. Saddened. Surely her mother had noticed my graying before me.

My Munise's hair was turning gray. She turned to me and laughed, still full of love.

Her laughter rings in my ears. That rare laughter of hers has somehow never faded from my memory. It clings, refusing to let go.

Love strikes me as something of a riddle. And that moment was the same: driven from motherhood to love, from love to friendship, from compassion to sexual desire. Blown from one to the next, such unthinkable precipices. And in these upheavals, objections rise up against all of the world's false prohibitions.

I paused for a moment on the wharf. The summery breeze was locked in an embrace with autumn as it blew over the island. That belligerent wind, portent of fall, soothed me.

My friends wanted to walk to the central market so we could take a carriage. When I went to the island as a child had there been a carriage stop there?

I objected, telling them that the autumn breeze was so pleasant. "Let's sit down," Semra said. "We'll have a coffee." I can't remember the name of the hotel café, the front of which was glassed in. There was no one sitting inside.

It was less windy there, but the sea churned with waves tinted glass-green and indigo that sloshed into turquoises and deep blues, frothed in whites and pale olive greens. I gazed out at the sea; that's where my life was. Clumps of dead seaweed drifted past.

After the crowds from the ferry went their way, the island appeared empty again. "It's so pleasant here," I said. "Why go to the house in Maden? We'll just be stuck inside." They insisted, saying that it was a lovely place. To get there, we'd walk through copses of pine trees. The house had a large garden, and Ali would light the barbecue. In the desolate market we found a butcher and greengrocer that were open, and we bought lamb chops, ground meat, tomatoes, peppers, onions and spices. After getting the rest of what we needed from a corner shop we boarded the horse carriage, everyone carrying bags.

The carriage made me dizzy—the sound of the horseshoes and sharp crack of the whip. We passed by mansions, their gardens full of wilting bougainvillea and blossomless jasmine and mimosa. All along the road were sycamores shedding their leaves, and there was a pattering as thick-shelled horse chestnuts fell to the road. And then there were languid, ponderous linden trees. The wind had died down.

There was an overgrown greenhouse, the glass of which was

cracked and broken in places, in the yard of an old mansion; it was filled with red flowers. "Camellias!" Semra exclaimed, clapping her hands, and Ali was suddenly transformed into Alfredo. As Ali sang, the coachman turned and looked, trying to hold back his laughter at that "odd" song.

'Those red camellias are etched in my memory. I asked the coachman to stop, and he reigned in the horses.

Below the red blossoms there were white and pale pink ones as well, and the reds were trying to conceal and cover them up. At least that's how it seemed from the garden gate. The short stems were adorned with glistening, thick leaves. The red, whites and pinks nestled among the waves of green.

I was drawn back to the carriage by Alfredo's song.

The clopping of the horseshoes resumed. Elem was telling them about Zeytin Island. "Maybe the next summer we could go together," she said.

At Maden we alighted from the carriage. A rusting iron gate opened onto the rather steep road. I saw a loquat tree laden with unpicked fruit that had dried on its branches; the scene was melancholic. A splendor was drawing to a close, and we were witnessing its demise.

A little further down there was a blue spruce, aged and decrepit, that had lost its silvery blue shimmer. But the pinecones on its branches, resembling toy barrels, still breathed hope for life.

The needles of the pine trees drooped as though afflicted by a disease. Crows and gulls filled the air with their raspy cawing and screeching. We reached the end of the road. A plump cat in the garden of a three-story apartment building, which seemed out of place on the island, scampered away when we approached. The cat ignored Elem when she called out to it.

Once she said to me, "We should get a cat of our own." That

memory sends a shudder through me. But there's nothing to be done.

I'm reminded of something else as well. She told me that in her childhood she'd had doves, which her father had bought for her from the animal market in Eminönü, near the Spice Bazaar. She and Hüseyin tried to get the doves to perch on their shoulders.

I want to be free of those memories. All of them.

The apartment smelled of mildew. We opened the curtains, the windows and the door leading to the veranda. Ali saw that the refrigerator was unplugged, and he plugged it in, disappointed that the raki wouldn't be cold. Semra and Elem rolled up their sleeves. Everyone set about working.

I laughed, "I feel like we're children skipping school."

The scent of linden and pine hung in the air. Across the way, I could see Sedef Island. In the neighboring garden, bright yellow fruit weighed down the branches of a quince tree. Sparrows flitted past like a summer rain. Ants were making their final preparations for winter. When I looked up, I saw a green fence and beyond that, as though at the edge of a precipice, the waterfront below, and then the wavy sea stretching into infinity—a Sunday afternoon in autumn!

In the afternoon, the air became thick with humidity, and it felt like we were swimming in steam. Ali lit the barbecue and it popped and crackled, sending up embers of fiery red and yellow. Which of us had said, "Autumn is breathing"?

But was it just autumn? I too was breathing. I was smitten with love for the day and sunset.

("Selim Bey, if only I could go to the island again! To all the islands in the world. If I could just relive everything again. To see Elem's smile, to make love with her, feel happiness . . . This time, that joy which I never understood wouldn't abandon us.")

Evening fell. From the ferry we saw the fall moon. Its oranges and reds paled to a white incandescence. Elem was sitting beside me, as though she were Liù, and I, Prince Calàf.

My Aunt Nadire, who came and went through Elem's life like a ghost, was perhaps our most refined yet gaudy friend.

What I mean to say is that she was a friend.

And I must make another correction: it wasn't my aunt, but rather Elem who came and went like a ghost. Never again did she call my aunt.

Aunt Nadire made cherry pies for Elem and served her cherry liqueur. They had evening tea together.

My aunt was like a dream of the past for Elem. In Aunt Nadire she saw one of those elegantly robed women that her grandmother had known and told Elem about. An aging young girl who wore a velvet robe.

Aunt Nadire's obsession with velvet was something new. "My body wants velvet," she said. "I don't know why, but I feel cold, winter and summer." Red and purple outfits with lace collars and cuffs. Like the clothes of a young woman of means sent abroad in exile.

"A little like Belgin Doruk," I said to my Munise, telling her about the years my aunt had dreamed of Belgin Doruk, who starred in those old black and white Turkish films.

That's why Elem was always entranced whenever an old film came on television. They spoke together about them: in her seventies, that old girl whose dreams and longings still pulsed in her heart would speak of the films from her youth as though they'd come out yesterday. Elem would call her up whenever she came across one of those films on television and tell Aunt Nadire which channel it was on. It was though they'd made a secret agreement.

The next morning, my aunt would call me, an accusing tone lurking in her voice: "Where were you last night? Bless her heart, Elem told me that *A Young Lady's Chauffeur* was coming on." Or, "If Elem hadn't called, I would've missed *A Summer Rain*."

Indeed, where had I been? Out on a night with Gelengül prowling for lust? Onstage, where I'd lost my beliefs and ideals, singing of the pangs of the heart? It no longer matters. Those pages have long been turned. When I remember them, a feeling of suffocation comes over me.

They would sit and chat. Sometimes they'd call each other during a film. My aunt, unable to hold out against Elem's persistence, would hesitate at the last moment about telling Elem about the end of the film. Did it have a happy or sad ending? "If I tell you, you'll just go to sleep."

There was so little that Elem and I both loved and shared. Not once did she call to tell me about a film she was watching, probably because she knew she'd just get the answering machine.

But they didn't talk on the weekends, on those Saturdays and Sundays when we met.

"You called my aunt. I got another scolding."

"Belgin Doruk was amazing in *You're Always in My Heart*. I couldn't help it."

I'd look out at my tired garden through the window. Mostly on winter days. Leafless, bare, flowerless. My hands knotted together, tortured by memories of the previous night.

And later, it wasn't just those old films. My Aunt Nadire would launch into tales about Ankara, her reminiscences of Ataturk's mausoleum and Kızılay Park, which she visited but once in her life.

She'd gone to Ankara with my grandmother. I'd heard about it maybe a hundred times. Each time she started talking about Ankara, I'd become terrified that she might start telling the story again.

But Elem never wearied of those remembrances; Aunt Nadire had found her audience. They'd gone to Ankara to "pay their respects" to Ataturk, as she said. But why hadn't my mother gone? What year had it been? Had I been born yet? It was unclear. Ankara had stolen her heart. "Our capital."

She'd probably been quite young, because she explained what she saw through the eyes of a child. The mausoleum was so grand and magnificent that it towered over you. The large, broad steps and rows upon rows of countless columns . . . And then she would go on about the park:

"The Kızılay building in the park is about belief, goodwill, solidarity and compassion. In fact they're twin buildings, side by side, embellished with a large red crescent moon. Elem, isn't that also like a new moon?"

"Yes, Aunt Nadire."

Ah, Elem, your voice, your excitement! Why does your voice still ring in my ears? That enthusiasm of yours which I'd found so pointless now stabs at my heart.

"At night they'd illuminate the crescent moon with red lights. I wonder if they still do that?" My Aunt Nadire would fall into reverie, as though those red lights were burning before her eyes.

My cruelty knew no bounds. "It was torn down long ago. Those lights are long gone, as is the crescent. There's nothing left." Even though I knew the answer, I asked, "Elem, have you ever been to Ankara?"

"No."

"One day you should go, Elem. Go with Handan. Perhaps she'll take me along too."

Damn it all! I close my eyes. The train begins to pull out of Haydarpaşa Station. My Aunt Nadire is sitting across from me in the dining car, and Elem is by my side—we can feel each other's heat. Why didn't it ever happen? The train sets out at night, rain pounding against the window with its star and crescent. She's content: Handan Sarp, with her dear aunt and Elemishka, going to Ankara.

That woman could've been happy. Now she has no one except herself. She begrudged her young seamstress the chance to see Ankara. And her aunt, as well, who put on her lace skirt and garish makeup and took young Handan to her entrance exam, waiting at the door for her.

Elem was generous with her affection: "What do you remember about the park, Aunt Nadire?"

"Ah, yes, dear child. Handan says it's gone now, but it was so beautiful! So green, clean and well-kept. And do you know what I remember? They'd put rubbish containers all around the park, and my mother said to me, 'If you see even the smallest piece of garbage, I want you to pick it up and put it in the rubbish bin.' It was like a game as I ran around picking up bits of trash, twigs and fallen leaves and putting them into the rubbish containers."

If only I could silence the memories, and release the tension in my heart. But I can't. Aunt Nadire goes on and on. In my imaginary train, snowflakes stick to the window. Soon my aunt will be confronted with Vronsky. And then an atmosphere reminiscent of *Anna Karenina* will be conjured up. I'm unable to put an end to this nightmare.

On another day:

"I'll always remember the circular fountain in the park with its streams of water. We went so many times to the park. Elem, roses had been planted all around the fountain. Such colorful, glorious roses. My mother said, 'You just can't get enough of looking at them.'"

And another evening:

"I also remember the small booth that sold Kızılay sparkling water. The building was whitewashed and lit up with red lights. And there was a large signboard that had a bottle lit up with a flashing red light. My mother and I drank sparkling water from crystal glasses."

They'd forgotten about me. My aunt, an eternally young girl, spoke as Elem, my young seamstress, listened. She couldn't get enough of telling her stories. As though from her imagined memories of Ankara she brought to life the excitement of the founding of the Republic. And Elem spoke to her about Ataturk. The naivete of it all pained me.

I'm in pursuit of the past, of the days when Elem still loved me. Deep down I miss the conversations she and my aunt used to have.

I remember that small old house, half brick and half wood, in the back streets of Bahariye. With flowerpots of begonia and fuchsia in front of the windows, the house seemed to be hopelessly trying to rekindle the life of a hundred years past. Although she receives a small monthly stipend from her father's retirement fund, Aunt Nadire is no longer able to make ends meet. The house was originally bought to tide over the family in case they ran into difficult times.

Soon, however, the place will be torn down. The contractors have promised her a floor of her own in the new building, but each time my aunt finds herself unable to give up the house. Again and again she argues with the contractor because she thinks they're trying to swindle her. "And so of course I kicked him out!" she said.

In the tiny sitting room she has a collection of wedding candies. There must be a hundred of them, some in little decorative boxes, others in lace sachets with ribbons and on miniature ceramic plates. How could she ever part with them? She insinuates that if she were to move in with me, I wouldn't let her bring those "wormy candies." She knows that if she even were to stay with me while construction was underway it would be a disaster. We both know that.

First she glares at me. Then she begins showing them to Elem, one by one, telling the story of each. That couple grew old together, and then there were those unlucky women whose husbands cheated on them; there was also the woman who, after years of marriage left her husband. And that couple had four children. Ah, and that poor woman died in a car accident . . . It was like the collected works of Émile Zola.

There were times when my aunt, who had flirted with marriage on a few occasions, was quite ambitious in life. Now and again she'd mourn that Handan Sarp hadn't (or wasn't able to) become a world-class soprano, a true prima donna. For years she was hung up on the idea that I needed to get closer to the maestros I worked with. "You should flirt more," she'd say. "You should start up an *amitié amoureuse.*"

I was never sure if she even liked opera, though she was pleased with her niece on the stage, Handan Sarp "backed by a huge chorus." But it always irritated her that I struck up friendships with the chorus members, and she never took a liking to Hikmet. "They are there to serve you!" she said.

At such moments, I'd become lost in thought. What could I do? In her opinion, chorus members were nothing more than extras. And there are many people who, though they claim to love opera, think the same way. Such ignorance has always made me uneasy.

At first, she was upset that I hadn't married. But then she changed her mind. "An artist should never marry. An artist should be happily married to her art." One day she was wearing an outfit of pale rose velvet with broad skirts and blue silk stitching along the collar and sleeves; it was obvious that she'd put it on for me. She made her announcement: "The marriage between an artist and their art is a truly happy one." For years she repeated this when people asked why I wasn't married: "She's an artist."

I've always believed that if opera will one day light the way for humanity, as Semra claims, we must first do away with those ostentatious opening night galas. The artificial splendor of the stage is more than enough—what need is there for gaudy gowns and suits? Opera has always spoken of loneliness.

But all the same, on my darker days I sometimes conceded that my aunt was right; indeed, regardless of whether or not I flirted with so and so director or producer, I could've appeared more often on television and had more interviews with newspapers and magazines. The turquoise tuxedo that Nedret wanted to make for me would certainly have garnered attention. Swelled with conceits and caprice, doted on by a poor young woman who would be half assistant, half servant . . . That's what would come to mind: a second-rate impresario or press manager.

Above all, what of my right to sexual liberation? I knew that changes were in the air. Little by little, Handan Sarp's sexuality could've become legendary, like that of Greta Garbo. And perhaps that would have served me well. Moralists have an odd curiosity about homosexuality, and their endless hunger demands satiation.

But I did nothing. Shrouded in seclusion, I remained buried in my own thoughts. Now, it's late, far too late. Sometimes I'm filled with regret, and not just about that but many other things as well.

As I said, many other things. Elem is among them. I was honest with her—after the very first time we made love, I asked her whether or not she was truly attracted to women's bodies; I wanted her to decide on her own. But such honesty hadn't been my intent. Compassion, kindness and love had no place in my life. I was going to just use her and then toss her aside, like everyone else in my life.

Everyone.

But still, I was overcome by a deep longing for innocence. And still am.

I worry that if Aunt Nadire's place is torn down, yet another stove-heated home will be lost.

The apartment where Elem's family lives also has a coal-burning stove. But her flat on Nemli Yufka Street is heated by gas. Everything changes.

The kitchen of my aunt's home, which overlooks a forlorn court-yard where the roots of fig trees strike down into stone, hasn't changed at all, and the old coal-fired range still rattles and sputters. When she and Elem had become close, Aunt Nadire used to invite us over.

A single window and door open onto the courtyard from the narrow kitchen, which is lined on each side with cupboards. If you were to rummage through them, you'd think she had a kitchen of palatial proportions. There were jams of all sorts, but especially cherry jam, Elem's favorite, as well as orange, bergamot, peach, apricot, fig, rose and cornelian cherry.

But Aunt Nadire wasn't about to give Elem her recipe for cherry jam, nor even a small jar of it. Smiling, she said, "If I did, you wouldn't come see me anymore." Her eyes glimmered with hope.

Those smiles, those pleasant moments. I mentioned it before—those are the ones I'd most like to forget.

In another cupboard were the pickles. One time she made pickled aubergine, especially for Elem, along with pickled slivers of red peppers wrapped in the stems of celery leaves and cabbage and garlic. Winking, Aunt Nadire said to Elem, "Just for you, the ones you like."

"You're going to put a pickle on your tart?" I asked. I was always taken aback when they did that. At the same moment, they'd say, "The sour brings out the sweet." There was nothing for me to do but smile along with them. Yes, I too smiled and laughed on those evenings we spent together.

My aunt's cheerfulness always came as a surprise. She'd dress up (inevitably putting on a velvet robe) and light the range, preparing tea and cherry tarts while she awaited our arrival. When she opened the door, her face would light up, and after hugging me tightly, she would pull Elem into a long embrace. Joy breathed youth into Aunt Nadire. It was as though, in her life of loneliness, she'd never grown out of childhood. "Will this woman ever grow old?" I'd ask myself. Her face had wrinkled, her hands trembled and her body had withered, but she stood as straight as ever. Somehow she'd transformed her loneliness into an elixir of youth which benefitted no one but herself.

"We should visit your aunt more often," Elem said. Most likely she wanted me to realize that, despite my solitary existence, I could create a "family life."

But our visits to my aunt remained few and far between.

I think my Aunt Nadire felt a certain sympathy for the relationship I had with Elem, but I don't know what she thought of it. She was just close to us, and after a life of longing for human warmth, she was at ease with that intimacy that society condemns.

Sometimes she calls and talks so much that I grow weary of listening. She drones on about how she still hasn't reached an agreement with the contractor. And then suddenly she asks about Elem. "She's fine," I say, "Elem is just fine." "Cherry tarts on Saturday," she tells me . . . But I can't bear to tell the rest. Aunt Nadire is waiting for Elem. Winter is coming and she'll light the range.

Elem, wasn't Aunt Nadire also like a grandmother to you?

---

* One night, Handan Sarp told me about her Aunt Nadire. It wasn't the heat that made that evening feel so stifling; it was Handan's description. The "aunt" in her heart-rending narrative was nothing like the "aging girl" she told me about that night. They were two different people. Aunt Nadire, who'd previously been described in rather unremarkable terms, was suddenly exalted, transformed into another person altogether through Handan's stirring narration. Such a sudden shift in character might appear to be a defect in the "reality" particular to the art of novel writing. But in life, our radical contradictions of thought and emotion fit seamlessly together. It struck me as being realistic; I was undisturbed by the existence of the two versions of Aunt Nadire. (Sİ)

"This morning I woke up and found myself surrounded by the glimmer of a white topaz," Mustafa said. As he fidgeted in his seat, he looked like a bleach-blond squirrel. "The world was floating in the topaz. It was just marvelous!"

The three of us sat speechless, glancing at one another.

But Mustafa (you can't just call him Mustafa—he'll tell you that his "real" name is Mustafa Hatice: "You can call me Mustafa Hatice Hanım, or just Hatice. But you must include Hatice.") wasn't content with this tale of topazes of white, yellow and blue. His attention slipped away, drifting from our conversation at the table, but we all tumbled into his reverie. We were all baffled by his tale—who was doing what, and where, and why?

That's exactly what he'd said: that he'd woken to a world suspended within a topaz. In contrast to the crisp yellows of the amber stone, which were golden and copper in hue, the yellows of the white topaz were pale, verging on pure white. And when he saw the world bathed in that pale yellowish white, all of his sorrows seemed to fade way.

Didn't we all desire that?

Elem's life was just beginning, in every possible way: her youth, our friendship, the new people she was meeting. I could sense that

Elem, who was also just starting to explore the world around her, felt the temptation to leave this hard reality behind and give herself over to the realm that he described. If she could cast off her shyness, she'd ask about that world floating in the glimmer of the white topaz. She contented herself with keeping silent, but her blinking eyes betrayed her excitement. She blinked like that when she was upset as well.

There was no need to ask the bleach-blond squirrel to go on; enraptured by our attention, he was exuberant. "There was the glimmer of crystal, and we were floating in its glow. Then we saw the colors of the rainbow in the glinting sparks. We'd been liberated from our physical bodies and were light as shadows."

It was up to me to summon him back to reality. "Hikmet, where are we now?"

Otherwise he would've rambled on about a white topaz joined by rubies, sapphires, amethysts of violet purple and sky-blue aquamarines.

He glared at me and fell silent. We'd all fallen silent. Then he said, "Nowhere. We aren't anywhere. We're here, in this heartless world."

Hikmet, my friend. An opera chorister in stubborn denial of the fact that, day by day, he was getting older.

("I've hardly mentioned him in our conversations because he has nothing to do with the story of me and Elem, and our separation. It never crossed his mind that we would separate. He imagined that we'd always be together, in an aquamarine bell jar.")

He left a mark on my life. And maybe on Elem's as well. Only time will tell. Perhaps one day Elem will ask herself, 'Just who was that peculiar man? Why did I meet him? What was it that he wanted to say?' One day. That is, if in her new life she has feelings to spare to dwell on Hikmet and Mustafa Hatice Hanım.")

As a chorister, Hikmet's voice was lost in the chorus. But in fact his voice was extraordinary, a booming bass the likes of which I've rarely heard.

He was able to create for himself and Mustafa (his "soul mate") a mysterious, secret world which he kept hidden from everyone else.

And in that world, he kept Mustafa Hatice concealed as well.

You may remember him from Yakup's meyhane in Asmalımescit, which was where all the artists and musicians used to go. On some evenings he would stride in, as if stepping onto a stage.

But not as a chorister. On those evenings, he was a fragile prima donna; he would sit very still, his right hand pressed to his left shoulder, fingers splayed ever so slightly.

With his dyed blond hair streaked with black, he was a striking figure. And he always wore brown leather suits when he went to Yakup's meyhane. He was an aging cowboy trimmed in fringe. Secretly he'd put on light pink lipstick and face cream.

The waiters served him fastidiously, and no one treated him any differently than the others. Many times I came across him there, and sometimes we went together. At Yakup's, he was a diva of the strange, of loneliness. Sipping his drink, he'd sit alone for hours on end, not speaking a word.

He never looked anyone in the eye as he sat at the end of the bar. If you went together, he'd insist that you sit down, but he always remained standing, as though he didn't want to take up too make space.

Sometimes even prima donnas can be humble in their own way . . .

We were at Yakup's. The wall across from us was covered with framed photographs. At first, I thought they were just pictures of meyhane nights. But I was wrong. It was only after I saw how Hikmet would sink into mournful melancholy as he gazed at the photographs that I noticed they were snapshots of youth.

Smiling women, all of them young. And there were men as well, some of them smiling, others glum. There were newspaper write-ups about the meyhane as well. And then photographs taken at Yakup's, tables crowded with people. Hikmet said, "One by one they've gone. It never occurred to me that I wouldn't see them here again."

He spoke as though they'd moved to another city or now went to other meyhanes. Perhaps that's why I was caught off guard: "Where did they go?"

Hikmet muttered a few lines of poetry from Yahya Kemal Beyatlı, who had enthralled me in my school years. But was he talking to me? To the emptiness? To the ones who'd left?

Disheartened by this journey, those remaining at the quay
Gaze, eyes moist, at the dark horizon for days and days.

(Maybe it was the name of the poet. Or maybe what the words evoked. At times, when she was talking with her friends at Yakup's, she was actually thinking of Elem.

Handan Sarp had only recently met Elem. At the time, there was no sign that they'd be dragged into a doomed relationship. In fact, there was a hidden hope. The meeting at the fashion boutique. That evening at the cafe in Nişantaşı. Were there problems? Nothing of importance. Elem and her brother and sister had attended the opening night of *La traviata*, because Semra invited them. The dinner with Elem's family at their home. All seemed well.

It must have been around the same time: Hikmet, whose last name Handan didn't know, was talking about the photographs of people who'd once frequented Yakup's and the obituaries he'd read that day. He also praised Handan for her performance in *La traviata*. As he spoke, the topics become entangled, shuttling from death to life and back again, from the capricious successes of the world to the shreds of memories left by the dead. That's how it seems to her.

There was a poet who wrote graceful poems but few knew of his work. Some nights he would go to Yakup's. The waiters knew nothing of his poetry. But the poet knew about the fatigue of the waiters and of workers. One day, he died.

There was a painter. An announcement for an exhibition of his work at a gallery had been framed and hung on the wall. The body of a young woman was sketched in a few sharply drawn lines, fleshed out it bright hues; it was strangely alluring. He used to go to Yakup's with his friends.

There was an actor who used to pack the theaters, stirring the audience to standing ovations. After he fell prey to alcohol, the roar of applause still thundered in his ears. Tears would spill down his cheeks as he talked about the roles to which he'd dedicated his life. But eventually he gave up on reminiscing about the past, his successes and acclaim. Two bottles of sleeping pills ended it all.

The soprano was pensive. The obituaries didn't interest her, nor the stories or her success as Violetta in *La traviata*.

Her mind drifted, echoing with words and lines of poetry from "The Silent Ship." Kocamustâpaşa. Scattered verses. Her thoughts were sent tumbling, driven on by the poetry, turning to a winter's night, a home, Elem's life. A neighborhood and the holy tomb of Şem-i Dede, where a car passes by. A young woman says, "This is the tomb of our holy grandfather. I pray for him every morning. He's the saint of our neighborhood."

Yahya Kemal Beyatlı wrote, "The people here find pleasure in sorrow."

Why such pleasure?

When there is resignation and poverty, is sorrow the inevitable result? Don't the poor have days and nights of joy, laughter and happiness?

Elem. Why would her parents give her a name that meant "sorrow"?

"What are you thinking about?" Hikmet asked.

"Nothing. Nothing at all."

Her thoughts, however, were swamped with memories. She felt torn. Tense.

Just as in Yahya Kemal Beyatlı's poem, the streets were narrow, bereft of sidewalks, and the houses huddled up against one another. Poverty drove them together, an echo of their suffering.

Every day Elem went to the boutique. When she returned to her neighborhood in the evenings, the only place she could see such dresses and evening gowns was on the television.

Were Elem's curtains drawn? In Yahya Kemal Beyatlı's poem, there was a hand pulling a curtain closed.

They were entering the apartment building. On the stairway, Elem said those stinging words: "Be careful, the third step is broken." Handan paused on the stairs. If sounds never die out—and the mystery of sound waves always tortured Handan—that sentence will ring out forever: "The third step is broken."

Elem stepped aside so they could enter the apartment. But there was no entryway. A piece of printed cloth lay draped over the shelf lined with shoes, an attempt to hide them from sight. There was a murmur: "Holy family silence."

As though wishing to flee the apartment and its sorrow, Handan Sarp stepped out onto the balcony.

The wax plant was weeping waxen tears.

Approaching Handan, the young woman says, "We like growing plants."

Don't you see, the plant is weeping!

On that winter evening, a final cascade of blue light suffused the neighborhood, lapping at the broken-down lives, at the patience and resignation. The other balconies and windows were illuminated by a feeble yellowish glow. In vain, the last blue light of day crept through crevices, seeking out an artery of life.

You killed that place. The luxury of your art killed it, your opera. On gala nights bathed in dark hues, you were Norma, Gioconda the street singer, Olympia in love with Hoffman.

"Let's go inside. You'll catch a chill, Handan Hanım."

Handan Sarp tried to smile at Elem, as she thought, "It's colder inside." The printed cloth covering the cheap shoes. The curtains. I was cold. It's colder. As cold as my heart.

There was nothing to do but take shelter in the tomb of Şem-i Dede at the side of the road on the way there in the taxi. You could see it: every morning on her way from Kocamustâpaşa to Nişantaşı, she—young Elem, the other one—would pray for the soul of Şem-i Dede, pleading for a heart of purity as she ate her pastry.

Casting aside her thoughts, Handan found herself back at Yakup's, sitting across from Hikmet. People were enjoying themselves, drinking, seeking out a few hours of happiness. And then they'd die, leaving the world behind. Those who were famous would get an obituary in a newspaper, their lifeless photographs imprisoned in frames now nailed to the cross.

"Yes," she said to Hikmet, "you're right. But I don't care much for Mozart. I find his playfulness irritating."

"He wanted to bring joy to life. Why does that bother you?"

Bother her? He'd died quite young, as a . . . She stopped herself. Regardless of how young he'd died, she couldn't relate to his music.

Later would come the sound of the ney. When she thought of the tomb of Şem-i Dede, it was as though she could hear the music of the reed flute shuddering through the narrow streets of Kocamustâpaşa, rising and falling in a moaning lament. Even if she were a stranger to it, the music of the ney struck something within her; she could hear in its melodies the pain of someone with a grief-plagued heart. But it wasn't a plea. Only such wails could move her.

Yahya Kemal Beyatlı's poem receded into the distance. Nobody had ever said to her, "Go live in Kocamustâpaşa." She wasn't of their kind. Nor of Mozart's. For her, his opera *Così fan tutte* was ludicrous.

Fleeing from everything that night at the meyhane, she sought solace in thoughts of her grandmother. Yakup's was transformed into a garden in Pendik; the season, of course, was autumn. As she spread out hollyhock flowers to dry in the sun, her grandmother told Handan the story about the bird known as *garip kuşu*.

Garip, as the name suggests, was far from Allah as if in exile, a strange being in a strange land. And souls far from the grace of Allah forever pine for home.

Handan Sarp, her voice tinged with reproach, spoke of an enigmatic exile that tugged her from the garden in Pendik back to the meyhane.

But then she returned to her grandmother. I sensed an untruth lurking in the narrative. A strangeness clutched in the grip of the faraway.

I, Selim İleri, am unable to conjure the rest. The scene remains half finished.)

He wasn't just a chorister—he was mad about poetry. But it was the older generation of poets that he liked; the new poetry left him cold. And, in secret, he wrote his own poetry as well, always in the old Persian prosody of *aruz wezni*. On rare moments he'd read them to me and Mustafa Hatice, his poems born of passion.

But his paintings were altogether different. I forget to mention that—he painted as well, beautiful paintings in oil and pastel. But never in watercolors. Not anymore.

His pastels were of flowers. Some were of branches in spring bloom, others depicted clusters of white forsythia, or a few daisies or scattered violets. But they always seemed to be shrouded in a gauze of mist.

His oil paintings stood in stark contrast.

Once he gave me one of his oil paintings. It depicted two women, one of them rather young. The other, slightly older, was in the grips of agony, her face twisted with pain. Perhaps both of them were suffering. But the younger one, despite this, was smiling. She was blond and roundish of face, her eyes of green flecked with amber. The other woman, writhing in pain, had dark eyes, verging on black.

The two women look out from the canvas, as though speaking to whoever looked at them, their words a surging torrent. But no matter how long you gaze upon them, you'll never understand what they say. It seems that they are about to burst into howls. You turn away in fear.

But at the last moment, you see the desolate landscape of the horizon. Where are these women? Where have they been left? The barren earth is silent. Parched, forsaken.

At first sight I liked it. Hikmet had just finished the painting, and it stood upon the easel, perhaps not even dry yet.

Mustafa Hatice was sitting by the window doing needlepoint, unaware of the painting and its women writhing pain and the barren landscape.

"What inspired you?" I asked. We'd only recently become friends. I wondered if the spark of inspiration had been none other than the stricken figure sitting beside the window.

"I don't know. The images just appear, as though I'd seen them in a dream but can't remember them very well. Then I see the image in a flash of light, and start painting."

"How lovely . . . I never see anything, neither in my waking or sleeping life. I suppose I do dream, but when I wake up I can't remember them."

As I said that, I had no idea that one day I'd be tormented by nightmares, that Elem would haunt my dreams, that I'd struggle night and day with thoughts of her. That conversation took place long before I met Elem. I was but a rising star in opera at the time, buoyed by hope as I set forth on my journey. But it's strange: even then, a certain weariness tugged at my soul.

"You're so lonely, Handan."

"Forget my loneliness—I'm used to it. Your painting is so beautiful! Come, let's take another look."

But then something unexpected happened. Mustafa Hatice, who'd seemed to be completely lost in thought, turned to us, and with a smile tinged with envy, held out the needlepoint he'd been working on: "What about this? Isn't this lovely too?" I'd thought he wasn't listening to our conversation.

A few days later, Hikmet showed up at my place with the painting, which he'd had framed.

That mark on the wall is where the painting used to be. It had become unbearable. After all those years of hanging there, I took it down. That was after Hikmet died, and after . . . No, I don't want to go into that.

I left the story about Hikmet and Mustafa Hatice to the end. But they were the first friends that Elem and I had.

"Elem," I'd said, "I'm going to take you to a rather strange place. You'll meet two peculiar men. They live together."

Her eyelids aflutter, she tried to look me in the eye. Behind her gaze I sensed all the questions that she couldn't bring herself to ask.

"No, they're not like us," I said, forcing a smile. "They might be gay, if there is such a thing, but they just don't know it."

She listened, not fully understanding what I was saying.

"Hikmet is a bass. A chorister at the opera. But he dreams of being a diva—that's how he lives his life, and that's how he'll die. His friend Mustafa thinks of himself as a woman. Hikmet just fantasizes, but Mustafa believes with all his heart that he's a woman. If you treat him any other way, he gets upset."

I'd thought that Elem would smile, maybe even laugh.

But my dear Elem merely frowned: "It's tragic. So terribly tragic."

"They have no sex life," I continued. "Perhaps when he was young, Hikmet did, when he tried to convince people he was a diva."

Those memories send a chill down my spine. Every day we see hundreds of people, on the road, in buses, in cars. And all of their stories are full of tragedy, but they don't even know it.

That's how they are. Two people, closed off to the world. Woman. Man. Diva. Gay. Schizophrenic. Or their minds are on the other shore, drifting afar. Two good-hearted people. Although they've never harmed a soul, you could put them on the dissection table, slice into them with scalpels. But it doesn't matter: Mustafa Hatice is unshaken, and Hikmet defiant.

No longer am I repulsed by the homes of hoarders. After having experienced that unrelenting pain, I share something with them, and that empathy stabs at my heart.

Hikmet came across Mustafa Hatice in the streets. He was dressed in rags and talking to himself, weeping and laughing in turns. His features were fine and delicate, his figure androgynous. A piece of thin rope held up his pants, and his coat was spotted with stains. But he had an old silk scarf, frayed at the ends, which he'd wound around his head. Hikmet used to laugh say, "It was like a scene from the old films of Muhterem Nur."

That's what he'd say. But Hikmet died. He'll never speak of anything or be a part of my life again.

"Who are you?" he'd asked. "Are you lost?" Always trying to make light of the situation, he'd say, "I knew he had a screw loose." Hikmet, my suffering friend, my confidant.

Mustafa Hatice remembered little of his life on the streets. He told murky, muddled stories. It was as though the past had been caked over with rust. Memories would surface, only to be quickly forgotten again, shunted aside by a desire to leave it all behind.

He'd been orphaned off. But why? In our patriarchal society, are male children orphaned off? Had his parents died? His eyes moist, he'd stop talking. Once his foster mother caught him putting on lipstick. "Even when I was really young I was drawn to girlish things."

That's what said. But it has been years since I saw Mustafa Hatice.

He told of his passion for lipstick, blush and red nail polish; his foster parents beat and punish him. "They tried to push down my femininity." In the end, they kicked him out. Sometimes you find yourself listening to the most horrific stories with cold indifference; like a character in a Dostoyevsky novel, he'd suddenly stop, unable to go on, but you could sense that the memory was playing over and over in his mind. He could read and write, and knew that he lived in the country of Turkey which has a red flag with a white star and crescent moon.

But that was all.

When I met him, he was terrified of going outside. On spring days, Hikmet would coax Mustafa Hatice, who fought tooth and nail, to make the trip with him from Kurtuluş to Belgrade Forest so they could get some fresh air. At the taxi stand near their flat, there was a driver who seemed to pity Mustafa Hatice. They would set off in the early hours of morning, when the park would be empty. When no one else was around, Mustafa Hatice wasn't ashamed of the men's clothing that Hikmet made him put on.

When Elem met him, Mustafa Hatice had long been saved from his life on the streets, and Hikmet had given up on dragging him to the park.

It was uncanny how much he resembled Gelengül, and that resemblance between Mustafa Hatice and Clark Gable always fascinated me. But although they appeared so similar on the outside, they couldn't have been more different in the depths of their hearts. Clark Gable sought to be a paragon of masculinity; manhood was all about being crass, pugnacious and conniving. But Mustafa Hatice, even if he didn't know the fairy tale, was waiting to be whisked away by a prince on a white horse, just like Aunt Nadire. And Mustafa Hatice, withdrawn so deeply into himself, never seemed to ponder the possibility that femininity has a sexual side as well. Perhaps it would be more correct to say that he simply knew nothing of sexuality.

In psychological terms, could his stories all have had their own categories?

Elem felt quite at home in the old neighborhood of Kurtuluş. "It's like a European version of Kocamustafapaşa," she said, which pleased me. Soon after, however, she sided with her own neighborhood: "But our churches are cozier, more Muslim," which struck me as a rather odd thing to say.

As we passed by the pickle shop, Elem stopped to look at the pickled aubergine, and mentioned Aunt Nadire in her comparison of the two neighborhoods. She said that the jars of pickled aubergine in the shop window just had to be the handiwork of Aunt Nadire; she was rather cheerful that day on the way to Hikmet's place.

But her mood quickly darkened when we arrived at his cramped apartment, the walls of which were covered in somber paintings, and even in the middle of the day the curtains were half drawn and black candles of all sizes burned on end tables cluttering the living room.

But it wasn't sadness that gripped her. Nor was it nervousness. She was simply overwhelmed by the "tragedy" of it all. It was like a "tragic" dream when I'd told her about Hikmet and Mustafa Hatice, but now she was face to face with the world they inhabited.

I watched my young seamstress from the corner of my eye.

The silent diva was suddenly transformed, brimming with ebullience as he greeted Elem, Handan's friend. Mustafa lingered a few steps behind, swaying ever so slightly on his heels. Elem looked at them, at the same time taking in the mournful paintings and the candles.

On the way, she'd asked me, "Do they know about us?"

Yes, they knew about us. There was no need to hide anything; our closest friends were all steeped in sorrow. Such realms of anguish granted us the right to live.

I'd said to Hikmet, "You'll be pleased to hear I'm no longer so alone."

And he replied with those words that always made me wince: "A soul mate?"

"Not exactly," I said bluntly.

Elem did something out of character that day. After quickly shaking Hikmet's hand, she approached Mustafa, who was wearing a hand-knit sweater and flannel gown, and kissed him on each cheek, hugging him tightly.

That was how their friendship started, a long-lasting friendship. I don't know if she still calls to ask after him.

Memories of our time together. Our first few years.

The apartment looked onto the side street below where children tried to play ball among the rows upon rows of parked cars, and in the distance a massive plane tree in a courtyard reigned over its domain. In that cluttered museum of knickknacks, everything looked like an antique. Through the paintings covering the wall—abstracts, figures, landscapes, portraits—you could trace the shifts in his style and inspiration; a sea, storm and moonlight whispered of Ivan Aivazovsky, and in a dark portrait of a young man, there were traces of the work of Burhan Uygur.

"Hikmet, why don't you sign your paintings?" I'd once asked.

"I do, but only some."

"Which ones?"

"Only those reflect my melancholy. The bitterest of them all."

I was examining a portrait of a young man shrouded in darkness. It was signed. As though he were standing before you, the young man seemed to be swept away by that darkness. I asked, "Whose portrait is this?"

"Mine. When I was young."

I realized that in all of his signed paintings there was a desolate, barren landscape, either in the background or off to the side, a strange steppe amidst those dark hues, drained of light.

I didn't ask. Perhaps it was the wasteland of his life.

But Mustafa Hatice didn't see that barrenness. Because we were coming to visit, he had started cooking that morning, even the night before: beans in sauce, aubergine with tomato and onions, leeks in olive oil, and Circassian chicken. He said, "One day, I'll cook bass braised in mayonnaise for you."

It was a mystery how he'd learned to cook. The life story of that androgynous man who grew up on the streets was lost in darkness.

He set the table with surprising grace. And yet all winter long he wore the same sweater and flannel gown; in the summer, he donned a vest and print dress, like a servant girl. In all, he had four outfits: two flannel gowns, two dresses. He washed one, and wore the other. But the dining table was covered with a fine cotton cloth, the cutlery was silver and the glasses pure crystal. For a long time he'd pressed Hikmet to buy them. "Because of the silverware, we starved for a year," Hikmet confessed.

Hikmet is deeply concerned, however, that his soul mate from the streets will one day be tossed back into a life of vagabondage.

"Why would that happen? And who would want to . . ."

He cut me short: "Handan, there are people who would hurt him."

Later he made me his confidante and told me the story.

It makes me think of *The Phantom of the Opera*; that's the only way I can sum it up. But in that story, some of the characters are truly malignant.

For years Hikmet had done watercolor paintings of Istanbul for a gallery, the name of which I won't mention. The gallery owner had forbidden him from signing his paintings, which were bought cheaply and then sold with the signature of a fictitious artist. After he'd done hundreds of watercolors, working like a slave, the owner began to fear that one day the true identity of the artist would come to light. After all the secret labor that went into those watercolors of the skylines of Istanbul, the Bosphorus, summer mansions and the Blue Mosque, he managed to scrape together a little money and buy the apartment he lives in, as well as another in the same building which he rents out.

And he has two rather greedy nephews who know about his property but have no idea how he made his money. Nor do they care; they're only interested in their inheritance.

"When I die . . ." he sighed, torn by desperation.

Never again did he take up watercolors, nor speak of them.

His only concern was Mustafa Hatice.

But wasn't there any way he could prevent his nephews from getting their hands on his property? We learned everything we could about inheritance law and consulted lawyers, but it was a conundrum. Everyone said something different. Even if you donate everything to charity, the beneficiary and ownership rights remain in your name.

It was maddening.

"I can't sign the ownership over to Mustafa," Hikmet said. "I don't know if he has any relatives. Perhaps he's afraid. He won't tell me anything."

"But how can you know that you'll die first?"

For such soul mates, family, society and law are horrifying. Marginalized again and again, forever cast out.

"Hasn't Hikmet come yet?" I asked. He would always come to my dressing room before the curtain was raised. But that night, he didn't come. "Where's Hikmet?"

I stood before the mirror. My face appeared drained and desperate in the frame of lights. For years I'd been doing my own makeup: first the powder, then the eyeliner, lipstick and blush. Soon Handan would disappear. Then my outfit arrived, and the costume assistant helped me into the folds and pleats of the dress. I was now someone else, a figure from the libretto.

"He hasn't come," they told me.

"That's impossible," I said. "He's never late."

But they ignored my questions.

I leaped up, flushed by a feeling of panic I couldn't control. If he hadn't come by now . . . It was an internal dialogue, as always, and my mind was a jumble of fears.

I called, but there was no answer. I was sure that something must've happened to Mustafa. I waited by the phone, and called again. It rang and rang; again no answer. I was panicked and couldn't put down the phone.

"You'll be late," I was warned. "The orchestra is ready."

The words seemed to come from far away. I went back to my dressing room, listless; the assistants finished dressing me. That evening's performance was *La Cenerentola*. In a few minutes I'd be on stage, giving the audience the entertainment it sought. My stepsisters Clorinda and Tisbe would scorn me, but I'd remain optimistic. Don Ramiro, Prince of Salerno, would soon fall in love with me.

Throughout the ball scene, my eyes were locked on the choir, seeking out Hikmet's face. I was tense, and the warm tones of Rossini's music only brought me pain; I simply couldn't be Cenerentola.

With my final strength, I sang the last notes. "It must have just been a small run-in with the police," I told myself; just a trifling concern. They probably wrote him a ticket, and the stage manager signed off on it.

When I left the opera house, the city was still thronging with people and traffic. A feeling of loneliness bore down on me. Neither Semra nor Ali had a part in *La Cenerentola*, and I had no friends among the cast.

Semra and Ali knew nothing of Hikmet's home life, including Mustafa Hatice, so I couldn't call them. I thought of calling Elem; but she was staying with her parents, and I couldn't call in the middle of the night. I got into a taxi and told the driver, "Kurtuluş."

What happened next terrified me. At the entrance of the apartment building, I rang the doorbell, but no one answered. I could see a dim light glowing in the window of his flat. I rang the doorbell again and again, to the point that I must have woken up everyone in the building, but no one opened the door. Lights were on in some of the windows, and I could see the insidious blue flicker of televisions, a deceitful blue.

A church in the distance seemed to gaze at me, soulless and cold.

I decided to go to the local police station, but I didn't know where it was. So I went to the Zorbela Özkurtuluş taxi stand, and explained the situation. They knew Hikmet, and a young driver, the one who used to take Hikmet and Mustafa Hatice to Belgrade Forest, drove me to the station.

"No, I'm not a relative," I told the police.

"Then we can't break down the door," the policeman said drowsily. The other officer was drinking tea, eyeing me up and down. It was the first time in my life I'd ever been to a police station.

"Abla, there's nothing we can do," the young taxi driver said. "Does he have any relatives?"

"A few cousins, probably," I said, but immediately regretted it.

"Have them come," the officer said.

"Look," I said, "I'm a soprano at the Istanbul City Opera. My name is on all the posters for the performance of *La Cenerentola*." But my attempts to sway them with my "fame" came to nothing.

I was utterly alone. I had no one I could turn to for help. Opera meant nothing.

There was nothing to be done. I couldn't even call a locksmith to open the door without permission from the police.

The air was filled with a quiet but steady drone, like a portent of dark things to come. I recalled that in recent days, Hikmet had spoken to me about his impending death. It was all he talked about; he no longer wanted to live in "this foul, evil world." Not a day would pass that he didn't talk about it. But I hadn't taken it seriously.

We went back to the apartment building, the dim light still glowing in the window. I rang the doorbells of the other flats. A few neighbors came down, and they became worried as well. I was exhausted; an elderly couple invited me in and brought me a glass of water. The wife smiled at me. A nephew of theirs knew one of Hikmet's tenants living on another floor, and he called the apartment.

It's impossible to put such heartrending pain into words. I saw death, face to face. It filled the room: a bleach-blond man lay in a heap on the floor, and opposite him Mustafa Hatice sat hunkered down, oblivious to the world.

It had been a heart attack.

I didn't go to the ceremony at the opera house, where they sang one majestic choral by Verdi, "Patria Oppressa." The voices came from a lost distance, searing my heart.

Until Elem came to my place after work, I hadn't shed a single tear. My dear Munise took me in her arms, and I burst into tears. "I keep seeing his face," I sobbed. "Elem, the two of us . . ."

"Shush," she said, kissing my tears. She tried to soothe the pain. Like a child, I ran to her, my Munise, for solace.

Few people carry a sea within them, but that night I saw it. Because of her tears. Because she embraced me.

Because the sliver of ice that slashed at my heart slowly melted away.

That night, I saw within Elem a vast sea opening up into infinity.

There are certain scenes that drive you to separation and then leave you in torment. They must surely exist in everyone's lives. People who have suffered the pangs of separation, or long to be in the bosom of God. They are similar, evoking one another, calling out to one another.

But sadly, the violence of separation, when it is still a fresh wound, becomes lost. When you want to speak of it, you falter; its colors fade and the feelings wither. A hush falls over everything, as if those emotions had gone into hiding. And when you dwell on them, wracked by an anguish akin to death, they deny your suffering.

But still, from time to time, especially when least expected, they reappear with barbed intensity, just as you'd first experienced them. The only difference is that the memories appear as though suspended, a constant reminder that they are from a time past.

I try to brush aside those feelings that conjure images from my life—from the days, months and years I spent with Elem. But if they are to haunt me, then let them appear as specters; it is only fitting. And as I wander among those flickering shadows of the past, I'm struck by a sense of being lost in the world, and then the pain rushes in.

That familiar pain: I've never been able to cast it off. But the pain of separation is different, because it's tempered with the hope that one day, perhaps, you may still come together again. The anguish that comes later is cold, distant—a phantom reminding you again and again that your beloved is gone forever. Either waves come crashing in and drive the feelings away, or they rustle among the scattered autumn leaves, which have always hinted at despair; or, ever so rarely, they say their final words and die.

And I, recalling the pasts of each and every one, cry out against life.

I'm but a stranger in that garden. In my garden. If it can even be called that. The garden expects nothing of me, its plants and weeds growing however they desire.

The blossoms of the coralbells withered long ago, but its leaves are still aglow in reds and yellows. But I was first drawn by the lilacs. When I was thinking of buying the flat, I saw the lilacs growing in the garden. Now, there is nothing. No lilacs, no coralbells. I simply gaze upon leaves, red as pomegranate. The lilacs have wilted. The first days of November, a dry southwest wind. An Indian summer.

One night as I was trying to seduce Elem beneath the blossoms of the coralbells I felt the permanence of love and the transience of sexual desire. But it didn't happen all at once; it was only after I'd accumulated layer upon layer of experience and suffering. I tried to stir my passion with false fervor. The love, however, hadn't faded.

I unbuttoned her blouse, my lust flushed by the fear that we might be seen. Our legs were pressed together, and soon our lips were joined. That was to be our last lovemaking set aflame by passion. All that would be left was a love that one day I alone would be left to bear.

Later, I told Elem that I'd known nothing of love, that I'd lived a life hemmed in by taboos and judgments. "But after the sexuality began fading away, I found love. I found it in you."

She believed, however, that when sexual attraction begins to ebb away, love dies along with it. She may not have put it in words, but I could see it in her eyes. For Elem, our relationship should have stayed the way it started.

I told her that she should sleep with other women. Especially women her own age, women with young bodies, just as Gelengül had always told me to do. I told her that if sexuality were roused by desire, it would bring her satisfaction. And because it was an animal lust, it was perfectly natural and would bring no harm to our love.

That which people call faithfulness is none other than hypocrisy and depravity. People who think of themselves as "faithful," I told her, are lying to themselves.

Elem listened, petrified.

But she loved me, and tried to save herself with her love. That's what I wanted her to understand. We were driven apart by her belief that her feeling of love had been tarnished. There's no other way I can explain it.

In our relationship, she sought the faithfulness of a husband and wife. That's what she'd been taught: physical fidelity is virtuousness.

I've never believed in that. Nor in the faithfulness of husbands and wives, in which lurk hidden passions and desires, their lives ravaged by "sin" when a husband sleeps with another woman or when the wife falls for another man. And women with women, and men with men. Our sex lives are nothing more than a tragedy.

"But why?" she would ask. "Don't you love me?"

I'd usually been drinking when we spoke of such things; I had to be. And I'm sure that I smiled when I said: "I love you, passionately.

But the same love can be felt for an object, an instrument or a souvenir."

She didn't understand me. She didn't trust me.

And I also may not have understood. But I trusted her, my Munise. Little by little, something motherly began slipping into my love. But it wasn't exactly motherly. As my love for her grew, my compassion and desire to protect her drove away my sexual attraction. It could have been a subconscious game, perhaps even an escape from social pressure; disregarding sexuality, stifling it and shoving it aside, may have been my own way of mocking nature yet again.

But nature is savage.

Dreams tormented me. Scenes echoed in my dreams, creating new scenes of anguish.

In one dream I awoke weeping. I said to Elem, "My dear, if you ever leave me . . ." In front of Şem-i Dede's tomb, we stood looking at one another. But I couldn't see the billowing blooms of purple wisteria.

An Indian summer. As day broke, the pattering rain stopped.

The fourth of November. A cold day. Winter was coming, and I wondered: how many years have passed since our separation?

I took out my old calendars and held all those years in my hands. After describing those scenes, there will be little left at all.

I did everything I could to forget. But I couldn't move on, especially in the first few months. The first year. If I were to see the painting now, that same heartache would throb anew. I took it down, and wrapped it in cloth. What else could I do? It hung there on the wall. Hikmet's painting. I'd hung it there before I met Elem. When she came into my life, it was there on the wall. When you stepped into the room, they gazed at you. Two women. Even if just for a moment, they would catch you in their gaze.

A trace was left on the wall and in my heart as well. What of Elem's heart?

Have I told you about it? I loved that painting. Perhaps my own torment wasn't enough, and I needed the anguish in that painting as well. That's why I'd hung it opposite the entryway, so that I could see it every time I came home. There they would be, staring at me.

I used to wonder: why are they together? I'd try to figure out why they stared out at us, side by side. Surely they needed to speak to one another. But they remained there, silent, with their smoldering gazes fixed upon me. Perhaps they had talked. Perhaps the conversation had come to an end. Her eyes were dark with anxiety. The older one, her eyes betraying a profound loneliness. The other, with her wry smile of resignation. Her silence seems fitting; in her moss green eyes, there is a flicker of submission. Her lips are curled into a smile, but her eyes, just her eyes, speak: that's how we must live . . .

I'd asked Hikmet. And Elem asked me as well. "Who are those women?"

Hikmet said he didn't know.

I told Elem, "That's you and me. The two of us. Even before he met us, he knew what was coming."

The one with green eyes was Elem, I said. The dark-eyed one, Handan Sarp. Stuck in that desolate wasteland, their hearts barren.

My Munise objected: she said that she was the one with dark eyes.

"You don't have dark eyes," I said. "And she's the older one, practically my age."

But she insisted. She smiled, and then pouted at that roundish face, saying that she didn't want to look like that. I remember being surprised, because Elem's face was in fact rather round. I smiled that day.

It must've been seven or eight years later. One evening, I saw her on my way from the kitchen to the bedroom; she was looking at Hikmet's painting of the two women, as if seeing it for the first time.

Yet again she smiled, but it was different; a hurt smile, stripped of joy, as she stood there withdrawn into herself. "You're right," she said eventually, "she looks like me."

At first I didn't understand what she meant.

"You once told me that she looks like me."

Such moments occur; the pain grips your heart, and you find yourself breathless. That was such a moment. I could sense Elem's exhaustion. No, that's not quite right; she seemed drained. Head bowed, she gazed blankly at something in the distance. She'd been pensive for weeks, months, her voice more tremulous than ever when she broke those silences of suffering. As she stood there, I sensed it: the silence of suffering. Without a word she sat down, and in that moment her youth vanished.

My grandmother used to say, "The sufferers in this world already have one foot in the next."

It was after we'd separated. A blow like a slap across the face. That memory came to me: Elem standing before that painting, head bowed. But in those days, hadn't she always been like that? Bowed, crushed. That scene tormented me like a sea without a horizon.

Memories can be cruel. I took down the painting, Hikmet's painting of the two of us. Together for years and years to come, the two of us. I couldn't bear it.

Have I gotten over our separation? I don't think so. If I had, I would no longer be tormented by dreams of her. Just last night we were together in my dream. In our hotel room on Zeytin Island. The walls were a pale turquoise, the curtains muslin. There was a side table between the two beds. Nothing had changed at the Mercan Hotel.

But the season was different. It was no longer summer, and there was no hint of the warm July sunshine. A chill hung in the air, and the sky was ashen. And when I looked from the window, the sea spread out before me, that sea I long for every day, aching to take shelter in its arms; but in my dream, its surface churned with the white froth of waves, and it seemed lit from within, a deep blue that rose up in challenge to the gray of the day's light. But it was unclear whether it was a churning of passion or spite.

Something had happened to us as well. No, it wasn't separation; we were still together. The idea of breaking up wasn't in my thoughts. It's difficult to explain: in my dream, it never even crossed our minds to separate. But suddenly a distance opened up between us, as if we were complete strangers.

When you awake from a deep, heavy sleep, you often cannot figure out where you are at first. That's how it was in the dream. That room in the Mercan Hotel in that autumn light was completely unfamiliar. I looked at the furnishings around me, bewildered; the window and the sea were gone. Elem and I had drifted even further apart. I felt that I loved her; at the same time, however, our separation seemed even closer than ever.

It's strange—until the day when she said that we had to go our own ways, I'd never felt that I loved her so much.

I awoke. I wasn't weeping. My eyes were stingingly dry. I was in my bedroom, but I didn't ask where I was; everything was in its place. But Elem wasn't there. Not in that room, nor on Zeytin Island.

But it's not just the dreams. If I could come to terms with our separation, those scenes would no longer swarm upon me. The moment I glance into the mirror, I take a step into the strange world of reflections. I turn my eyes away, but it's too late; the scene has begun.

Elem is here, in my home. But I'm not there. She's alone. That happened at times, when I left Istanbul; there was the summer that I went abroad with Ali and Semra on a trip without Elem. She had my key and would come after work to water the plants and look after the place.

Until now, it had never occurred to me to ask: what did Elem feel when she was alone in my home? In the last rays of daylight, my furniture, records and Hikmet's painting on the wall would all be set aglow. Did my absence pain her?

I don't know. But I'm sure that she'll never come again. When I'm abroad, she won't step alone into my garden or sit for a moment beneath the coralbell's blossoms; the hose coiled there like a snake, the plants wilted from the summer heat, the withering leaves of the lilac, and a young woman watering my plants . . . I wonder, did she ever listen to "Suicidio!" when I was away, even just once? I should've told her to, so that she'd think of me.

When she washed her hands, did she catch the scent of my Amazone perfume on the towel or notice my lipstick left uncapped in front of the bathroom mirror?

She probably quietly left the apartment, turning off the lights and locking the door behind her. My home that had been left in her care. The garden watered, she would head off toward Kocamustâpaşa in the summer evening, thinking of Handan, the woman she loved. Once loved!

She had been filled with love.

And so had I. Like a howl in the night.

The rain poured down. It had begun lightly at first, a tremulous drizzle. And now, for two days it has been raining, gushing down in torrents. A biting wind blows. The petals of the crimson geraniums that Kadriye Hanım had planted in the garden are scattered by the wind. But where have they gone? The dead geranium with its scarlet blossoms, where has it gone and to whom?

Who could have imagined that one day Elem would never visit Handan again? That she wouldn't call? That she could go through life without missing her?

But that's how it is. You've gone one way, and I another. Our paths will never cross again.

Two armchairs, and between them a low table on which sat our glasses, a bottle of wine, a bowl of nuts and a few books of poetry; passionately, I read poems to you on those nights. Saturday nights, which as time went by, were fewer and further between.

To purify our souls, I prepared the table for yet another Saturday night: the glasses, the cherry wine that you loved. Perhaps that night, our night, would last into the early hours of morning, and we'd open other bottles of wine.

Soon you'll ring the doorbell and say, "Handan, it's good that we have these Saturdays together."

Those Saturdays were suffocating. The time dragged on, burdened by awkwardness and tediousness.

In the dim light of the lamp, I'm reunited with the shadows. In the darkness. The darkness pulls me in; a shudder runs through me. Sitting there in front of the large window looking onto the garden. The armchair you sat in for years is empty. But you're with me. At the very least, I can imagine that I'm holding a letter from you. I need such lies. But these letters I've written—how could I send them to you? Who can I entrust them to?

The stubborn autumn rain falls endlessly. I turn on the garden light and can see everything rotting away, the entire garden.

It won't be like those Saturday nights when I'd be silent—when the both of us would be silent. First I'll talk. I'll say everything: that which you knew and that which you didn't know. All the things you kept inside, locked away in silence. If I have the strength.

Elem, this same very night, Saturday night, you're on the threshold of your new life, there, in your home. That life will go on like that. You'll live a life that I rejected.

You once said, "I'll never have a home like yours." That's where I am now, if I can really call it my home. Here, I've lived completely alone, like the homeless, the vagabonds, those who don't belong in this world. And tomorrow I'll be alone, and the day after.

The furniture, the tables, the walls, they all seem to be closing in on me.

I can sit, gazing out the window. I can go out into the rainy garden. It's as though I've fallen in love with the rain all over again. I can hope. The doorbell may ring. An impossible dream: you could return.

"I'm back, Handan. Let go of it all, you'll see that I've returned."

But the heartache won't fade away. My suffering will never bring back what I—what you and I both—lost. Some things can only be lost once.

And it's because of that irrevocable loss that I can speak. When you give yourself over to reminiscing, the fear and timidity pull back into the shadows. What's left for us to take offense at?

This apartment once brought us life but it's now filled with a deathly silence. There is the same bed. It was in the beginning, one of the Saturdays, or a Sunday, even a Friday. We met more often back then.

It was the same bed. We'd fallen asleep after lovemaking, our limbs entwined, completely naked. The phone rang, and I leaped up. It was your mother: "Handan Hanım, I'm sorry for disturbing you, but Elem hasn't come home yet. She said she was going to meet up with you." It was well after midnight, your mother said. I was irritated; but was it our carelessness that bothered me, or the fact that she had the audaciousness to call?

You awoke and sat up in the bed, naked, listening to me speak on the phone. I had an urge to start kissing your breasts again. "She just left," I told your mother. "Don't worry, a friend of mine is bringing her home."

But your mother did worry. She always did. Especially about the friendship between her daughter and Handan Sarp, the older woman. About our relationship, and life together. About my private life. What a dull word, "private life." Everyone wonders about everyone else's "private lives."

I began kissing your breasts again. But you didn't know; for me it was just passion, while for you it was love. You always opened your heart to me.

"Quick, get dressed," I said, hurriedly pulling on a dress. I tried to laugh it off: "A friend of mine is taking you home now."

You were angry because she'd called and embarrassed you. "I'm going to erase your number when I get home," you said.

And now, have you erased it?

As though you wanted to repay me, you were stroking my face, lips and hair. Trying to make love with me again.

I pulled my lips away from yours, and reached out to pick up the phone to call a taxi.

If she'd known my address, that woman would have shown up on my doorstep. That's what I'd been thinking about your mother, without trying to betray my concern, appearing indifferent to the worries of mothers. You weren't yet my dear Munise—you were just a lover.

Today I passed down the same street where we sped off in a taxi: "We're late, could you drive a little faster?" On the same streets I walked as the rain pelted down; I was pensive, despairing. Handan Sarp walks for hours. In the rain, in the mist, in the biting cold. Every day she walks, comparing her life to the mists, to the rain, to the mud she slogs through. Days under leaden skies.

Was it after we kissed and embraced that you sang that song to me in your timid voice, the song that your grandmother sang to you? On this journey of longing, don't forget me . . .

No, it was somewhere else; a place full of people, and I was laughing.

The wedding was absurdly crowded: İnci, Elem's older sister, was getting married. Where? At an officer's club.

Weddings have always been tedious for me.

But perhaps when I was a child I enjoyed them. It was always the same group: my grandmother, mother, Aunt Nadire and me, going to the weddings of neighbors and relatives.

In those days we had neighbors and relatives. But not anymore. There is no one who would invite me to the weddings of their sons and daughters. And I'm perfectly content with that.

It was the ignorance of childhood; I enjoyed going to the weddings because everyone got dressed up: Aunt Nadire in her billowing under-skirts, the scent of my mother's perfume, my grandmother's flower brooch.

With every step the glittering diamonds of her brooch would twinkle, flashing with the colors of the rainbow.

For a long time now, Aunt Nadire has had the brooch, which has always only been worn at weddings. She'd dreamed of wearing it at her own. "If I get married," she told me, "I want you to pin it on my gown." After her dreams of marriage had withered away, she boasted of the brooch, showing it off as a sign of her heritage.

But ever since I cut myself off from my family, weddings have remained a distant memory.

As we were going into the officer's club—was it the groom who was an officer?—I was telling Semra and Ali about the weddings I'd gone to as a child, but I didn't dare show my feelings. Not about my excitement when the jazz band played, nor my irritation with the mournful, awkward dancing of the older people, the crotchety mothers stamping about with their permed hair, the roar of applause when the wedding cakes were cut . . .

I was tense, but I kept it hidden. I kept myself hidden. What was İnci's wedding to me? I knew, however, that if I didn't go, it would seem snobbish on my part and reflect badly on Elem. There was no choice.

Elem invited Semra and Ali as well.

The wedding hall was garishly lit. Such ceremonies are always melancholy; you know that soon they'll be over and the lights will go out. That night, I felt out of place and irritated by the meaningless greetings and fake laughter as the music played and children dashed among the tables.

For her wedding and dowry, İnci's family had been saving up money, and Elem had been giving all of her weekly earnings to her mother. Every day they went shopping, buying pots and pans, an oven, bed sheets, towels . . . I told Elem that I thought it was a little absurd.

"But her fiancé's family is paying for the wedding," she said.

Her wedding gown was made at Nedret's boutique. At İnci's insistence, I even went to the final fitting. Nedret was surprised, unable to understand why I was there; her lips twitching, she kept stealing glances at me. Indeed, why had I come?

In her dress, the bride looked beautiful, but a little childish, like the *jeune fille* in old Turkish films. Her eyes sparkled with joy. I was introduced to a dour-faced woman wearing a headscarf: "This is my mother-in-law." Even then İnci addressed her directly as "mother."

"Your gown is quite beautiful," I told İnci, "and you look beautiful as well."

She smiled and thanked me, blushing.

I was trying to stand as far from Elem as I could.

Nedret, unable to conceal her confusion, whispered to me that she'd only asked for the cost of the fabric. But of course, she said, she'd give another wedding present as well. "I didn't know that you spent time with Elem and her family," she added with a questioning smile.

Nedret didn't attend the wedding.

I kissed Elem's mother on the cheeks.

She was wearing a poorly cut brown dress, which obviously hadn't been made by Elem. Her lips were smeared in lipstick; it was clear that she wasn't used to wearing makeup. She was a typical housewife with trembling hands and suffering etched in her face.

"Thank you for coming, Handan Hanım."

Then she kissed Semra on the cheeks and shook Ali's hand, although she didn't know them. I introduced them as friends from the opera: tenor Ali Arkın, and mezzo-soprano Semra Arkın. Apparently Elem had spoken a lot about them. She shook Semra's hand, and smiled at Ali. Elem's mother was wearing a gaudy fake gold necklace; it was probably İnci's, I thought.

At that moment Elem came up.

But she wasn't the same Elem that I knew; she'd been transformed into the Elem of Kocamustâpaşa and gone back to her people. It always disconcerted me when I saw that transformation.

But I was at ease that night at the wedding, even a little indifferent.

I trusted Elem. No matter what happened, I knew that we'd never be daunted by anything, not weddings, parents or society. And I knew that Elem saw the same pitiful absurdities at the wedding that I saw. When we came eye to eye, we whispered to one another. My fears were dispelled; Elem wouldn't go back to her people. That night, she was just taking on the role she had to play.

My Munise brought us to our table. Her father was sitting there, wearing a cheap suit and a necktie, speaking to no one. He seemed hesitant to speak to us. But who were we? He had the air of a man who'd been broken down, having worked day in and day out his entire life, and he tried to be welcoming to us, those strange guests who for some reason were above him in life.

We caused a slight stir: singers from the Istanbul City Opera! That pitiable opera, which Semra believed in so ardently, was yet again causing us to be objects of curiosity. But was it just opera? Our clothes, our behavior, our way of walking, and the fact that our table was set off from the rest, overlooking the crowd, already made us strange.

When her father left the table for a moment, Elem said, "Hüseyin is going to bring some drinks."

"But if no one else is going to . . ." I started to say, but couldn't finish the sentence. What were we doing there? I let Semra and Ali take the lead.

In the end, alcohol was served. İnci's sister-in-law usually drank beer in the evenings, and was a bit "wild," Elem whispered to me. In that case, Semra, Ali and I were also a bit "wild."

"But there isn't any whiskey," Elem whispered.

I stroked her hand. "Don't worry about us, we'll manage. In any case, we won't stay long." But in fact I badly wanted a drink. I have no patience for the constraints of such morality. I even had the urge to shout, "Yes, I drink! I, Handan Sarp, drink like the rest of us whores!"

Hüseyin had grown up. He was quite mature for his age. He wasn't like the others in his "community," nor was he like the spoiled snobby children of the rich or the other men in the officers' club.

And he was bringing us alcohol. He approached with a waiter who asked what we wanted to drink. I realized that alcoholic drinks would have to be bought and that Hüseyin was going to pay for ours. My mood darkened. Semra probably realized that as well, because she didn't order anything. Ali asked for a double rakı. I froze for a moment. "And you, Handan Hanım?" Hüseyin asked.

I felt suffocated; a line of poetry came to mind:

To go, to go someplace else. My heart yearns from this night on.[*]

What was the rest? "And now I must leave," I thought. But I knew that there were hours before we could leave.

"It probably wouldn't be appropriate if I were to drink rakı," I said, with the pouting, languid smile of a condescending diva.

"Handan Hanım, of course it would be fine," Hüseyin said.

I asked for rakı.

So that was the diva's trite victory: drinking a glass of rakı at the wedding of the officer and the bride from Kocamustâpaşa, and forgetting about her Munise, as though she didn't exist.

Diva, that's all you were.

Everything seemed to be out to disparage me and break down my heartless pride.

Unbeknownst to me, I'd been made one of the witnesses to their marriage, out of the courtesy of Elem's family. I was just about to start drinking my glass of rakı when her mother and father came to

---

[*] If memory serves me correctly, this was written by Baudelaire, but I don't know who the translator was. (Sİ)

the table. I thought, "I'll never get away from them tonight," as I looked at her thickly painted lips. Timidly, the poor woman said, "As a close friend of the family, would you mind?"

"Thank you. But wouldn't someone else be more appropriate?" I asked, pushing the glass of rakı in front of Ali.

Elem's father, who had been silent up to that point, said, "It would be honor for us, Handan Hanım."

"Well then, by all means," I murmured, like a passive daughter in the films of old. We walked toward a table that had been set up in the middle of the wedding hall. That night I'd worn a dark gray gown and a diamond-studded hair clip, and had only put on mascara. But as I strode toward the table, I noticed the slump-shouldered husband and wife plodding along beside me; I tried not to look at them. A darkness flooded through me, tinged with the bitterness of poison.

A pianist started hammering out a song. Perhaps it was a wedding march? I saw İnci and the groom. She looked beautiful, innocent; he was short, timid. As I walked, I pled silently that it would all be over and done with.

The witness for the groom was an elderly woman, apparently his primary school teacher. She was wearing a matching skirt and jacket that had been tailored who knows how many years before; the dark blue fabric was faded. "Handan Hanım," she said to me, holding out her hand, "I saw you, a few years ago, in *La traviata*. Your voice was beautiful." I started thinking about the price of tickets at the Istanbul City Opera. How much were seats? Mezzanine seats?

We stood by the table and then were seated. The teacher sat across from me. I saw the large black notebook in front of the marriage officer. After their names were entered into the book and I signed off as witness, they could live their lives in the "decent" sanctity of marriage. Was that why İnci was so pleased? She was beaming.

But in my ears echoed the roar of a distant sea.

I'd bought a gold coin threaded with a ribbon, and as my last duty at the wedding, I pinned it to İnci's gown.

"If you'd like, let's go," I said to Semra and Ali. It was still early, so we had time to go somewhere else.

Semra said, "Let's say good-bye to Elem and thank her." Semra was sitting beside Ali, who at the time was quite handsome and hadn't yet put on weight; she appeared happy, but anxious.

Elem was nowhere to be seen.

I smiled when I saw Elem standing beside the pianist. "She's over there," I said. But the smile fell from my face when I saw the microphone in her hand.

As we were leaving, she began to sing:
On this journey of longing, don't forget me . . .

Perhaps I thought of it now, or maybe it occurred to me that night:

A young girl approaches the stage, holding a bouquet of red carnations. She loves the singer, who is a rather young man, and he takes up her up onstage and embraces her. Together they wave red carnations at the audience. It was that young girl who told me the story. She's always been a child. But she never told me that she wanted to be a singer.

Who did you sing that song to? Your friends sitting at the tables? They were the same age as you. Had they asked you to sing? Did you sometimes go out with them and sing, and I never knew about it?

Semra said, "We should've stayed and listened."
I didn't have time. I was on a journey of longing.

It was around the middle of November; the weather had warmed, and there was a southwest wind. The sky was the color of smoke. In those days, I'd wake up early and go into the garden. My life had changed. To escape from life, I was going to bed before ten in the evening. In my garden, which seemed to shift from day to day, I'd turn to the past, looking around me, as though seeking something out. But soon after, those ventures to the past became lost in a haze. I was losing my "scenes."

In fact, I didn't know what I was looking for or what I'd lost. Waking up early and taking shelter in the garden was a way for me to resist and go on with life. That new order in my life was like that of a soldier's, and I let its rules guide me.

There was nothing holding me to that flat, to my dilapidated garden, not even to that city. In those foggy mornings, I knew that, no matter where I went, the person I longed for would never appear. And even longing began to fade, as though shrouded in mist or smoke.

Those scenes are painful, because I don't know any other way to live. I still haven't rescued myself from life; nor am I yet in the other-world of my grandmother.

I listen to the voice of Handan Sarp on cassettes, but the recordings weren't done very well. Later they were transferred to compact disc and given to me as a gift.

It moves me. I should confess that I'm profoundly affected by that voice; my own voice, which I destroyed. I lived through one of world's grandest disasters; that's how it is for me, though others may laugh it off. There have been so many catastrophes in the world, I know. But that voice!

When no one is around, I listen, tense with fear. I'd always tried to sing of humanity's hope. At one time, like Semra, I'd believed in opera. In the end, I took revenge by ruining my voice.

I listen to music, songs, the singing of my friends. But those nights when I truly lived opera can never be revived.

Beyond the crying out of passion, that voice also speaks of melancholy and longing. But few people hear it. There is also that infinite compassion that follows rebellion and hate.

Just the other morning a woman stopped me in the street: "I've missed listening to you sing! There was a time," she said, "when your voice soothed my loneliness." After we parted ways, those words rang in my ears: "There was a time . . ."

Those songs remind me of the past, of joys and excitement that are gone forever. "There was a time . . ." Most of the time, I'm unable to restrain my sobs. But it makes no difference; I'm alone. No one sees my tears.

But at times I talk as though there were someone there with me. Yes, I say, I used to play this song for Elem. I played it again and again. That's why the tape is worn out. We would sit and listen. She liked hearing my voice, even if the music was strange for her. The sound of the instruments, as though coming from a distance, and the sounds of the opera house itself, and my voice: elegant, piercing.

Some nights I'd sing along with the recordings. My Munise called them "private concerts." The opera would continue, and we'd lose ourselves in the music.

Without telling me, she'd written on the recordings of *La traviata*, *Norma* and *Tosca*: *Violetta*, HANDAN SARP. *Norma*, HANDAN SARP. *Tosca*, HANDAN SARP. Remembering destroys nothing; I've grown accustomed to that. Memories are like a hidden, unconscious reflex of pain.

The pain of one memory in particular—a New Year's Eve—has never gone away, and even now it makes me blush in despair. When there's pain, there can be no forgiveness. And I've never forgiven myself for what I did. It was utterly despicable; there's no other way to describe it. Despicable, as only I could do.

After we'd separated, that particular memory tormented me, leaving me writhing in flames of regret. Just when I thought that the pain of our separation would suspend all else, that scene would arise in my mind, that New Year's Eve.

Gelengül had invited me to her home, but I was undecided. "I'll let you know later," I said. But without asking me, she'd already called Elem and invited her. I had no desire to be seen in that gaudy home of hers.

Elem said, "Shall we go?" I knew that she didn't like Gelengül, and she'd only gone in the past because I insisted.

I was perplexed. "Do you want to go?" I asked.

"It would be something different. And we'd be together." She hadn't yet moved into her own place, and if we didn't go, she'd have to spend New Year's Eve with her family. If she were just with me, her family would find it odd. And she was incapable of lying. Gelengül was an opportunity, she explained, and to make it even better, no one in her family knew who she was.

I said nothing. It struck me as both absurd and pitiful. Family pressure, I thought to myself, creates such traps. Although they knew Handan Sarp, they'd find it strange if Elem spent the evening with her; but they wouldn't object to an evening with Clark Gable, who they didn't even know.

"Okay then, let's go," I finally said.

My thoughts turned to four or five years before, to a night I recalled with aversion. Elem was going to stay with me; it was the first night, when I told her about Kaya. She called her parents to tell them she wasn't coming home, but they told her that she couldn't stay the night out. Sulking, she returned to her parents' apartment. What had they prevented? Our relationship? My mouth curled into a bitter smile.

And Elem sensed it. "What are you thinking about?" she asked.

"Nothing."

"If we go, I'll stay the night with you. But if you don't want me to stay, we won't go."

I didn't answer. But I picked up the phone and called Gelengül, telling her that we would come. I didn't ask if she'd called Elem.

I despise New Year's Eve, just like all other special days—birthdays, holidays, it makes no difference.

My Munise was working that night. It was probably Friday. There was no end to the requests that those capricious strumpets made for evening gowns, especially when it came to the New Year. At one point, Elem managed to call me to say that she wouldn't finish work until eight o'clock, which was fine with me because we'd avoid the holiday traffic. Women whose dresses had been delivered long before were calling and having their drivers bring over their gowns for adjustments.

What else could they do? Elem knew those women better than me. And the other girls who worked there knew as well. They just bowed their heads, going about life, not seeking a way out. The order of things lays out your lot in life.

As usual, I was at home alone. It was a cold gray day, and the sun was starting to set. Both the day and I were wrapped in a deep melancholy. I was tormented by fears about the nightmarishly absurd evening awaiting me; I knew it would drag on. Then, for some reason, I became caught up in a flurry of ideas about what I should wear to the party. "I should be stunning," I thought, "as ravishing as possible." I have no idea why I was suddenly so captivated by the idea. Spurred on by this frenzy for beauty, I rushed to the hairdresser; needless to say, I already had an appointment.

I'd originally planned on having my hair pulled into a bun. But that frenzy tugged at my mind, and I decided to leave my hair down. "Layer by layer, comb it up and out," I told the hairdresser. "Like Carmen." That night I would be just that: Carmen. I would enchant the men, drive the women mad with jealousy. "If only I had a red dress!" I thought. I would rend to pieces society's notions of woman-hood and manhood.

The hairdresser, a young man, was taken aback at first. He'd always known me to be rather restrained, but now I was asking him to make me look like a femme fatale.

As the sky shaded into black, like an evening of mourning, I returned home. Mourning becomes Handan Sarp. But that night, she would disavow her grieving. All thoughts of Elem fell from my mind. My old life was a wisp of a memory; Carmen would seduce everyone!

What I did next surprised even me, when I looked back on it: I adorned my black evening gown with the red velvet roses which Elem had once given me. They weren't Carmen red, but they would do. Then I put on my makeup, heavier than I'd ever dared before. And then a full bottle of perfume. My dear Mevlevi grandmother had called it "parfume"—for the briefest of moments, a wave of sentimentality washed over me, but when I looked in the mirror, I couldn't even recognize myself.

I picked up the phone: "Gelengül, tonight I'm going to seduce them all! Even you will fall at my feet."

She laughed, crystalline and crisp. "Come, come! Drive them mad with passion!"

It's strange, but just that once I wasn't repulsed by her laughter. Narcissism had swept me away.

Again and again I found myself gazing at myself in the mirror: before me stood a woman who looked at least ten years younger than her age. Someone could easily call me a "young woman." And I wasn't unattractive at all; beautiful, in fact. Alluring. If there were such a thing as masculinity and femininity, men's hearts would be set pounding, and women's envy set aflame.

When Elem saw me looking like that . . .

Elem didn't see me in that state, not exactly.

Eight o'clock. Fifteen past. Forty past. Nine o'clock. I heard nothing from Elem. In the past hour or two, I'd already had a few drinks. That old familiar feeling of incertitude weighed heavy on my heart, and I turned to alcohol to give me strength. But I felt hemmed in; the evening gown, my hair dyed coal black, my forlorn eyes already bloodshot, my eyelashes thick with mascara. The scent of my perfume was cloying in the heat of the apartment. I rushed out onto the balcony: I needed to feel the cool of the night, fresh air. Why was Elem so late? Why was she ruining my evening? Wasn't I Carmen that night?

But when I looked in the mirror one last time, I saw it: nothing but a wreck and ruin remained of Carmen, of that whore of the opera, harlot of the novel. She was no star. What I saw in the mirror was a woman feigning youth, her face painted like a clown; her cheeks were sunken and her eyes shot with blood. Her lips twitched, as though she were trying to say something to herself, like a sleepwalker. But I wasn't drunk. Not in the very least.

In fact I was sober, more so than I'd ever been in my life. At that moment, I saw the truth: a woman who was trying to be as "female" as other women expected her to be—hence the fixation with Carmen—and so she'd dolled herself up, trying to escape her own life, and was going to play at being a woman at Gelengül's party, at the home of a lesbian named Clark Gable!

A woman on the threshold of femininity, ravaged by alcohol.

That's how Elem found me. In the armchair, clutching a bottle of J&B, the whiskey glass on the kitchen counter.

My Munise stood there, holding a bundle of chrysanthemums: light orange, white, golden yellow.

"Ah," I said, "I see you've brought some flowers from the graveyard."

Elem was wearing her old coat, a dull-colored cardigan, a thread-bare blouse and a long skirt, the color of which matched nothing else. And her worn-out shoes.

Elem saw a woman at the end of her days . . . A lesbian . . . A soprano . . . A diva.

"I'm late, aren't I?" she murmured.

"Yes, you are," I snapped. "And look how badly you're dressed. Did you buy those flowers for Gelengül? They're preposterous."

I didn't kiss her. We always kissed each other on the cheek when we met up. "Quick," I said. "We'll find you something to wear." She couldn't go dressed like that. Not with me. Not to Gelengül's home, filled with those snobbish women in their flamboyant gowns and arrogant men wearing suits. Was it that I wanted to protect her? Or that I wanted to protect my image as a diva?

Exhausted from working all day, she didn't have the strength to object.

I took the bouquet of flowers from her hands and tossed it aside. "Take off your coat."

Rushing into my bedroom, I began shuffling through the dresses in my wardrobe. "Take off what you're wearing!"

Only then did she resist. "Handan, I'm bigger than you. It'll be obvious that I'm wearing someone else's clothes."

I screamed at her: "Did you think you could wear that to Gelengül's party? Everyone's there. Who am I going to introduce you as? My servant?!"

Silently she removed her sweater and blouse, weeping. Tears poured from her moss-green eyes.

It was despicable.

I was despicable.

And the regret still throbs.

Handing her the brown outfit and green coat that she'd made for me, I hissed, "Put this on. We're late already."

After Munise died, Feride slept for seventeen days, brought down by a brain fever. I was afflicted with nothing.

I have no expectation that people will understand a Çalıkuşu who's not like Feride. But I have no need for people or so-called "humanity." I feel nothing but hatred for such things. After we separated, I lived on through memories of my Munise. And I tasted the bitterness of my own despicability.

My God, how similar I am to Feride! She also had dressed up Munise in fine clothes. But there is a difference, of course: Munise hadn't made those clothes herself.

How strange; on this long, haggard autumn evening, I can't remember how my Munise died. I remember that they forced Feride to leave the room. And there was that perfume, heliotrope. Feride hadn't let her use it because Munise was so young. But I didn't begrudge my Munise my clothes. She may have made them, but that outfit and jacket belonged to me.

When Fikret Bey came, he was filled with enthusiasm. On the telephone he'd dropped a few hints, but it never occurred to me that the piece he wanted to compose for me would be the *Çalıkuşu Opera*.

At first I wanted to put off our meeting. Perhaps it would be yet another one of those "legendary operas," or, even worse, the story of a "female hero" from some long forgotten historical tale or epic. I didn't have the stomach for such works.

And I was in the clutches of a deep melancholy. That was the summer I'd told Elem, "It's over. There's nothing left between us," and she'd gone with her family to Zeytin Island. Days went by, and she never called. I wondered, was it really over? I was tormented by doubts. Did I really want it to end? What was she doing on the island? My feelings swung between anger and spite; I was completely alone in the world. Meeting up with Fikret Bey seemed pointless, but I didn't dare risk hurting his feelings.

Sitting across from me, he said, "Çalıkuşu, the story of Çalıkuşu. We all know the story . . . It will go splendidly. Splendidly."

As I got ready for his visit, Kadriye Hanım prepared a few appetizers. We sat in the garden. It was summer, and the evening offered a cool respite from the heat of the day. The scent of moist earth was in the air and the sky was shading into a purplish blue.

I found myself drawn to the idea. The legend of my childhood, of my first steps toward adolescence, my heartache. I was swept back to my grandmother's home in Pendik, where my adventure with *Çalıkuşu* first began: "Çalıkuşu, you'll catch cold if you sweat too much!"—as if the past would never let me go. And Munise . . . For a moment, I recoiled in fear. What of my feelings for Munise and Feride?

Did Fikret Bey know what I carried in my heart, did he know my secret? How could he? I'd never spoken of anyone about the "guilty passions" that I'd forged from Feride's tenderness. No one knew. Not Nilüfer, not Elem. I'd never spoken to Semra and Ali about it. Not once did Hikmet and I ever talk about *Çalıkuşu*.

A feeling of unease settled over me. In the beginning, when Elem and I were closer, maybe I'd told her in a moment of drunkenness? Perhaps I had, but I have no memory of it. But what would change? Fikret Bey doesn't know Elem. She was my confidante; she would never betray my trust. This was nothing but a deep anxiety, simple paranoia.

Fikret Bey was swept away by the story of Feride. As he sipped his glass of rakı tinged a bluish white, he told me that Reşat Nuri had once turned it into a play titled *Istanbul Girl*, but the city theater had never performed it. The manuscript was missing, he said, but if we could find the text it might help him write the libretto.

"But Fikret Bey, aren't I a little old to play Feride?" I was already in my forties. The cicadas buzzed in the trees above. Suddenly I remembered the sound of my mother's voice calling out to me: "Çalıkuşuuu!" I remembered the sound of the cicadas at the summer house in Pendik.

The whirring of the cicadas apparently meant nothing to Fikret Bey; he was telling me about Montserrat Caballé, and how she continued performing after all those years.

A bitterness seeped into my thoughts. I would've liked to have played Feride with the energy of my youth, when my ideals still soared. There should be a freshness about the performance, a roughness; I shouldn't yet know the full potential of my voice. As sincere as Feride herself.

Was I fooling myself to think that I could conjure the passion of my youth for the part of Feride? "First I played Liù, and then Turandot. Just like Montserrat Caballé," I said to Fikret Bey.

The idea had its allure. Aside from a few minor performances abroad, I'd never been given a role in an opera written by a bel canto composer.

"Handan Hanım, to the *Çalıkuşu Opera*," Fikret Bey said, raising his glass. "To us and the *Çalıkuşu Opera*." It was a bold claim, as though we'd already conquered the world without leaving our chairs.

I don't know why, but the final song of Liù suddenly began playing in my mind, her last plea, followed by the sharp rebuke of the chorus. The melody merged with Fikret Bey's dream, and I was overtaken by a strange yearning: after the global premiere of *Çalıkuşu Opera*, we'd be invited to perform everywhere, and I'd sing Feride to the world, to life.

My ambition knew no bounds:

"And Munise?" I asked, serving the cheese canapés I'd taken out of the oven. It seemed as though even the cicadas had fallen silent. "Will Munise be a soprano as well?"

Poor Fikret Bey thought for a moment that I was jealous of her role. For a moment his gaze lingered on the canapés garnished with slices of tomato and green pepper, and he turned to me and cautiously said, "She'll just have a minor part. We'll focus on Feride and Kâmran."

But he didn't say "Kâmran." He said something more akin to "Kâm*u*ran."

The alcohol was taking effect. I'd only had maybe two glasses, but that melancholy, the hollow hopes, the darkened dreams about *Çalıkuşu Opera* were enough to bring out the other Handan.

I objected: "For me, the relationship between Munise and Çalıkuşu is critical. And, if it were possible, I think that *Çalıkuşu Opera* should end with Munise's death."

He didn't understand, and just stared at me. Oblivious, he had no idea that I was turning against him as he sat there chewing canapés. A sliver of tomato skin had stuck to his lip. Was that short, plump man who said "Kâmuran, Kâmuran" and blinked at me behind his ridiculously thick glasses going to compose *Çalıkuşu Opera*? My contempt was palpable.

They come to your home and speak to you about *Çalıkuşu*, that novel everyone has read. But they've never considered how that story resonates for you, in your heart. Not once. Who was this man? What business did he have in my home, when I'd suffered so much because of Feride's compassion, because of her kindness veiled between the lines, her love and motherly care?

With blatant mockery, I said, "There's no reason for Feride to go back to Kâmran. Just a final duet, with Munise and Feride . . ." My explanation was verging on madness; I knew I had brazenly bared my heart, but was beyond caring.

"Handan Hanım, how could that be? For generations, *Çalıkuşu* has been so popular because of the love between Feride and Kâmran. Look at it however you will, but it's a love story like Leyla and Majnun." He looked like a child who has seen the toy of his dreams shatter into pieces before his eyes.

And I derived immense pride in that moment, staring scornfully into his face, watching his pride and greed shrivel.

And what of my *Çalıkuşu* opera? After Munise's death, all would be perpetually lost for Feride: the motherly kisses, the gramophone playing in the distance, the afternoon sun, blond bangs, the singing of the birds . . . But darkness would not fall over the scene. No, a sharp triangular beam of light would shine downward, growing more and more distinct. And then there would be an aria of heartrending lament, and Munise, who died in my arms, would remain on stage and the orchestra would continue playing in the pit as I slip out of the spotlight, stepping off the stage and moving through the hall, my voice a fading vibrato faltering before the surge of music it sought to taunt, and I'd leave everything behind, never to return. And of course, I wouldn't join the curtain call.

Summer night. The cicadas began buzzing again.

As I was planning the stage directions I caught myself: "But Feride doesn't join the curtain call." The infinite sea in my heart had vanished, along with my fervor; I fell silent. The child whose imaginary toy had fallen to pieces was now Handan Sarp.

Opposite me, he sat stunned by my unexpected proposal. I knew what he was after; he wanted to use me in the drafting of a vile opera based on the book that was my most beloved. An opportunist. We'd have to "talk about it," he said, as though I were falling for the scheme. "Your ideas are powerful. But everyone expects Feride and Kâmuran to . . ."

I was no longer listening.

It seemed like everyone was conspiring against me to tear down my dreams.

I won't deny that I probably frightened that plump man out of doing the *Çalıkuşu Opera*. But who did he think he was, trying to shuffle off my proposal? Verdi? Puccini, Bellini, Wagner? He just wanted to take advantage of the fame of the novel. But *Çalıkuşu Opera* could have been . . .

No, I don't believe anyone.

Getting rid of Fikret Bey was the only thing I could do.

Just as I'd had to give the slip to that "Daisy Hanım" who'd invited me to "five-star restaurants" to eat lobster.

The dream was short-lived, inoculated against ever becoming reality. Fikret Bey, who'd said, "Let's get started right away," was never seen or heard from again. Even if I hadn't gone on about Munise and Feride, the same would have happened.

I longed to tell Elem about *Çalıkuşu Opera* and my evening with Fikret Bey. Down to the last detail.

But on Zeytin Island she met an older woman and made love with her, and then told me about it. Everyone seemed to be against me. But while they railed against my arrogance, egotism and selfishness, they never saw how afraid or downtrodden I felt inside, as though I'd been shoved to the margin and left there alone.

Could I have told Elem?

I could sense that *Çalıkuşu* had somehow withdrawn from my life. We're all affected differently by works of art, and I'll never be able to explain to another person how that novel touched me. My Munise will die there, alone. They pluck you, dear reader, away from the corpse. Day by day I'm losing my Çalıkuşu.

It was said that Feride had yet again begun to take on the scent of mountains of exile. A scent accompanied by the parched chime of weeping bells.

From the mountains? If your life is one of exile, you have no need of weeping bells and mountains.

Characters in novels also have mothers and fathers.

I haven't talked about them much: my mother, Leyla Mahmure Yönder, who thought that the man she divorced from years ago is still her husband, and my father, Şevket Sarp, whom I hardly know.

My silence regarding them is not because the issue is unimportant to me. Nor is it because they have no place in this novel. Perhaps it is simply due to the fact that I don't feel any connection to my family.

I never have. Aware of the savagery of nature, I've always found empty nests more alluring. The next year, the parents and children won't recognize one another. Empty nests of dry twigs, vanished loves. The urge to protect.

We moved my father into a retirement home surrounded by pine trees in Maslak. It was his decision.

Elem and I went together. He'd prepared his belongings—just the necessities, what the retirement home requested. A whole life packed into a few suitcases.

"Don't leave me alone with him," I told Elem. "I don't know if he's my father, or just some stranger." I didn't know. A woman you don't know behaves like a mother toward you, and a man you don't know says he's your father. You're just a child; you know those people the way you've been taught to know them. But couldn't I have been adopted when I was a child? I tried to laugh it off with a sneer.

Elem listened, horrified.

"Don't be afraid. He probably is my father. How do I know? Because I like strangers." I was a cruel traitor.

She sniffled like a child: "Handan, he could move into your place. Every day after work I could come and look after him. And during the day Kadriye Hanım could as well."

"But what's there to look after?" I thought. "He hasn't fallen on hard times, he's not bedridden. He's just old and wants others to look after him, nothing more."

She needed to know the truth: "Since I was four years old, he'd visit me just once a week, sometimes once every two weeks. Sometimes I wouldn't see him for months. Even if I'd seen him more often, he still would've been a stranger to me. I've never wanted my parents around, just as I didn't want to come into this world. Unless you want me to move out of my own place, don't push the issue."

Elem arrived early that morning, pale, her lips trembling. That was probably how she'd been when she took her grandmother to the hospital. My father, on the other hand, was just moving into a rather luxurious retirement home.

I'd guessed that Elem would come early. That day I'd put on a nice dress and done my makeup; I saw no need to make a tragedy out of it.

Since Friday, my father, Şevket Sarp, had been adamant about moving in to the İsmet Aysal Retirement Home. Without telling me, he'd already gone and spoken to the management and made the financial arrangements for him to stay in a single room. And there he could stay until the day of his death, under the care of doctors and nurses.

Elem noted with a hint of surprise that I'd carefully done my makeup: "You look beautiful."

I laughed. "At this age, I have to work hard to make myself beautiful." Indeed, it was a lot of makeup for a Sunday morning.

"I have a friend, a young woman, who helps me out," I'd told my father. "But she works all week and Saturdays, so let's go on Sunday morning."

We arrived at the small flat in Maçka. Is that all that was left after a life of relative affluence? His last home. A den of dotage, mildewed with damp. To hide the pain welling up within me and the tears stinging the corners of my eyes, I fled to the bathroom. On the counter was a tube of toothpaste, squeezed into a curl.

It had fallen on me to tidy the place up and put it up for rent, the kind of work I despise. Kadriye Hanım was going to help me. But it needed repairs and painting—who would want to live in such a wreck of a apartment?

So this was old age and death: a retirement home and a flattened-out tube of toothpaste. I looked at my face in the mirror, and swore to myself: "I'm not going to fall to pieces because of a tube of toothpaste." Angrily I wiped the tears from my eyes.

When I came out, he was talking with Elem. My father said that he was "so proud" of me and that he'd always kept up with all my performances. It was true, he did come to the operas in which I sang, and he brought along his young lovers, which he no longer bothered keeping a secret. As he aged, he became increasingly fond of young women, and I'd shake their hands before my performances. If I saw those women on the streets, however, I always ignored them. They displayed a certain admiration, but it wasn't because they understood opera. Rather, it was because of what they saw on stage and that I was playing the lead role.

Elem was nearly brought to tears, as though she too felt honored that she knew me.

"We can talk about all this later," I said. An absurd, hollow scene from *King Lear*; we were running late, and I was no Cordelia. A taxi, which I had tracked down after much effort, was waiting for us at the curb.

Şevket Sarp wanted to carry one of the suitcases.

"Don't tire yourself, Dad," I said. The word "dad" stuck in my throat.

Elem picked up two of the suitcases, but my father insisted on carrying one as well. Something within me snapped, and as I picked up two of the others, I grumbled, "Please, leave it. We'll carry it. Why do you need all these clothes and things anyway? I could've brought them later."

Despicable. How could someone be so cruel? Images flashed through my mind, and I found myself on a massive ship during a sea journey. There's a man who'd lost himself in the throes of his sexuality; he looks a little like the broken-down Şevket Sarp before me now as he dances with a spoiled coquette of a woman. A child senses that they're drawn to each other and is terrified. That frightened child is Handan; the young woman pretends not to see the child Handan. Perhaps it would be better to put it this way: the woman doesn't condescend to see her. And the child feels that at that moment, she lost her mother Leyla Mahmure, lost her forever on that ship even though she isn't there. Terrifying! There I was, sitting at the captain's table with all those well-dressed people I didn't know. There was the clatter of silverware and of plates, of soupspoons scraping bowls, and everyone seemed aglow with happiness.

There was the sea, opaque, dark, viscous. I could disappear into it. We traverse that sea.

Was it a desire for revenge? I don't think so. I'm not a vengeful person, but I cannot bear people who bring pain into my life.

I wasn't jealous of the woman on the ship, nor of any of my father's girlfriends. It was just the way they ignored and looked down on me that hurt. And then their false flattery, and my father's aloofness. Should I deny that Şevket Sarp brought great suffering to my life?

An image: Aunt Nadire, trembling head to toe. My father is shouting at my mother: "A conservatory? Do you want your daughter to become a whore?"

As we left the apartment, I tried to cast the memories from my thoughts. My father gave me the key, and I locked the door. Brushing aside his hypocrisy, I took the key—never again would he return there. The taxi was waiting below, and Elem rushed down the stairs with the suitcases. I called the elevator.

Our composure came as a surprise to the employees at the retirement home. The elderly usually arrive to that home full of fury and anguish. But we—my father, myself, and young Elem—were calm and composed, which they surely saw as a sign that something was amiss.

And what kind of "nest" was that? For me, such places are empty of meaning.

We were shown to the room, which had stone floors. I asked if the floors were heated in the winter. "A rug can be put down," the woman said. But I was confused. Who would bring the rug? The nurse? "You can bring one from home," she said.

I counted the blades of the radiator. A strange fear surged through me; where will I live out my final days?

I thought to myself, "Such stubbornness to live! Why doesn't he just die?"

"It's nice, very nice!" my father said. But there was nothing nice about it at all. Even in summer it was cold and soulless. In winter it would summon death. Autumn would pass miserably in those stone-floored rooms for the elderly who have no one else in life. The copse of pines outside the window was a lie. It would snow, and the pine trees with their sharp needles would be blanketed in snow.

I thought again of my own end. Maybe they would even mention me on television: Handan Sarp, a well-known soprano, lives utterly alone at the state hospice, forgotten by her fans and acquaintances. I smile proudly. One day, filled with pride. At a retirement home, in the hospice.

Preposterous things happened that day. My father, who had just met Elem, was holding her hands, making sounds reminiscent of sobbing. Elem embraced him; she was probably making him promises: "We won't leave you here alone. We'll come every weekend to see you."

We may well have to come.

I may.

Is it in the nature of things that the dead and the aging are a burden to others? My grandmother passed away at her home in Pendik silently, in secret. She'd harbored no hopes of retirement homes or the clasping of hands, the carrying of suitcases or compassionate words.

"Father, we're leaving," I said. "I'll call you in the evening." But I didn't even know the phone number of the İsmet Aysal Retirement Home.

That woman, the nurse or whatever she was, gave me a long look and then held out her hand. I must confess: at that point, after everything was finished and done and I had nothing left to hide, I shook her hand with disgust. She'd grown used to exploiting the shame of people who dropped off their elderly. I squeezed a small roll of money into her hand: "Please look after my father."

Making no secret of her pleasure, she said, "Of course I will, Handan Hanım."

I knew nothing of my fame among the caretakers at the retirement home.

Our taxi had been waiting for us, and we left behind the sloping hills of pine.

In Sarıyer we had lunch at a small fish restaurant. It was early afternoon; I drank rakı. Elem burst into sobs.

In the evening, I squeezed the tube of toothpaste into the sink.

Fog. A foggy night. The mist seeps into my memories. All those years ago, the day we went to the İsmet Aysal Retirement Home. The entire city was blanketed. Even the ferries were canceled. I walked through the fog, alone. There wasn't a single island to which I could flee. A night carpeted in a gray haze. Whitish gray. Bluish gray. I was emptied out. Hollow.

In the very beginning there are hints of scenes that speak to you of your loneliness and the dark future looming over the horizon.

But at the time, you're blind.

Now, you find yourself face-to-face with those scenes, rent asunder in the midst of your solitude and the howling silence. Ever receding into the distance is your beloved with whom you walked along the same path for years on end. But you're so ruined that as your yesterdays writhe in vain, you speak of them—in vain.

There is a song that rings out, echoing in my memory. At our home, we didn't sing or listen to music. If I were doing my homework, the radio was always silent. But the words of that one song never left my thoughts—I could even sing it now. Did I once try to teach it to Elem?

So many nights gazing upon the moon, so many nights of weeping . . .

But for me there were no nights of weeping in the moonlight. As I said, for a long time I've been hard as stone. I won't deny that in the early days of our separation I did cry. In the early days: I wrote page after page, somniloquies, entreaties. I wanted Elem to read them, I wanted Elem's heart to fill with sadness for me, for my life.

Day after day: the feelings of wretchedness and anger lashing out.

No, in my memory it wasn't a moonlit night. We weren't even in the garden. We were sitting in the living room, and the curtains were drawn.

Gelengül was showing us her thick, heavy boots: they were repulsive, but she was infatuated with them. Then she began insisting that we go out. "I'm bored of being here," she said. It was a lie, of course; she was on the prowl.

But I was also tormented by my apartment. Gelengül's words seemed to be a warning. I couldn't bear it when they were at my home parched by the heat of the radiators; everything was aging, cracking around the edges: the furniture, Hikmet's painting of the two women, the other paintings. My life was growing stale, crackling apart.

Elem, however, was still young. My feelings for her, not yet overcome by motherly affection, were still shuttling between lust and tenderness.

Led by Gelengül, we hurtled into a night of vampires. I don't remember where we went, but it was a shadowy den of a club. The kind of place where people think they can be saved from themselves.

It was dark. Crowded. Music like the booming of the apocalypse. There was a throng of feminine men, their faces ravaged by age, and a few mannish women, their faces made up. And scattered here and there were small groups of gawking young men from the outskirts of the city—poor, but obsessed by luxury, wealth and vanity—some of them trying to look tough, others effeminate. It was a gay club, but they had opened their doors to lesbians as well; money is money, after all. Everyone seemed to be trying to find themselves, to find a cure for the pains they carried within, in pursuit of the false freedom of Saturday night.

And that's when I saw Kaya. Her face would appear in the crowd, and then vanish again, like the beacon of a lighthouse. I couldn't tell—did her expression seem sorrowful? Weary? A shudder ran through me.

No, that wasn't our last meeting; it was our second-to-last.

The last time I saw her was in Beyoğlu, in the evening. We saw each other, then looked away. That was the last time.

But that night at the club was the most painful encounter with her.

Seeing her tormented me. Whatever it was, we'd shared something and brought each other pleasure; despite her disappearances, I knew that she'd loved me. She was continuing her life as a street hustler, and I, Handan Sarp, gazed at her from a distance with the air of a fallen aristocrat. I'd never been able to help her. No one had.

With the manliest voice she could muster, Gelengül was rambling on about something to Elem, trying to pull her from me into the frenzy of the crowd. But I clung to Elem. At another time in my life, I wouldn't have. "It's Kaya," I whispered, clutching Elem's arm. My words were lost in the roar of the club. "Kaya is sitting at the bar." I pointed her out. Elem glanced in her direction.

Just as I was about to suggest that we leave, Kaya caught sight of me. She probably smiled, a token of our days past.

I don't know what Kaya thought at that moment or what she was feeling.

I found myself drowning in memories of that tumultuous period of my life, as though the wound hadn't healed. There was an attachment, tatters of memories binding me to that street girl. But I despised myself for my lack of will, for my convoluted feelings. Perhaps I was afraid that I missed her.

"You look at her," Elem said, "like a mother would."

Kaya was approaching us.

Did Elem's words sink in at that moment? I don't think so. I was too concerned about Kaya, who was drawing nearer as she made her way through the crowd.

Later, Elem's comment struck me: you always prided yourself on not having "family feelings" and even claimed to loathe what family stood for; you had nothing to do with men, and—at that time anyway—had never wanted children. Despite all that, your closest friends and the women you made love with see you as a mother, and even say that you look at others like a mother. No matter what you do, motherhood clings to you, and you can't shake it off.

"Like a mother reunited with a long-lost daughter . . ."

What if that's the truth? What if, in the end, there's nothing but motherly tenderness behind those storms of passion we call love and the sexuality that enslaves us? If such compassion is all that's left after teetering on the razor's edge of encounters of lust, what then? The ground falls out beneath you. The dilemma of my life.

Reeling, you find yourself in the grip of the motherhood you rejected: on the one hand, I thought that I'd made a mistake by bringing Elem there. Should I really be showing her this side of life? I wondered. On the other, there was that other "girl" who inhabited that world of clubs and the streets, Kaya, and I pitied her.

But I remained composed. I had to.

There was nothing I could do for Kaya. That was her life. She was used to it, perhaps even preferred it. And she wasn't weak; indeed, I was far more fragile. As for Elem, I bore no responsibility for the choices she'd made. Hadn't she slept with another woman before me? Who was she? One of the other seamstresses at the boutique?

I caught hold of myself, and by introducing Elem to Kaya, I dealt a blow to that sense of motherhood.

It dawned on Kaya that Elem was my lover. I could see it in her eyes, that gleam of love of the moment of separation; she'd come to my place one morning, pounding at the door: "Handan, aren't we even friends anymore?" That embittered passion. For me, for Elem.

I knew that Elem sensed it as well.

Kaya was wearing an outfit of billowing blue silk. In the dark of the club, you could almost believe the fake silk was real. Her splendor spoke for itself; hers was the kingdom of night. But in a few hours, under the light of day, that heap of blue would be seen for what it was: pitiable, desperate fervor.

Gelengül disappeared into the crowd.

For us, a miracle was taking place. We stood in the midst of that swarming crowd as though completely alone; no one showed the slightest interest in us, nor did we in them. People thronged past as we drew closer in a moment of rapture. It felt as though the three of us had always been together, that night and every night. Together!

There was no holding back. As we were enshrouded in the pulsing mist of fuchsia and violet neon lights, a surge of pleasure rushed through me as our bodies touched, and I could feel the heat of our contact. Was I losing my mind? Was it just a delusion brought on by the alcohol?

But the miracle persisted: I embraced Kaya, and then she hugged Elem. The three of us were hugging each other. What had brought on that intimacy? How long did we stay like that? A vortex was pulling us inward, spinning us out of control, threatening to pull us in forever.

We were talking. Kaya's petite plump lips were nearly caressing my cheek. She was in the middle, and she turned to Elem, again her lips nearly brushing her cheek as well. A rare openness had come over Elem that night, and over the thunder of the apocalyptic music she was telling Kaya about her work at the boutique. That life was something alien to me; the decadently dressed woman and Nedret's haughty glances. But there, at that moment, their world of pomp and splendor crumbled at our feet. They would've been driven mad by the sight of the three of us! Kaya was holding Elem's hand. And although we were speaking of trivial matters, our behavior verged on the lascivious.

But soon after, I'd find myself slipping away from the conversation. But why? To face reality? Far from it. For me, the thunderous music suddenly fell silent, and I could hear the rustle of leaves and a faint breeze, perhaps a summer wind, or wisp of fall. The artificial fuchsia of the grotesque neon lights gave way to the melancholic reds and pinks of a sunset.

As we stood at the threshold of the door leading out to my garden, we saw that in the dark of night it had been transformed into a Japanese garden of exquisite grace. We stood gazing in awe, lost in our thoughts. We stopped time. We stopped all the wickedness of life, all the monstrosities. But where was that sound coming from, that tremulous plaint of a flute?

The melodies in the song of the flute soothed our pain. Beside Elem, the flower buds of a cherry tree suddenly bloomed, and Kaya's squat laurel billowed into blossom and greenery. And over there, a mysterious pine swaggered. That's how it happens. In the garden after the rain has stopped, you find yourself consumed by thoughts. I showed them a spider web, its strands glistening silver with droplets of rain. The web spoke so much of us, the three of us and our lives.

That was the most painful night for me. The night that was seared into the memory of Handan Sarp.

Did we leave and go to one of Kaya's favorite dives that sell tripe soup, rife with the stench of a slaughterhouse? As the scent of tripe hung heavy in the air, that lucid moment of blossoms and budding green faded away. The horizon seemed to fold in on itself. No sea would ever take me into its arms, and the more I longed to embrace the infinite, the tighter I coiled into myself. I felt as though everything was slipping into darkness but I could sense Kaya's desire for Elem, and despite Elem's innocence and purity, I felt that she was responding to that lust.

Later that night, they dropped me off at home.

It wasn't jealousy. Far from it. I simply wanted to protect my Munise. And I knew that if it were just another one of Kaya's one-night stands, my Munise would be unable to bear it.

I opened the door of the garden: dark, bereft of a cherry tree. Just a squat laurel in the desolate night.

("You're quiet. Are you sure you want to talk?"

"At first, I liked talking with you here in the confines of my home, telling you about everything that happened. It was a new kind of heartbreak. I'd hoped that it would do some good."

"Good? What kind of good?"

"I wanted you to write about me. I thought that something would be left of my separation from Elem—this novel."

"But you've only told me about your life. And what you've told me has been just scattered fragments. More and more these days you lapse into silence when we meet."

"I've told you so much. More than I can stand. Aren't novels based on life?"

"In a way."

"In any case, I'm not as happy with this as I'd been before. Are you going to write the novel?"

"I'm not exactly sure what you want it to be."

"Sometimes, Selim Bey, talking about all these past experiences strikes me as completely absurd. They'll never come back to life. I feel as though I'm poisoning myself to death."

"You wanted to relive them, didn't you?"

"Of course I could've been mistaken. It was a slip, a falling . . .")

But falling doesn't just happen. At least, that's not how it happened to me. And I don't think anyone just suddenly tumbles down.

It's probably more like this: the person who is falling thinks that it happened all at once. But if you think that disaster just suddenly comes crashing down on you, you're mistaken. You simply didn't hear the sirens.

Before, it was all about going out. Going anywhere, it didn't matter. Just getting out of my apartment, which was suffocating me. The need would pounce on me, and I actually feared that I'd go mad. The fact that I was talking to myself also made me feel I was toeing the brink of sanity. The torment would begin as evening drew near. But it's always been like that in my life; sunsets are simply unbearable.

Every day Elem and I spoke on the phone, but our evenings we spent apart.

I don't know why. Maybe that was how we were summoning the eventual, final separation.

And perhaps the torment and sunsets were the wail of the siren. I never heard it.

In appearance, it was Handan Sarp, a soprano from the Istanbul City Opera, who wanted to spend our evenings apart. Later, during one of our bitter fights, Elem would say that I, the soprano, had looked down on her, the seamstress—she would say that I'd treated her with contempt. And then another accusation: "At night, you always had your own life to live!"

Nights were death for me. Slowly, death would approach and quietly nuzzle up to me. I liked it.

I must have believed Elem because I didn't object. Nor did I tell her about the evenings of death. "You always had your own life to live!" After our final separation, that's what I thought as well, and that's how I describe it. It's strange, however; like a child, I believe in what I tell people.

Because I thought Elem was right. I wanted her to be right, and I wanted to find a reason, or the reasons, for our separation. In my entire being I believed that I, Handan Sarp, was the reason why we stopped seeing each other.

In the middle of the day, we had short phone conversations. For years that went on. Elem would call in secret so that Nedret wouldn't notice. The voice of my Munise was always soothing, and I'd feel better after she called. Able to get through the day. But as time went by, the calls became routine. It could've been a call from anyone. My heart no longer thumped when the phone rang.

Apparently it was me who wanted to meet up on the weekends. No, that's a lie. Even if it's not true, Elem never sought out the answer. Couldn't she have asked? If she had, I would've told her that it was because on Saturday nights we could stay together later into the night. Even on those Saturday nights when I was at the opera, didn't I rush to her after the performance?

Most evenings, Elem was alone at home. After work, she'd return to her small apartment on Nemli Yufka Street, probably exhausted. She'd turn on the light, change her clothes, and go into the kitchen to prepare something to eat. Warming up something, making a salad. Did she set the dinner table, or just eat standing in the kitchen? Then she'd watch television. An old film, or a popular show. Sometimes she'd turn on the radio with the volume ever so low and lie down to sleep.

I know that kind of life; to me it was no stranger at all, and I could understand those evenings of hers. And if the pain weren't enough, there were those nights when I went out and she was at home alone, in that boundless solitude. What did she think of? Where I was, who I was with? The monotony of her days was matched by the monotony of her nights. As though she didn't have her own world, her own private life; it was always the same. Her expectations, her hopes, had vanished. With each passing day, the passion of her youth faded away. There was a woman in your life, Handan Sarp, both near and far from your heart.

Sometimes she went to her parents' house and stayed the night. Her mother, father, Hüseyin. Her grandmother had died, and İnci had her children to look after.

Our last four years together were like that. Elem said so.

She screamed, "What life of ours? There's nothing left between us! I'm all alone here. When I go to my mother's place, I'm all alone! How long could it go on like that?" Her voice faltered, trembling.

I know, just as I knew then, that we could go back to how things were.

But I didn't know that it wouldn't continue. I'd always thought that we would go on being together, ever since we'd made that promise to each other on Zeytin Island.

Her voice filled with desperation, she said, "Won't I ever have my own life? That's all I've wanted . . ."

Why didn't she come more often, why didn't she invite me out? Why didn't she insist? Was it because of her upbringing? Her shyness? But no matter how shy you are, you would tell the person you love—if you really love them—that you want to see them more. She could have told me. Especially if you're afraid of separating, if you know that being apart will bring you such pain.

It's obvious that for her the love and friendship we shared had faded away. She couldn't say it; she tried to avoid speaking of the fact that there was nothing left of our love. It was over for me as well, but there was a difference: as time went by, I found myself more closely attached to that spent love and began to find the meaning of my life in it.

Aware that our passion for each other was dwindling, she still remained silent. How was I to interpret her silence and refusal to say anything? Piece by piece, let it fall apart, and Elem will get her freedom. She'll be saved from Handan Sarp. It collapsed. Just as Elem wanted.

I was just as reserved as she was, afraid that I'd be imposing on her life. Even though Elem was so young, the exhaustion of day-to-day life was apparent in her face. I didn't want to inflict any more weariness on her than she already had.

There were nights when I'd hear from no one, and in the afternoon the terrors would start. Was I discovering the secret of creation? Or just going through menopause?

All I knew was that Elem was far way.

Opera gave me the breath of life. In that period Elem referred to as "those last four or five years," opera saved me yet again. Mockingly I referred to it as "my last stand." But being on stage, exuberant in the heart of the music and feeling my existence thrive through opera brought me to life again, if just for a while. It made it possible for me to forget myself, Elem's lonely days and nights, and the shadows haunting life.

And then those unbearable nights weighed upon me in their silence; no opera, no music. The worst were the nights that ended early. You go out, people come, and after spending some time together, everyone decides that it's a "proper" time to go home, and suddenly it's over. For them, that is. I was left destitute, facing the long, interminable night.

Spouses and friends are of no avail. They're all measured, solemn people; nothing can be expected of them.

There were weeknights that I went to see Elem. But as I said, she slept early, exhausted from the day's work, but she never let on that she had to get up early in the morning. She'd been promoted to manager at the boutique and had to be attentive; Nedret spared no one.

After bidding her goodnight, I'd go down the stairs, heavy at heart.

At the window she'd wave me off as I got in a taxi. A shudder would run through me. Not always, but sometimes, as a vague childhood memory came to mind: a woman standing under a tree as a girl walked away, ascending a hill, turning around every few steps to wave, again and again. It was summer. Behind tulle curtains, housewives sat observing the scene. I wonder: did they watch us as well? What business did this woman, Handan Sarp, have at the home of young Elem on Nemli Yufka Street? Getting into the taxi, I'd take one last look back at my Munise, who would stay at the window until we reached the curve in the road.

Waving farewell has always had a special place in my heart.

As soon as we arrived in Teşvikiye I'd get out of the taxi and walk. Elem would call to see if I'd gotten home and leave a message on the answering machine. Sometimes I'd take the long way around and walk all the way down to Valikonağı, hoping to tire myself out and save myself from the temptations of the night. In the dark of evening, wealthy neighborhoods have no objection to the presence of women like me, walking alone through the shadows.

Opening the door to my silent home, I'd stand for a moment and watch as the light from the garden glowed faintly in the dark of the room.

Then I'd listen to her message; her voice shy, hesitant, asking if I was okay, saying she'd been worried.

"Where were you?" Elem would ask after a moment, drowsy. Or am I imagining those details?

"I went for a walk, just a little walk." Or: "I stopped in the court-yard of Teşvikiye Mosque and then walked along the boulevard, looking at the lights glowing in the windows." Or: "The night came at me like a giantess of the dark seeking to pluck the life from my body, but I fought back."

After she got a cell phone, I'd call her: "I'm on the way home." Or: "I stopped here for a minute." Unconcerned, she'd fall back asleep. I didn't blame her. There was no reason for her to share in those long tortuous nights of mine.

Later, it was Elem who blamed me.

Gelengül, knowing that I was unable to bear the night, would slyly offer prescriptions for escape: at this place and that place, some people like us—enemies of the night—will be getting together, she'd say, as though telling a fairy tale. I'd wonder, but what was the point? Laughing in her deepest voice, she'd say that we'd enjoy ourselves.

Did I enjoy myself? It was a nightmare. I'd always sought out wounded souls like myself. People who needed to forget. In the beginning, I'd thought Gelengül was one of those. Allowing myself to be dragged from place to place, however, I saw that those people had pristine souls devoid of feelings.

The places that Gelengül chose for those nights out weren't the dingy bars we used to go to; long before we'd given up on those, and now Gelengül had her sights on the high-class establishments frequented by the self-styled rich. A few people would recognize Handan Sarp the soprano, and it was only through their attentions that I could afford such places. With concealed pride, Gelengül would say, "And this is my friend, Handan Sarp . . ." Her generosity never failed to impress.

If that bitter farce had stopped there, it would've been a blessing. But the men I was meeting were falling in love with me.

At Gelengül's insistence, we'd go to Nedret's to have new outfits made, right in front of Elem. Not once did she ever ask, "Where are you going to wear that?" Measured as ever, she kept a distance.

They were stylish outfits. My Munise's grandmother had probably dreamed of having dresses with lace yokes like that.

After all those years, my youth long faded, I was constantly the center of attention. Yet again I was charming the hearts of men. Seducing them.

It is impossible to understand Gelengül. At first, I thought she'd scorn such scenes of seduction. On the contrary, however, she was driving them on, introducing me to those "gentlemen" as though they were potential grooms.

Businessmen, most of them. Take, for example, that man in his mid-fifties who was doing his best to stay fit; he was an importer of rare whiskies. And he was making advances to me right in front of his wife. Never one to miss a chance, Gelengül whisked off his wife somewhere so that we could be alone.

"Why are you doing this?" I asked her. "What interest could I have in these men?"

But my behavior said something else altogether. I don't know why I was betraying myself in that way: even though I didn't like them, I was smiling, practically flirting, encouraging them. Why? To see their wives suffer. Happy people irritate me. Or maybe it was to throw the lie of marriage into their faces. I found myself transformed into a woman acting like a man.

"Sweetie, he's just the right type for you," Gelengül whispered.

That "gentleman" had a factory in Beylikdüzü and lived in Bahçeşehir. The two of us had been invited for an evening at his place. The garishly dressed woman beside him, she said, wasn't his wife but they'd been living together for years. Every day she went to fortune-tellers, pleading for hope that one day her dreams of marriage would come true.

And there was a younger man, also in business, though no one knew what he did. But he had money, which he spent freely, as well as a fleet of the latest model cars. Exceedingly handsome, he was athletic, and smoked cigarettes but not cigars.

Brows furrowed, I'd listen as Gelengül ranted on, her massive body trembling with an excitement that was beyond my comprehension.

I'd chosen for myself a world of loneliness which had no place for men or for women. Elem had been nothing more than a chance encounter, but I'd fallen defeated before her connection to me. My loneliness had been eclipsed.

As for Gelengül, she wanted to be the padishah of the harem. Like an elder sister trying to find a husband for a widowed younger sibling. And it was terrifying to watch her try to play the innocent match-maker. But I couldn't figure out why that change had come over her.

Strangely, I began to enjoy the compliments those men lavished on me. They stroked my ego: the meaningful glances, the handshakes and the way they vied to sit next to me and light my cigarettes. And I was forty-five years old! My youth had returned. In the past, I'd been indifferent to such behavior, but I seemed to have entered a new period in my life. At the detriment to who I am, I was letting them see me how they wanted.

"They're just crazy about you," Gelengül would say. "Those rascals have good taste!" And then she'd burst into that raucous laughter of hers, which everyone knew. I should look more "available," she told tell me, saying that my coyness could raise suspicions. She was, in short, the perfect madam of a bordello of one.

However, I owed those gentlemen a debt of gratitude because if it weren't for their attentions, people may have thought I was Gelengül's lover or consort. They saw in Handan Sarp a woman of allure and charm.

Winking like Clark Gable, Gelengül once said to me, "Maybe you should have a taste of men for a change. Have you ever slept with any of them?"

"Gelengül, don't be ridiculous. And since when are we on such familiar terms?"

With a laugh, she brushed aside my complaint. Just because I was forty-five meant nothing, she said, trying to convince me that I looked ravishingly young, and that as a woman who'd never slept with any of them, I held all the cards: "They've been through it a thousand times with these other women," she said.

I had no idea she was trying to drive a wedge between me and Elem's innocence. A shadow falls over my heart at the thought.

I struck up friendships with those men, but I never let them into my confidence and kept my secret concealed. They asked for my number, and I'd give it to them. They'd call, wanting to meet up somewhere far from prying eyes, and I'd tell them how full my days and nights were, saying that I simply didn't have time.

Laughing, I'd tell Elem about these little adventures, hoping she'd find humor in them.

Silent and distant, she tried to smile.

I slept with them. There was that one young man, for example, the one whose job was shrouded in mystery.

He knew nothing of pleasuring a woman. Even if I am attracted to my own sex, I know about the lovemaking between a man and woman. And he was a miserable failure. As soon as we started making love, that dashing young man turned into a timid little girl.

It may have been tragic for him, but for me it was a marvelous beginning; I couldn't have been happier. Being with a completely naked man was a sobering experience. Aside from the pictures and occasional photographs I'd come across, most of which were of Michelangelo's sculptures of youths, that was the first time I'd seen a man naked in the flesh—at my age! I was ashamed. But I found his shyness attractive in a way.

We were alone, a woman and a man. Everything was wrong. Not only was I much older than him, I was a lesbian. Still, going against nature has always stirred my sexual desires.

He held me in his arms, but couldn't get an erection; all that passionate thrashing around had been for nothing. Unaware of what I was doing, I reached down between his legs. For the first time in my life. He pulled away, trying to hide his limp manhood. But he didn't realize that his failure to get hard actually aroused me.

"How about if I hold you," I said, sliding my hands down his back, digging my fingernails in.

"Hold me," he said, as though relieved. His long-lashed eyes fluttered shut.

"Do you like men?" I asked.

He gave himself over to me with pleasure. He confessed that he enjoyed fantasizing that women were men; he'd seduce women but then imagine he was making love with a man. And out of respect for this tragedy of sex, I kissed him on the lips.

He liked being stroked and touched, something I was used to doing, and he tried to bring himself to pleasure as my fingertips trailed across his skin.

I wasn't repulsed in the least. On the contrary, I was learning about the traumas of the heart. Women and men. Women and women. Men and men. Always traumas, abysses, suicides.

"You're so understanding," he said, oblivious to my true desires. He imagined that this woman in the autumn of her life sought happiness in his young body.

I was understanding, because he was a wounded soul.

He hadn't gone after success like Bedia, but when he was at his peak, he was imprisoned for fictitious exports. A well-known holding company had set up a firm in his name through which they sent their so-called exports. They'd used him, and he'd grown greedy for more money. For weeks people talked about it, but no one was saddened by the news.

I slept with them.

Including the one sent to prison, there were four. Those were nights when I didn't have Elem, when I didn't have anyone, and was driven by a need for human touch. It was immature, but I needed that warmth so I could overcome the fear that life stirred within me.

Why had sex between men and women terrified and repulsed me for so many years? It isn't so different; in the end, you're left feeling empty. If only Elem had been there; if only she'd saved me.

I'm sure that I never brought much pleasure to the men I slept with, but it didn't matter, nor did the fact that after they had their orgasms, they'd become so indescribably full of themselves.

What was important, and so terrifying, was the darkness of my sexuality. It was suffused in gloom, and I began to see that neither women nor men could set it free. Always that darkness of my lust and desires!

Fits of longing for Elem would come over me. In the hours before dawn, as soon as I was alone, I'd call her, weeping. "Hello?" she'd say, again and again, but I never let her hear the sound of my sobs. "Who is this?" she'd ask. Did she know it was me? I'd see flashes of our days when we were happy together.

I may have liked the compliments and attention, but I felt no attraction for the male body. And I was exasperated by their possessiveness, their boasting and swaggering, especially when they'd ask, "So, how good was I?"

Although I may not have liked their bodies, I did feel a rather strange sexual satisfaction. By sleeping with those men, I was putting on display their wives and the women they slept with. At one time, love had flashed in their eyes when they gazed upon one another, but now, the man they loved was sleeping with Handan Sarp. It was all a lie. They were saying those same words to me, the same lies. False whispers of passion.

There are two tragedies in life: poverty and sexuality. While I still believe the first can be solved once society is freed from capital and money, the second will torture people as long as humanity exists.

I don't think that a sexual relationship can stay fulfilling forever. In the end, your beloved will turn out to be an abyss.

That's how I was for the people I slept with, regardless of whether they were women or men, and that's how they were for me. Nothing but an abyss.

It's all sexual darkness.

And I had no confidante with whom I could share my feelings. My weekends with Elem were filled by silence.

Alcohol flowed through those interminable nights until dawn, and the hours passed with agonizing slowness. My trembling fingers would trace Elem's number on the phone, and I smoked cigarettes with reckless abandon. You may ask, "But what about opera?" The words of Jesus come to mind: "My God, why hast Thou forsaken me?!"

December was warm that year, one of those mild Istanbul winters. But the days were gray, always the dull hue of twilight.

I was trying to put my life in order. And except for a few minor indiscretions, I can say that I succeeded. I knew that the pain of separation wouldn't pass, nor did I want it to. The fervor of that howl I carried within in me during the first few months had begun to subside. I was just like anyone else who had learned how to hide their true feelings and stopped trying to seek revenge against themselves. I bore my grief with pride. If she were going to forget me, let her forget. If she doesn't want to remember me, so be it. The storm in my heart grew calm. And I knew that one day, the memories would haunt her as well.

That shuttling between life and death needed to come to an end. But when I ruined my voice, the world came to an end as well. It was Elem who brought me to that. Was it truly a demise? Or had that haze simply shrouded everything, making it all freeze in place? My feelings were numbed. I was cast out, utterly alone, my voice ruined. Despite that, wasn't it enough that I lived through my separation from Elem? Never once did I betray the memories.

At times, I was overtaken by strange moments of joy. A desire to live and start again would come over me, and I'd think of tending my neglected garden and my memories of Elem. Çalıkuşu would have brushed aside the sadness. It was good that Munise had died.

But then I'd be stricken down again.

And when that happened, I longed for Elem. I hadn't been saved, and I found myself writhing in the midst of that despondency. Phantasms of memories I'd thrust away suddenly appeared, speaking to me of passions and lovemaking as though calling me to a new love. But was it new? My despairing love after our separation was fading.

After our separation. That's when I really fell in love with Elem. With memories of days past. That's how it seems—that I fell in love with our memories. Everything seems to slip away, blanketed in mist.

The rains began. I'd been wrong about the mild winter, and December turned out to be cold and damp.

On those ashen days, I'd see visions of Elem lying naked on the bed, as though in the flesh and blood. The scent of her soap would fill the room, stirring my longing for her.

In the past, I'd pleaded for those apparitions to come, but now I screamed at them to leave me in peace.

We're at the door of the small bedroom, and I find myself in Elem's arms, kissing her and inhaling the scent of her hair. For some reason, in these visions I'm always clothed and she's naked; stroking her bare skin always leaves me feeling exhausted.

Again and again, it's the same illusion that comes on cold rainy days when the gray of the sky weighs down. The rain sends a shiver through me, reminding me of a bitterly painful evening, a phone call. That memory also leaves me feeling drained as I recall the night I'd called her when I'd broken down in tears.

I watched people holding their umbrellas as they walked in the rain. I knew it was raining but had left my umbrella at home, savoring the cold.

It was as though I wanted to punish myself, but not just by getting wet. I imagine Elem's naked body yet again, in the middle of the road in front of the Maçka Palace Hotel.

After our separation, my mind was flooded by memories, desires, and flights of the imagination as I reminisced over the things Elem had wanted to give me and what I'd given her. I wrote her long rambling letters, my somniloquies which I never sent, even though I knew her address. Most likely I told her about how I'd "popped my cherry."

Elem, I must have written to you about that. What an expression: "popping a cherry"! And they saw me walking silently as the storm subsided, a woman walking in the rain. You'd wanted that woman to take your virginity.

"Bistro" was written over the door. I went inside and sat down, and ordered a cognac. There, in the middle of the day, I had two more, one right after the other. On those nights when I was tormented by our separation I drank as well. Toward the end, I was always half-drunk when we met up. And now, it's daytime. When my mind is clouded by drinking, it's as though I can forget the pain of the bursting of my virginity, as well as the cruelty of nature and morals.

The owner of the bistro was a mournful-looking woman. "You've gotten wet in the rain," she said.

As I said, altogether there were four men: the fictitious exporter and three others. Did I mention that I can't remember their faces?

They thought they were going to make love with a mature and passionate woman of experience. But I was Handan Sarp, who'd never been with a man. They didn't know who she was; they didn't know the story of her life.

They asked, "Are you married?"

"Have you ever been married?"

"How many times have you been married?"

"Once," I said, "it was a very short marriage." And by saying so, I could take that step into womanhood with the dignity expected of a woman.

More despairing than ever, I'd step into the morning, having fallen even further in the eyes of that lie they call morality.

Sometimes it was a hotel and sometimes a luxurious weekend house in the suburbs. I never brought them into the privacy of my home, though even I felt like a stranger there and the idea of privacy seemed pathetic.

At times I'd take a taxi, and other times they'd drive me. If it were a taxi, I'd be alone, and if I were in their car, I'd sit in silence. Was I playing the game of regret? They played at being the seducer.

It was a winter morning. Why couldn't it have been summer or fall? I was shivering in the cold and dawn hadn't yet broken. Through the windows of the car, I could see people on the streets, starting yet another day in the struggle to survive. After having lived such a long and pointless life in this city, you realize that you know nothing of the people who live here. You have absolutely nothing in common with them. They crowd around the bus stops and walk hurriedly down the streets. I looked, but that's all it was—looking on. There was a man pushing his cart filled with rice and boiled chickpeas; where was he going? I closed my eyes. I recalled how Elem would pray at the tomb of Şem-i Dede and then buy a pastry. At that hour, she'd probably already left for work and was going to the boutique in Nişantaşı. No longer could I call and hear the sound of her voice.

The sun hadn't risen yet. I was returning down streets where I'd hoped to flee the night. My home, enveloped in murderous silence, was cold and dark, unwelcoming. The corpse undressed and slipped into bed.

Here and there, I scribbled notes. Jumbled sentences in notebooks. In the daytime, in the middle of the night. The screams I couldn't hold back.

The conversations echoing in my memory are like that: scattered words. We shouted, hurling insults at one another, filled with rage. Slowly, we were drifting apart. I thought it wasn't over. But it was.

Scenes from the abyss: a woman pulling into herself. She looks so much like me. And there's a young woman who'd lived a life of silence; she's shouting. The older of the two is walking toward autumn, thinking that's how life will be, filled with the scents of fall. The young woman has forgotten; but what? Can we ever forget autumn? Scenes of sorrow.

When we lose someone we love, we're filled with pain. My suffering persisted, refusing to fade. I'd awake, wondering why my heart throbbed with sorrow. Then I'd remember: no, my Munise would never leave me! The ache tears at your heart, day and night.

Pain and separation.

In my memory, fragments of sentences:

"Handan, we have to . . ."

"No one has ever . . ."

The voices are jumbled. Is it Elem speaking, or me? And there is always the sound of the rain:

"I gave you my youth . . ."

"What else could I . . ."

"Have you no pride?"

It was then I found out that we'd "decided" to separate. I was alone, unwanted. I had always walked that thorny path by myself, and now I would set off toward autumn.

Tonight, however, I want to speak of other things.

Yesterday I went into my garden. For a long while, I haven't felt at home in my own home. But the small garden, with its tattered remnants of autumn, warmed my heart. I saw something of myself: the leaves and flowers may have fallen away, but it was holding out against the ravages of the season. Clumps of weeds sprouted among the dry stalks, the leaves had blown into scattered heaps, and sparrows flitted about, defiant of the rain. I had a sudden desire to make peace with the garden, and with life as well.

There was a cat sleeping in a corner of the garden, a tabby that seemed to have made itself quite at home. Elem had always wanted us to get a cat. It's memories like those that I'm trying to forget; they only bring me to tears. I brought some food for the cat, which had nestled up to me. Perhaps it'll stay. "Elem, if only we had gotten one," I said to myself.

The rain dripping off the eaves looks like a curtain of beads.

I like it this way, but when spring comes, I'm going to clean up my garden. There are all those untended gardens between apartment buildings, forgotten and forlorn. But I'm going to tend to mine. At last, I now know that I have the strength.

I'm going to plant flowers. Somewhere I have some unopened

packets of seeds that rattle when you shake them, and some bulbs as well, perhaps hyacinth and tulips. But yet again I'm caught in the grip of memories: Elem and I had bought them at a shop near the Spice Bazaar. Seeds never die. That's what they say. Years have gone by, but it doesn't feel that way. I don't remember what flowers they are. There are pictures on the packets of seeds. And when they bloom . . . Will they bloom at all? If seeds don't die.

Daydreaming of flowers, I went inside. It had been cold in the rain, and the flat was warm. My clothes were wet, so I went into my bedroom to change.

After our separation, that's where I spent my nights of mourning. My furniture made me uneasy. I even thought of ways to destroy my bed.

No time seemed to have passed at all. Perhaps it hadn't. Maybe Handan Sarp had simply made up all those months and years. Maybe she'd made up her lesbian life and the woman named Elem who'd once fallen in love with her. It can't be known.

"No one has ever loved you," I whispered.

Yet again I was confronted with the sameness of time. Only the daylight was different. In the past—if there is such a thing as "the past" after our separation—it was always at dawn that I'd awake from uneasy sleep, bathed in sweat, stricken by the pain of losing someone I loved. But who had died?

It was Elem, my Munise.

Now, even if it's evening, my garden is like that. The light of day, the waning evening light. The lilacs are withering. Over the summer, they probably didn't even bloom. I've even neglected the crepe myrtle, which had once been so dear to me. With its dry brittle branches, it looks like the skeleton of some prehistoric creature. Aster flowers used to bloom as fall drew near, but one year they caught Fusarium wilt and then the blossoms drooped and the stems blackened. Never again did I plant asters. But Elem's rose, as though conspiring in a cruel joke, has started budding.

An image: Handan Sarp wrapped in her thoughts as she gazes upon the few remaining plants in the garden, their yellowed leaves drooping in the evening light. At first they seem to envelop her and soothe her pain, but soon she feels trapped, as though the Fusarium wilt is seeping into her soul.

It's the same here in the bedroom. She needs to feel the chill deep in her bones to sleep, so she goes out into the garden at night. Later, she awakes drenched in sweat, the pain of loss wrenching her heart. She's alone and has no one to console her. There, in the garden, she leans her head against the trunk of the crepe myrtle, murmuring: "Help me, help me . . ." Then she goes back to bed, shivering, clutching the pillows as she weeps. But why is she hiding her tears?

My Munise wasn't with me. No; I merely made her up. The days passed, full of my deceptions. I embellished and destroyed this life with lies.

It was autumn when we separated, and I was left to face it alone.

My fingers clasped, I press my hands to my chest. I see Handan Sarp in the wardrobe mirror. It's strange; she hasn't aged, as though the pain and heartache keep her young. And it's strange that, just as in her youth, she looks at the world, at life, with such malevolence. She's always been a stranger here.

"This spring we'll plant the seeds."

"Yes, this spring."

I listen to the voices. They lie.

As I lay down to sleep, my thoughts are filled with the flowers Elem and I would plant. The flowers in my dream were all pale: the pinks, yellows, blues and fiery reds all light shades of pastel, even the green of the budding saplings. They grew ever upward, and I drifted into sleep among their pale blossoms.

I don't remember waking up. But I was awake, and Elem was by my side, gazing tenderly down at me, and in her eyes which flickered amber and green, I could see the passion, shame and fear she felt when we first made love. I wanted the fear to melt away; there was nothing to be afraid of. We would never hurt each other, would we Elem?

She was naked and so was I. But I felt ashamed, because we'd separated. Months, years had passed.

"Our first lovemaking," Elem said.

Our first lovemaking, all that time ago. Impassioned, the body feels no shame, and when you're making love, your masks fall away. But when the love has faded, your bodies become estranged, timid; you want to turn away and cover yourself. You're wounded, in body and soul.

Confused, I wanted to get up and put something over my naked body. It felt wrong to see each other naked.

When was our final night of embraces, of making love? How could I have known it would be the last? Our caresses of compassion and desire were tinged with tedium and unease.

It was as though we'd forgotten about our separation and yet another night we'd be in each other's arms. We didn't know that tomorrow, or the day after, another life would begin. Perhaps only Handan Sarp didn't know.

I sat up, but Elem held me back by the shoulders: "Don't be ashamed of your nakedness. Don't be ashamed of anything."

I wanted to tell her that we'd separated, that she'd left me one day and I'd grown old. As though she knew what I was going to say, she put her finger over my lips, and then began lightly kissing my neck. I felt as though I'd burst into sobs at any moment. I was lonely, and my Munise was consoling me. But she was a stranger to me. I'd made love with a stranger and hoped for a life with her.

"Let's take refuge in each other," she said.

I let go. Handan gave herself over to the young seamstress. A song began, from *Samson and Delilah*: "My heart opens itself to your voice." It seemed to come from afar but was full of sincerity.

"Do you hear that song?" Elem asked.

I nodded, smiling.

Is it possible to love somebody more than yourself? I loved Elem more than anything. Just as, at one time, she'd loved me.

I've never sung that aria. And never will.

My voice is gone forever.

As the song rose to its plaintive crescendo, Handan Sarp was lying on my bed of solitude, still dressed. She'd forgotten to pull up the blanket. Perhaps she'd been stricken by a fever; her throat burned, her head throbbed. This time, the wardrobe mirror reflected the truth: a homely, unkempt woman, wrinkles around her swollen eyes.

Sudden is the only way to describe it.

Handan Sarp thought that everything was fine. For both of them. Two inseparable confidantes, she thought, drawn even closer together by their occasional crises and bouts of tedium.

Didn't she understand what lay behind Elem's questions?

"What's going to happen to us, Handan?"

"Are we destroying our love?"

"Were you with Gelengül last night?"

"Handan, do we have a future together?"

I was blind: "Won't we just keep going on like this?"

Phone conversations on Saturday nights. Whispered questions.

I was on the verge of collapse for fear of losing her. Long before I'd already lost myself. There was the hope, however, of winning her back. I know that this is tiresome. But we went through a separation—a period of separation—that was maddening. As I speak of it, I feel as though I were suffocating.

Why those days, that separation? And why is it raining yet again today? Because of what I've said?

On our Saturdays together, I controlled myself. What did she expect me to think about for the future? There were many long years ahead. Together, sharing the pain of an exhausted love. Seeing each other but rarely, lapsing into silence. Grieving even more on the days we were apart.

It happens suddenly. That's it. You find yourself utterly alone in this terrifying world. When the only person who understands your pain disappears from your life, that pain no longer soothes you.

She couldn't say, "I love you." All she could say was, "Handan, I've changed a lot. You're like a sister to me now." I felt I'd been crushed under all the sorrow in the world, all the hunger, wars, oppression and torture. Impaled upon a passion, a duet of love I'd been blind to until the day of our separation.

I couldn't leave her. We had yet to bring new pain to all the suffering of the world. I was afraid. Sooner or later, Elem would understand this suffering, I thought. She would feel it, and so I waited. Wasn't she more softhearted than me?

How meaningless: ashes in the ashtray, cigarette butts. On the wall, the traces of that painting—who was he? My friend, how could I forget his name?—a portrait of two women. When it should drive a person to madness, I did nothing, staring at the ashes. Can I tell you that the rotting leaves in the garden are trembling in the cold?

She said, "I'm going to tell you something. But I don't want to hurt you . . ." And then silence.

Suddenly. That's how it started, with Elem not wanting to hurt anyone. Unable to say, "I'm leaving you. I'm in love with a man."

Where were we? At her place or mine? One of us was about to open the door; it was probably me. Meaning that we were at her flat. At the end of the night. Elem standing across from me. "If I take her in my arms," I thought, "everything could change." As she looked away, I could sense a distance in her compassionate eyes.

"Tell me."

"I made a promise to my family. I'm getting married." Her head was bowed, face ashen.

These are the things I've blanketed in silence. The things I remembered and cowered before. But I always returned to silence, wanting to cast them from my thoughts. But since I'm speaking of those stifled memories:

They remain distant, just as Elem.

After we'd decided to separate, we would meet up—yes, we continued to see each other, perhaps because we couldn't bear letting go, or maybe I couldn't let go and Elem pitied me—and I'd call her when I arrived back at my apartment: "I'm back home." Then I'd ask, "Why did I call you?" Her answer: "Like in the old days . . ."

I try to drive those memories away: the phone calls, the sorrow that tormented me and her strange reply: "Like in the old days." My home, where I never felt at home. The streets, where I walked for hours, unknown streets. Sleeping pills, madly, pill after pill.

It wasn't real. For either of us. It was just a nightmare and soon after I'd wake up bathed in sweat. I wasn't in love; all my life I made sure that I never fell in love. That dark dream would come to an end. I still hope that it will.

It wasn't real. I'm slandering Elem. She never did anything to me. I was lost in this world.

But it was real: Handan was opening the door. She turned, as though she'd been stabbed in the back. She wanted to leave, but couldn't.

"I'm getting married."

The words rang in her ears. Closing the door, she walked toward Elem. At that moment, Handan fell into the trap of hopeless love. Not once in her life had she felt so desperate. "Never," she said, "have I ever believed anyone. Except for you. Just you. I never believed even my mother and father."

Elem squeezed her eyes shut.

"Is there someone else?" Handan believed she'd composed herself. A haughty gesture. Again: "Is there someone else?" She knew she'd asked twice. It was a stranger she was addressing.

The stranger nodded, turning her gaze away.

Rigid, Handan Sarp stood there, unable to move. She looked around the flat, at the windows and curtains. "The balcony is over there," she thought. Didn't we eat dinner on that balcony? The garden next door, the lilies. She wanted to hug her. Like she'd do in her dreams, like she'd done time and time again. But who? A woman approaching thirty she didn't know, a lesbian; no, you can't embrace her. I can see it, as though she were right there in front of me. Handan sat down. "Who is it?" Her voice was cold.

Elem was standing in the same place, her back to Handan. The curtains were half open. Was she looking out at the street? "What does it matter, Handan?"

"Handan"?

"How dare she be so familiar," Handan thought. "How many years older than her am I? She should remember that she's addressing me, Handan Sarp, the diva!" But then she relented: "Elem is the closest friend I have. If she leaves, my life will be left in ruins."

"Who is it? Tell me!" Trying to understand what she was struggling against, she was left in confusion. A woman she didn't even know was saying that she was getting married. Estrangement came suddenly. There was nothing left between them. Was she the same woman who'd once said, "I love you"? For now, she wasn't an enemy. But she would be, in her new life. In that life, her past would be hidden away. But there would be a difference between that and what she kept secret now. Having fallen prey to that malevolence known as morality, she hid her true self out of fear for her existence. But in the future, that past would simply be denied. Handan Sarp would be left helpless, unable to do anything. "I should just get up and leave," she thought, "the night's already over." That night was years ago. There is no night. The night is a lie.

"You can't leave me!" she cried, bursting into tears.

Evening. The sea, long absent, suddenly churned thunderous. The murky blue pulling me into its depths. I was powerless, unable to resist. I'd hoped that my friend would never let me go and together we'd disappear beneath the waves.

I longed to call out to her: "Why are you doing this? Why are you running from the sea?" To throw my arms around her neck. To weep.

When Elem vanishes from my heart, I'll be left alone facing that murky blue sea. Once you've begun to speak, you can't go back; I'll explain what happened afterward. But evening is falling. The lights in the windows will all flicker on, glowing in the thick gloom of night. What comes next is the sea.

Heaving sea, pounding sea. The waves, crashing against boulders which I liken to my life, rise up, rumbling. The boulders want to be seen just once more. There I see Handan Sarp, and this time she looks so much like Elem, hiding her pain. As though there were nothing left to do.

The reddish brown of the boulders—Handan Sarp has disappeared—are veined with mossy greens. My home, the garden and the city are all lost to me. The sea has taken me. As the wind howls, in the distance I see a battered weary ship pulled down beneath the waves.

I was mistaken. We were at this apartment, at the kitchen door. The wind whistled through the transom window, which was ajar.

A long, long life. I felt as though I was trapped in a pit, trying to resist, to object. Four months later my voice would succumb to death, abandoning me. We were here, in this home.

Never would it have occurred to me. It was one of the Saturday nights of our fading love. Out of nostalgia for the early days of our passion, I'd probably prepared some food, and after taking a shower and doing my hair, put on a dress. I'd been drinking and smoking cigarettes one after the other. I wondered: "Why doesn't life just end?" Tedium. Emptiness.

It wasn't a night of dizzying dances. No, my dear; that night will never happen again, never again will you save me with your embraces and kisses. It's gone, spent. Let that night stay with you as you remember it. The tears in your eyes are meaningless. You have no right to cry; those who leave are unafraid of separation. You left and then forgot everything. They are all faded stars—look at the night, at your loneliness, until those stars sear your heart.

Elem came late that night. At the kitchen door, she wanted to kiss. Not on the lips, but on the cheeks. Tears in those beautiful eyes. "I'm going to tell you something. But I don't want to hurt you, Handan . . ." And then silence.

I looked at the tears in her eyes. I'd been unable to close the transom window all the way. Was it March? The beginnings of a storm. Offhand, I asked, "What is it?"

"Handan, I have to change my life."

Now I can remember it more clearly. Even the lights; the light in the hall was on, but I hadn't turned on the kitchen light. Elem stood in the light, and the other woman was in the dappled shadows.

"How are you going to change your life?"

Reaching out to take my hand, she said, "Come, let's sit and talk."

"I can't close the transom window. The wind is whistling." I told her that I couldn't close it without a ladder.

"Handan, my family wants me to get married."

I smiled. "That again. They've always wanted that."

"It's different this time. I don't want to disappoint them."

Now I understood why she had tears in her eyes and why she'd come late. Perhaps she had desperately walked the streets, trying to think of how to tell me.

I was unmoved. Her life would be nothing without me. I thought that it would pass, as it had before. In any case we were together, day and night.

Her face was pale. Maybe she'd been like that since she'd come and I hadn't noticed.

"Do you want to get married?" I asked.

"Yes, I want to start a new life for myself."

I felt faint. I forgot about the window as waves of anger rose up within me. "That's it? So it's that easy." Had I said something like that before? For some reason, I thought of Zeytin Island, the summer heat on my skin.

The way she rose up against me was breaking my heart. "In the last few years we haven't been close at all," she said. "You just live your own life. I waited, thinking that you might change. But now I've made my decision."

I bolted from the kitchen and swung open the front door. "Get out!"

"Handan . . ."

"Out!"

She turned and left. As she was going down the stairs, I closed the door, leaving her in the dark. The howling of the wind filled my flat, filled everything.

Was it because of the alcohol? It's a blur. Whatever happened, the sound of rushing water drowns it out. What did Handan do? Did she pause by the door? She went inside. In the living room she saw a yellow chick with matted feathers. The night was cold; but now, I remember it as crackling with sparks. At night, on the counter, chicks were shivering in the cold. A young woman, practically a girl, had once fallen in love with them. She bought three. The yellow one is yours. It's yours now.

Taking the chick in her palm, she said, "I should find a medicant." The word struck her as anguished somehow, antiquated: "medicant." She wondered: How could a toy chick stab the heart so deeply? To catch up with her, that young woman who had such pity for chicks but none for Handan. To chase after Elem: "What will happen to the chick?" Teetering on the brink of death. She snatched up her raincoat from the rack.

Tatters. The raincoat seemed to be in tatters. The street was empty, though it was early and a Saturday night. "Taxi!" she called out as a taxi approached: driver in front, two passengers in the rear, a man and a woman. The taxi didn't stop.

She ran to the taxi stand: "Taxi!"

Was it Serencebey or Yıldız, or the Conrad Hotel? She couldn't remember. Her only thought: "Take me to Elem!" That was all she knew: Elem. Where was she? What if she hadn't gone home? Would Handan Sarp go to Kocamustâpaşa? Her family's home. No, she'd never find the way. Pulling the raincoat tightly around herself, she said, "To Yıldız."

She was trembling. The roads were a blur; had they gone down to Ihlamur, or along Barbaros Boulevard? Streetlights, headlights. To stop themselves from crying, people bite their lip. I was biting my lip. There's nothing else you can do.

"Right. Turn right here."

I rummaged through my pockets, only to find I hadn't brought my wallet. The red taillights of cars in the distance flickered like a warning. We were drawing near that desolate street.

The taxi's headlights illuminated the street. Then I saw her, just going up the street. Elem. The corner shop was closed. I saw the owner locking the door behind him.

"I'll get out here," I told the driver.

I found a banknote in my pocket and handed it to him, not even looking at the meter or thinking to get the change. I had to catch up with Elem. The driver stopped me, and gave me the change: "You should be more careful," he said. He said something else, but I couldn't hear him. The roaring had begun, the thundering of the sea echoing in my ears.

I thanked him. My words ran together.

The street was lined on both sides with crumbling apartments. In the triangle of light under a streetlamp, my Munise walked, her back to me.

"Elem!" A cry in the night. It was like a scene from an opera. I was losing myself. I was saved. Handan Sarp was on a stage. A night scene, a street at night. Soon she'll sing one of the opera's laments.

My friend on the stage turns, stunned. That's when the song begins. My song.

("Even before we started meeting up, I'd lose myself in dreams, wondering if I could compose it. An opera about the love between two women. The form would be traditional, more or less. In the first act: meeting, and falling in love. In the second act, romance, but then the passion dwindles to one-sided love. In the final act, separation and torment. Eternal torment. Under a street lamp, everything comes to an end. But Selim, I don't have the talent for that. Every time I'm thrust back by the roaring of the sea, the crashing waves and howling wind. Driven into darkness. Lost.")

She turned, illuminated in the triangle of light, toward the sound of my scream. "I knew you'd come."

I was relieved. "It's good that I came," I told myself. She'd wanted me to. It was a game of coquetry, of wanting to know you're loved. But my joy was short lived.

In the middle of the street, we stood facing one another. A space between us. But I couldn't take a step toward her. My Munise. At one time, we'd gaze at each other, feeling that life would be impossible if we were ever driven apart. But now, Handan Sarp stands there slumped, pathetic, wounded. Elem smiles, compassion in her eyes. What about the other woman? I can't see her face.

On the stairs: a different flight of stairs that came into my life.

The stone steps come alive, each of them a part of that life; I'm stunned, as though I'd been slapped. My heart aflame, I find myself tumbling down the stairs of the past, down the steps of a dirty stairwell—but they'd been clean!—of a run-down apartment building in Kocamustâpaşa. Where's Semra? She should be with me. We'll be welcomed again as the wax plant weeps in the deep blue of evening. Which step was broken? And Elem is young, not yet ravaged by life. She stands aside to let us pass. It's there, from the balcony, that I can see the darkening blue of the night sky. The city is cruelly divided; this is where the young seamstress who works in Nişantaşı lives. I'd put on Amazone perfume, a cashmere shawl. We passed the tomb of a saint.

I wanted to smoke a cigarette. I desperately needed one.

Elem turned on the light. Traces of my influence could be seen in the apartment: a candelabra on the table, glimmering in meaningless bronze magnificence. She'd asked me what I thought of the armchair, the sofa.

"A cigarette and something to drink. Whatever you have."

When she started smoking regularly—which was because of me—she bought a cheap brand of foreign cigarettes. Now, she handed me a pack of Maltepe. For the first time, I noticed that she was smoking Maltepe, the cheapest local brand. "Do you have any other cigarettes?" I asked. As though such a question could be asked on a night like that.

"No." Her voice was cold, clipped. "There's nothing to drink either. I'll get something from the shop." She opened her purse and took out her wallet.

"Don't bother." That same fear came over me. It would haunt me: what if she leaves, if I never see her again?

On the first drag of the cigarette I started coughing. Some people smoke Maltepe, Samsun or Birinci, while others have packs of Marlboro, Parliament, Eve or Davidoff in their pockets and purses . . . Nedret paid her a meager weekly salary as though it were a gift from the gods. But still Elem managed to look after her own flat and help out her parents and İnci's children, and buy me gifts as well. Hüseyin still hadn't found a job. Most likely, he'd join the military.

It's strange: the sky was aglow like an Aegean dawn and the stars hadn't yet faded. Nilüfer and her friends were singing songs of revolution. But I gave myself over to silence, withdrawing into myself. Was I seeing the future, or was the future silencing me? Was I nothing but a coward?

Smiling, Elem came into the living room holding a bottle of whiskey, still half full. Nearly a year before I'd brought it. Most likely in spring.

Her pleasure at finding the bottle was childlike. But I was trying to remember that spring night, when I wasn't in the grip of that pain. I'd probably had a sudden desire for whiskey, perhaps on my way back from the opera. Where had I bought it at that hour of the night?

I must have been losing my mind. At such a moment, why would I think about a bottle of whiskey? My heart was thudding in my chest. I couldn't make sense of my urge to drink or why I was obsessing over her Maltepe cigarettes. I could see it clear as day: Elem was leaving me.

"You can't leave me. I'm begging you." I'd never heard that voice before.

She was standing beside me, pouring whiskey into a glass. As her eyes began to well with tears—I was probably imagining that—they seemed larger, more luminous. And what love was in those eyes, such compassion and goodness. Her love for Handan Sarp, however, had faded; that was all. Nothing would come of her pleadings: "You can't leave m . . . Don't." On the verge of tears. But then this beseeching lover began pulling away; no, I drove her out, along with my feelings of love and tenderness. The wind began howling. Shrieking in the night. Here, in this home too. I carve it all into the niches of my memory. Above all, the night of our separation.

Whispering of heartache, the duet between Violetta and Alfredo:
My love, we shall leave Paris, and we shall always . . .

They must go far from Paris, far from the prying eyes of the city. In that small, drowsy summer house, Violetta, that faded rose, would bloom again.

I put out the cigarette.

"Couldn't you smoke it? They're not like your Eve cigarettes." Her tone was mocking.

We should've gone far away. Perhaps to a summer house, like Violetta and Alfredo. No, it was impossible; everywhere seemed hostile to our presence.

I was on the verge of tears. Silent tears, cowardly and pitiful. But somehow they pulled back. All that was left was a throbbing: in my head, my heart, my entire being.

I lit another Maltepe.

"Do you want ice?" Before I could reply, she went into the kitchen.

As she walked away, I didn't look after her. I lowered my head. Wishing the night would be over.

There were three half-melted candles in the bronze candelabra. I wondered: when had she lit them? Was I here? You have one just like it, Handan. The same candelabra. It will whisper to you of your love. You'll hear it, but Elem never will.

Unable to speak, buried in silence. Helpless. It snows. When it snowed, we would call each other. "Hello, Handan." "Hello, Elem." "The roads are frozen." We were saddened that we couldn't see each other that Saturday. Please, remember.

Unable to speak, to call out to her. But I knew. I knew that it would come to an end. I'd felt it. Emptied out inside. In this room: put the sofa over there. Maybe put the dining table up against the wall. And just there, the bedroom. As we kissed, our hands moved over each other's bodies, familiar with every curve. My memories will forever remain here. My God, why does it have to be like this?

I sat, rigid.

As she poured me a glass of water, she said, "Handan, nothing's going to change. It will be just the same. Aren't we friends? That's what will be left behind. A sweet friendship. I don't . . . I don't want anyone to get hurt." Her voice faltered.

I threw the glass. Whiskey spilled onto the white rug, and Elem stepped back, stunned.

"Make love with me!" I cried. "I'm begging you, make love with me!" I fell to her feet, throwing my arms around her legs. I thought, "If we make love, everything will be fine. Elem, if we make love, we'll never be apart again!" But I couldn't say it, just why I wanted to make love. She tried to pull me up. I kissed her feet, again and again. She had put on her house slippers when she'd come home, as though everything in life were normal.

Probably she thought it was an outburst of sexual passion. But it wasn't. On the contrary, we were as distant from each other as ever. And sex was the furthest away.

Lightly, she tried to push me away, but I clung to her legs. "Don't you have any pride left?" she asked.

But her words fell on deaf ears. Pride meant nothing to me.

I thought, "If we make love, everything will be fine." That was my hope. Naked, no masks, our bodies entwined. No, it's not over, we're meant for each other.

I refused to get up. That was the first time she'd seen me so desperate. She held out her hand to pull me up, but I pressed it to my lips.

"Elemishka, I beg of you. I've been all alone in my life. But you've always been with me, Elemishka, everywhere in the world, no matter where I go."

A pained expression on her face. And concealed disgust. But I was blind to it, as my heart split open and gushed forth:

"At night, at Gelengül's parties, in the mornings . . . I talk to you, Elemishka. I say, 'This is what I'm doing tonight, Elemishka.' I miss you, how could I live without you! I see people as they go to work in the mornings, they are so lonely. I know you see them too. Elemishka, I . . ."

She cut me off: "Elemishka? You've never said that to me before. Where did this 'Elemishka' come from?"

"When I'm alone, your name is Elemishka. That's how I call you. Elemishka . . ." At last, my tears found courage and I was shaken by sobs.

She blinked in confusion. "Why haven't you ever told me this before? Tonight you're so strange. Why now?"

"Tonight and every night," I moaned. "I was always ashamed of our life. Of our love."

Stunned into silence, she stood there.

I begged: "Hold me. Please, don't . . ."

"I can't go back on my word, Handan. I made a promise." Gently pulling me to my feet, she led me to the sofa. Her hands were cold as ice.

"Who is it?"

She picked up the bottle of whiskey and took a drink. I could tell she didn't want to answer.

My heart ached. I knew I was losing her forever. "Who is it?"

"Please try to understand. I've always been close to my family. I can't just walk away from them," she said, collapsing onto the sofa.

I stood across from her. My knees felt weak. "Is it your mother's side of the family?"

"Yes."

"Why didn't you tell me?"

"I didn't think you even cared. You . . . You've never loved me. Never."

I'd always called her Elemishka on those days and nights of loneliness, lost in thronging crowds of solitude, calling out to her, talking to her, to myself.

Her eyes filled with tears. "I waited, thinking you might change. You abandoned me long ago, Handan. We weren't even lovers anymore. We were nothing. And I had no one in my life. Even with you I was alone, with my family I was alone, everywhere. Like an orphan. At the very least, my mother wanted me to start a new life. But you said nothing." She began weeping.

"Make love with me," I said, leaning toward her. I tried to kiss her on the lips.

"That wasn't lovemaking." She smiled bitterly. "We just played at making love. You despised me. You hated my body and my love for you. Always so distant and cold. For you, lovemaking was nothing but a game."

"It's a pity." That's all I could manage to say. I sat on the sofa beside my Munise.

"What is?" she asked, pulling away.

"Everything. The years that went by. My respect for you . . ."

"I gave you my youth."

It was like a slap to the face. I never wanted your youth, Elemishka!

No, just pure compassion and us, together, but not in the way that other people are together. In our own way, free of lies and deception. That's all a person can give another.

I stood up, trying to hide my feelings. I didn't realize it—Elem told me later—but a vicious smile twisted my lips: "Your youth?"

"Yes, my youth. It meant nothing to you."

I didn't say good-bye. "No, it won't end here," I told myself. I walked to the door. She didn't try to stop me.

I went home.

It was dark. I didn't turn on the lights. The living room was bathed in the sickly pale light that trickled through the glass door of the garden. It was almost spring, but the chill of winter hung in the air. I missed her hands, the warmth of her touch. There were nights when I wept as I poured out my heart. Painful memories. You held my hands. The touch of a friend. It was like a moment of trust, of happiness. But it was an illusion.

The telephone didn't ring. I waited.

No longer would she wonder about me. "Has Handan gotten home?" She didn't call after me, asking me to come back. She probably didn't look out the window. No, the love and compassion was gone.

My mind was a blur. "I should die," I thought. No, we'd never leave each other like that. The telephone will ring. "Handan, I'll always love you. Forget what I said, I must have lost my mind." The phone didn't ring.

I called her: "Who are you marrying?"

If you're not in love, if the love has faded away, what's left? Sadly, but with a certain coolness, she said, "A carpenter. He has a workshop in the neighborhood."

"Which neighborhood?"

"Ours. They say he's liked me for a long time."

With a calm, steady voice she told me everything. I asked questions, trying to understand, but I just couldn't bring myself to accept it. As though in a single night I'd forgotten how to breathe, to live.

"Did you know each other?" I was repulsed by myself, but unable to stop asking questions.

"No, Handan. He came with his family to talk to my parents about it."

"So you've met him."

"Yes."

"Okay," I said. I wouldn't humiliate myself any further. "I see." I'd lived a decent life. I may not have been a Maria Callas, but in my own small way I'd become a diva. No, I wouldn't let myself break down in grief and tears.

A photograph of my mother glowed wanly in the light from the garden. I looked at her; she may as well have been a stranger. Memories of my childhood and youth flickered through my mind as though I were sifting through them in the palm of my hand. And then a curtain call: I was bowing yet again on an unfamiliar stage, and the applause roared as my voice echoed in the hall. It would all dwindle to nothing in the end.

After a long silence, I said, "Give me your forgiveness."

"What do you mean?"

"I've had a long life."

"Handan, don't talk like that!" she said in a panic. I could hear desperation in her voice for the first time that night. The night she made her final decision.

"I've forgiven you. Now, it's your turn. Give me your forgiveness!"

"Handan, what are you doing?!"

Suddenly everything seemed to empty out: words, emotions, the world around me. I wasn't even aware of what I was doing. Elem was afraid, unsure of how far my madness would take me.

I hung up the phone and unplugged it, and then turned off my cell phone as well. Never again would I speak with anyone. Elem would never see me again. The pills were in that small cabinet. My grandmother used to say, "The taste is bitter but it'll make you well again. Medicine is made to heal." She called it a remedy cabinet. Such a spiritual, sensitive woman. Elem's grandmother had wanted a shimmering velvet gown. And Elem loved me. Truly loved me. I'll say it forever: she loved me passionately.

Lesbians have grandmothers. I opened my grandmother's cabinet of remedies. What good will a bottle of Novalgin do me? Who am I, what have I done? Won't a handful of pills put an end to this empty life? Closing her eyes, she'd embrace me. Not once did I think of us ever being apart. "Go, make love," I said, "make love with women your own age." But I always shouted, "But come back to me!" Go, feel the pain of life, suffer the trials of love, and come back to me; know that I'm your only love in this world. One by one I took the pills from the dark green bottle. I was even smiling. I must have looked like a jeweler carefully handling her emeralds and rubies.

It wasn't a beautiful death. Nilüfer, my ex-lover, wanted to be Hedda Gabler. Hedda wanted to kill someone else, the man she loved. But I won't be Hedda; I'm killing myself. Only Handan Sarp will die.

We made love. She was the first person I could trust when making love. Whom else could I trust? I had no one. No mother, no father. With a flicker of a smile she came into my life; she knew nothing of opera. It made her laugh. Like a mournful autumn evening, I pulled the smile from her lips. My love, my child, my sister. Only compassion. So much that she didn't know about my callousness brought on by passion. Tearing her down, exhausting her in tempests of sex, more and more madness. She wanted compassion. And much later, that's all I had left. I couldn't sleep with her; the sexuality had faded, pulled away from compassion, and I was left with the bitterest of pleasures.

The first pill.

Elem didn't come. How long had it been? Half an hour? How long would it take her to get here? Elem won't come. The second, the third Novalgin. It would end just as beautifully as Hedda wanted. Nilüfer had also wanted to give the gift of death: "Who is she? Her name is Esma, isn't it?" No, her name is Elem. I'd never heard that name before. I didn't know the story behind her name. I didn't ask.

I won't tear down Hedda Gabler's dreams; it will be beautiful, poetic. But I'm a diva; I shouldn't die at home. News of my death, my suicide, would appear in the newspapers. No one will be responsible for my death. I'll leave behind a knot of secrets. Scenes of me on television: in *La traviata*, I die in Ali Arkın's arms; in *Norma*, I walk toward the flames; the fake stove in *La bohème* brings no warmth to Mimi. Ah, *Tosca*, as I gaze at the starry sky, enveloped in the scent of jasmine! No one's responsible for my death. None of those people I let into my life.

I'm not resentful. "It was the hope of sorrow!" I'd read that somewhere: the hope of sorrow. The first round of Novalgin is finished. So that's how it is; you gave Handan Sarp your youth. Now give her separation, cruelty and death. Never come again.

I leave the kitchen. My mother's photograph gazes at me. But this time I won't be defeated by Leyla Mahmure Yönder; I swallow the pills, ignoring her summons to life, a mother's summons, my mother's. Her daughter suffered such pain.

I don't know if I'm defeated. I thought of a beautiful end: I'd go to Sarayburnu and await death on a bench by the sea. That's where they'll find my body, lying on the ground. Toward morning, by the churning sea. It'll all be over by the time the sun rises. At first, no one will know who I am. Just a dead woman, hair in tangles, eyeliner running down her cheeks. Dead, a cigarette between her fingers. Elem would hear about it on the news.

As I get into a taxi, an urge to live fills me. Life, just a little more. "Go," I tell the driver, "leave me here and go." He looks at this drunk woman and drives away. I need to vomit. But what if I vomit blood? What have I done? Elem, I don't want to die. I force myself to vomit. The instinct to live drives my finger down my throat. In the middle of the street, a scene of disgrace: Handan Sarp, vomiting.

It didn't end at home.
It didn't end anywhere.

It didn't end. Until gangrene sets in, it won't.

Spring came but didn't blossom. A long drawn out winter. Every day brought frost. Storms raged on the sea inside me. I was always shivering from the cold. The sky was a permanent gray, which filled me with dark joy. Pulling into myself, withdrawing further and further. Those were the days when my garden began growing wild.

As always, I was living as a recluse. I didn't see anyone; I'd cut off contact with everyone I knew.

Except Elem. We saw each other, perhaps even more often than before, to convince ourselves that the separation was real. Every evening we spoke on the phone. I waited by the phone for her to return home from work.

Sometimes during the day I'd call her, knowing she wasn't at home, and listen to the phone ring. One time toward evening her mother answered the phone, and I hung up. It sounded like her mother's voice, but it could have been İnci. Her family sometimes met up at Elem's apartment. That place that was meant to set Elem free . . .

Elem and I met up from time to time. Our relationship carried on. We weren't bitter. Nor were we close. An ambiguous relationship, wounded. And there was no hope of healing.

That winter seemed to go on and on.

My rather ridiculous attempt at suicide had left Elem shaken. The next morning she came to see me. Stubbornly she hadn't come the night before, not wanting to play into my "caprice," as she said. She'd rung the doorbell, but I couldn't rouse myself from bed. She waited, and rang the bell again. When I finally opened the door, she said, "I was afraid. I kept thinking of Hikmet's death." The sight of me had frightened her; bags below my eyes swollen purple, lined with spider veins. "I'm fine," I told her.

Had the pain subsided? I felt numb. That morning I didn't tell her about my escapade with the bottle of Novalgin. "You're going to be late. Nedret will be upset." I needed to be alone. I was exhausted and wanted to sleep.

She wouldn't go. "Handan, your lips . . ." The corners of my lips were cracked. She sensed that something was wrong. For a moment, I thought that if I hugged her, begged her, that the engagement would somehow vanish from our lives. I could forget about the night before. But I just stood there, blankly looking at Elem. I felt as though I'd been emptied out. My pride held me back; I didn't reach out for her.

After that sudden separation, I began thinking about winters of the past. The seasons, always coming and going. It begins in fall and with unsettling bounty prepares us for winter. Wherever we go, the branches of trees are heavy with fruit: plump quince, crimson pomegranate, citrus swelling in the orchards. We must've seen it together. We'd buy chestnuts, Elem would make jam from cornelian cherries, and I'd put chrysanthemums in the vase that Elem had bought. At the time, I didn't understand that we were happy. Winter, looming over the horizon, brought us joy. So many winters passed that way.

Had it passed, or was it lingering? It didn't matter. Only the snowfall made us uneasy; would we be able to see each other on the weekend? And then winter would fade away.

I was oblivious to those seasons, the most beautiful in my life.

Unending winter. Even though spring had arrived, the biting chill of winter evenings persisted. I was trying to cling to something, to keep myself afloat. I wanted to live. But day by day I withered, sinking into despair.

Some evenings we met up. At the beginning, toward the end. Until the very last night, that final night. But always outside. Our homes had been lost to us.

During the days of our separation only once did I go to her home.*
Never again did Elem come to mine.

At times I imagine that I can mend everything. I think to myself: there's no need for us to destroy one another. Elem is a child of the earth, and I of the sea. People born of the earth experience the world with narrow horizons, their lives are like everyone else's; they'll never know the infinite. And that's how it should be. When I set out over the waves, the world means nothing to me. Alone on the open sea, I can bring my Munise to life. Let her live out her life like everyone else. Let me be forgotten . . . But I couldn't bear it. Our separation weighed on me, crushing me.

I scribbled absurd things in my notebook; it was unclear what they were: notes, memoirs or sorrows.

MEMORIES ARE RINGING OVER THERE. IT'S NOT THE PHONE. WHEN I LOOK OUT THE WINDOW, WHEN I GO

---

* Handan Sarp never told me why she went to Elem's that last time or what happened. That significant detail eluded me at the time. (Sİ)

INTO THE GARDEN, SEAGULLS FLY PAST, SEAGULLS THAT HAVE LOST THEIR SEA.

I wrote it in red pen, all capital letters. Looking at it now, I'm reminded of clots of blood. Just what were my feelings that day? Or was it night? My eyes had probably been filled with death.

ELEM, WE'RE FRIENDS TO THE DEATH.

AMONG PEOPLE, OUR LOVE HAD NO NAME. ONE DAY, WE'LL BOTH LONG FOR THIS NAMELESS LOVE.

It was a Tuesday evening. Which year? Yes, it was evening. I'd called Elem and written that down after our conversation. What had we talked about? We always spoke of the same things. My fear of separation. She tried to console me: I had friends—who, I wonder?—I was famous, I'd start a new life.

How can I describe it? Those nights linger in my memory. I pitied that woman who struggled through those nights, clinging to life. She always recalled the early years, the first meetings, the nervousness and timidity. I couldn't explain it to anyone, not even Elem.

It's impossible to describe what you experience. Slowly I began to understand that. All you have are a few words, dry as dust, to express what you went through in your torment. And not just one torment, but many. A single word, emptied of meaning, is incapable of expressing itself, much less our suffering. Because of the insufficiency of words, of sentences, all that ruin and despair is diluted and stripped of sorrow. When we try to describe it, we simply butcher the experience.

Still:

My heart pounded with excitement on the nights we would meet. Why? Nothing was going to change. I was a stranger to Elem. She had her own life; I didn't ask about it, and she didn't tell me. Nothing I could do would make any difference. She was walking her own path.

I decided to act as though the despair didn't exist. But was it a decision? No, that's just how it happened; we erased the past. And we didn't speak of the future. As for me, nothing was left: no future, nor a separate new life.

But that desire to see her, my Munise!

It seemed that if we didn't meet up, if I didn't see my Munise in the body and flesh, death would come all the sooner. I'd been infected with the cruel sickness of love. Being able to see her soothed my pain as I moved ever closer to death. Perhaps, in fact, it made it worse, but there was nothing else I could do.

When we met, we didn't talk about her marriage. When was the wedding? How much longer would this separation go on? In the end, even that would be taken from me. We didn't speak of her mother or father, and I never asked about İnci or Hüseyin. As for the "carpenter," I didn't even know his name. Was he young? Elem had never mentioned his age. I spoke of such things only with myself.

I wished that the evenings would never draw to an end so that I could see her just a little longer. That was my sole desire. Was I awake or dreaming? I couldn't be sure.

One thing had changed: we no longer met on the weekends. Only one day a week, on Tuesday or Wednesday. But we never talked about why. There were no more Fridays, Saturdays or Sundays in our lives. Occasionally, we may have met up on a Monday or Thursday. Or it could just be my imagination.

If we were going to meet up in the evening, I'd start getting ready during the day. I felt a desire to look beautiful in her eyes, as though I could rekindle our love; a reminiscence of the early days of our passion. I hoped that fine dresses, makeup and jewelry would bring me beauty. I forced myself to go to the beauty parlor to have my hair done. A few times our eyes met in the mirror and I saw the hairdresser's concerned looks. "Handan Hanım, are you okay?" I nodded yes in the mirror. It took all my strength to not break down in tears: I'm not well, somehow I must win over Elem's heart. No, it wasn't about winning her heart.

Back at home I couldn't decide what to wear; my wardrobe seemed to be set against me. I thought often of Necmi. Which performance of *La traviata* was it? Because of my costume I'd shouted at him. I was brash, spoiled. Blushing, he stammered: "Handan Hanım, I'm just . . . I just want you to look beautiful, young and beautiful." At the time, I didn't need his help.

The afternoon would drag on interminably. You'd never guess what I did one time: I looked for the blue folder Elem had once given me. When I found it, I sat and flipped slowly through the articles about me, the newspaper and magazine clippings, the interviews and announcements from the Istanbul City Opera. Withdrawing from the world, I sat and read.

My Munise had underlined words of praise with a felt-tip pen. She'd collected everything she could find about me. At the time, she carried me in her heart. But tomorrow or the next day, if she reads something about me, will she linger over the text, cutting it out and saving it?

Sometimes I lie in bed, motionless, not wanting to think, trying not to think. "Elem," I say to myself, "how is this going to end, how will we forget each other? What about these articles you cut out for me, the photographs of us which you insisted on having taken, Hikmet's painting hanging on the wall, the two women he painted? So, you'll forget it all." From the sea I hear a thunderous voice: "Long ago!" it roars, echoing. "Elem forgot you long ago." A stupor reminiscent of sleep.

Even more listless, lethargic. With all my being I know it, I feel it: when lovers separate, it's always like this. Everything falling into ruin, and you're silent, filled with regret. Woman or man, femininity and masculinity come to an end.

I began wearing blacks and grays. The only splash of color was the flowers that she'd knitted for me once, which I'd pin to my lapel: a bright red rose, or a bouquet of violets, the flowers drooping ever so slightly. A reddish starflower, or a spray of spring plum blossoms. Perhaps they would remind Elem of the days when she made them for me. Mimi used to knit flowers as well. Once, I was Mimi. Later, much later, if she remembers me and my loneliness: blacks and grays.

In the eyes of men, or in the eyes of a lesbian, my charm is irresistible. I'm resplendent, ready for the stage. Wearing just a little makeup, with the exception of my eyelashes which are heavily mascaraed, I'm a despairing Butterfly who failed at suicide. I put on perfume, lavender by Guerlain, hoping its sharp scent will remind you of me. I want everything to remind you of me.

And as though Elem were there with me, as though she'll come home with me tonight to my home on Sakızlı Street, I put a bowl of nuts on the radiator to keep them warm. Broken dreams for a broken life.

But succumbing to broken dreams isn't the way. Handan Sarp will never forget.

The sixteenth of May. Which year? The year of our separation.
FOR YOU, I'LL REMAIN AS A MOMENTARY SOB, NOTHING MORE.

Was it May? No, March. I cringe when I see that word. "Ma" could just as easily be the first two letters of "May." I know: time should pass more quickly. Quickly I spin the hour and minute hands. Time rushes forward. No, not a momentary sob; a ceaseless wail on a cold March night.

NOTHING WILL BE LEFT OF ME FOR ANYONE ELSE.

I'd written it in red pen, all capital letters.

I don't want to be a sob for anyone.

Actually, I didn't want anything. From a distance, I watched as she took the first steps toward her new life. I gave myself over to idleness, nothingness, observing the adventures of others in the world like us.

"This year, bridal gowns . . ."

"What bridal gowns, Elem?"

She blushed: "Veils are in style again."

"Elem, one day I should take you to . . ."

"Why did you stop?"

I'd stopped talking because that's how our intimacy had begun. Now, she was talking about bridal gowns. I'd gone with her to the boutique for İnci's gown. And now, she was going for herself. I fell silent.

I'd also written this:

Elem, they're going to ask me about you. "She's fine," I'll say. "She's doing well." We meet up now and then. The people who know I love you will flash me a knowing smile. Will you smile so cruelly as well?

I should tear it up and throw it away.

People like us—women, men, it makes no difference—are lonely, steeped in solitude. On the path that leads to love, you'll be eternally lonely, no matter who or what you are. Your femininity, your masculinity, is of no use. You'll be stung by love as it passes through your life or you'll be left completely alone.

On one of those evenings during that long winter, I must've read that to her because I remember her asking, "People like us?"

Elem said to me, "I've changed a lot. I don't know, it's like I see you as a sister, Handan."

I'll never forget the way she smiled with such happiness. "They've put a spell on you," I said. The conversation struck me as mundane.

"You've been bewitched." I was saying to myself, "You'll always be my sister, my lover, my child . . ." This is a secret; how many people would understand?

I usually left home early. Neither the blue folder nor lying in bed would make the time pass. I was probably reliving the same day again and again. The day that we decided to separate.

We'd meet at a cafe somewhere in Beyoğlu or Nişantaşı. Feeling emptied out, she walks, unable to restrain the sorrow welling up within, her entire being in tatters, hoping that walking will bring some respite. Then a moment comes: regardless of where she is, Handan Sarp suddenly places her hands over her face for no apparent reason. She notices that her hands are cold.

People passing by pause to look at this woman standing perfectly still in the middle of the sidewalk, her hands over her face and her shoulders beginning to shudder. I didn't know that woman either and when I pulled my hands away, I'd smile at the people staring in surprise as though saying that I thought it was strange as well. At least I thought I was smiling. Time and time again I caught myself, standing there with my hands over my face: it was absurd, pathetic. A reflection of my ruined state.

It was still early. I'd walk the streets, passing the time until I'd meet Elem in the evening, looking in window shops at all that luxury, the clothes that millions of people would never be able to afford, the furniture and jewelry and ostentation, the pomp of prosperity. I would seem to have forgotten my pain or scowl at my suffering. Soon, however, I'd be overcome by anxiety.

One cold evening it was raining, a piercing rain that made me think of broken mirrors. In vain I struggled with my umbrella which had been blown inside out. After walking a little further I went into a cafe, but not the one where we were going to meet. It was still early for that. I needed to pass the time somewhere; I needed shelter. The sky began darkening. Time seemed frozen.

For a long while I'd been unable to shake off that feeling of emptiness. Drops of rain gathered in tiny streams on the window. No one else was in the cafe. Yet another evening of solitude slipping toward a lonely night.

In those days I'd begun carrying a purse for my bottle of sedatives and packet of tissues, and sometimes a book. After taking off my raincoat, I leaned the umbrella against my chair, and a moment later it clattered to the ground. I ordered an espresso and gazed out the window at the small garden that had been set up on the terrace. Water ran off the lemon trees, vines and cherry laurels, making me long for spring. They were cold, battered by the wind; I could feel it. Some of the flowerpots had toppled over.

I took my book from my purse. I was reading long novels in those days, books I'd never been able to finish; not because I didn't like them, but because they too might come to an end. I fanned through the pages, thinking of having a drink, an early evening cognac to warm me.

Perhaps it was the book I was reading that made me want to drink. The main character was an alcoholic intentionally drinking himself to death. The author, Malcom Lowry, had been the same. I hadn't heard of him before. At the age of forty-eight he committed suicide. It wasn't an easy novel to read.* But if you can ignore the tumult around you, it speaks of secrets.

The tumult died down. The cafe was always empty at that hour, and the waiters knew that this woman reading a book and drinking cognac needed to be alone. It was silent except for the pattering of

* Handan Sarp must have been reading Malcolm Lowry's *Under the Volcano*, which I'm also quite fond of. (Sİ)

the rain, a lovely sound. It fit well with the novel, which, if I'm not mistaken, is set in a hot, tropical climate. There, the rain was warm. A chill runs through you. Lights, the lights of dusk. The lines of the novel whisper of your own sorrow.

A second cognac. I'd begin to feel like I was myself again. The pain dwindled. That's how I'd begin the evening, preparing myself to see Elem. In my imagination, our meeting would be gentle, as though it had become part of the novel. In vain, I'd try to find traces of our past, the days when we were happy, in the novel and in life. Blood and pus would flow. I didn't want to lose Elem, so I made a decision: even if she gets married, what's going to change? Love can be one-sided, like the man and woman in the novel . . . I began to feel ever so slightly dizzy.

I asked for the bill, even though it wasn't yet time for us to meet. But the sky was completely dark, meaning night had fallen. I could wait at the other cafe.

Stepping out into the rain, I knew that even though I would see Elem, a night of eternal loneliness awaited me.

I don't know how many times we met.

They sit opposite each other at a table. As they talk of trivialities, the woman tries to solve the riddles she sees in the face of the younger woman and bring them to life in her heart.

If I saw a mirror, I'd look at my own face: an outpouring of longing and love.

In that season of separation, those meetings brought nothing. All they did was feed the separation, mature it, making it our own. As we sat there speaking of nothing, a glance, a question, the clothes Elem was wearing, all pushed me to the brink of madness. That young woman who for years had worn muted tones—like she had at İnci's wedding—had now taken to bright, showy colors. I could make no sense of it. And I was already slipping away. "You've had a lot to drink, haven't you?" she asked once, concern in her eyes. "Yes, probably." Did I expect her to pity me? But she asked nothing else.

"Elem, I can't manage unless I drink." I lit another cigarette.

As she gazed at my cigarette, it seemed as though the worry in her expression had disappeared.

I engraved the riddle in her face into my memory, knowing that one day it would disappear. If one day she no longer recognized herself, she could come to me and I could tell her.

"Aren't you worried about your voice? You're ruining it."

I'd forgotten about my voice.

Then an argument would erupt. I'd start insulting her, saying things I'd never said before, humiliating and scorning her. Most of the time, she said nothing. Although she didn't respond, she didn't seem to be sad. Her expression was peaceful. On one of the nights we met, she said that she'd changed, that she was "another person." That was how she replied to my insults.

When we walked out the door, we went our separate ways without a word, without saying good-bye or hugging. I'd get into a taxi, not caring how she got home. But when I arrived at my apartment, haunted by specters of memory, I'd be flooded with fear and regret and run to the mirror, gazing at my howling face, wishing I could weep. I'd call and apologize, promising it would never happen again, Elem . . . I opened the windows and doors, stepping into the garden, trying to sing. But the songs were abandoning Handan Sarp.

What didn't bring me suffering, poundings of the heart and madness? There were flowers of spring that, in spite of the gray skies, began to bloom. On my long walks in Istanbul, city of stone and concrete, I unexpectedly came upon them as I drifted through the gardens of my youth.

There were nettles and hibiscus in the cemeteries, and clumps of daisies as well. In some places they all blossomed together. The poppies hadn't yet bloomed, but there were buds of blue sweet alyssum along the edges of sidewalks and the Spanish broom was just about to blossom. And when the poppies bloomed . . . I don't know if it was just a conjuring of thought, but images of Elem raced through my mind: Elem, at her wedding, a bridal bouquet in her hands, and I wondered when she'd get married. No, I never dared to ask.

And the poppies did bloom. Along with the blossoming of poppies, green plums swelled on the branches. Soon there were heaps of green plums at greengrocers and street sellers sold them in paper sacks. All those years ago, Elem would bring overflowing sacks of the season's first green plums when she came to see me. They smelled of grass, flowers and spring. At the same time we'd bite into a plum, and Elem's face would pucker at the tartness. I felt alive, like I truly existed and was loved.

Now, whenever I see green plums my heart sinks.

Later the magnolias blossomed. They were the color of ash, just like the season. During the summer of our separation I saw them in Kireçburnu, blooming from behind a wall. It's an ancient tree, and every year it bursts forth with more and more blooms. I looked up to admire the flowers. I could hear the sound of the sea, the waves crashing against the shore.

I'd gone to see the tree before. It was morning and I remembered that one summer Elem and I had looked at it together. Just then, a group of children went past, running, laughing, in pursuit of some hidden joy. It's difficult to explain: time may pass, but I'll never forget how I smiled bitterly at that moment.

Then it was cherries.

As she was cleaning my flat, Kadriye Hanım showed me two bottles: cherry vodka and cherry cognac. There was just a little dark liquid at the bottom of each. "Can I throw them out?" she asked. I shrugged. "They've lovely bottles," she said, "if I wash them, I can get the cherry stains out." I had no choice but to be indifferent: "Take them if you like." Cherry season was approaching. Let the sky be as gray as it wants. No cherry vodka or cognac, no cherry jam sent by her mother. Cherry liqueur chocolates in pink foil, cherry wine. This tale should end like that: the end of cherries.

"Don't make any cherry pies," I told Aunt Nadire. "Elem is so busy at work these days I haven't even seen her." And then I hung up the phone. The end of cherries.

Waiting for the evenings when we'd meet. I had no other life. I just stayed at home, usually wearing an old, threadbare dress. Where had I gotten it? My hands and arms felt as if they belonged to someone else. My entire body felt foreign. I was terrified that they'd call from the opera. When Semra rang, I didn't answer; her voice on the answering machine was tense with concern. To live, just for Elem! No, that was no longer possible. To live, just to see Elem!

When the weather warmed, I spent my days in the garden. Yet another thick novel, more suffering; there were so many tragic books I'd never discovered: now it was *Black and Blue*.

As the sun began to set, the hazy gray would fade. Patches of peach-pink flitted across the sky. Swallows warbled, darting above. That sick woman will think she's getting better, almost completely well. But ill people like her know that the heartache will return. A few minutes of easy breathing is just a deception. Soon enough, she'll be locked in struggle with that old pain. Mournfully you look up at the swallows, deaf to their trilling. A sigh escapes your lips: the evening will melt away into memories, and every day we lose each other just a little more. Every day, the distance grows.

Then, you plead, practically begging on your knees, and she agrees: so and so day, around eight in the evening, a cafe . . .

"No excuses!" she said. It was almost the end of May. "Ali misses you too. He has a surprise for you."

It dawned on me that nearly two months had passed since we decided to separate.

"Handan, what's wrong?" Semra asked.

"Nothing, I'm fine. There's nothing wrong," I lied, ashamed that I couldn't tell the truth. My voice faltered: "I don't want to talk. I just can't."

As before, she suggested we go to the islands. I knew she wouldn't hang up until I agreed. Thursday? No, perhaps Elem would want to meet up on Thursday. I didn't tell Semra about my meetings with Elem. "Friday," I said, trying to end the conversation. Fridays and Saturdays were no longer Elem's days. "We can go on Friday."

I had no interest in going to the islands. That week, Elem and I didn't meet. It was the first week we didn't meet. And that's how it would be. Weeks. Perhaps a month. I can't bring myself to say it: months.

Even if I can't say the word, I find myself haunted—a rush of fears, memories, worries—and as my mind is tossed into turmoil, my mouth goes dry as ash and my lips feel as though they will crack open. The only accompaniment I have is a shadowy melancholy.

Days passed and then Friday arrived. We'd arranged to meet according to the departure of the high-speed ferry, and Ali and Semra picked me up. No one mentioned Elem. The fact that they didn't ask about her meant that they sensed something. In silence, the issue was closed.

Although it wasn't fall, the sunshine seemed to whisper of autumn. On deck, Elem's hair didn't shimmer in the light. But we weren't even on deck. The sunshine was only visible through the small window of the ferry. I recalled seeing a strand of gray in her light brown hair.

The ferry slowed, drawing near the pier. As we alighted on the island I felt an unexpected sense of joy. Was it because I saw the cafe where we'd sat before? It had been painted dark teal. "That's where we sat," Semra said. The same waiter took our order: coffee, just as before. That autumn day, the sea had been rough. But now, in mid-morning, all was calm. Summer had begun on the island, and there was no trace of the gray skies of Istanbul. "Even in early March the mimosas began to bloom," Ali said but stopped himself, because I would've wept.

We weren't going to the house in Maden. It was being repaired and painted.

The day was ours, idle, spreading out before us. A trip around the island in a horse-drawn carriage, a walk, early dinner. They were trying to cheer me up. "What am I doing here?" I wondered.

We got in a carriage. A memory: Ali had been transformed into Alfredo, the coachman smiled through his mustache and Elem spoke of Zeytin Island. It was probably that summer that we'd gone to Zeytin Island for the fourth time, Elem and I. Yes, the fourth time.

We never went all together, with Ali and Semra. Nor will we ever. I didn't tell them.

I'd told Elem about the imaginary islands of mapmakers of old. "Handan Island," she'd said on the ferry to Zeytin Island, on the seas, the horizon, in dreams. And later we decided that we'd live on the island, summer and winter, far from everyone. The two of us.

Ali revealed his surprise as we walked through the copse of pines. During the carriage ride, we'd hardly spoken, sitting in silence. No, that's not quite right: out of respect for my silence they didn't speak. We walked under the dazzling light fanning through the pines; but the trees seemed to be afflicted, ravaged by a fungus perhaps, in the throes of death—like me. Ali told me about a proposal he'd received; it was a performance in which we'd sing a love duet, a benefit for some foundation to be organized by a holding company. I wasn't listening.

The pines were ill.

He said that he'd first thought of doing a piece from *La traviata* and then considered something from *Aida* or *La sonnambula*. Yes, that woman walking in her sleep dreamed of the trees toppling down, one by one.

"There's still time. It will be at the end of October."

"I don't know what will come of my life by the end of October," I said, unable to control my thoughts.

Semra and Ali were visibly startled.

Brushing aside their surprise, I went on: "Do you remember the camellias? Are we going to pass by that mansion and the greenhouse? There were all those red camellias. And pink ones too, do you remember? Hiding among the red ones."

In the gardens along the road, only the oleanders were about to bloom. Red, pink and white flowers. I smiled. "If mosquitoes fly around the leaves of an oleander, they get poisoned and die. That's why they plant so many of them here." I bit my lip: "The poor mosquitoes . . ."

But there was still the matter of the performance. Would I dare hurt Ali Arkın's feelings? We would make a fine pair: Alfredo, plump as a cow, singing with Violetta, her voice raspy from alcohol and cigarettes: "We could sing 'O terra, addio' from *Aida*," I suggested.

We must have drawn near Maden at that point.

Weren't the pines ill then as well? They were hanging on to life.

The house was somewhere nearby. We were there, the four of us. Just opposite was Sedef Island. A drink in my hand, descending the steep steps to the shore; the sea would save me from my friends, from my Munise. I'd walked along the seaside. The full moon from *Turandot* had not yet risen.

Fine, I decided, I'll turn my thoughts from that house and autumn evening. We selected a duet and decided to start practicing immediately. Of everyone, Semra was the most pleased. "It'll be wonderful," Ali said naively. We reached the road to the pier. Being on the island became more bearable. I almost started enjoying the day as it drew to a close.

There was a row of restaurants. Randomly we chose one and went inside. It was like we'd traveled in time; a song was playing, a song by Paul Anka: "Tonight my love, tonight!" Paul Anka meant nothing to Semra and Ali. But it brought me back to my childhood, to the days when I knew nothing of falling in love, and also to Elem and our separation: "Tonight my love, tonight!"

If the song "You are My Destiny" hadn't played and if there hadn't been flowers in small glass vases on the table, would I have trembled like that? I don't think so. White wine and fish. We raised our glasses in a toast to our upcoming performance, to our success. "No," I said, "let's drink to my relationship with Elem. It's over, we broke up." And just at that moment, the song "Crazy Love" began to play.

In the beginning, you don't feel the pain so intensely. Or perhaps it's so harsh that you are numbed to the pain. In any case, it was melodramatic: the intertwining of our separation and the loss of my voice.

I made a decision. During our first rehearsal I realized it was pointless to push a voice that could no longer perform, and I paid no heed when Ali and the pianist asked to start again at the beginning. Why had we started with "Parigi, o cara"? Probably to do justice to the melodrama unfolding. I had listened to a record, the wondrous voices of a man and woman singing, and the record spun endlessly. That was before Alfredo accompanied me, before Ali Arkın:

We'll be together forever!

No, we aren't together. Our paths have parted:
She's arrived, at long last!

I couldn't sing. "I'll never be able to do this," I thought, my hands on my throat. My voice trailed off in a moan. Alfredo wasn't there. Let's try again, they said. "What's this? Is it a song?" I once asked, my hair pulled into a ponytail by my grandmother; the Çalıkuşu of old. "It's opera."

I left without saying good-bye. A broad stairway, the steps seeming to never end, white marble. Perfectly suitable for a melodrama.

I don't know if there's anything left to tell, or if there's any need, for that matter.

Summer dragged on, the color of smoke. At last, that interminable winter had come to an end, giving way to haze. Days under a bell jar, humid and sticky. Summer was at our throats.

When we met—which was less and less often—we only fought, and I hurled hurtful words and accusations at her. But Elem had changed; no longer did she cower in defeat but stood up for herself and her family. Our separation, however, seemed abstract. We never talked about her marriage or her fiancé.

The next day, my conscience would torment me. Actually it was more like a disappointment, the kind that lulls your mind into stagnation. But I'd become enslaved by it. I wanted to see Elem so that I could taste that disappointment, live through it again and again. In desperation I even once called the boutique.

"Can we meet up tonight?"

"No, I'm busy tonight."

"Okay, tomorrow night . . ."

I'd call, trying to find a way, surprised at what my anger and suffering did to me. The Handan Sarp I knew never loved, pursued anyone or begged. But I was begging:

"When can I see you? I've missed you."

"You just don't seem to understand!" she shouted. "I'm starting a new life, Handan. You want the past. But the past is gone, it'll never be the same."

I knew that she wanted to be set free of me. Insisting was pointless. Elem had erased the past, and she was behaving as though our coming together and drifting apart were merely random events. It was Handan Sarp who couldn't break free of the past. Why had I become bound to this woman? People who are heart-bound to another know what it means to be parted from the ones they love. As she became more and more distant, I came to realize that even in the past when we'd been most intimate I'd felt her pulling away. Separation had already filled my life. It always had.

The end of summer. We'd forgotten each other. Elem forgot me. I pretended as though I had. We no longer called each other.

If only I had a child. A daughter. If I were a mother, I could say, "I think I'm going through a menopausal crisis." Zeytin Island, the shoreline road, my fertility drying up like a mockery. At the moment when Handan Sarp, who loathed femininity and masculinity, was denied her nature, she suddenly found herself overcome by maternal desires.

The image of her engagement ring was seared into my memory: a graceful, elegant ring. I saw it on her finger. I didn't ask, nor did she tell me. It struck a blow to my heart. Such childlike fingers, I wondered if she pricked them when sewing. For days I was tormented by the image of that ring. Haunted. Separation filled my life.

I stopped calling her. And she stopped calling me. In that horrifying darkness, I gave myself over to silence. Handan Sarp had ruined her voice. That voice. She told no one. I didn't ask about the ring. And Elem didn't ask about my singing or what had become of me.

One day, I told myself, she'll move the ring to the finger on her left hand. The thought echoed in my mind as I walked, sat, awoke breathlessly from sleep. "There must be a ceremony," I thought, "when the man takes his wife's ring and . . ." I don't know. It never occurred to me. Ceremonies like that mean nothing for people who are in love with separation.

Weeks would pass, and then months.

It was the end of summer. I'd forgotten; not Elem, but that our separation and love had come to an end. One night I called her. I was sitting in the dark. Most nights I sat in the dark; it somehow made me feel better, seeing the wan light coming in from the garden.

I heard her scream. The darkness was torn asunder. The other woman screamed, and it was the same refrain: she wanted to hear Elem's voice. I tried to cover my ears, but the sound rang out.

I stepped out into the garden, hoping the scream would stop. Autumn was being swallowed up by my vines, which ruled the unkempt garden like a despot. A feeling of revulsion for the place shuddered through me.

In the dark, I dialed the number by touch. It began to ring. A man's voice answered: it wasn't Hüseyin, nor her father. I didn't recognize it. For a moment, I considered hanging up.

"Can I speak with Elem Hanım?" I wasn't thinking. It didn't occur to me that she might be married already.

"Of course. Who should I say is calling?" The voice was deep, masculine. Some men's voices are more masculine than they should be.

I could still hang up. "Handan Sarp."

The phone went silent; he must have put his hand over the receiver. Then the sounds began again: someone talking, a clatter as the phone was set down, probably on the sideboard. I waited, listening to the sounds of her home: laughter and music, but not opera of course. A woman was singing, her voice a long vibrato, probably on the television. It was too late, I couldn't hang up now: I'd said my name, diva of the past. A woman, most likely Elem's mother, was talking about something.

I felt exhausted: so much love, and hate.

Elem picked up the phone. "Yes, Handan." That's all: "Yes, Handan."

"Good evening," I said, my voice already showing signs of huskiness that would only get worse with age. "It is evening, I thought, isn't it?" "I was just wondering how you're doing," I said.

"I was going to call . . . I'm sorry, we've just been in a rush about moving. I'm moving back to Kocamustafapaşa. Our wedding is at the end of October."

I wasn't listening. It was like a slap: Kocamustâfapaşa. We were sitting across from each other at Hristo's. Without blinking an eye, I snubbed Elem about Kocamustâpaşa and Reşat Nuri's novel. My hands were shaking. I sought in vain for my packet of cigarettes and lighter.

The word "wedding" brought me back. That was even more painful. I'd always thought that a woman like Elem would want nothing to do with weddings.

"Wedding?" My lips trembled.

"I was going to tell you. This weekend I'm moving to Kocamustafapaşa, so I need to bring everything to my husband's place."

We set up her apartment together. An armchair here, maybe a vase of flowers there, some begonias . . .

At her new home in Kocamustâpaşa, no one would hear my voice speaking through the memories.

"I'll bring your invitation. The wedding will be on the twenty-first of October."

"Are you going to invite Semra and Ali?"

She paused. "Yes, I suppose I should."

"I won't come alone to the wedding."

Ali and I went to the wedding together. Semra had made up an excuse.

They were both surprised that I wanted to go. Why wouldn't I want to? I had nothing to look forward to; all I had were my monotonous nights. My attempt at suicide was a fiasco. If I was going to go on living, I had to deal with it and get used to the idea.

But what lingered in my mind was that 17th of December: the howl of the storm, the candlelight, Feride "in a fever" waiting for Munise. I imagined Feride in that dingy room in the village of Zeyniler. The candle flame flickers in the wind coming in through the windows. Feride is sitting on the bed, her eyes burning. There was no hope for Munise. She was buried under the snow. Munise had been buried under the drifts.

We met up at Cafe Bliss. Ali arrived before me. "Let's have a drink before we go," I said. The wedding was at the Hilal Wedding Hall in Aksaray. Elem hadn't found time to bring me the invitation, so she called and explained in detail how to get there. She'd also invited Ali and Semra by telephone. "It'll be easy to find," Ali said.

I nodded, waiting for the waiter to bring my whiskey. Ali was nervous. But there was an odd peacefulness about Handan Sarp. When your worldly emotions are lost, the separation of bodies, the physical separation, no longer seems to matter. And I know that I've paid the price.

Physically, I don't miss her like I did before. It was my body that seemed to believe there was no cure for our separation. Being ashamed of your sexuality inflicts a wound. And the price? Her marriage.

"Your outfit is very nice," Ali said.

Who would have guessed that I would wear what Nedret had proposed all those years before: a black suit, not unlike a tuxedo. Of course, I didn't have Nedret tailor it. I wasn't sure if she'd attend the wedding that night. But if she came and saw Handan Sarp in that outfit, she would be stunned: a black jacket, black trousers, collarless black silk blouse. I had masacaraed my lashes and put on sparkling silver eyeshadow, as well as deep red lipstick that verged on black. My hair, which had been dyed with a few streaks, was pulled into a bun and I wore a headband.

Ali added: "You look beautiful."

I smiled, and took a sip of whiskey. The first sip always feels good. With a bluntness unbecoming Handan Sarp, I said, "Even if she were to come back, I don't think I'd sleep with her. But I would take her in my arms and cry."

My eyes were dry.

The next morning, I'd be smothered in loneliness.

A light rain was falling. We entered the building.

My feelings had changed, just as my feelings now aren't what they were when I first called and started telling you about our separation.

I'd hoped that on the wedding night our separation and my suffering would bud into something, just as a seemingly dry branch sprouts blossoms. That's why I wasn't afraid to open myself to the pain. Perhaps it was my own *Çalıkuşu* opera.

When I came to you, I wanted this separation of ours to go on living in a book because it truly was alive, as vibrant as an opera. I believed that this lie which people call morals means absolutely nothing when it comes to love. If Handan Sarp had been lost in the name of that false morality, then perhaps others could rise up in revolt.

But now, that sea has turned flat and stagnant. A dead, muddied sea choking on filth.

When we went inside, children were running around near the entrance of the wedding hall, dashing among the thick, crude columns. The colors were hideous: the walls were blue, the ceiling was white, and the columns were a pale pink, and the floor was covered in vinyl tiles. There were restrooms just across from the cloakroom. I could hear music and people talking coming from inside, but there was no laughter. Even the children's expressions were dull. Could I share this thought with Ali? A wedding of the poor.

There was a full-length mirror, the secrets of which seemed to have rusted over. I looked and saw a woman in black, wearing a suit like a tuxedo. On the breast of her jacket there was a brooch, a cluster of grapes made of rubies, and it had green leaves embellished in gold. No one there would ever be able to buy the likes of it.

I turned to Ali and, not caring whether or not he'd tell anyone, said, "This is a wedding of poor people."

Ali told me that he had grown up there. He'd said that once before. I remembered the colorful paper lanterns from our party that night. It was night, and the lanterns were beautiful. The wedding hall had been decorated with glittering stars, streamers and crepe paper chains that were used wedding after wedding.

That neighborhood . . . What was it about the place? Did the people who were born and grew up there think they were special somehow? Why that sense of superiority? Tomorrow, the next day, what would come of it? What would come of this story? What would opera, which Semra believed so passionately in, bring to that neighborhood, and what would its inhabitants bring to opera? I felt exhausted, like I'd been abandoned on my own path. Bid me farewell.

As we entered the hall, I heard someone say, "It started raining."

I turned to look; a man with a mustache was talking to the young attendant of the cloakroom. "We didn't realize how cold it was getting."

At the entrance of the hall there was a sign: "It is forbidden to bring your own alcohol." Just like at İnci's wedding. I saw İnci; she was wearing the wedding gown she'd ordered from Nedret. I felt as though I were at her wedding yet again, with Hüseyin and Elem's father.

Gathering up my confidence, I granted Elem the loneliness that she gave me.

The stars and paper decorations continued down the garish hall. Up ahead, I saw the flickering of lights. More children were running around. Ali smiled, stroking their heads, and they smiled back. We were standing at the top of the stairs.

Handan Sarp committed suicide last night. It sounds absurd to say. I shrug; so what if she did?

The wedding hall reminded me of a barn. The stairs led downward. As I stood there with Ali, everything was coming to an end. More guests started coming in, and the end was drawing near.

I descended the stairs. There were hundreds of people, all from the neighborhood; simple people living in their own world. But I knew that I'd create a stir: the crowd in the hall turned to look. That strange woman in black entered the final scene of the melodrama like a cancer.

Where would we sit?

Ali Arkın had studied at Davutpaşa High School and now he's a tenor in the opera; he saw some of his relatives at the Hilal Wedding Hall. I'm a stranger. Always a stranger.

I couldn't see Elem. Just as I hadn't seen her at her grandmother's funeral.

There were rows upon rows of tables, all crowded together. If this wedding wasn't a funeral, then what was it? There were the same groups of weeping women wearing headscarves and men with loosened neckties. And all the children who would share the same fate. Weddings of the poor are funerals. It is forbidden to bring your own alcohol.

I'll return to Elem that which I stole from her youth. I'll give her back the path that everyone follows, and to those who showed her what life "should be," I give our love. For myself, I'll take a bouquet of oleander and grant life to everyone aside from myself.

During my descent, I stopped on one of the steps. Ali took me by the arm. The people in the terraced rows of tables turned to look at Handan Sarp. She had retired from the Istanbul City Opera. Below, at the very bottom, she saw Elem sitting at a table that faced the hall. The bride and the man she would take to bed.

For a moment I felt as if I would vomit.

For the first time, Elem and I were coming face to face. I was seeing you for the first time. But you hadn't seen Handan Sarp yet.

My Munise was sweating, and with a small white kerchief she wiped the droplets of sweat from her forehead. Her veil had been pulled back.

"Ali, it's so strange. We'd been so close, but no one knows us here. There's nowhere for us to sit."

Ali's grip tightened on my arm; I had probably begun to sway.

A small white kerchief. It was trying to tell me so much, but I couldn't understand. Perhaps later. Perhaps tomorrow, when I remembered everything.

On the table in front of that handsome young man there was a glass of rakı. Every once in a while he took a sip. His face was flushed, maybe out of nervousness.

An elderly man approached us.

I didn't recognize him.

"Handan Hanım, welcome. Didn't Elem arrange a place for you?"

"I don't know."

Ali whispered: "Elem's father."

I didn't even know his name. "Where would you like us to sit?" I was on the verge of turning back. Going back ten years of my life, saving myself from Elem, her father, the wedding, Ali from Davutpaşa High School.

Hüseyin approached: "Handan Abla."

I recognized Hüseyin. His eyes looked moist. How much did he know about my intimacy with his sister?

He held my hands, which I held out to him.

I felt the warmth of his hands. I was wearing a suit like a tuxedo, and he was wearing a dark colored suit as well, his necktie neatly tied. He represented new, hopeful times. I hugged him.

"Welcome, Handan Abla."

But I didn't feel welcome. I would've liked to, but I didn't. I thanked him.

Before she moved out of her parents' house, Elem had once told me: "You can tell everything to Hüseyin. He's my confidant." No one can have a confidant. Right now, Elem, Hüseyin cannot be the bearer of our secrets.

"Quick, find us a place to sit." A strange boldness had come over me, and I was on the verge of making a scene. "Are people bringing their own drinks?" I asked. He didn't seem to understand what I meant. "It was written at the door," I explained. I was doing a fine job of humiliating myself. Elem's father was standing beside Hüseyin, but for me he had vanished. Dead. "Before coming, we drank some whiskey," I told him. Hüseyin blushed, and Ali looked away.

The music changed. They were playing something lively. Something I wouldn't understand.

Was that Elem, dancing the *halay*? Halay? That's what they call it, arms linked in arms. And there was Elem. Could that tall woman be the mother of the groom? İnci joined the people dancing, and others joined in as well. There were more men than women. Some of the men approached the groom and hugged him. They spread love like an infection. Elem's wedding gown was stunning, putting the Hilal Wedding Hall to shame. Never in my life had I seen her look so beautiful. She was holding hands with her husband. Her gown was white, pure as snow. And it was snowing, the white of the flakes shimmering pale blue.

No one was looking anymore at the woman in black with her brooch of ruby grapes as she stood there in dazed shock. She was no longer the center of attention.

Everyone cheered for the bride and groom, applauding the dance but also love, family and life. There was a man rushing about taking photographs of everything, the flash popping again and again in a silvery ball of light.

We'd been seated next to a husband and wife. As Ali spoke to them, I sat in stiff silence. Hüseyin had probably gone to get us drinks. "Hanımefendi," I heard someone say. They wanted to know which television show I starred in.

I swore to myself: the next morning, there wouldn't be an ounce of pain left.

Waiters brought us plates of cookies and orange juice in plastic cups. I didn't touch them. The sight of the cookies brought an ache to my heart.

I kept thinking of the wax plant and the light of evening. The sky was a deep blue. And then night fell. We were sitting on the balcony.

The wax plant was weeping. The blue radiance of night. The flicker of fireflies, some glowing yellow, others lavender. Elem turned and said, "Look, Handan, the fireflies are praying for us."

The music stopped. At least, for me it went silent. But I could see Elem dancing the halay on a stage of some kind; or was it the *horon*? They were trying to get her mother to join. She'd once given me a gift: a piece of cross-stitch, which she had made herself.

Hüseyin brought us glasses of whiskey. Ali thanked him, and Hüseyin slid in beside us.

Why did Elem look so glum? At İnci's wedding she was all smiles.

I couldn't understand what was happening to me: I wanted to hug Ali and weep to my heart's content.

The dance vanished. All I could hear was the song "Casta diva" ringing in my ears. Revolt and imploring; rejection and resignation. I'm on stage, a wreath of golden laurel leaves on my head. I walk toward the fire.

But you are Handan Sarp, you've never been Norma. Turandot. You've always been Turandot.

The woman sitting beside me said something but I couldn't hear her. "Someone's waving," she said. But who would wave at me? "Elem's waving to you." I gave Norma's howl back to Elem and kept Turandot's wickedness for myself.

From so far away, we came eye to eye for a fleeting moment. I raised my right hand. That was my final bow in the curtain call. I stood a few steps in front, and behind me were the lives of everyone else.

The following is from a letter Handan Sarp sent to me:

What surprised me most was when you said, "Lately, you've been strug-gling to tell your story." Who's struggling? I've bared my heart and soul to you, knowing full well that it is something I never should've done. What else can I do?

I'd hoped that a "work of art" would help me endure this shattered life of mine, that something would remain of my dark tale.

But I saw the worry in your eyes: you were afraid of writing this sinis-ter tale. You were afraid of the darkness.

When listening, you didn't keep yourself distant from the pain of the heart. But when it came time to write Handan Sarp's book, you became evasive and reluctant.

You asked questions. You asked why I wanted this book to be written. You wanted to know what I expected from it and why I'd chosen you.

You tried to disregard what I said, and then you tried to bury me and all that happened in my life.

Were you afraid I'd be a stain on your dignity as a writer?

Rather than saying this openly, you wrote: "What you've told me is jumbled, disconnected." You could've told me your thoughts to my face. We could've talked in person. You even wrote that you were hesitant to call. You're a coward.

As I write this letter, I'm looking at the notes that have been sitting on my desk for at least three years. What good could they do me? That's why I wanted you to write the book, that's why I told you everything. Just as I brought my voice to ruin.

But in a certain sense, you're right. If you had written the book—if you'd been able to—who knows how my bared soul may have been torn up and abused in today's world where even the most profound suffering is defiled. You thought that the consequences would fall on your shoulders alone.

Selim Bey, I once thought that I was a wild, unknown sea. I thought that whoever came into my life would drown there. But it was only me who drowned.

I hope that in the future you don't regret having tried to silence my life.*

There were four or five ridiculous balloons tied to the bridal car. As I left the wedding, I noticed that it was raining even harder. The night air was frigid.

I walked, passing down streets, lanes, boulevards, alleys. But where was I going? My heart was leading the way.

When I leaned my forehead against the iron bars of the tomb, I felt them pressing against my skin, cold as ice. But Şem-i Dede offered me no words of solace.

---

* Needless to say, I never responded to Handan Sarp's last "somniloquy." (Sİ)